KNIGHTS OF DARK RENOWN

Errin's eyes grew cold and he stepped back from the Knight. 'I will meet you, sir, on the field at noon. When I am dead I ask—as one Knight to another—that you allow me to be buried alongside Dianu. I think it inappropriate for us to talk further.'

Cairbre sighed and stood. He drew his sword and tossed it to Errin: it was wonderously light and razor-sharp.

'The blade has magic properties,' he said. 'It will enhance your skill and cut through anything—ultimately even this armour I wear. Use it today and I will take your blade.'

'It is not necessary,' said Errin.

'No, it is not,' Cairbre agreed. 'But at least your lady will see a battle for her life and not a meaningless slaughter. Until noon, then.'

KNIGHTS OF DARK RENOWN

David Gemmell

LEGEND

First published in Legend 1989

9 10 8

First Legend edition published in 1989 by Century Hutchinson

Arrow Books Limited
Random House UK Ltd, 20 Vauxhall Bridge Road, London SW1V 2SA

Random House Australia (Pty) Limited
20 Alfred Street, Milsons Point, Sydney,
New South Wales 2061, Australia

Random House New Zealand Limited
18 Poland Road, Glenfield
Auckland 10, New Zealand

Random House South Africa (Pty) Limited
PO Box 337, Bergvlei, South Africa

Random House UK Limited Reg. No. 954009

A CIP catalogue record for this book
is available from the British Library

ISBN 0 09 963950 5

Printed and bound in Great Britain by
Cox & Wyman Ltd, Reading, Berkshire

Dedication

True friends are rare, but without them life would lack all quality.

Knights of Dark Renown is dedicated with love to Val and Mike Adams, good neighbours, good friends. And also to Ivan Kellham, Sue Blackman, and the staff at Village Video, Hastings, who put up with a quirky author serving behind the counter whenever he feels the need to run away from his word processor.

Acknowledgements

As always grateful thanks to Liza Reeves for the guidance, Jean Maund for the copy editing, and Stella Graham, Tom Taylor, Edith Graham for the test reading. Special thanks to Roger Garland for the inspired cover art.

And to Val, the safe haven in the sometimes treacherous sea of life.

Prologue

He was nine years old, torn between grief and joy, and he was flying beneath the stars and above a land bathed in moonlight. It was a dream. Even at nine years old he knew that people did not really fly. But still, at this moment, dream or no, he was alone and free.

No one to chastise him for stealing a honey-cake, no one to beat him for failing to see a finger-mark on the silver as he polished and polished hour upon hour.

Somewhere – though he knew not where   his mother lay cold in death, and the grief was like hot knives in his soul. But, as children will, he forced it from his mind and looked to the bright, diamond stars. They seemed so close and he tried to soar towards them. But ever they remained, glittering and cold, far from his reach. He slowed in his flight and gazed down.

The land of the Gabala was so small now, and the world so large. The Forest of the Ocean lay beneath him like a wolf pelt, the mountains merely wrinkles in an old man's skin. He dropped lower, falling, spinning towards the ground, and screamed in his fear as the mountains roared up towards him, jagged and threatening. His dizzy fall slowed and he floated once more. On the sea beyond Pertia Port he could see the great triremes with their square sails, their oars lifted – and on the land the lights of the towns and cities. Four huge braziers were lit on the walls of Mactha fortress, twinkling like candles on a cake. He sped away from the lights towards the distant mountains.

He wished he might never go home; wished he could float like this for ever, safe from the many tortures of slavery. While his mother had been alive there had been someone who cared for him – not as a slave boy but as Lug, the child, flesh of her flesh. Her arms had always been open to him.

Grief and pain swamped him once more. When she had become ill Lug had been told she needed rest . . . but it did not help. They had sent for the healer, Gwydion, but he was away in the city of Furbolg. Lug had watched the flesh vanish from his mother's features, seen her change from a living, loving woman to a skeletal creature whose eyes could look at him without recognition, and whose arms did not have the strength to open for him.

And then she was gone . . . while he slept. He had kissed her good-night and been led away to a room he now shared with five other boys. In the morning he had finished his chores and run to her chamber, only to find her covered with a white linen sheet. This he had pulled back from her face. The eyes were closed, the mouth open. And no trace of breath or movement could be seen.

The elderly house slave Patricaeus had found him there and carried him back to his own room. Lug had been aware of the old man, but he could not move. He was frozen in shock. He felt himself tucked up into Patricaeus' bed, the warm blankets around his shoulders, but he could not even close his eyes. The old man had stroked his face, and gently closed his lids.

For a long while Lug had slept. Then something inside him snapped – and his spirit had sailed free into the night air.

He shivered, though he felt no cold, and wished he could bring his mother back. Just then his eye was caught by movement far below. A line of riders, nine of them, were riding out into the night on tall white horses. Lug dropped towards them and saw that they were Knights dressed in silver armour, white cloaks draping to their saddles. They formed into a line in a meadow, and white mist billowed around the horses' hooves like a ghostly sea. On a nearby hillside Lug saw a man, his face partly hidden by a dark hood on a velvet cloak. The man was chanting, but the language was unknown to the boy. The Knights sat silently as the mist deepened.

Lug came closer, avoiding the chanting man and settling himself on another hillside near some trees. As he came to the ground he sank through it; a touch of panic spurred him and he rose again, wishing that he were solid. The wish became reality and he sat down upon the grass. The mist had not reached the upper slopes of the hill and he settled down to watch the Knights.

Their armour glistened in the moonlight, round helms under tall black plumes, silver neck-plates linked to curving shoulder-guards, engraved breastplates, thigh-guards and greaves. Yet they carried no shields.

Nine riders on nine white stallions. . . .

Lug remembered the stories Patricaeus told in the Slaves' Hall at the Solstice Feast – and he knew then upon whom he spied.

The legendary Knights of the Gabala.

Lug did not know their names – save that the Lord Knight was Samildanach, the greatest swordsman in the realm. The boy scanned the group. There at the centre, taller than the others, shining silver raven wings adorning his helmet, was Samildanach, sitting silently . . . waiting.

But for what?

Lug transferred his gaze to the chanting man and suddenly the horses began to whinny in fear. The Knights held them steady, and Lug's mouth dropped open, for the stars were disappearing from the sky as a great black gateway formed before the riders. A sliver of silver grey appeared in the rectangle of black and a bitter wind howled through the opening. Then the mist rose like a huge wave to engulf the Knights, and unearthly screams sounded from beyond the black Gate.

'Follow the Sword,' came the cry, and Lug saw the blade of Samildanach shining like a lantern, and heard the drumming of hooves as the Knights thundered forward.

Then there was silence and the darkness faded, leaving the stars to shine once more.

Lug looked across at the far hillside, but the chanting man had gone.

The mist gathered and flowed up the hillside and Lug rose and tried to fly. But he could not. His body was solid, and rooted to the earth. The cold wind touched him and he shivered.

The dream was no longer comforting and he was desperate to return home. But where was home? How far had he flown?

A noise came to him through the mist – a slithering, rustling sound. He spun and tried to scan the ground, but the grey fog was everywhere. Lug ran back up the hill, heart pounding, but he slipped and fell in the muddy grass and rolled to his back. A black shadow reared over him and sharp talons raked down at his body; he rolled again desperately as they scored the skin of his chest.

'No!' he screamed, as the slavering jaws of the beast dropped towards his face. He threw up his arm. A blazing beam of golden light sprang from his fingers to engulf the creature and with a scream of agony it disappeared as Lug sank back to the grass. Another shadow fell across him and he cowered to the ground.

'Do not be afraid,' said a voice.

Lug looked up to see the outline of a man. The moon was shining over the stranger's shoulder and his face was in silhouette, his features impossible to see.

'I'm frightened,' said Lug. 'I want to go home.'

'And so you shall, my boy. And then this . . . dream . . . will be forgotten.'

'What was the beast?'

'It came from beyond the Gate. But it is dead. You destroyed it, boy – as I knew you would – for within you is the Power. Farewell. We will meet again.'

'Who are you?'

'I am the Dagda. Sleep now – and return home.'

Lug had closed his eyes and slipped from awareness. When he opened them again he was lying in Patricaeus' bed; the old man was sitting beside him, dozing in a chair.

Lug rolled over. The bed creaked and the old man awoke.

'How are you feeling, Lug?'

'What am I doing here, sir? Where is my mother?'

'She is dead, boy,' said Patricaeus sadly. 'We buried her this afternoon.' The blanket slid from the boy's chest as he sat up.

'Dear Gods!' whispered Patricaeus. 'What have you done?' Lug looked down; his chest was scored in four shallow cuts which had bled profusely, drenching the sheet below the blanket. When Patricaeus pulled the bedding aside, the boy's legs were covered in dried mud.

'Explain this, Lug. Where did you go while I was sleeping?'

'I don't know,' said Lug. 'I don't know anything. I want my mother! Please?'

The old man sat beside the weeping boy and placed his arms around him.

'I am sorry, Lug. Truly.'

1

The rider paused at the crest of the pass, the wind
swirling about him and screeching through the moun-
tain-tops. Far below him the lands of the Gabala stretched green and verdant, ribbon streams and shimmering rivers, hills and vales, forests and woods – all
as he remembered, echoing his dreams, calling for his
return.

'Home, Kuan,' he whispered, but his words were
whipped away by the wind and the tall grey stallion
did not hear him. Touching his heels to the horse's
side, the rider leaned back in the saddle as his mount
began the long descent. The wind dropped as they
neared the deserted Border fort, its gates of oak and
bronze hanging on broken hinges. The Gabala Eagle
had been hacked from them – only the edge of a wing-
tip left on the rotting wood, and this covered by a
brown and green patina that all but merged it with the
timber.

The rider dismounted here. He was a tall man
wearing a long hooded cloak, a heavy scarf wound
about his face and holding the hood in place. He led
the stallion into the derelict fort and halted before the
statue of Manannan. The left arm was broken, and
lying on the cobbles. Someone had taken an axe or a
hammer to the face and the chin was smashed, the
nose split.

'How soon they forget,' said the newcomer. Hearing
his voice the stallion moved forward, nuzzling at his
back. He turned, removed his thick woollen gloves and
stroked the beast's neck. It was warmer here and he
unwound the scarf, draping it over the pommel of his

saddle. As he pushed back the hood, sunlight flashed from the silver helm he wore.

'Let us find you a drink, Kuan,' he said, moving to the walled well at the centre of the courtyard. The bucket was warped by the sun, gaping cracks showing beneath the iron rings. The rope was tinder-dry, but still usable if handled with care. He searched the deserted outbuildings and returned with a clay jug and a deep plate, then stood the jug in the bucket before lowering both into the well. When he carefully drew the bucket up, water was gushing from the cracks, but the jug was full and he lifted it clear and drank deeply. Placing the plate on the cobbles, he filled it. The stallion dropped its head and drank. The rider loosened the saddle girth and poured more water into the plate, then climbed the rampart steps and sat in the sunshine.

This was the end of empire, he knew. Not the blood-drenched battlegrounds, the screaming hordes, the discordant clash of steel on steel. Just the dust blowing across the cobbles, limbless statues, warped buckets and the silence of the grave.

'You would have hated this, Samildanach,' he said. 'This would have broken your heart.'

He searched inside himself for any grief over the Fall of the Gabala. But there was no room . . . all his grief was for himself as he gazed down at his statue.

Manannan, Knight of the Gabala. One of the Nine. Greater than princes, more than men. He delved into his hip-pouch, pulling clear a silvered mirror which he held up before his face.

The Once-Knight looked into his own deep blue eyes, then at the square face and the silver steel which surrounded it. The plume was gone from the helm, hacked away in some skirmish to the north; the visor, raised now, dented by an axe-blade in the Fomorian War. The runic number that named him had been torn from the brow in a battle to the east. He could not remember the blow; it was one of so many he had endured during the six lonely years since the Gate closed. His gaze shifted to the plate rings that circled his throat and pictured the beard growing beneath them, slowly – oh, so slowly – preparing to choke him to death.

What a death for a Gabala Knight, imprisoned within his helm, strangled by his own beard. Such was the price of betrayal, Manannan told himself. Such was the penalty for cowardice.

Cowardice? He rolled the word in his mind. During the last, lonely, aimless years of wandering he had proved his physical courage time and time again, in sword-play, in the charge, in the long wait before the onslaught. But it was not his body which had let him down on that dark night six years before, when the Black Gate yawned and the stars died. It was altogether a different cowardice which had robbed him of the power to move.

Not so the others. But then Samildanach would have braved the fires of Hell with a handful of snow. As would the others: Pateus, Edrin . . . all of them.

'Damn you, Ollathair,' hissed the Once-Knight. 'Damn your arrogance!'

Manannan returned his mirror to its pouch.

He rested for another hour and then stepped into the saddle. The Citadel was three days' ride west. He avoided towns and settlements, buying his food at isolated farms and sleeping in meadows. On the morning of the fourth day he approached the Citadel.

Manannan steered his stallion through the trees and into what had once been the rose garden. It was overgrown now, but here and there a bloom still flourished, stretching above the choking weeds. The paved path was mostly covered by grass and small blue flowers. It was only natural, thought the Once-Knight – six years of wind-blown soil settling over the carefully laid

14

stones. The side gate was open and he rode into the courtyard. Here and there grass seeds had settled in the cracks of the pavement, fed by the fountain pool which overflowed its marble parapet.

He dismounted, his silver armour creaking and his movements slow. The stallion stood motionless.

'Not as you remember it, Kuan,' whispered the Knight, removing his gauntlet and stroking the beast's neck. 'They have all gone.' He led the horse to the pool and waited as it drank. A wooden shutter nearby was caught by the wind, which cracked it against the window-frame. The horse's head came up, ears laid flat against its skull.

'It's all right, boy,' Manannan soothed. 'There is no danger here.'

As the stallion drank, he loosened the saddle girth and lifted the pack from its back. Hoisting this to his shoulder, he walked up the steps to the double doors and entered the Welcome Hall. Dust had gathered here and the long carpet smelt of mildew and corruption. The statues stood staring at him with sightless eyes.

He felt the burden of his guilt grow even stronger and pushed on past the figures to the chapel at the rear of the building. The hinges groaned as he forced open the leaf-shaped door. No dust disturbed this place, with its low altar, but the golden candlesticks were gone – as were the silver chalice and the silken hangings. Yet still the chapel emanated peace. He lowered his pack and unfastened the leather binding thongs. Then he moved to the altar, removed his baldric and scabbard and unbuckled his breastplate, slipping it under the protruding shoulder-plates. Carefully he placed the armour on the altar. Shoulder-plates and habergeon followed. He would miss the sleeveless coat of mail; it had saved his life more than once. Hip-shields, thigh-guards and greaves he laid upon the stone, placing his black and silver gauntlets atop the breastplate.

'Let it be over,' he said, reaching up to release the helm, but his fingers froze as fear flowed in him. The spell had been cast by Ollathair in this room six years before – but without the wizard, was the peace of the chapel enough to remove it? Manannan calmed himself. His finger touched the spring-lock, but the bar did not move. He pressed harder, then dropped his hand. Fear fled from the onset of his anger: 'What more do you want of me?' he screamed. Sinking to his knees he prayed for deliverance, but although his thoughts streamed out, there was no sense of their reaching a destination. Exhausted, he rose – a knight without armour. Moving to his pack, he dressed swiftly in well-fitting woollen trews and leather tunic, then looped his baldric over his shoulder with the sword and scabbard nestling at his right side. Finally he pulled on a pair of soft doeskin riding boots and gathered his blanket. The pack he left where it lay.

Outside the stallion was cropping grass at the far wall. The man who had been a knight walked past the beast and on to the smithy. It too was dust-covered, the tools rusted and useless, the great bellows torn and tattered, the forge open – a nesting-place for rats.

Manannan picked up a rusted saw-blade. Even had it been gleaming and new, it would have been useless to him. The silver steel of the helm was strong enough in its own right, but with the added power of Ollathair's enchantment it was impervious to everything but heat. He had once endured two hours of agony as a smith sought to burn the bar loose. At last, defeated, the craftsman had knelt before him.

'I could do it, sir, but there would be no point. The heat needed would turn your flesh to liquid, your brain to steam. You need a sorcerer, not a smith.'

And he had found sorcerers, and would-be wizards, seers and Wyccha women. But none could counter the spell of the Armourer.

'I need you, Ollathair,' said the Once-Knight. 'I need your wizardry and your skills. But where did you go?'

Ollathair had been above all a patriot. He would not have left the realm unless forced. And who could force the Armourer of the Gabala Knights? Manannan sat silently among the rusted remains of Ollathair's equipment and fought to remember conversations of long ago.

Considering the size of the empire it had once ruled, the lands of the Gabala were not large. From the borders of Fomoria in the south to the coastal routes to Cithaeron was a journey of less than a thousand miles. East to west, from the Nomad steppes to the western sea and Asripur, was a mere four hundred. One fact was sure – Ollathair would avoid cities; he had always hated the marble monstrosity of Furbolg.

Where then? And under what guise?

Ollathair had been merely the name chosen by the Armourer, but there was another name he used when wishing to travel alone and unreported. Manannan had discovered this by chance ten years before, during a visit to the northernmost of the nine Duchies. He had stopped at a wayhouse and seen the owner showing off a small bird of shining bronze that sang in four languages. As the man lifted his hand, the bird circled the room and a sweet perfume filled the air.

Manannan had approached the man, who had bowed low upon seeing the Gabala armour.

'Where did you come by the bird?' he had asked.

'It was not stolen, sir, I promise you. On the lives of my children.'

'I am not here to judge you, man. It was merely a question.'

'It was a traveller, sir . . . two days ago. A stocky man, ugly as sin. He had no money for a room and paid with this. Am I right to keep it?'

'Keep it, sell it; it is not my concern. Where did this traveller go?'

'South, sir. Along the Royal Road.'

'Did he give you a name?'

'Yes, sir – as is the law. And he signed the register. I have it here.' He lifted the leather-bound book and showed it to the Knight.

Manannan caught up with Ollathair the following afternoon on a long open stretch of road. The Armourer was riding a fat pony.

'Is there no peace?' Ollathair asked. 'What is the problem?'

'There is no problem that I know of,' Manannan told him. 'This is a chance meeting. I saw your handi-work at the inn; a little extravagant for a night's lodging, was it not?'

'It's flawed; it will not last out the week. Now ride on and leave me to a little serenity. I will see you at the Citadel in a week.'

Now as Manannan looked about him at the cobwebs and the decay, he shivered.

Perhaps Ollathair would have chosen another name. Perhaps he was dead.

But with no other clues the Once-Knight had no choice. He would ride to the north and seek news of a craftsman called Ruad Ro-fhessa.

The boy gripped the tweezers, lifted the tiny bronze sliver and took a deep breath. He licked his lips as he leaned over the bench, his hand shaking.

'Easy, now,' said the ugly man, sitting beside him. 'Be calm and breathe easily. You are too tense.' The boy nodded and rolled his shoulders, seeking to ease the knots of tension. His hand steadied and the bronze sliver slid into place at the back of the model. 'There!' said the man triumphantly, his one good eye examining the metal hawk. 'Now take the wing and lift it – carefully now!'

The boy did so and the wing spread effortlessly, the bronze feathers gleaming. 'And release.' The wing snapped back into place against the scaled body.

'I did it, Ruad. I made it!' cried the boy, clapping his hands.

'Indeed you did,' the man agreed, a wide grin showing his crooked teeth. 'In only a year you have duplicated that which took me three, when I was your age. But then you had a better teacher than I!'

'Will it fly?' asked the boy. Ruad Ro-fhessa ruffled the lad's tightly curled blond hair. He shrugged his huge shoulders and stood, stretching his back.

'That will depend on your ability to draw the air-magic. Come, we will sit for a while.' Ruad moved away from the bench and through the workshop to a wide room where two deep chairs were set before a hearth in which a log-fire blazed. There he settled himself, stretching his short legs towards the blaze and resting his massive arms across his chest. The firelight gleamed on the bronze patch covering his left eye and highlighted the silver streaks in his thinning black hair. The boy joined him; he was tall for his age, and had almost outgrown the tunic of his House.

'You did well, Lug,' said Ruad. 'One day you will be a Master Craftsman. I am greatly pleased with you.' Lug blushed and looked away. Compliments were rare from Ruad, and never before had he been asked to sit by the fire.

'Will she fly?'

'Can you feel the magic in the air?' countered Ruad.

'No.'

'Close your eyes and rest your head back against the chair.' Ruad lifted a heavy poker and stirred the blaze to life, adding three fresh logs to the fire. 'The currents of magic are many, the colours deep and sometimes

19

startling. You must begin with the colours. Think of White, which is peace. Harmony. Picture the colour, flow with it. Can you see it?'

'Yes,' whispered Lug.

'When there is anger, or hatred, or pain, other than that of the flesh, White is the answer. Summon it. Blue is the sky, the power of the air, the dream of things which fly. Blue is what calls them on halting wings. Can you see the Blue?'

'I can, Master.'

'Then call on the Blue.' Ruad closed his good eye and aided the boy in his search. 'Do you have it, Lug?'

'I do, Master.'

'And how do you feel?'

'I can sense the sky calling me. I feel the need for wings.'

Ruad smiled. 'Then let us return to the hawk. Hold to your feeling.'

The two craftsmen made their way to the workshop, where the boy lifted a tiny knife. 'Am I ready?' he asked.

'We shall see,' answered Ruad. 'Release the magic of the Blue.'

Lug nicked the skin at the base of his right palm and held his hand over the bird's metallic head. A single drop of blood splashed on the beak.

'Now the wings,' Ruad ordered. 'Swiftly now.' Lug followed the instructions, then stepped back. 'Press your finger over the cut and stop the bleeding.' Lug did so, but his blue eyes were fixed on the bird. At first there was no movement, but then the golden head jerked, the plate rings grinding together. Slowly the wings spread and the hawk rose from the bench, soaring through the open window in search of the sky. The man and the boy ran out on to the mountainside to see the golden bird fly higher and higher. Suddenly it faltered, and Lug watched as a bronze feather floated away from the hawk . . . then another . . . and another. The flight was ungainly now.

'No!' screamed Lug, raising a slender hand to point at the struggling bird. Ruad watched in amazement as two fragile bronze feathers which had dropped from the bird reversed their flight and pinned themselves to the wings once more. For a few seconds the hawk steadied. Then the wings snapped shut and it plummeted to the ground, lifeless and ruined. Lug ran to it, gathering the feathers and cradling the twisted body.

Ruad Ro-fhessa came up silently, laying his hand on the boy's shoulder. 'Do not let this dismay you, Lug. My first bird did not even make the window. It was a great achievement.'

'But I wanted it to live,' he protested.

'I know. And it did; it found the sky. Next time we will check the neck joints more thoroughly.'

'Next time?' repeated Lug sadly. 'I reach the Age next week. There is no place for me in the House and I shall be sold.'

'That is next week. Many things can happen,' said Ruad. 'Bring the bird back to the forge and we will see what can be saved.'

'I think I will run away. I will join Llaw Gyffes.'

'Stronghand may not be an easy man to follow – but we will talk about this on another day. Trust me, Lug. And now let us see to the bird.'

Ruad watched as the youth wandered the hillside gathering the fragments of metal. The feathers had fallen away – and then reversed their flight – albeit for only a few seconds. Yet Lug had only reached the Yellow, the least of the Colours.

Back at the workshop, they left the bronze fragments and sat by the fireside. Lug was silent and sorrowful.

'Tell me,' said Ruad softly. 'What did you feel when you shouted to the sky?'

The youth looked up. 'Despair,' he answered simply.

21

'No, I mean at the moment when you screamed.'

Lug shrugged. 'I do not know what you mean, sir. I . . . wanted it to fly.'

'Did you notice what happened when you called out to it?'

'No. It fell.'

'Not immediately,' said Ruad. 'It tried to gather itself; in some way you were still linked with it. But you say you felt nothing. What Colour did you feel? Was it the Blue?'

Lug sat for a moment, trying to remember. 'No, it was the Yellow. I can only reach the other Colours through you, sir.'

'No matter, Lug. I will think on it. It is almost time for you to be going; your free time ends at dusk, does it not?'

'I have a little while,' said the youth. 'Marshin says the family will not return from Furbolg until tomorrow. They are bringing guests for the auction.'

'It may not be as bad as you think,' offered Ruad. 'There are many good Houses. The Lady Dianu may need a house servant – or the Lord Errin. Both have good names for their treatment of slaves.'

'Why should I be a slave?' Lug snapped. 'Why? The empire has gone. All the lands are now being ruled by peoples who were once slaves. Why should *I* remain? It isn't fair!'

'Life has a habit of not being fair, boy. The Fomorian War was the last, and you were a victim of it. But you will have an opportunity to buy your freedom; it is not so bad a life.'

'Have you ever been a slave, sir?'

'Only to my Craft,' admitted Ruad. 'But that does not count, does it? You were taken . . . what, five years ago? How old were you? Ten, eleven? It is the way of things, Lug. Wars cost money and that is recouped by plunder and slavery. The Gabala fought that war for national pride, for the right to give away their empire and not have it taken from them. You were one of the last victims. I know it is not fair, but a man who goes through life complaining about fairness will make nothing of himself. Trust me on this, boy. There are three kinds of men: winners, losers and fighters. The winners are blessed by the Colours; no matter what they do, life treats them like gods. The losers waste their energies whining like scolded children; they will amount to nothing. The fighters keep their swords sharp and their shields high; they expect nothing they do not battle for, but they fight until they drop.'

'I do not want to be a warrior,' said Lug.

'Listen to me, boy!' snapped Ruad. 'And with your whole mind. I am not speaking of swordsmen, I am speaking of life. Your wits are both sword and shield; it is a matter of perspective. If you want something, then plan for it. Think of all that could go wrong, and picture all that can be done to make it right. Then do it. Don't talk about it endlessly. Do it! Set your mind to the task. You have a good mind and a great Talent. I do not know how you held that bird in the air, but there is in you a power. So search for it. Build upon it. And never allow despair to rule your heart. You understand me?'

'I will try, sir.'

'That is a good enough answer. Now go home and I will examine the bird.'

Lug stood and smiled. 'You have been very good to me, sir. Why do you take the time?'

'Why should I not?'

'I don't know. In Mactha they say you are a hermit who dislikes the company of people. They say you are . . . rude and surly, ill-tempered and short of patience. But *I* have never found you to be so.'

Ruad rose and laid a huge hand on the boy's shoulder. 'I am what they say, Lug. Make no mistake

23

on that. I do not like people; I never have. Greedy, grasping, selfish and self-serving. But I have a way with Talent, boy. I can make it flourish – as a gardener with blooms. You remember the day I caught you hiding in the bushes behind the workshop?'

'Yes,' said Lug, grinning. 'I thought you were going to kill me.'

'On each Tiernsday for seven weeks you had hidden in that spot and watched me work. You showed patience – and that is rare in the young. That is why I decided to teach you a little of the Colours. And you have been a good student. If the Source is willing, you will continue so to be. Now be off with you!'

After the boy had gone, Ruad gathered together the remains of the metal bird, examining the points below the neck which had given way. The pinions were too slender, but only by a fraction. Lug had good hands and a sure eye, but as yet his soul was not attuned to the magic of the sky. But then, Ruad knew, magic was built on harmony and a slave boy reaching his majority was unlikely to find it. He could be sold to a ship's captain and spend his life below decks, or to a prince and suffer castration to serve in a harem. And there were other, even less savoury ends for a youth of his looks. Yet these perils were not great. The vast majority of bright young slaves were bought by good masters who used them well in their businesses, giving them opportunities to buy their freedom at the age of thirty.

Still, who could blame a boy for fearing the worst?

Ruad locked his front door and saddled the old bay mare. He rarely rode into Mactha, but now he needed supplies – salt and sugar, dried meat and herbs and, most of all, more ingots of bronze and gold.

Bronze was a good metal for an apprentice to work with, but it did not take to magic like gold. Had Lug's bird been Fomorian gold, it would have flown over the highest mountain and returned at a thought. But gold was scarcer than a woman's virtue.

Ruad heaved his ungainly body into the saddle and steered the old mare down the trail between the pines. The ride took two hours and the sight of the white stone buildings of Mactha brought him little pleasure. He waved to the guard on the North Gate and rode on to the livery stable owned by Hyam. The old man himself was sitting at the paddock fence, bartering furiously with a Nomad trader.

Ruad unsaddled the mare and led her to the hay-box. Then he brushed her back and returned to the fence, where the debate was hotting up.

'Wait! Wait!' said Hyam, waving his slender fingers in the Nomad's face. 'We'll put it to this traveller.' He turned to Ruad and winked. 'Good sir, be so kind as to examine the two horses by the rail and give me your honest opinion as to their worth. Whatever you say, I will abide by.'

Ruad glanced down at Hyam's fingers, which swiftly flickered in archaic Roadsign. The burly craftsman wandered to the first beast, a seventeen-hands-high chestnut stallion of some eight years. He ran his hands over the strong legs and down the flanks, then moved on to the gelding. This animal was of sixteen hands, perhaps five years older than the stallion, and showed some evidence of a sway back. Hyam had signalled forty silver halves for the pair.

'I'd say thirty-eight silver halves,' stated Ruad.

'You ruin me!' squealed Hyam, dancing on the spot. 'How can this happen to an honest man?'

'You agreed to abide by this man's decision,' the Nomad reminded him. 'And though it is five pieces more than I offered, I will accept.'

'There is a conspiracy in Heaven against me,' said Hyam, shaking his head. 'But I have been trapped by my own stupidity. I thought this man knew horses. Take them; you have a bargain beyond your dreams.'

The man grinned and counted out the money; then he led the horses from the paddock. Hyam transferred the silver to a hip-pouch and sat back, grinning.

'You are a rascal,' said Ruad. 'The stallion has an inflamed tendon; it could be lame within the week. And the gelding? Its spirit has gone.'

'Hardly surprising,' said the old man softly. 'They are from the Duke's stables and he is not kind to them.'

'How is life for you, Hyam?'

'It could always be better,' answered Hyam, running his hand through his thinning white hair. 'But there are bad times coming.'

'According to you – and all horse-traders – times are always bad,' said Ruad, smiling.

'I cannot deny it, Ruad, my friend. But this is different, believe me. You can see the signs throughout Mactha. The number of beggars has increased since your last visit. And whores? The town swims in new whores. Ten years ago I wouldn't have complained about that, but now? Now I see it for what it is. Many are good women who have lost their husbands or their homes. Walk down the Streets of Trade and see the closed shops with their barred windows. And the price of slaves is dropping . . . that is never a good sign. The beggars fight among themselves for the best sites, and the number of robberies has doubled since last year.'

'Does the Duke take no action?'

Hyam hawked and spat. 'What does he care about Mactha? I hear news from all over the Duke's realm. He has almost doubled the taxes everywhere. Farmers must give him twenty per cent of their crops, or else yearlings. And since most of the farmers rent their lands from the nobility, they are left with about ten per cent to feed their families and plan for the coming year.'

Several men had gathered to view the horses. Hyam signalled Ruad to silence, and they continued their conversation using Roadsign.

'There is madness in the air, my friend. The Duke ordered three men impaled last month. Their crime? They wrote to the King, asking for justice against the raised taxes. The King sent Earl Tollibar, the Duke's cousin. Now justice is to be served against the three men who asked for it. There's a sort of dark poetry there.'

'Impaling was outlawed more than twenty years ago,' said Ruad.

'But in those days the Knights rode the land and the old King ruled. Do not look to yesterday, Ruad. Yesterday is dead – gone, like the Knights.'

'All the counsellors cannot be dead,' protested Ruad. 'What of Kalib?'

'Poisoned, so they say.'

'Rulic?'

'Killed in a hunting accident. I should get in supplies for the winter, Ruad; there is a bad feeling in the air.'

'Look after the mare,' said Ruad, aloud. He walked out through the crowd gathering for the horse auction and on to the Streets of Trade. As Hyam had said, many traders had closed their businesses. It was not a good sign.

A young woman approached him. 'Your pleasure, sir.'

He smiled at her. 'Business must be bad for you to approach one so ugly.'

She did not return his smile. 'Only three copper quarters,' she said, her eyes avoiding his.

He took her hands and turned them over. They were clean, the nails scrubbed. 'Why not?' he told her, and followed her through a maze of alleys to a dismal structure with a broken door. Inside it was clean but dingy, and a baby slept on a pile of blankets by the far wall.

She led him to a pallet bed and swiftly lay back, hauling her woollen dress up around her hips. Ruad was about to loosen his belt when he heard a movement behind him and stepped sideways so that the club whistled harmlessly past his shoulder. Turning, he hammered a blow to the assailant's midriff, doubling him over, then cracked the blade of his right hand to the man's neck. He was unconscious before he hit the ground.

The woman sat up, her hand over her mouth.

'We needed money,' she said. 'He's not dead, is he?'

'No,' said Ruad, 'and you'll get your money when you've earned it.'

He loosened his belt.

Ruad stepped from the gloom of the dwelling into the sunlit street – his good eye narrowing, his senses alert. The woman had been a disappointment, bursting into tears as he moved to her. She had made him angry and, unlike some men, anger had no part in Ruad's sexual desires. He had dressed and left her.

He found his way back to the main street, brushing aside beggars as he walked. Hyam was right; Mactha was becoming a running sore.

The Street of Ore was near deserted and Ruad was surprised to see boards being hammered across the windows of Cartain's establishment. The front door was open and he stepped inside. The former Nomad was supervising the packing of several large crates, but he spotted Ruad and waved him through to the back room.

Cartain joined him there, and poured a goblet of apple juice which he passed to the bemused Craftsman.

'You are leaving, too?' said Ruad. 'Why?'

The tall, angular merchant sat down at his desk, his dark slanted eyes fixing on Ruad. 'You know why I am rich?' he asked, stroking his hawk beak of a nose.

'I have always disliked my questions being answered by questions,' Ruad snapped.

Cartain grinned, showing a golden tooth. 'I like you, Ruad – but answer my question.'

'You buy cheap and sell dear. Now, why are you leaving?'

'I am rich,' said the merchant, smiling at Ruad's increasing annoyance, 'because I read the wind. When it blows fresh there is money to be made; when it blows bad, there is money to be made. But when it does not blow, it is time to move on.'

'You are an irritating man,' Ruad told him, 'but I shall miss you. Where now shall I peddle my toys?'

'I will send someone to you. Your work is still highly sought after. Do you have something for me?'

'Perhaps. But I need gold ingots and more bronze – also a quantity of that Eastern oil.'

'How much gold?' Cartain asked, leaning back and averting his eyes.

'You will earn three hundred Raq for my little singer. I will take the equivalent of one hundred.'

'Show me.'

Ruad opened the leather pouch at his side and took from it a small golden bird with emerald eyes. He stroked its back and stood it on his palm. Then, lifting it to his lips, he whispered a word. The bird's metallic wings spread and it rose from his hand to circle the room. Soft music sang from its beak and a heady perfume filled the air.

'Beautiful,' said Cartain. 'Simply exquisite. How long will the magic last?'

'Three years. Four.' Ruad lifted his hand and the bird spread its wings and glided to his palm. He passed it to Cartain.

'And the words of command?'

'The name of its maker.'

'Perfect. You are a Master. There is a king far to the

29

east who desires a giant eagle to carry him into the sky. He would pay in diamonds as large as skulls.'

'It is not possible,' said Ruad.

'That cannot be true, my dear partner. All things are possible.'

Ruad shook his head. 'You do not understand the limits. Magic is a finite power. A long time ago Zinazar sought to extend it; he used the blood of innocence. It did not work then and it will not now.'

'But supposing a thousand people were willing to give their blood?'

'There are not a thousand people in all the world who can drink the Colours. Forget his diamonds, Cartain. How rich can one man be?'

Cartain chuckled. 'He can have all the wealth of the world – and one copper piece more.'

Ruad drained his apple juice. 'Now tell me why you are leaving – and not a single word about the wind, if you please.'

Cartain's smile faded. 'There are bad times coming and I want no part of them. My messengers tell me of evil deeds in the capital. This in itself would be of no consequence to a Nomad like me, but King Ahak's mismanagement has left him with a thin treasury. Several Nomad merchants have been arrested, accused of treason and tortured to death. Their wealth has accrued to the King. Old Cartain will not feed the vulture's treasury.'

'I had my problems with the King,' said Ruad. 'He is arrogant and headstrong, but he is no despot.'

'He has changed, my friend,' Cartain told him. 'He has surrounded himself with men of evil – even recruited men for a group he called the Knights of the New Gabala . . . and they are terrible. It is said he was gravely ill and a sorcerer cured him, but his soul died. I do not know. These stories abound. But then men will always talk of kings. What I do know is that the climate is not good for Nomads – or those of Nomad blood. I have seen these things before – in other lands. No good will come of it.'

'Where will you go?'

'Across the Inner Sea to Cithaeron. I have relatives there . . . and a young wife.'

'You have a wife here, as I recall?'

'A rich man cannot have too many wives! Why not come with me? We could make a fortune.'

'I do not desire a fortune,' Ruad told him. 'Have my goods sent to the mountains tomorrow.'

'I will. Take care, Craftsman. All secrets have a habit of becoming known and yours, I fear, will prove no exception. And this time you would lose more than an eye.'

Ruad left the merchant and wandered back towards the stables, stopping to eat at a small inn.

Cartain's planned departure bothered him, leaving him uneasy. Cunning as the merchant was, he was also a man to be trusted. There were few like him, and Ruad needed him. He finished his meal and sat staring at the gathering clouds.

All secrets become known.

There was truth in that, but it was a problem for another day. He paid the innkeeper and, carrying a sack of provisions, returned to the stable. Hyam had gone, but his youngest son saddled Ruad's mare. The boy was sharp-eyed, with a flashing smile.

'You should buy a new horse,' said the lad. 'This one is worn out.'

Ruad mounted and grinned down at him. 'This is the beast your father sold me two months ago, swearing on the souls of his sons that she would run for ever.'

'Ah,' replied the boy, 'but then Father is not as young as he was. Now, I have a gelding that was sired by Buesecus and even a man of your size could ride him all day and see not a mark of sweat upon him.'

31

'Show me,' said Ruad, following the boy back into the paddock. The black gelding was almost seventeen hands high, with a strong back and good legs.

Ruad dismounted. 'Is it true?' he asked the horse, 'that your sire was Buesecus?'

The gelding swung its head. 'No,' it replied. 'The boy is as big a liar as his father.'

The lad backed away, his eyes wide and fearful.

Ruad shook his head. 'And you looked so innocent!'

'You are a sorcerer?' the boy whispered.

'Indeed I am. And you have offended me,' said Ruad, fixing the boy with a bleak look.

'I am sorry, sir. Truly. Please forgive me.'

Ruad turned away and remounted his mare. 'Your father may be old, boy, but he was never stupid.' He heeled his mount and set off for the mountains. The lad was gullible and deserved to be fooled. Even as a child Hyam would have known the difference between magic and trickery.

All secrets become known.

He calmed his mind and reached into the Colours. It took him time to find the White and ease his fears. At the top of a rise he swung in the saddle to look back at Mactha. The sun was dropping behind the mountains and the town was bathed in crimson.

Ruad shivered and, before he could steel himself, a vision shook him. Eight Knights in red armour, their faces ghostly white, their eyes filled with blood, were riding across the sky with dark swords in their hands.

With a great effort Ruad tore himself clear of the vision. Rubbing the sweat from his face, he kicked the mare into a run.

2

The six soldiers lay sprawled in death near the carriage and the two women stood side by side facing the attackers. Groundsel waited with his men behind him, eyeing the women with deep appreciation.

That they were sisters was as obvious as the fact that they were patricians. The taller of the two, dressed in a billowing skirt of green silk and a white blouse gathered at the throat, was holding a short sword she had swept up from the ground. The other was standing beside her, no sign of fear in her wide grey eyes. Both were beautiful. The girl with the sword had short curly hair, dark and glowing like a beaver pelt. Her sister wore her raven hair long, curling to her shoulders; she was dressed in a flowing robe of ash-grey silk, gathered at the waist with a belt braided with gold.

Groundsel felt arousal washing over him. He had never enjoyed sisters before – and these would fight, scratch and claw. He swallowed hard. Which of them should be first? The tall, proud one or the smaller, well-rounded woman with the haughty grey eyes?

One of his men darted forward and the taller woman's sword snaked out in a fierce backhand cut. At the last second the man hurled himself aside, the blade slicing open his brown leather jerkin. He scrambled back on all fours, to the laughter of his comrades. Yes, thought Groundsel, the swordswoman would be first.

The sound of a trotting horse came to him and Groundsel swung to see a rider entering the hollow. He was a tall man, riding a tall horse, and though he was dressed in tunic and trews he wore a silver helm with the visor raised. He halted his grey stallion some ten paces from the twelve outlaws.

'Good morning, ladies,' he said. 'Are you in need of assistance?'

Groundsel stepped forward. 'Be on your way,' he hissed, 'or we'll drag you from the saddle and leave you for the crows.'

'I was not addressing you, peasant,' said the rider softly. 'Where are your manners?'

Groundsel reddened and drew his two short swords, while the eleven outlaws spread themselves out in a circle. The rider slid from the saddle and drew a longsword that shimmered in the sunlight; he held it double-handed.

Just then the thunder of hooves filled the clearing.

'Back!' yelled Groundsel and the outlaws sprinted away into the undergrowth as a troop of soldiers rode in.

Manannan sheathed his sword and walked over to the women. He bowed.

'Are you hurt?' he asked.

'No, sir,' replied the smaller of the women. 'Our thanks for your gallantry. I am Dianu; this is my younger sister, Sheera.'

Manannan turned. 'My compliments on your sword-skills, lady. You have a fine wrist.'

A slender fair-haired man joined them; he was clean-shaven and wore no sword, but carried a fine bow of horn. His clothes were of the softest tan leather and, though unadorned, were cut to perfection. His eyes were brown, flecked with gold, making them tawny like those of a great cat. He took Dianu in his arms and kissed her cheek, then he turned to Manannan; his smile was warm and friendly, the eyes open and honest.

'Thank you, sir. Your courage does you credit.'

'As does your timing,' responded Manannan, holding out his hand.

'I wish it had been better – these loyal men would still be alive. I am Lord Errin of Laene,' he said.

'You have grown since last I saw you. Were you not page to the Duke of Mactha?'

'Indeed I was – the year he won the Silver Lance. I am sorry but I do not recall you, sir.'

'My name is Manannan. I was clad somewhat differently then and sported no beard. Now, if you will excuse me, I must be on my way.'

'Surely not?' said Dianu. 'You cannot ride alone in this forest. That robber was Groundsel and even now he will be watching us. You would be in great danger.'

'As will he, my lady, if he crosses my path again! But do not fear for me. I have no wealth and Kuan rides far – and very fast.'

'You are welcome to stay with us, sir Knight,' put in Errin. 'My estates are less than half a day away. Shelter for the night, and a good meal?'

'Thank you, but no. There is a man I must find.' Manannan bowed to the women and walked to his horse.

Dianu watched as he rode away. 'A strange man,' she said. 'He could not have defeated them all – and yet he was prepared to take them on.'

'I do not remember him,' mused Errin. 'Perhaps he was a sentry, or a soldier on duty.'

'He would have been more than that,' Sheera said. 'He walks like a prince.'

'Well, he must – I fear – remain a mystery,' said Errin. 'Come, let us get out of this cursed forest before Groundsel returns with more cut-throats.'

For a week Ruad stayed in his cabin workshop – melting his ingots, creating gold and silver wire, delicate leaves and curious rings. On the eighth night he awoke from a light sleep to hear the sound of horses galloping on the trail. He swung from his bed, stretched, pulled a cloak about his shoulders and moved through the cabin and out into the yard beyond.

Six riders had pulled up before the dwelling.

'Whom do you seek?' asked Ruad, straining to recognize the men.

'Who says we seek anyone?' asked a rider, leaning forward across his saddle.

'It's late for hunting,' offered Ruad, 'and I'm tired, so state your business.'

'He's here,' hissed the rider. 'Where else would he be? I'll search the cabin.' He swung down from the saddle and marched across the yard. Ruad stepped aside, but as the man drew abreast of him his left hand flashed out to circle the rider's throat and lift him from his feet.

'I didn't hear you ask permission,' said Ruad softly. The man's feet lashed out weakly and his fingers scrabbled against Ruad's iron grip.

'Let him go!' ordered another man, heeling his horse forward. Just then the moon broke clear of the clouds and by its light Ruad recognized the speaker.

'I would not have expected an educated man to be riding with dross such as this, Lord Errin,' said Ruad, flinging his victim aside. The man fell to the ground, gasping for breath.

'I am sorry to disturb you, Craftsman, but a slave escaped today after the auction and he is said to frequent your company. We thought he might be here.'

'Does this slave have a name, Lord Errin?'

'I believe he is called Lug – an ugly name for such an attractive boy.'

'Did you buy him?'

'Yes; he was to be a present for the Duke. Unfortunately, now he will not be suitable. It will be necessary to brand his head and perhaps hamstring him.'

'Harsh   treatment   indeed,'   said   Ruad,   'but

warranted. Please search my cabin and then allow me to return to my bed.'

'I would hardly doubt your word, Craftsman. If you assure me he is not here, we will leave you in peace.'

'Be assured, Lord Errin, I have not seen the boy since last Tiernsday. Now, good night to you.' Ruad walked to the fallen man, who was struggling to sit; hoisting him to his feet by his hair, he led him to his horse and bundled him over the saddle. Lord Errin grinned, tugged on the reins of his stallion and galloped from the yard.

The man with the bruised throat lagged behind, then rode to where Ruad stood.

'I tell you . . .' he began. Ruad cut him short.

'Please,' he said, spreading his hands, 'do not promise we will meet again. Insults make me angry, but threats bore me. And when I am bored, I am sometimes violent. And neither of us wants that, little man.' The rider jerked the reins savagely and kicked his mount into a canter.

After he had gone Ruad wandered to the well, hauled up a bucket of cool water and sat on the wooden bench to drink and watch the stars.

Lug had been right to be fearful. The Duke would have been a poor slave-master. The Craftsman closed his eye and searched through the Colours. The boy would be frightened, his emotions racing. Ruad never liked to use the Red, for it always led to paths where evil walked. But the Red was strong and it knew fear. He found the current and concentrated on Lug. Within seconds he snapped clear and turned.

'Come out, boy,' he called, and the door of the wood-shed opened and Lug stepped into the moonlight. 'You almost made a liar of me!'

'I had nowhere else, Master. But tomorrow I will find Llaw Gyffes – if he will have me.'

'Come inside,' said Ruad softly. 'I have a few . . . toys . . . that may help you on your way.'

Inside the cabin, Ruad stoked the coals to life and hung the old iron flat pan above the flames. Into this he scooped a little fat and as it began to sizzle he cracked four eggs into the pan.

'I take it you are hungry, young Lug?'

'Yes, Master. Thank you. But, with respect, I reached my majority yesterday. I am Lug no longer; I am a man, and it is not fitting to carry a child's name.'

'Indeed it is not,' agreed Ruad. 'What name have you chosen?'

'Lámfhada, Master. I have long coveted the name.'

'LongArm. Yes, it is a good name. The first Knight of the Gabala was called Lámfhada. If you bring to it a fraction of his fame, you will do well.'

'I will do my best, Master. But I am no hero.'

Ruad slid the eggs from the pan to a wooden platter. Then, slicing several pieces from the dark loaf he had made the day before, he passed the meal to the newly-named Lámfhada.

'Do not judge yourself too harshly yet. I knew no Knights who sprang, fully-armoured, from the womb. All were striplings once.'

'Have you known many Knights?' Lámfhada asked.

'Many,' agreed Ruad, pouring a goblet of water and cutting himself a slice of bread.

'Why did they leave, Master?'

'You are full of questions, young man. And stop calling me Master — a man such as yourself may now address me as Craftsman. Or, as when you completed the bird, you may call me Ruad.'

'You would allow me to use your given name?' whispered the boy.

'It is not my given name,' Ruad told him, 'but I would be pleased if you used it.' The boy nodded and finished his meal, wiping the bread over the platter to scour the last traces of egg-yolk.

'I hope my coming here will not bring you trouble. They will use the Seer, Okessa, to find me; he will know I was here.'

'No,' said Ruad, showing his crooked teeth in a wide grin. 'They do not have a Seer good enough to penetrate my secrets – not even Okessa. Do not fear for me. Now, let me give you a present. Come.' He led the runaway through to the workshop where he opened an oak chest that lay against the far wall. From it he took a pair of doehide boots, edged with silver thread. 'Try them on,' he told the boy.

Lámfhada pulled off his sandals and struggled into the boots. 'They are a little big.'

Ruad pressed his fingers against the boy's toes.

'Thick socks should make them more comfortable, and you can grow into them.'

'Are they magic, Ruad?'

'Of course they are magic,' snapped the Craftsman. 'Do I look like a cobbler?'

'What will they do?'

'There is a word which I will write down for you, and when you say that word, the boots will give you speed and strength. You will be able to outrun any man and, over rough ground, even a horseman.'

'I don't know how to thank you. They must be priceless.'

'Unfortunately they are a failure. Yes, even I fail, young Lámfhada. They will not hold the magic. They will give you an hour, maybe two; then they are just boots. But they are good boots.'

'Can I not restore the magic?' asked the lad.

Ruad grinned. 'It will be good practice for you to try, at least. You need the Power of the Black, which is Earth Magic. But the Black is capricious and not easily drawn . . . and you can only find it at night, under moonlight. I used gold thread, and there is no metal better attuned to the Currents. The difficulty is control. Too much gold and the power is such that no man could wear them and still keep his balance; one leap would carry you so high you'd die of the subsequent fall. Yet too little and the power is exhausted within an hour. The problem has irritated me for a decade.'

'And the Word?' Lámfhada asked.

Ruad took a piece of charcoal and wrote it on the table-top. 'Do you know how to pronounce it? And don't do it!'

'I know,' said the runaway, his blue eyes locking to Ruad's face. 'That is your given name, is it not?'

'It is, boy, and no man must know of it. That is why I asked you never to talk of your work here.'

'You have shown great trust in me, Ruad. I will not betray it. How is it that men think you dead? And why would you want them to?'

'You and I are no different, boy,' Ruad told him. 'All men are slaves. My joy is that I understand magic better than any man alive. I love to create things of beauty. The Knights of the Gabala were beautiful – their armour beyond compare, their hearts as pure as the hearts of men could be. But there are in the world other powers, aligned to the Red, linked to the Dark-light. My work was sought after by those powers and it still is. But you do not understand me, do you? And indeed, why should you?'

'Your skill was desired by evil men,' said Lámfhada. 'I understand that.'

'I was captured five years ago by the King's men and taken to Furbolg; there they burned out my eye. The King wanted magic weapons, but I would give him none.'

'How did you escape?'

'By dying. My body was thrown into a pit beyond the castle walls.'

Lámfhada made the sign of the Protective Horn and shivered, but Ruad chuckled. 'By *appearing* to die! No heartbeat. No breath. They buried me – thankfully – in a shallow grave. I dug myself clear and staggered to the home of a friend. He nursed me for eight days; then I was smuggled out of the city and made my way here.'

'One day they will find you, Master. Why not come with me to Llaw Gyffes?'

'Because I am not ready. And I fear there is something I must undo. But you go. Live your life. Be free – or as free as any man can be.'

'If only the Knights were still here,' said Lámfhada sadly.

'It is childish to dream of what can never be,' Ruad whispered. 'Now it is time for you to go.' He opened a drawer under the bench, taking from it a long knife of razor-sharp steel. 'Here, you may need this.'

'Is it magic also?'

'The worst kind of magic there is. With one thrust, you can destroy a lifetime of dreams and hopes.'

Llaw Gyffes stood alone at the crest of the wooded hill on the edge of the forest, one hand resting on the broad trunk of a twisted oak, the other hooked into his wide leather belt. It had begun to rain, but the tall man appeared not to notice. His eyes were fixed on the jagged plain beyond the forest where several deer were grazing alongside a group of big-horn sheep. In the distance six riders were slowly making their way among the boulders and Llaw watched them for some time. It was obvious they were seeking tracks and they were not hunting deer, for the small herd could clearly be seen from their position and they showed no interest in them. The season was too early for wolf-hunting, the

41

grey timber beasts still high in the mountains. That left only Man.

The sky darkened and rain lashed down, streaming from Llaw's oiled leather shirt and drenching his green woollen leggings. Reaching up, he took hold of a thick branch and smoothly hauled himself into the sanctuary of the tree, climbing swiftly to the uppermost boughs where a crude wooden platform had been fastened and the branches above interwoven to form a thick roof. He sat down and parted the leaves so that he could see the riders. They were closer now, but still he could recognize none of them.

He pushed his blond hair from his eyes and lay back, willing himself to relax. Why should he care who they were hunting? Had anyone cared when Llaw Gyffes had been taken? Had anyone come forward to speak in his defence? Feeling his anger mount, he swallowed it swiftly. What point would there have been? You cannot blame them, Llaw. The decision was set from the moment he had smashed the bastard's skull!

One moment was all it took to change a life. In that single heartbeat, the blacksmith had become the outlaw.

The Duke's soldiers had been seeking a Nomad merchant accused of treason and had already ransacked several homes – stealing what they wished – when they had come upon Lydia. The officer in charge of the search ordered his men out, but stayed within himself. Seconds later Lydia's scream was heard by many of the neighbours, but they did nothing. Only a young slave boy had the courage to run to the smithy. Llaw had dropped his tools and raced back through the narrow streets. Two soldiers were outside his door, but before they could draw their swords he fell upon them, his huge fists hammering them senseless. One suffered a broken jaw, the other three fractured ribs. When the smith kicked in the door, smashing the bronze hinges, Lydia was lying across the bed, her eyes lifeless; the officer was buckling his belt.

As Llaw Gyffes advanced into the room, the officer drew his sword and lunged. Batting the blade aside with the back of his hand, Llaw crashed a ferocious blow to the man's face and the officer fell to his knees, the sword slipping from his fingers. Llaw moved to the body of his wife, seeing the purple bruising at her throat. Then a strangled cry of horror escaped from him and he turned on the stunned killer. Blow after blow he ripped into the man until at last the punished skull split and Llaw found himself kneeling over something unrecognizable. He staggered to his feet, his hands drenched in blood and brain, and stumbled from the house – into a fresh squad of soldiers. Llaw made no attempt to defend himself and they dragged him to the prison at Mactha.

For two months he was kept in an airless dungeon, chained to a wall. They fed him maggoty bread and stale water and left him sitting amidst his own filth. It was in this state that he was dragged before the court.

The trial was held in the Duke's Hall, and many were the faces Llaw recognized in the balconies above, to his left and his right: friends, neighbours, associates. The Duke sat on a raised dais, flanked by his knights, as the prosecutor outlined the facts. Llaw's anger flared as he heard the twisted version of events: there was a disturbance in the home of the blacksmith and a squad of soldiers, led by the Duke's nephew, entered the house. There they found that the blacksmith, Llaw Gyffes, had murdered his wife. Valiantly Maradin had tried to subdue the man, but the blacksmith's strength was prodigious and he had fought like a demon, killing Maradin and severely injuring two other soldiers.

The Duke leaned forward, his baleful eyes locking to Llaw's. 'What do you say?' he asked.

'It does not matter, I think, what I have to say,'

Llaw replied. 'All around this hall are men who know the truth. This . . . Maradin . . . raped and murdered my Lydia . . . and he paid for it. That is all.'

'Then bring forward these men to bear witness for you,' said the Duke. 'Where are they?'

Llaw looked up, his eyes sweeping the balconies. No one met his gaze.

'That brands you for the liar you are,' the Duke stated. 'Tomorrow morning you will be quartered and impaled. Take the wretch away.'

Returned to his dungeon, Llaw was once more chained to the wall. But gone now was the malaise that had gripped him during his captivity and in its place was a burning hatred. Hooking his hands around the chains, he hauled on them, feeling for a weakness. There was some movement in the right-hand chain; throwing the weight of his arm forward, he strained at the metal, then relaxed. Pushing his back against the wall, he hooked his fingers into the bracket fixing the chain to the stone. It seemed loose, and he could feel rust on the bolts.

Three times more he tried to loosen it. The bracket was bent now, almost U-shaped, but still it held. He tried the left-hand side, but this was immovable. Breathing deeply and easily he gathered his strength, hooking his right hand once more around the links. The muscles in his shoulders bulged as he fought to straighten his arm . . . the metal groaned and slowly, agonizingly, the bolts slipped from the mortar binding them and the chain snapped loose. Turning, Llaw could now put both hands to the left chain and pushing his right foot against the wall, he tore the bracket loose.

Free of the wall, there was still the barred dungeon door. Gathering his chains, he moved towards it and listened. There was no sound from the corridor beyond.

Returning to the wall, he loosely fitted the brackets back into place.

'Guard!' he yelled. 'Guard!' He heard the sound of footsteps.

'What is it? Why are you screaming?'

'Guard!'

'Damn you, be quiet!'

But Llaw continued to shout at the top of his voice and finally a grille opened at the centre of the door, the guard looking in to see the huge prisoner still chained to the wall.

'Be quiet, you whoreson, or I'll come in there and cut out your tongue!'

'You haven't the nerve,' hissed Llaw. 'You're a gutless sack of cow droppings!'

The grille slammed shut and Llaw heard the sound of the bar being lifted clear. Then the door opened and he blinked hard against the sudden light from the torches beyond as the guard advanced.

'I know what you want,' whispered the man. 'You want me to kill you. You can't stand the thought of your limbs being cut off; you don't want to think about the sharp stake rising through your body, ripping and tearing. Well, I won't kill you! I'll just make you *wish* you were dead.' From his belt he pulled a hide-handled whip.

Llaw hurled himself forward, his body cannoning into the startled guard. They fell to the floor, Llaw's hands circling the guard's throat with increasing pressure until his neck snapped and his body jerked. Llaw rose and stared down at the body. He had no regrets; Lydia's death and the injustice of the trial had conspired to alter the soul of the blacksmith. Gathering up the chains, he moved to the corridor. Some twenty feet to his left was the table and chair at which the guard had been stationed, and hanging from a hook on the wall were the keys to the chains. Llaw unfastened the manacles and left the chains on the table.

He was not yet free. He did not know the layout of

the dungeons, nor had he any idea of a way of escape. He knew he was on the fourth level below ground, and that the stair-well led to the Great Hall. There would be no way to freedom by that route. But where the other stairs led he had no idea. He sat back on the table, thinking. To come this far and still be a prisoner was galling. Returning to his cell, he stripped the liveried tunic from the body of the guard. At the man's belt was a knife, its edge razor-sharp. Slowly and painfully Llaw scraped away his red-gold beard, leaving only his moustache. Then, donning the guard's tunic, he moved back to the table. The corridor was some sixty feet long, with six barred doors on either side. Swiftly Llaw opened them all, freeing the prisoners and removing their manacles.

They staggered into the corridor. All were covered in filth and many had weeping sores on their skeletal limbs.

'You have a chance at freedom,' whispered Llaw. 'But stay silent and follow me.'

He climbed the stairs at a run, not bothering to look back, while the prisoners shuffled after him. On the next level a guard sat at a table, idly rolling dice. Llaw waved the prisoners back and boldly approached the man, who glanced at a marked candle.

'You're early,' said the guard, grinning, 'but I'll not complain.' Scooping up his dice he rose – straight into a clubbing fist – and slumped back to his seat, his head dropping to thud against the table-top. Once again Llaw opened the cell doors, freeing the prisoners. He neither knew nor cared what crimes they had committed; all that mattered was his own escape.

'Now you may do as you please,' he told them.

'But how do we get out?' asked a thick-set bearded man, with a jagged scar on his cheek.

'Take the stairs and free the others. There are two more levels,' Llaw told him.

46

'What about you?'

'I have other business.'

'Who are you?' another man asked.

'Llaw Gyffes,' he told them.

'Stronghand? I'll remember it, my friend,' the bearded man promised.

Llaw nodded and moved away into the shadows, climbing a narrow stair-well which led to a carpeted hallway with curtained windows. Drawing back the hangings, he looked out over the courtyard less than ten feet below. The great gates were open and two sentries stood chatting in the shadows. On the walls he counted five bowmen. Beyond the gates he could see the lights of Mactha and the far mountains shining in the moonlight. Easing himself through the window, he silently dropped to the cobbles. A sudden shout froze him in his tracks, but it came from within the castle.

'The prisoners are free!' came the call as Llaw ran to the gates.

'What's happening?' asked a sentry.

'The prisoners have broken out,' Llaw told him. 'Quickly, get to the Hall and guard the stair-wells!'

The two sentries raced towards the doors and Llaw glanced at the men on the battlements. 'Help them,' he shouted. 'Guard the Hall!'

The bowmen ran to join their comrades and Llaw slowly walked from the fortress, skirting Mactha and heading for the distant mountains.

He learned later that the twenty-three men he had freed had opened the cell doors for forty more. Thirty of the prisoners died in the hand-to-hand fighting inside the castle, twenty-two more had been captured in the first three days, but eleven had escaped.

Now, seven months later, as Llaw sat in his tree hideaway, the hunters were once more seeking a runaway.

Llaw hoped they caught him.

He didn't want armed men riding through his forest, disturbing the deer and putting Llaw himself in peril.

Lámfhada crouched behind two jagged boulders and watched the horsemen. The rain was lashing at their eyes, but still they came on, led by the tracker – a wizened Nomad with slanted eyes. Lámfhada was sure the Nomad was a man of magic. How else could he track him across rocks and scree?

The youth glanced back at the mountains and the forest's edge. There lay security – but it was at least a mile distant and uphill. He was chilled by the biting rain and his empty belly gnawed at him. Here in this desolate place he wondered at his decision to flee, cursing himself for his stupidity. Was the Duke's service so bad, compared with this? It was . . . he knew that well enough. The Duke often had his servants whipped and, at the Midwinter Solstice, had ordered an elderly slave to be flayed alive for some indiscretion. No, thought Lámfhada, better to be a runaway.

The Nomad tracker stopped some two hundred paces away from the boulders and suddenly pointed. Lámfhada blinked and shrank back as the riders spurred their mounts into a gallop. The youth leapt from his hiding place and sprinted towards the mountains, slipping and slithering on the mud and the greasy rocks. The horses thundered after him and he could hear the shouts of the riders.

In panic Lámfhada screamed the magic name and instantly felt his weight lessen, his stride lengthen. He was almost floating over the rocks. Swerving to the left, he leapt ten feet to a boulder, cutting to the right up a narrow trail towards the trees. The horsemen could not follow directly and were forced to skirt the boulder, losing ground on the runner in the process. Once more the chase was on.

Lord Errin spurred his giant black gelding into a gallop and bore down on the runaway, scarcely able to believe the speed at which the youth was moving. Had he known he was this swift, he would never have dreamt of giving him to the Duke but would have kept him and taken him to Furbolg for the races. Too late now, thought Errin, as he closed on the boy.

Hearing the hoofbeats Lámfhada cut left, clambering up a scree slope and clawing his way over the jutting boulders. Errin cursed and guided the gelding on to the treacherous slope but the horse slithered, dropping to its haunches. Another rider galloped up.

'Give me your bow,' shouted Errin, taking the weapon and notching an arrow to the string. Lámfhada was almost in the clear as Errin drew back the string, took a deep breath, allowed the air to drift from his lungs and, between breaths, loosed the shaft. The arrow sped to its target, catching the youth high in the back. He staggered, but did not fall and reached the sanctuary of the trees.

'Should we follow, my Lord?' asked the Nomad.

'No, we are not strong enough to face the rebels. Anyway, the arrow went deep; he will not survive.' Errin threw the bow back to the rider and led the black gelding from the scree slope. 'What was it the boy shouted?' he asked.

The Nomad shrugged. 'It sounded like a name, Lord: Ollathair.'

'That is what I heard. Now why would a runaway use the name of a dead wizard? And why did his speed increase so greatly?' Again the Nomad shrugged and Errin smiled. 'You do not care, do you, Ubadai?'

'No, Lord,' the Nomad agreed. 'I track him. I do my job very good.'

'Indeed you did. But it is intriguing; I will ask

49

Okessa when we return.' The Nomad hawked and spat and Errin chuckled. 'He does not like you either, my friend. But beware, for he is a powerful man to have as an enemy.'

'A man may be judged by his enemies, Lord. Sooner strong ones than weak ones, I think.'

Errin grinned at him and led the group back towards the safety of Mactha.

Just beyond the tree line Lámfhada stumbled to a halt, a great weariness rising within him. He tried to move on, but his vision blurred and the trees seemed to move and sway before him. The ground swept up at him and his eyes closed.

A slender man stepped from behind a thick pine and advanced towards the fallen youth. He was dressed in a shirt of sky-blue silk, leather trews and silver-buckled shoes, with around his shoulders a fine cloak of sheepskin. His long hair was gathered at the nape of his neck by a silver band, and his eyes were violet. Kneeling by Lámfhada, he saw the blood seeping from the arrow wound and turned away his head.

'Well, are you going to take it out?' came a voice and the man jerked and rose swiftly to his feet, turning to face the newcomer – a tall, broad-shouldered warrior with blond hair and a red-gold beard.

'I don't know anything about wounds. I think he could be dead.'

Llaw Gyffes grinned. 'Your face is as grey as a winter sky.' Ignoring the man, he strode to the stricken youth and ripped away his shirt. The arrow was deep and lodged under the shoulder-blade, the flesh around the wound already swollen and puffy. Llaw gripped the shaft.

'Wait!' said the other. 'If it is barbed, it will rip him to pieces.'

'Then pray it is not,' replied Llaw, suddenly wrenching the shaft clear. Lámfhada groaned, but did not wake. Llaw held up the arrow; the head was not barbed. Blood was pouring from the wound now and Llaw plugged it with a piece of torn shirt. Lifting the youth, he draped the body over his right shoulder and walked away into the shadow-haunted forest.

The other man followed. 'Where are we going?' he asked.

'There is a settlement about an hour ahead. They have an apothecary and a Wyccha woman,' Llaw told him.

'My name is Nuada.'

Llaw walked on without speaking.

The sun was sinking behind the mountains when they crested a small rise above the village. There were seven cabins and a longer hall to the south, while at the northern end was a paddock in which five ponies were gathered.

Llaw turned to his companion. 'Check if the boy still lives,' he ordered.

Gingerly Nuada took Lámfhada's arm, feeling for a pulse. 'Yes,' he said, 'but the heart is beating erratically.'

Llaw made no comment and began the long walk down the hill. As they approached two men came from the nearest hut; both were armed with longbows and had knives at their belts. Llaw waved at them and, recognizing him, they returned the arrows to their quivers.

Llaw took Lámfhada to the furthest cabin, mounted the steps to the rough-hewn porch and tapped at the door, which was opened by a middle-aged woman. Seeing his burden, she stepped aside; he entered the cabin and made straight for the narrow bed beneath the eastern window.

The woman helped him to lay the youth on the bed and pulled the blood-drenched plug from the wound. More blood began to flow and she watched it carefully.

'It did not pierce the lung,' she said. 'Leave him here; I will see to him.'

Llaw said nothing. He rose and stretched his neck, then noticed Nuada standing in the doorway.

'What do you want here?' he asked.

'A meal would be pleasant,' Nuada said.

'Can you pay?'

'I usually sing for my supper,' stated Nuada. 'I am a saga poet.'

Llaw shook his head and pushed past, stepping into the gathering darkness. Nuada joined him. 'I am a *good* poet. I have been welcomed in the palace at Furbolg and have sung before the Duke in Mactha. And I have been east.'

'Good poets are rich poets,' said Llaw. 'It is the nature of things. But it does not matter; I expect the villagers will be glad of a song. Do you know the saga of Petric?'

'Of course, but I tend towards the contemporaneous. That's why I am here – gathering material.'

'Take my advice – and give them Petric,' advised Llaw, walking away towards the long hall.

Nuada ran to catch up. 'You are not very sociable, my friend.'

'I have no friends,' Llaw told him, 'and I need none.'

The hall was some seventy feet long, with two stone hearths set on opposite sides at the centre. There were a dozen tables and, at the far end, a long trestle stand behind which were several barrels. Llaw elbowed his way through the crowd and lifted a tankard from a hook on the wall. This he filled with ale from a smaller barrel placed on the trestle table. Nuada saw that he left no payment, so he too gathered a tankard.

'What do you think you're doing?' asked a swarthy man, poking a thick finger into Nuada's chest.

'Getting a drink,' the poet answered.

'Not with my jug, you don't,' he said, snatching the tankard away.

'My apologies,' said Nuada. Turning, he saw the blond warrior talking to a man nearby. The man – thickset and with a swelling belly – swung to stare at the poet, then smiled and made his way over.

'You are a saga sayer?' the man asked.

'Indeed I am, sir.'

'Have you travelled far?'

'From Furbolg. I sang at the court.'

'Good. You have news, then. I'll introduce you. What's your name?'

'Nuada. Sometimes called Silverhand – when I play the harp.'

'We have no harps – but there's a meal and a bed if you tell us what is happening in the world. Nothing too flowery, mind,' he warned. 'Keep it simple.'

Llaw Gyffes sat down on a bench seat against the wall, pushing his long legs out before him. He grinned as he experienced a moment of sympathy for the poet. This was not Furbolg, nor even Mactha. The courtly saga-sayer was about to practise his art before a group of nithings, wolfsheads, men who knew the difference between romance and reality. He watched as Nuada climbed atop a broad table, then the hallkeeper called for quiet and introduced the poet. Conversations ceased momentarily, then began again as Nuada started to speak. Men turned away and a joke told in the far corner of the hall brought hearty laughter.

Suddenly Nuada's voice rose above the clamour, rich and resonant.

'When a hero dies,' he said, 'the gods give him a gift. But it is double-edged. You!' he stormed, pointing at a stout man wearing a wolfskin jerkin. 'Do you know the gift? Yes, you, the pig in wolf's clothing!' A ripple of laughter sounded and the man's face flushed red as his hand reached for the dagger at his belt. Nuada swung to point at another man. 'What about you? Do you know the gift?' The man shook his head. 'Then I'll tell you. When a hero dies, his soul wanders, called hither and yon by saga-sayers and poets. When they speak of him before a crowd – even such a pack of beggars as is gathered here – then his soul appears in their midst. That is magic! That is a kind of sorcery no wizard can create. And why is it double-edged?

'Because that hero will stand among you and see that you care nothing for his deeds. They are less than shadows.

'By that fire stands Petric, greatest of warriors, noblest of men. He fought evil and he stood for something greater than glory. And what does he see when he looks around him? Sniggerers and loafers, runaways and lechers. Such a man deserves far better.'

Llaw Gyffes glanced nervously at the fire, but could see nothing apart from the dancing flames. But the hall was quiet now and the poet held that silence for several moments; then his voice softened.

'It was at the dawn of a different age,' Nuada began, 'when Petric walked from the Forest. Tall he was . . .'

Llaw listened as the familiar tale unfolded. Not a sound disturbed the telling and Nuada's magic wove its spell. At the close, when he recounted the treachery and the gallantry when Petric was slain at the Pass of Souls, all eyes were on the poet. But he did not end the tale there, with the winged demons closing in on the body. He spoke of Petric's warrior soul rising from the slain corpse and continuing his battle in a ghostly sky – his sword a blade of moonlight, his eyes two shining stars. When Nuada's voice finally faded to silence the applause was thunderous.

For an hour he spoke, telling stories of ancient heroes, ending with the tale of the Knights of the Gabala and their journey to slay the essence of evil. Despite himself, Llaw found his own cynicism drowned by the poet's eloquence and applauded as loudly as the rest when the tales were over.

The hallkeeper brought Nuada a tankard of ale, which he downed swiftly. Then he called for a chair and set it at the centre of the table, sitting down for the questions.

Men gathered around, asking of events in the world outside. He told them of the purge in the capital, of Nomad merchants hunted like rats; of rising prices, and food shortages in the north. He talked of the Great Race and the stallion, Lancer, a giant grey which had beaten the best horses in the empire.

At last he stepped from the table and rejoined Llaw Gyffes.

'You have talent,' said the outlaw. 'But was Petric really here?'

Nuada smiled. 'He was, if you felt his presence.'

'How is it that a man of your skills should find himself in such a place as this? You should be rich, and living in a palace.'

Nuada shrugged and his violet eyes narrowed. 'I have lived in a palace. I have dined from gold plates.' He touched his blue silk shirt. 'Once I would have worn this shirt for one day only, and then given it to a slave or thrown it upon a fire.'

Llaw smiled. 'But you are going to tell me that all this was as nothing compared with the freedom of life in the forest?'

'Not at all. Look at me, man! What do you see?'

'You are handsome enough, with that long dark hair and those odd eyes. What is there to see?'

'I am a Nomad. My father was one of the richest merchants in Furbolg.'

Llaw nodded. 'I understand; it was all taken from you.'

'Worse than that. My family were slain. I was not

55

at home when the soldiers came; I was with . . . a friend. She smuggled me from the city.'

'These are bad days, right enough. What made you choose this forest?'

'I heard there was a rebellion here, led by a hero, and I came to learn his tale. Then I will travel east to kingdoms where sanity still rules.'

'You'll find no rebellion here. Outlaws and thieves, perhaps, but no heroes.'

Nuada said nothing for a moment, then leaned close to the outlaw.

'There is a new saga being told in Furbolg and many other towns. It is about a hero who has defied both Duke and King. He slew the Duke's nephew and was sentenced to death; but he escaped the dungeons of Mactha and released all the prisoners there. All over the country his name is a byword in the fight against tyranny.'

Llaw chuckled. 'The fight against tyranny? What nonsense is this, poet? Fighting tyrants is like spitting against a storm.'

'You are wrong. This man exists and I will find him.'

'He has a name, this paragon?'

'He is called Stronghand. Llaw Gyffes.' Nuada's eyes gleamed as he spoke the name.

'Good luck in your quest, poet.'

'Then you do not know him?'

'No, I do not know the man you speak of. Come, let us eat.'

3

The Once-Knight rode along the narrow trails far from any settlements. He lived by hunting his meat with his longbow and taking what herbs he needed from the clearings in the woods and meadows. Time was running short for him now, and the pressure on his throat was greater. But nowhere had he heard of a craftsman with special skills, and the name Ruad Rofhessa was unknown. Only the large town of Mactha was left now in the north and he was loth to travel there, for the Duke would remember him – even if his page did not.

It was fifteen days since he had stopped at a town to purchase supplies of salt, a wax-sealed jug of brandy and a sack of grain for his stallion. Grass was plentiful, but a grain-fed horse could outrun any wild beast. The town had been small – some sixteen houses, a smithy and a store – and the prices of his supplies more than double what he expected. But he had paid and ridden on to camp just outside the town in a wooded meadow by a stream.

It was hot and sweat trickled on his scalp under the suffocating helm. As he opened the brandy and drank deeply, his mind fled back to the worst moment of terror in his childhood. He had climbed a dead tree and was traversing from one side to the other when a dry branch snapped beneath him and he had plunged through the leaves and fallen into the rotted heart, his feet hammering through an ants' nest. His arms were pinned at his sides, the trunk surrounding him like a narrow upright coffin. He had cried out, but he was far from home and had told no one where he was going.

Ants began to crawl over his skin . . . up along his face, across his eyelids, into his ears. He screamed and screamed, but they crawled into his mouth. With his arms pinned he could not climb out, and he waited for hour upon tormented hour until at last a forester heard his feeble cries. Six men laboured for an hour to cut him free and from that day he had avoided confined spaces. Even into manhood the terror had stayed with him.

And when the Black Gate opened the nightmare had rushed from his memories, engulfing him in a tidal wave of fear.

Yet now he was trapped again, this time by a cylinder of silver steel locked to the neck-plates of his Gabala armour. He could not wipe away the sweat that trickled on his scalp . . . that felt like ants upon his skin. He drank more of the brandy.

Where was Ollathair? Manannan had tried the sword-jewel often, but so far it had offered no hope. But then the Armourer had to be within a day's ride of the wielder.

Damn you, wizard! Where did you go?

During his six years of self-imposed exile, Manannan had listened avidly to all the news from home; but mostly it concerned the new King, Ahak, fresh from his victory in the last Fomorian War. He had negotiated the dissolution of the empire with rare brilliance, agreeing treaties with all the territories the Gabala had once ruled. But the Knights had passed into legend and of the Armourer there was no word at all. Had he changed his mind and travelled with Samildanach? On that terrible night there was a deep, fine mist; that was how Manannan had been able to slip away unseen.

But no . . . Ollathair had said he must remain to re-open the Gate when the Evil Ones had been defeated. Five days, he said he would wait. So where could he be after six years?

Manannan sat with his back to a broad oak and continued to drink. After a while he began to sing a ribald song he had learned as a mercenary far to the east. It was a good song – about a girl, her husband and her two lovers, and the various ploys she used to keep them all apart. He could not remember the last verse. The stallion moved away from him, cropping grass at the edge of the stream.

'It is no joy to sing alone, Kuan. Even in such a beautiful spot,' said the Once-Knight. 'Come, stay by me and I'll give you grain. Come!'

The stallion lifted its great grey head and stared at the man.

'I am not drunk, I am happy. There is a difference, although I would not expect a horse to understand.' He struggled to rise, but tripped over his scabbard. Pulling it from his belt, he dropped it to the grass and stood. 'See? I can stand.'

'Look at that, lads. He really can stand!'

The Once-Knight turned and peered at the newcomers. There were four men, three of them bearded and the fourth a youngster of maybe fifteen years. 'Welcome, gentlemen, may I offer you a drink?'

'Oh, we think you can do better than that, sir. We are in need of money and a fine horse.'

The Once-Knight sank to the ground and chuckled. 'I only have the one horse, and he is not for sale.'

'But then,' said the first man, a broad-shouldered fellow with a dark forked beard, 'we are not planning to buy him, sir.'

'I understand,' said the Once-Knight slowly. 'But he is not for stealing, either. Now be off with you!'

'That is not friendly, sir, and you risk much with such an attitude. Look around you – there are four of us, all armed and not one of us drunk.'

'I've offered you the jug,' the Once-Knight told him. Pulling his sword clear of its scabbard, he hauled himself upright by gripping the trunk of the oak. 'Now be warned,' he said, his voice slurred, 'I am a Knight of the Gabala. To face me in battle is to die.'

'Well, my boys,' jeered the first man, 'here is an interesting sight – a regular Knight – a Gabala Knight, no less. Strange that he should wear no armour save that dented helm. Even stranger that he should be drunk. I would not doubt your word, sir, but was strong drink not frowned upon by your Order?'

'It was,' admitted the Once-Knight. 'We were . . .' he struggled for the word.

'Pure?' offered the man.

'That's it! Pure. Noble Knights.' He laughed. 'Noble like gods! And proud. Proud. Yes. All gone now. Gone away,' he said, waving his hand in the air. 'Off to fight the Demon Lord.'

'But you don't appear to have gone with them, sir?'

'No. I was . . . frightened. The Black Gate. Ollathair conjured it and I would not pass it. I couldn't, you see. Something inside just . . . snapped. We were all mounted and ready – and the Gate opened. The others, Edrin, Pateus . . . they all rode in. But not me. No. Not I. All gone!'

'You are – and forgive the bluntness of my language, sir – a coward, then?'

'Yes, yes. That is me: the coward-Knight. And yet the truth does not hurt the way it once did. Are you sure you will not share my jug?'

'Thank you, but no. We will, however, relieve you of your horse and your purse.'

'I do wish you would not attempt this,' said the Once-Knight. 'We have known each other but a short time and already I like you.'

'Kill him,' said the man and the other three drew their knives and rushed forward while the leader walked towards the stallion. The Once-Knight rolled his wrists and the longsword hissed as it swept up, sunlight flashing on the blade. The first man tried to halt his charge, but it was too late and the blade sang down to slice his jugular before smashing his collarbone and opening a great wound all the way to his lungs. He was dead before he hit the ground. The blade slid clear and slashed back in a reverse cut that opened the second man's belly clean through to his backbone; he alone had time to scream. The youngster had circled behind the Knight and now he leapt forward with knife raised. Without turning the Once-Knight dropped to his knee, spinning his sword so that the blade was between his right arm and his side. The boy did not see the danger until he was almost upon the kneeling man and the sword clove into his chest, dissecting his heart.

The Once-Knight dragged his blade clear and stood. In the several seconds that the fight had lasted, the robbers' leader had reached Kuan and grabbed for the reins. The stallion reared, his front hooves cracking into the thief's face so that he stumbled back and fell heavily. A shadow moved across him and he looked up.

'It was a foolish move, and your friends have suffered for it.' The man rolled to his knees, eyes wide in disbelief as he stared at the bodies.

'My son!' he screamed, scrambling to the boy. 'You've killed my son.' For some seconds he cradled the body, then stood and drew his own knife. The Once-Knight said nothing, for he knew no words could dissuade him. With a piercing scream the robber raced towards him.

The longsword sang out . . .

Sober now, the Once-Knight climbed into the saddle. 'Come, Kuan, this place is no longer beautiful.'

Since that day he had avoided towns, settlements and even lonely cabins until he reached the Duchy of Mactha. If Ollathair was anywhere it would be here, in his homeland. The Once-Knight drew his sword and gazed into the ruby pommel. 'Ollathair,' he whispered. The jewel shimmered and darkened, an image forming at its heart; there, by a well, stood the Armourer.

And armed men were moving towards him, their swords bright in the moonlight . . .

'No!' shouted the Once-Knight. But the image faded.

Errin rose from his bath and stepped into the thick robe held out for him by Ubadai. His body glowing from the hot water, he moved to the window and felt the freshness of the night breeze. Ubadai poured a goblet of watered wine and carried it to his master, but Errin waved it away.

'No drink tonight,' he said.

'Something troubles you, Lord?'

'Why do you stay in my service, Ubadai? I freed you two years ago and you could go wherever you want – back to the Steppes; across the sea to Cithaeron, or into the east. Why do you stay?'

Ubadai shrugged, his dark, slanted eyes showing no emotion. 'You should drink. Drink very much. Fall down, maybe.'

'I do not think so. Go. Leave me.'

Errin watched as the Nomad turned on his heel and strode from the room. He gazed down at the wine and shivered. Having closed the window, he walked to the far side of the room where a log-fire blazed in a stone hearth. Dragging a heavy chair to the fireside, he sat and stared into the flames.

The meeting with the Seer, Okessa, haunted him – forcing its way into his mind again and again. He had never liked the man, whose shaven head and curved nose gave the impression of a vulture. And his eyes always seemed to shine with a malevolent gleam. No, Errin did not like Okessa.

'It is rare that you take the time to consult me,' the Seer had said as Errin entered his study.

'Our paths seldom cross,' Errin replied, gazing at the shelves and the tomes placed there. 'You have some interesting books. Perhaps I could borrow some?'

'Of course, my Lord. I did not know you were expert in the Dead Languages.'

'I am not.'

'Then, sadly, the books would be of no value. How can I help you?'

Errin sat in a high-backed chair opposite thc Seer, who carefully laid his quill on the desk, pushing aside the book on which he had been working.

'I have come to seek your advice. A youth – a runaway – shouted a word. I think it was some kind of spell casting, for his running speed increased. I wounded him, but he escaped to the Great Forest.'

'And the word?'

'Ollathair.'

'You are sure?'

'I believe so. My man, Ubadai, heard it also. What does it signify?'

Okessa leaned back and stroked his long nose with the index finger of his right hand, his pale eyes fixed on Errin. 'A dead wizard – he shouted the name of a dead wizard. Are you sure his speed increased? Could not fear have spurred him to greater urgency?'

'It is possible – but only just. I have never seen a man run faster and, as you know, I was Master of the Games last autumn in Furbolg. No, I think the word was one of Power. Is that possible?'

'All things are possible, Lord Errin. Some . . . artefacts . . . of Ollathair's survive, I believe. The King beyond Cithaeron has a golden falcon, and King Ahak possesses a Gabalic sword which can cut through anything, even steel. But these are priceless. How would a runaway slave obtain such an artefact?'

Okessa stood and moved to the bookshelves, drawing down a leather-covered tome. Returning to his seat, he opened the book and carefully began to turn the pages.

'Ollathair,' he said at last. 'Yes, here it is. The son of Calibal, fifteenth Armourer to the Knights of the Gabala. Ollathair was apprentice to his father in 1157 at the age of thirteen. He succeeded his father in 1170, so, he would have been twenty-six then. In 1190 the Knights vanished from history and we are left with merely legend, the most enduring of which is that they rode into Hell to destroy the essence of all evil. Ollathair was arrested as a traitor the following year, and was put to death in the dungeons of Furbolg. There is also a brief description of his interrogation. No, I do not think you heard the boy correctly.'

'Could there be more than one Ollathair?' Errin asked.

'If there was, my Lord, be assured I would have heard of him. Was there anything else?'

'No, my Lord Seer, but I am grateful for your time and effort,' said Errin, rising.

'Please, do not leave quite so soon: there is a matter I wish to discuss.' Errin sat down. 'It is the question of your household, my Lord. You have some six Nomad retainers, I believe?'

'Yes – and all loyal, both to myself and to the crown.'

'The crown sees it differently. The King is about to issue an edict that all Nomads be detained and sent to Gar-aden.'

'It is a desert!'

'You question the King's wishes?' asked Okessa softly.

'It is not for me to question my sovereign; it was merely an observation. However, the Nomads in my employ are not slaves and they are free to travel where they wish.'

'Not so,' said Okessa, smiling. 'No Nomad can now

enjoy citizenship, and all are under the King's express command to gather at Gar-aden. Those who do not obey are to be hunted down and slain, their goods and chattels taken by the crown or the crown's agents. In Mactha the agent will, of course, be the Duke.'

'And how, may I ask, are we to describe who is a Nomad? They have been among us for hundreds of years; it is said that many noble families have Nomad blood.'

'You know of such families?' Okessa asked, leaning forward, his eyes gleaming.

'Not with any certainty.'

'Then be careful of what you say. It is decreed that the Nomads are a tainted people and they must be removed from the kingdom.'

'Thank you for this advance intelligence,' said Errin, forcing a smile. 'Be assured I shall act upon it.'

'I hope that you do. By the way, this matter of Ollathair intrigues me. Tell me, would you know of any craftsman or landholder around Mactha with only one good eye?'

'I do not make it my business to mix with the lower orders, Lord Seer, but I shall have enquiries made for you.'

'Thank you. Would you treat the matter with some urgency?'

'I will indeed.'

Errin had gone straight to the Duke, who took him to his private apartments in the west tower.

'It is not for us to question a royal decree,' the Duke pointed out. 'And let us not forget the question of increased wealth. You and I are in a fortunate position. Neither of us has any Nomad blood in our family lines; we can only benefit.'

Errin had nodded. He had always known the Duke was a hard and cruel man, but he had believed there was also a certain nobility of spirit in him. Now as he looked into the Duke's dark eyes he saw only greed. The Duke of Mactha stood and smiled. Taller than Errin – who had once been his page – he was a handsome man approaching forty years of age, with a carefully cut and combed forked beard. 'Do not fret about a few peasants, Errin. Life is too short.'

'I am thinking of my manservant, Ubadai. He has been a faithful companion – and he saved my life. You remember? The bear hunt, when my horse fell? The beast would have torn me to pieces, but Ubadai leapt from his horse to the bear's back.'

'A brave move, but is that not what we expect from our followers? Give him money and send him to Garaden. Now, let us move to happier matters. The King is coming to Mactha in the spring and I want you to be the Lord of the Feast.'

'Thank you, my Lord. You do me great honour.'

'Nonsense, Errin, you are one of the finest organizers I know. The worst swordsman and the finest cook!' The Duke had chuckled, and Errin had bowed and left the room.

Now, here before the fire, his heart was heavy and his mind full of foreboding.

Okessa was a snake, and it would be long before Errin would forget the malevolence in his eyes as he had asked, '*You know of such families?*' It was that alone which had saved the one-eyed Craftsman, Ruad Rofhessa. Errin would never deliver any man into the hands of the Lord Seer. But where did that leave him?

Lost in thought, he did not notice Ubadai approaching. 'Food,' said the servant, placing a silver tray beside Errin's chair.

'I am not hungry.'

Ubadai looked long into Errin's pale face. 'Some bad thing, hey? No drink. No food.'

'You must leave Mactha ... tonight. Take all Nomad servants with you and make for the forest.

Beyond it is the sea. Get as far from the realm as you can.'

'Why?'

'To stay is to die. All Nomads are to be herded to Gar-aden. It is a place of death, Ubadai; I can feel it. Prepare the servants.'

'It is done,' Ubadai assured him.

Ruad adjusted the silvered mirror and stropped his shaving blade against the leather hanging from the wall. Satisfied with the edge, he wetted his face with warmed water and carefully cut away the black and grey stubble.

The face he saw was one that merited a beard, he thought: a heavy, all-disguising beard, to cover the lantern jaw and mask the gash of a mouth with its crooked teeth.

'You are uglier now than ever,' he told his reflection. Returning to his table he pushed aside the remains of his breakfast and removed the bronze eye-patch, polishing it with a soft cloth until it gleamed. Replacing it, he poured himself a goblet of apple juice and watched the coming dawn, the shadows shrinking back from the trees outside his window.

He had been happier here than at the Citadel, for the old fortress held too many memories of his father. Calibal had been a stern parent to the son he had not wanted and the boy – ugly and awkward – could do nothing to please him. Every day of his youth had been spent trying to win his father's love. At last he had succeeded in the Colours, proving himself a greater magician than Calibal; then his father's indifference had turned to hatred, and he put the boy from him. Even when he was dying, he would not allow his son to sit by his death-bed.

Poor Calibal, thought Ruad. Poor, lonely Calibal.

He stood and forced the memories from his mind. For three hours he worked on his designs, then wandered out into the meadow beyond the woods to sit and enjoy the autumn sunshine. Soon the dark clouds would gather, the north wind howl and the blizzards cover the mountains with freezing ice and snow. Already the leaves were turning to gold, the flowers fading.

A distant figure caught his eye, making slow progress up the hill. Ruad waited as Gwydion approached.

'Lazing in the sunshine?' said the newcomer, his lined face red with the exertion of the climb, his white shoulder-length hair shining with sweat.

'You should buy yourself a horse,' responded Ruad, rising to his feet. 'You're too old for mountain walking.'

The old man smiled, took a deep breath and leaned on his staff. 'I have not the energy to argue,' he admitted, 'but a glass of your apple juice will revive me.'

Ruad led him into the house and poured him a drink, while Gwydion sat down at the table.

'How is life treating you?' the old man asked.

'I do not complain,' said Ruad. 'You?'

'There is always work for a Healer – even one with fading powers.'

Ruad cut several slices of dark bread and a wedge of cheese, passing them to Gwydion. While the man ate Ruad walked to the doorway, scanning the road to Mactha. All was still.

'Okessa is seeking news of a one-eyed craftsman,' said Gwydion as Ruad returned.

'I do not doubt it. I made a mistake.'

'You gave magic to the boy, Lug?'

'Yes.'

'That was not wise.'

'Wisdom should be tempered with compassion,' observed Ruad. 'Did you come all this way to warn me?'

'Yes and no,' replied Gwydion. 'I would have sent a message, but there is a pressing matter you might help me to resolve.'

'You speak of the change in the Colours?'

'Then it is not all in my mind? Good,' said Gwydion. 'So my powers are not fading as fast as I believed?'

'No. The Red is swelling, the other Colours fading. Green is suffering the worst, for it is the furthest.'

'What is the cause?' Gwydion asked. 'I know that the Colours shift and dance, but never in such an extreme way. The Green is now a shimmering thread – I am hard pressed to heal a sick calf.'

Ruad moved to the hearth, cleared away the ash and prepared a new fire. 'I do not have any answers, Gwydion. There is an imbalance; the Colours have lost their harmony.'

'Has this, to your knowledge, happened before? I have never heard of such a thing.'

'Nor I. Perhaps it will right itself.'

'You think so?' asked Gwydion. Ruad shrugged. 'There is an ugly feeling in the air,' whispered the old man. 'In Mactha there have been three murders in the last week. There is fear, Ruad.'

'It is the influence of the Red; it stirs the emotions. I have felt it too – an impatience, an anger, that affects my work. Lately I have been unable to use the Blue, so I have resorted to the Black, but even that is fading.'

The old man shivered as a cold wind blew through the open doorway. 'Light the fire, Ruad. These ageing bones cannot take the cold.'

Lifting a thick branch from the hearth, Ruad ran his fingers along its length. Fire leapt instantly from the wood and he thrust it into the prepared tinder. 'The Red, of course, still has its uses,' he said, adding fuel to the blaze.

Gwydion grinned. 'Not for Healing, from which I earn my meagre income.'

Ruad closed the door and pulled two chairs before the fire. Gwydion seated himself, holding out his hands to the dancing flames, and Ruad joined him.

'You will, of course, stay the night? You are most welcome.'

'Thank you,' Gwydion accepted.

'What other news have you?'

The Healer shivered. 'None that is good, I fear. A traveller from Furbolg says the city is in the grip of terror – a killer is stalking the streets. So far the bodies of eleven young women have been found, and five young men. The King has promised to hunt down the killer, but as yet there is no sign of any success. Added to this are rumours concerning the Nomads. More than a thousand were taken to Gar-aden to what was described as a settlement. I have it on good authority . . .' Gwydion shuddered. 'Strange how fire does not warm me as once it did. Do you think I am close to death, Ruad?'

'I am not a seer, my friend,' said Ruad softly. 'You were talking of the Nomads?'

'There is a pit near the mountains. I am told a thousand bodies lie there, with room for many thousands more.'

'It cannot be,' Ruad whispered. 'Where is the logic? Who could gain from such a slaughter?'

Gwydion said nothing for a moment, then he turned towards the Craftsman. 'The King has decreed that the Nomads are tainted, that they corrupt the purity of the realm. He blames them for all ills. You have heard of the nobleman, Kester?'

'I met him once: an irascible old man.'

'Put to death,' said Gwydion. 'His grandfather wed a Nomad princess.'

'I have never heard the like. Is there no opposition to the King?'

'There was,' replied Gwydion. 'The King's champion, the knight Elodan, left his service. He stood up for Kester and demanded the ancient right to champion his honour. The King agreed, which surprised everyone, for there was not a finer swordsman than Elodan anywhere in the empire.

'A great crowd assembled for the combat in the jousting fields outside the city. The King did not attend – but his new Knights were there, and it was one of these who stepped forward to face Elodan. The battle was fierce, but all who saw it – I am told – realized at once that Elodan had no chance against this new champion. The end was brutal. Elodan's sword was smashed to shards and a blow to the helm sent him to his knees. Then the Red Knight calmly cut Elodan's right hand from his arm.'

'A Red Knight, you say?' whispered Ruad. 'Describe him.'

'I was not there, Ruad. But I am told they appear only in full armour, their helm visors closed.'

'*They?* How many are there?'

'Eight. They are deadly. Six times now they have fought in single combat for the King and on each occasion a different Knight takes the field. But all are invincible.' The old man shuddered. 'What does it all mean, Ruad?'

The one-eyed Craftsman did not reply. Moving to the window, he pushed it shut, drawing the heavy woollen curtains to block any draught of cold air.

'Treat this house as your home,' he told Gwydion. 'If you are thirsty, drink; if you are hungry, there is food in the pantry.'

Ruad strode through to his workshop, opening the chest by the far wall and rummaging through its contents. At last he found what he was seeking: a gold-and silver-rimmed plate, round and black as ebony. He carried it to his work bench and slowly polished it with a soft cloth.

Satisfied, he closed his eye and reached into the Colours. The Red almost swamped him but he rose through it, seeking the White. The Colours were shimmering, receding . . . the White was a slender ribbon now but he fastened to it, finding calm.

His eye snapped open. Taking a curved knife from the bench he pricked his thumb, allowing a single drop of blood to fall to the plate. As it touched the ebony it disappeared, and the black plate became a silver mirror in which Ruad gazed down at his reflection.

'Ollathair,' he said. A mist covered his image, then cleared as if a ghostly wind was blowing, and Ruad found himself staring down at the Great Hall in Furbolg. The King was seated on his throne and around him stood eight Knights in red armour. Ruad's concentration increased; the scene grew closer still.

The Knights' armour was of a strange design, yet similar to the work he himself had designed for the Gabala. The helms were round, the neckrings overlapping. The shoulder-plates were perfectly fitted, but boasted a high collar that would stop any swinging blade from harming the neck.

Suddenly, as his examination continued, the tallest of the Knights swung round; his head jerked up and through the visor Ruad saw a pair of blood-red eyes staring at him. The Knight's sword flashed up . . . Ruad hurled himself back from his seat as the plate exploded, shards of burning metal slashing the air. One thudded into the door-frame, smouldering into flame as Ruad rose trembling from the floor. The smell of burning wood hung in the air. Taking a deep breath and steadying himself he moved around the room stamping out the smouldering pieces.

When he had finished, he returned to his seat. Gwydion entered.

'I am afraid to ask,' said the old man, 'but I must. What did you find?'

'Evil,' said Ruad. 'And there is worse to come — much worse.'

'Can it be countered?'

'Not by the likes of you and me.'

'Then it must be terrible indeed, if Ollathair is powerless against it.'

Ruad smiled. 'I am not powerless, my friend. I am just not powerful enough.'

'Is there any force in the world that could make you so?'

'The Knights of the Gabala,' Ruad answered.

'But they are gone.'

'Exactly. And I have surrendered the one weapon I had.'

'What weapon is that?' asked Gwydion.

'Secrecy. They know who I am, and worse, where I am.'

Towards midnight Ruad stirred in his chair. In the back room he could hear Gwydion snoring and outside the autumn winds were rattling the window-frames. He could not recall dropping off to sleep, but he had awoken refreshed and now he stretched and rose. The fire was dying down; he thought of the old man, and his inability to take the cold. Stepping outside, he walked to the wood store and gathered an armful of logs. The night was cold and, but for the sighing of the wind, quiet. Three times more he carried wood to the hearth, building up the fire so that some warmth would remain at the dawn.

Wide awake now, he wandered outside to the well. Just as he was about to lower the bucket he glimpsed a moving shadow to his left and stood stock still, not turning his head. Then he sat down on the well wall and waited.

They came in a rush, seven swordsmen all wearing

the livery of the Duke – a black raven, wings spread on a field of green.

'I need you!' bellowed Ruad. From the rear of the house came the sound of wood being splintered and three golden forms bounded into the clearing. Shaped like hounds, yet larger than lions, they ran to Ruad and stood facing the armed men – jaws gaping, steel teeth shining in the moonlight.

'Good evening to you,' said Ruad, standing to face the soldiers.

They stood very still, gazing at their leader, a slim young man carrying a longsword. He licked his lips nervously, tearing his eyes from the golden hounds. 'Good evening, Craftsman. We have been sent to escort you to Mactha.'

'For what purpose?'

'The Lord Seer, Okessa, has ordered your presence. I do not know his reason.'

'But he asked you to come in the dead of night? Armed and ready for war?'

'He said you were to be brought at once, Craftsman,' said the young man, avoiding Ruad's gaze.

'Return to Mactha and tell the Lord Ckessa I am not subject to his bidding. Further, tell him I like not his method of invitation.'

The young man stared at the golden hounds and their slavering steel jaws. 'You would be wise, Craftsman, to come with us. You will be declared a nithing, an outlaw.'

'I think, boy, it is time for you to leave.' Ruad knelt by the hounds, whispering words that the soldiers could not hear. The beasts moved forward, their eyes gleaming like red stars, and suddenly a ferocious howling came from them. As the men panicked and fled, sprinting down the hill, the golden hounds bounded after them, baying in the moonlight.

Gwydion walked from the house to stand beside the Craftsman.

'How did they find you with such speed?'

'I do not know; but it does not matter now. I must leave here at once.'

'I will come with you – if you think I will not slow you down.'

Ruad grinned. 'I would be glad of the company.'

'Those hounds . . . they tore through the back of the house. How many of those men will get back alive?'

'All of them. I did not order the hounds to kill. They will follow the men until they reach their horses, then they will return. Come, you can help me to gather my belongings. I wish to leave nothing behind me that can be used by the Duke or Okessa.'

Together the two men gathered the smaller artefacts in Ruad's workshop, placing them in a large canvas bag. There were also gold and silver ingots hidden behind the chest and these Ruad loaded into two saddlebags, carrying them out on to the main porch.

The hounds returned after an hour and stood like statues under the stars.

'Can I approach them?' asked Gwydion.

'Of course; they will not harm you.' The old man knelt by the lead animal, running his fingers over the overlapping plates of the beast's neck. 'This is marvellous workmanship. Are the eyes rubies?'

'Yes. You think it overly dramatic? I had thought to make them emeralds, but they are scarce.'

'They are perfect. I take it you cast the limbs from actual bones?'

'No, I copied a design of my father's. Hounds were his speciality. I just made them bigger.'

Ruad carried the saddlebags from the porch, draping them across the gleaming backs of two hounds. Then he tied the canvas bag to the back of the third.

'Wait here,' he told Gwydion. The Craftsman

returned to the house and the old Healer saw a bright flame spring up in the main room. Ruad wandered from his blazing home without a backward glance.

'Let us go,' he said. The hounds silently padded alongside him.

4

Lámfhada awoke, his eyes unfocused, his vision swimming. Lines ran above his head – dark lines, like the panelled lid of a coffin.

'No!' he groaned, struggling to rise. A gentle hand pushed him back, and soothing words calmed him. His head rolled on the pillow and he saw a young woman with dark brown eyes who stroked his brow.

'Rest,' she whispered. 'You are safe. Safe. Rest. I am with you.'

When his eyes opened again he saw that the lines were timbers, supported by a central beam. He turned his head, hoping the young woman was close by. Instead he saw a man sitting by his bed, a handsome man in a sky-blue shirt; he had long, shoulder-length hair and was beardless; his eyes were violet. He smiled as he saw Lámfhada looking at him.

'Welcome back to the world, my friend.' The voice was soft and almost musical. 'I am Nuada. I found you in the forest.'

'You saved me,' Lámfhada whispered.

'Not quite; there was another man with me. How do you feel?'

'My back is sore.' Lámfhada licked his lips. 'Thirsty,' he said.

Nuada brought him a cup of water, supporting his head as he drank. 'You were struck by an arrow which lodged deep. You have been in a fever for five days but Arian says you will live.' Nuada spoke on, but sleep once more overcame the youth and he dreamt of golden birds flying around the sun.

He awoke during a storm, hearing the shutters on

the windows rattling and the rain pounding on the slanted roof. This time there was another man beside his bed – yellow-haired, with a red-gold beard and eyes the colour of storm-clouds.

'It is time you roused yourself, boy,' the man told him. 'You are costing me dear.'

'Costing?'

'You think Arian and her mother do this for love? Much more time in bed and I will be penniless.'

'I am sorry,' said Lámfhada. 'Truly. I will repay.'

'With what? I have already sold your dagger.'

'Leave him be, Llaw,' said a voice and Lámfhada saw a middle-aged woman come into view. 'He's not ready yet; it will be days before he can rise. Get out with you!'

'Into the storm? Your charity fails to impress me. And the food smells too good to miss.'

'Then behave.' The woman came to the bedside and rested a calloused hand on Lámfhada's brow. 'Good, the fever is passing.' She leaned over the youth and smiled. 'You will be weak for a few days, but your strength will return.'

'Thank you, lady. Where is . . . the other woman?'

'Arian is hunting. She will not be back tonight; she will have taken shelter from the storm. But you will see her tomorrow.'

'A few more days,' snapped Llaw. 'Already he is thinking of a pretty face. Put some broth into him and I'll wager he'll proposition her.'

'Why should he not?' replied the woman, grinning. 'Every other man has – but for you, Llaw Gyffes.'

'I have no need of a woman,' he said, and reddened as she laughed.

Lámfhada slept again.

The storm had passed by the time he woke. He seemed to remember being fed, but the memory was hazy and his hunger was great. He sat up, but winced as a sharp pain pulled at his back. The young woman was kneeling by the hearth, striking flint against iron to light the tinder in the grate. Lámfhada watched as a thin spiral of smoke rewarded her efforts and, bending over the hearth, Arian blew the fire to life. He found himself staring at her hips, and the stretched buckskin trews she wore.

'It is rude to stare,' she said, without turning.

'How did you know I was staring?'

'The bed creaked as you sat up.' With the fire lit she rose smoothly and walked to his bedside, pulling up a chair. Her hair was honey-gold, her eyes deep brown, her mouth full, her smile an enchantment.

'Well?' she asked.

'Well, what?' he stammered.

'Am I fit for market?'

'I don't understand.'

'You are staring at me as you would a prize cow.'

He looked away. 'Forgive me. I am not usually rude.'

She laughed and took his hand. 'And I am not usually so easily offended. I am Arian. You?'

'Lu . . . Lámfhada.'

'Are you sure? There seems to be some confusion.'

'I am sure. I was called Lug, but I gave myself a good name – a man's name.'

'Very wise. Lug does not suit such a pretty face. Why did you run away?'

'I was sold to the Duke. I thought it was better to run. Where am I?'

'In the Forest of the Ocean. Llaw Gyffes brought you to my mother. You nearly died. He should not have pulled the arrow out; you almost bled to death.'

'I do not know why he saved me. I seem to be causing him trouble.'

'Do not concern yourself with Llaw; he is a contrary man and few people understand him. What are your talents?'

'I can cook . . . clean – and I have skill with horses. I play the flute.'

'Can you hunt? Make clothing, fashion wood?'

'No.'

'Can you work clay?'

'No.'

'What about herbs? Would you recognize *amarian* or *desarta*?'

'I'm afraid not,' the young man admitted.

'Then life will be difficult for you, Lámfhada. It would seem you are about as useful as a dead sparrow.'

'I can learn. Will you teach me?'

'You think I have nothing better to do?'

'Of course you have. But will you?'

'We will see. Are you hungry?'

'Ravenous!' he admitted. She brought him some cold venison and cheese, then gathered her bow and a quiver of arrows. 'Where are you going?'

She looked at him and smiled. 'Isn't it obvious?' she said, holding up the bow. 'I'm going to pick flowers!'

After she had gone, Lámfhada pulled back the blanket and eased himself from the bed. He looked around for his clothes, and padded across to the hearth. His trews lay across the back of a chair and he slipped them on; his shirt was hanging on a hook by the far wall and he saw that someone had expertly sewn the hole made by the arrow. Once dressed, he sat down by the fire; his legs felt weak and unsteady. He added wood to the blaze and sat quietly, thinking of the terror of his flight and the sudden hammer-blow as the arrow struck his back.

He had been saved by Llaw Gyffes, the man he had come to join, but – as Arian had pointed out – he had little to offer the rebel leader. He felt suddenly foolish and, worse, useless. The door opened and a blast of cold air touched him.

'How the young recover,' said Nuada. 'Good morning to you!'

Lámfhada smiled. 'I remember you . . . like a dream. You were sitting by my bed. Nuada, isn't it?'

'It is. I can see you're feeling stronger, but you shouldn't overstretch yourself. You really were extremely ill. Arian tells me you are called Lámfhada. A good name. A Gabala Knight, no less – one of the first, I think.'

'Yes, so I am told. Are you a rebel?'

Nuada chuckled. 'You know, I think that I am. But I fear I will strike no terror in the hearts of the King's soldiers. Saga poets are rarely swordsmen.'

'You are a poet?'

Nuada bowed and sat down beside the youth. 'I am. Probably the best in the realm.'

'Do you know many stories?'

'Hundreds. When you are feeling better you must come to the hall. I perform there every night. I have become famous here and men travel from settlements all over the forest to hear me. If they had any money, I would be rich.'

'Tell me of the Gabala Knights.'

'A rather wide area, covering two hundred years. Could you not be more specific? The tale of Lámfhada, perhaps?'

'Tell me of Ollathair,' said Lámfhada.

'Ah, a student of modern history,' commented Nuada. 'Do you know the origins of the Knights?'

'No, not really. Weren't they rebels at one time?'

'Not quite. The Order was formed in 921 by the then King, Albaras. They were judges; there were nine of them and they travelled the land adjudicating on disputes in the name of the King. But in 970, during the War of the Rebellion, they saved the King from execution and spirited him away to Cithaeron. When he returned in triumph in 976, he granted the Knights

81

lands for a Citadel and freed them from the jurisdiction of monarchs. They were still judges and they travelled the nine Duchies of the realm. They were the arbiters, scrupulously fair. As the years passed, the Order gained more rules. No wealth, for that could lead to corruption. Wives were forbidden to the Gabala Knights, for families could be threatened in order to extort favourable decisions. It was an honour to be chosen, but the price was high.'

'But what of Ollathair?' Lámfhada asked.

'Patience, boy. The Knights were chosen by the Armourer. When one died, or was killed, the Armourer would travel the lands to find a successor.'

'Why the Armourer? Was he not a servant?'

'The Armourer was the Father of the Order. He supplied not only the magic armour they wore, but also the spiritual armour. He alone could command the Gabala. Ollathair was the last Armourer.'

'What happened to the Knights?'

'No one truly knows. But the King sent a messenger to Samildanach, the Lord Knight, requesting a special favour. It is said that his request took the Knights to a world of demons, where they battle still for the good of the Realm. I do not know what became of them. It was the first year of the new King's reign. Perhaps he had them poisoned, for they ruled against him in several disputes. Or perhaps they were killed by assassins. Perhaps they fled to another land. Whatever their fate, the Armourer Ollathair was taken by the King's men and imprisoned. He died in Furbolg. Why the interest in a dead sorcerer?'

'I don't know,' Lámfhada lied. 'It just interests me.'

'The Realm could do with them now – the Knights I mean,' said Nuada.

'Just what we need,' agreed Llaw Gyffes sardonically, pushing shut the door behind him and walking to the fire. 'A handful of Knights in pretty armour! I am sure they would sway the King.'

'They were more than Knights,' said Nuada, 'and greater than heroes. Do not mock them.'

Llaw warmed his hands before the fire. 'You poets never see reality, do you? Everything is part of some great Romance. You came here looking for a rebel leader and found only an outlawed blacksmith. *That* is reality. The Knights were just men, and they knew greed and lust and despair just like all of us. Don't make gods of them, Nuada.'

'I'll agree to that, Llaw Gyffes. But do not make fools of them either, for they were all better men than you.'

'That is not difficult,' Llaw agreed, slapping Nuada on the shoulder. 'But I am alive, when many better men are dead. And I will remain so – by looking after my own interests and leaving the heroics to you and your sagas.'

The Once-Knight rode up the hill, dismounting before the charred remains of the house of Ollathair. The stallion, Kuan, stood nervous and afraid; as the acrid smoke swirled to his flaring nostrils, he whinnied and backed away. The Once-Knight stroked the stallion's neck.

'It's all right, Greatheart. It is only the ruins of a house; there is no harm here. Wait for me.' Carefully he picked his way through the embers, searching for any sign of a body. But there was nothing.

Returning to the stallion, he loosened the saddle cloth and lifted his food sack from the pommel. There was precious little left: three honeycakes and a canvas bag of oats. He fed one of the cakes to Kuan and ate the other two. Then he drew water from the well and drank, leaving the bucket for the stallion to slake his thirst.

Ollathair was gone. Taken by the armed men? He doubted it. Would they have destroyed the house? Perhaps. But there was no sign of a struggle. He saw tracks close to the well and knelt by them. Paw-marks, deep and sharp. Lions? Here, so close to a town? He stood and followed the tracks for a little way. Men running, slipping and sliding down the hill, the beasts bounding after them. He grinned, then laughed aloud, but this increased the pressure on his throat and he calmed himself. The beasts had padded back to the house, where two men had stood. The Once-Knight knelt again. The paw-marks suddenly became deeper. He thought for a moment, then noticed that some of the boot-marks coming from the house were deep also. Ollathair had loaded the lions with packs and set off towards the forested mountains . . . four, maybe five hours ago.

Kuan whinnied, his head turning towards the trail to the town. The Once-Knight stood and saw a party of riders galloping towards the gutted house. Swiftly he dragged his foot over the tracks; then he tightened Kuan's saddle cinch and mounted, leading the stallion forward to disturb the ground still further.

As the riders neared, he saw they were all wearing breastplates bearing a painted raven on the chest. There were some fifteen men in the party.

'Good day to you,' said the Once-Knight.

'What are you doing here?' demanded a lean, hawk-faced man.

'I saw the smoke and wondered if anyone needed help. I take it you are upon the same business?'

'My business is none of your concern. Who are you?'

'I, sir, am a man of manners,' the Once-Knight replied, 'and ill suited to conversation with men of no breeding.'

The riders sat very quietly, waiting for a response from their captain. His face burned red and his dark eyes narrowed as he heeled his mount forward.

'It ill becomes a stranger to insult an officer of the Duke. Apologize, sir, or I shall be forced to deal with you.'

The Once-Knight leaned forward on the pommel of his saddle. 'When last I met the Duke, he had won the Silver Lance for his prowess on the jousting field. I recall him saying that a gentleman should learn three things: honour, that he might bring it to his name; swordsmanship, so that none could take his honour from him; and humility, so that he could always see where honour lay.'

'You are a friend of the Duke?'

'I am the man he beat in the tourney – but then I was always better with the sword than with the lance.'

The captain thought for a moment, then came to a swift decision. 'My apologies, sir, if my words caused offence, but we are hunting an outlaw and the Duke has charged me with his capture.'

'Your apology is accepted – and allow me to offer my own. I have travelled far and I fear my temper is short. Tell me, do you seek a heavy-set man, travelling with three large beasts?'

'I do indeed, sir. Have you seen him?'

'About two hours ago, that way,' answered the Once-Knight, pointing away from the forest. 'I thought the creatures might be lions, but I did not see them closely.'

'My thanks to you, sir Knight. Are you heading for Mactha? The Duke is in residence, and I am sure he would be delighted to see you again.'

'I think perhaps I will. Good luck in your hunt.'

As the riders thundered away, the Once-Knight tugged on the reins and touched his heels to Kuan's side. The forest was maybe two hours' ride, and with luck he would find Ollathair before nightfall.

As he rode, he remembered his joust with the Duke. The man was a skilled horseman and a deadly lancer. Had the tips of the weapons not been covered with wooden plugs, the lance would have pierced his heart; even so, he had endured the pain of two cracked ribs. It was a shame the man's character was not as well honed as his skills. The Duke had not uttered the words he credited him with – these had been said by the Lord Knight Samildanach, as a reproof to the Duke.

The Once-Knight grinned as he thought of Samildanach: a true Knight, and a man of great humility. Had the Duke found the temerity to challenge Samildanach, the outcome would have been considerably different.

Memories of his friend flooded back, filling him with sadness . . .

Samildanach riding to the joust against the King of Cithaeron's champion, or in single combat against the rebel Duke of Tarain, or leading the prayers at the Citadel, or dancing with Morrigan at the Feast of Souls. There never was a better Knight of the Gabala, he thought. Or a better friend.

'I am sorry I betrayed you,' murmured the Once-Knight.

Furious when the report of the escape of Errin's Nomad servants was brought to him, Okessa took the news to the Duke and demanded Errin's arrest. The Duke in turn berated Errin, but accepted his assurance that his servants had run away, stealing some two hundred Raq in gold in the process.

'You are a dreadful fool, Errin,' said the Duke. 'But then you have always believed the best of people. Now you see, do you not, that these people cannot be trusted?'

'Indeed I do, my Lord. I curse myself for my stupidity.'

'It cannot be helped. Okessa would like you hanged, but it is one pleasure I shall deny him. After all, where would I find another Lord of the Feast? And who would prepare the swans cooked in wine?'

Errin smiled. 'And the quail, my Lord.'

'Indeed, the quail. Far more simple to acquire another Lord Seer! By the way, one of the King's Knights will be here some time today, to finalize the arrangements for the visit. Make him welcome, would you?'

'Of course, my Lord,' Errin answered, bowing and leaving the room. Okessa was waiting in the hallway; his eyes shone with malice and sweat gleamed on his bald pate.

'Do not think,' he hissed, 'that you fool me. You conspired to allow those Nomads to escape justice – just as you did not tell me about Ruad Ro-fhessa. But you will fall, Lord Errin, and I will spit upon your grave!'

'What a charmless man you are, Okessa. And as for this Ruad, do not forget that I came to you concerning Ollathair. How was I to know that he was alive and living in the Duchy under another name? You are said to be a Seer. Surely you should have been able to find him? Or are your powers fading?'

Okessa smiled. 'We will see, Lord Errin. I cast your horoscope this morning. In five days your life will face a critical time – so critical that you might not survive. How does that please you?'

Errin swallowed hard and tried to force a smile, but it did not fool Okessa, who chuckled and stalked away. Errin lifted a trembling hand to his face. He was angry with himself for showing fear, but he knew Okessa would not have lied to him. What would be his purpose? No, Errin was sentenced to death. How would it come? Poison? Suffocation? A fall? A stray arrow?

His first urge was to run to his home and flee to Furbolg; he had friends there. But what would the Duke make of his flight? No, he was trapped. He wished Ubadai was close. The little Nomad had a nose for trouble and would die to protect him. Not that Errin wanted anyone to die for him, but it was pleasant to know that Ubadai was asleep outside his door. If an ant broke wind in the meadow outside, the Nomad would be instantly awake. Without him Errin felt isolated and vulnerable.

That night he slept badly, his door barred, the windows shuttered and locked. In the morning he bathed and dressed in a green tunic of eastern silk embroidered with gold thread, soft boots and a cape of yellow-dyed wool edged with the softest leather. Okessa's threat seemed less dreadful on this bright morning, and with the King's Knight due the Lord Seer was unlikely to risk an assassination. Errin was determined to make a fine impression on the Knight; as matters stood, he needed all the friends he could get.

It was sunset before the Knight arrived, and Errin was relieved when the guard on the watch-tower signalled a rider approaching. Errin and the Duke hurried down to the gate to greet him. The Knight wore crimson armour and rode a great black stallion of some seventeen hands. The rider's visor was down, and the sun was setting behind him as he made his slow progress to the castle gate where he drew to a halt under the portcullis.

'Welcome, sir Knight,' said the Duke.

'My horse is to be stabled alone,' said the Knight, his voice muffled by the helm. 'No other beast must be present.'

'Of course,' said the Duke, nonplussed, turning to

Errin who whispered instructions to a sentry. The man ran off to warn the ostler.

'We have a fine feast for you,' said the Duke. 'It will be ready within the hour. And there are rooms prepared in the north tower.'

The Knight dismounted. 'Where is the stable?'

'Errin,' said the Duke, biting back his anger, 'show the King's messenger to the stable. I will see you both in the great hall.'

As the Duke departed, Errin approached the Knight. 'Was your journey arduous?'

'The stable, if you please.'

'Certainly. Follow me.' Errin led the Knight across the square and into the stable yard, where the other horses were being led away. As the stranger entered the yard leading the stallion, several horses began to whinny and rear. Their handlers fought to control them, but the Knight's horse remained motionless, its head still.

'He is well trained,' said Errin.

The Red Knight did not reply but walked past Errin, leading his horse. Errin reached up to pat the beast's back but his hand recoiled as it touched the flesh of the creature's flank; it was cold as ice.

Inside the stable the Knight unsaddled the stallion and led him into a stall. The horse stood silently, ignoring the feed box.

'There are blankets close by. I'll have them fetched,' said Errin.

'There is no need.'

'I beg to differ, sir Knight. The horse is cold.'

The Red Knight swung on Errin. 'Do not touch him again. I do not like to see others place their hands upon what is mine.'

'As you please,' said Errin. 'What is your name?'

'I am the King's messenger. You, I take it, are Errin, the Lord of the Feast?'

'I am.'

'Show me to my rooms. And have a woman brought to me . . . a young woman.'

'With respect, sir Knight, I am not a procurer of women. There are many inns in Mactha, and many women who sell their services. I would suggest you attend to the Duke and then make your way there after the Feast of Welcome.'

The Knight stood silently for a moment. 'You are quite right, Errin,' he said at last. 'I am tired after my journey, and my . . . manners are lacking.'

'Think nothing of it, sir. Let me show you to your rooms,' replied Errin coolly.

In the main room a fire blazed and a hip-bath had been filled with warmed, scented water. Errin left the Knight to prepare himself and rejoined the Duke in the great hall.

'What a humourless, mannerless dolt!' stormed the Duke. 'Is the King trying to insult me, do you think?'

'I would think not, my Lord. The King has always held you in high esteem – and quite rightly. Perhaps the Knight is tired; he did apologize to me at the stable.'

'Yes – and that's another matter. His horse is to be stabled alone! Is this a prince among horses?'

'It is a strange beast, my Lord. When the other horses were being led away, they seemed terrified of it. I think that is what he was thinking of.'

'Well, his attitude will not do, Errin. I am of a mind to write to the King about him.'

'Might I suggest – respectfully – that you suspend judgement until we have seen him again? The King obviously favours and trusts him.'

'Wise words, Errin. But he would do well to show good manners this time.'

'I am sure that he will, my Lord.'

As he spoke, the Crimson Knight came into view at

the top of the staircase. He was still in full armour, but had removed his helm. His face was ivory pale and extraordinarily beautiful, his hair white and cropped close to his skull. He seemed in his early twenties. Errin moved forward, greeting him with a smile. Seen closer he looked older – perhaps thirty, perhaps more. The Knight bowed; his eyes were dark and bloodshot and he seemed weary beyond words.

'Are you well, sir?' Errin asked.

'Well enough, Lord Errin.'

'Your armour will wear you down. Tonight is a time for feasting and dancing.'

'I do not dance. I am here to inspect the Duchy on behalf of the King. Dancing I leave to others. But do not concern yourself about my armour; it never leaves me. That is part of an oath I have sworn.'

'I see,' said Errin. 'Tell me your name, sir, so that we may introduce you?'

The Knight hesitated for a moment, then responded with a swift, almost shy, smile. 'My name is . . . Cairbre.'

Errin, resplendent in hose and doublet of blue silk shot with silver, sat at the Duke's left hand during the Feast of Welcome, the Red Knight taking his place on the Duke's right. There were some thirty of the Duke's retainers present at the great square table, nobles all, from minor gentlemen of the Duchy to Knights of the Order. Errin had surpassed himself and the food, as all agreed, was exquisite: giant mushrooms, filled with minced beef and coated with Northern Duchy cheese; ten roast swans; honeyed ham, spiced beef and cakes of surpassing sweetness. But Errin noticed that the Knight scarcely touched his food, and asked for water to replace the wine he was served.

The Duke grew more ill at ease during the feast and was unable to draw his guest into any lengthy conversation. Finally he gave up altogether and turned his attention to Errin.

'Splendidly organized! Fit for a king,' said the Duke, wiping sweat from his brow with a scented handkerchief.

'I can assure you that the King's feast will be even finer, my lord. In the spring there will be many other delights which, sadly, the autumn denies us.'

As the slaves cleared away the dishes, Errin clapped his hands and rose.

The guests fell silent. 'Friends, the Duke hopes you have enjoyed the meal, and now asks that you make your way to the Narrow Hall where musicians are waiting for the dances to begin.'

As the guests filed away a flute began to play in the Narrow Hall, joined by a harp. The sound was lilting and light, and the Duke's mood changed.

'By heavens, Errin, is that Corius playing?'

'It is, my Lord. I took the liberty of requesting his presence for the evening.'

'The man charges a fortune!'

'I hope you will accept his performance as a gift, sir.'

The Duke bowed his head. 'You have outdone your-self. Well done!' Turning to the Red Knight, he said, 'I overheard you tell Errin you did not dance. Would you prefer to retire?'

'I will watch the dancing,' said the Knight, rising. Errin followed him into the hall, where many couples were now engaged in the Dance of the Winter Sun. The music was merry and Errin saw Dianu dancing with the young knight, Goan. Her dark hair was bound with silver thread and she wore a dress of shimmering white silk.

'I think,' said the Knight, 'that you would prefer to dance rather than to stand with such a sombre guest.' The ghost of a smile touched his lips as he spoke.

Errin grinned. 'That is the woman I hope to marry.'

'Then lead her to the music, sir.'

Errin needed no second invitation. Moving smoothly across the hall to the dancers, he tapped Goan on the shoulder. 'Goan, my dear fellow, would you introduce the King's messenger to the other guests?'

'Yes, sir.'

'Thank you.' Errin took Dianu's arm and led her into the dance. When the music stopped he took her to the rear of the hall, where slaves were stationed carrying silver trays on which were goblets of light, white wine. Errin took one and passed it to his companion.

'You are looking exceedingly beautiful this evening,' he told her.

'I only came because you asked me,' said Dianu. 'What do you know of that strange young man with the white hair?'

'His name is Cairbre. I know nothing of him, save that he is the King's messenger.'

'His face is very sad.'

'These are sad times,' he whispered. 'Come, let us seek some air.'

They left unnoticed through a side door and mounted the steps to a small chamber, where Errin had ordered a fire lit. The room was warm, the window open. Dianu wandered to it, staring out over the town of Mactha and its twinkling lights.

'I am leaving for Cithaeron,' she said.

'Leaving? But why?'

She turned suddenly. 'Oh, Errin, don't be such a fool! The King is murdering Nomads, the kingdom is falling ever more deeply in debt. Every day there are stories of unrest, of murder and robbery. Where will it end?'

He moved to her and led her from the window. 'Best not to speak of such things where you can be overheard,' he said, keeping his voice low. 'But Furbolg is a long way away, and in Mactha we do not suffer.'

'*We* do not suffer. But there are food shortages in the countryside – and winter is not yet here. It is all right for the nobility, with its roast swans. But swans will not feed a nation, Errin.'

'I had hoped we could be married at Midwinter,' he said. 'Are you saying the marriage will not take place?'

She took his hand and kissed it. 'Of course I am not saying that. I love you. But we could be married in Cithaeron?'

Errin shook his head. 'You cannot leave without the King's blessing,' he said, 'and he will not give it. The Duke was telling me that seven noble families have secretly left the realm, taking their riches with them. They have been branded traitors and their lands forfeited. This is your home, Dianu. Do you want to live the rest of your life in a foreign land, hated and despised by your countrymen?'

'You do not see as I see,' she answered sadly. 'There is evil here, Errin. Real, terrible evil, waiting to engulf all of us. The King is mad and surrounded by madmen. Did the death of Kester not trouble you? A fine man. A noble man. Put to death for having a Nomad grandmother? Sweet Heaven, Errin! Why do you not see?'

Pulling her to him, he kissed her face. 'I do see,' he told her. 'These *are* dangerous times. But they will pass . . . we can ride out the storm.'

She pushed him from her. 'It is not enough to ride out the storm. I am leaving here in two days; all the arrangements are made. My father, rest his soul, had many contacts in Cithaeron and I have transferred funds through the merchant, Cartain. All that is left here is the palace – and I can live without that.'

'All that is left here?' he said softly. 'You will leave me here, Dianu . . . and I cannot leave.'

For a long moment she looked into his eyes, saying nothing.

'It is your choice,' she said at last.

'I know that,' he answered, backing away. 'May fortune follow you.'

He turned swiftly, opened the door and made his way to the Narrow Hall. The music was faster now, punctuated by the laughter of the dancers as they swept into the furious pace of the Dance of the Storm. Unnoticed, Errin passed through the double doors and out into the night.

5

Arian ran smoothly up the game trail – her stride long, her footing sure. Every evening the deer travelled this trail, but these she never hunted for they were too close to the settlement. As her father had warned her during her training, 'When you are fit and strong, hunt far from home. You never know when disaster may strike – a sudden blizzard, or a lame leg – and you may come to need the meat you allowed to live. But hunt within sight of the settlement and you will drive the game far from you.'

He had been a good man and a better father, until the wasting disease hit him. It had been hard watching his strength melt from his bones, despite all his wife's skills. As the end drew near Arian's mother prepared him a goblet of wine mixed with foxglove. He had died peacefully and the two women had wept together beside his corpse.

Arian's mind dwelt on that image as she ran – and she did not see the slender wire, taut across her path. Hitting it with her lead leg, she tumbled to the trail and instantly three men raced from the trees. Dropping her bow Arian reached for her hunting-knife, but a diving body struck the air from her lungs and coarse hands held her down.

'Well, now,' said the man sitting astride her and pressing a grimy hand to her breast. 'What have we here?' She felt hands tearing at her trews and kicked out. The man above her slapped her viciously across the cheek. 'Watched you for days, we have,' he said, casually hitting her with his other hand. 'Watched you and wanted you. Beg, will you? Beg Grian to spare you?'

Arching her neck, she spat in Grian's face. Another casual blow snapped her head back to the ground. He ripped open her shirt and gazed down at her body; his face was round and brutal, his mouth open, showing blackened teeth.

'You pack of whoresons!' came a voice and the man above Arian stiffened and turned.

Standing at the centre of the trail was a hooded man in a black cloak. The sun was behind him and his face was hidden. Two of the men pulled knives from their belts and Grian also drew a knife, but remained kneeling on the stunned girl.

The hooded man threw his cloak back over his shoulders. His right arm ended at the wrist, the stump covered by a black leather cap laced along his arm. And he carried no weapons. Grian smiled and stood.

'You picked the wrong time and the wrong place, cripple,' he said, advancing. 'You are dead – food for maggots!'

Grian's two companions eased out to the newcomer's left and right, but he did not move back. Instead he stepped forward. The attacker to his left leapt for him with knife arm extended. The cripple swayed back and the knife flashed by him. At the same moment his elbow hammered into the attacker's throat and he staggered, his face turning blue. Then he slumped, dying, to his knees, his fingers scrabbling at his throat. As the second knifeman charged in the hooded man spun on his heel and leapt, his booted foot thundering into the man's jaw. The knifeman's neck cracked like a dry stick. The hooded man landed lightly and turned back to Grian.

'You won't take me with your fancy tricks,' Grian snarled.

'No, I won't,' said the man softly.

Grian stepped forward. Arian's knife entered his lower back, driving up through his lungs and into his heart. A strangled cry escaped him as he fell face down in the earth.

Arian found her trews and pulled them on. The laces were cut, but she roughly fastened them. When she looked back the stranger was sitting on a tree-trunk with his face turned from her. Gathering her bow, she moved to him.

'My thanks, for your gallantry.'

He pushed back his hood and she saw a square face and deep brown eyes. He was not handsome, but he radiated strength. He smiled and became handsome.

'It was not gallant, it was merely necessary. Are you hurt?'

'Only my pride. I should have seen their trap.'

'It is only from such mistakes that we learn. How are you called?'

'I am Arian.'

He nodded and rose. He was a head taller than Arian, which made him tall indeed. 'Is your home close by?' he asked.

'About an hour to the west.'

'May I escort you there?'

'There is no need,' she told him, reddening.

'No offence was intended, Arian. It is just that I am hungry, and a meal would not be unpleasant.'

'You have not told me your name.'

'I am Elodan.'

She looked into his dark eyes and kept the pity from her own. 'The King's champion?'

'Once upon a time. Shall we go?'

'You really should not walk in the forest un . . . without weapons. It is not safe,' she said.

'No, I will be more careful,' he told her with a wry smile. She looked back at the bodies and grinned.

'There are some larger bands of wolfsheads – and despite your skill, you are no match for a bowman.'

'Indeed I am not.' Together they set off down the trail, Arian leading. After a while she looked back at him. 'You are very quiet,' she said.

'I was thinking.'

'What about?'

'Are you married?' he asked.

'No. Why do you ask?'

'Merely to make conversation. How old are you?'

'Seventeen. And you?'

'Older than time.' He chuckled. 'At least, it feels like it sometimes.'

'You don't look more than thirty.'

'As I said, older than time – to a seventeen-year-old.'

Waking with a sore head and a stomach that seemed to be on wheels, Errin groaned and rolled to his side. The empty flagon of wine lay in pieces where he had hurled it at dawn. He opened his eyes slowly and groaned again as he remembered the events of the previous evening. Dianu was going away. He could not quite believe it, yet he knew her well enough to realize that she meant what she said. He decided to ride to her palace later in the afternoon.

His new manservant, Boran, entered silently. 'Your bath is ready, my Lord,' he said.

'For pity's sake, don't shout,' Errin told him.

'I hear it was a good feast, sir.'

Errin looked up at the balding servant, taking in his tanned healthy face and his sickeningly clear eyes. 'I feel that if I blink too quickly I will bleed to death,' he said.

'The bath will revive you, my Lord, and the Council meets in an hour.'

Errin flopped back on his pillows and pulled the blankets over his head. Boran sighed, cleared away the broken flagon, opened the velvet curtains and left the room. Alone once more, Errin sat up. The Council of Nobles was a deadly dull affair and usually no more than three or four of them turned up for the meeting. But today was different. Today the Red Knight, Cairbre, would be present, along with the Lord Seer, Okessa. Everyone would be there, vying to show their loyalty to the King.

'A pox on it,' said Errin, sliding from the bed and walking through to the outer room and his steaming bath. The water was rose-scented, which Errin had never liked, and Ubadai had never forgotten that. But Boran was new and had yet to learn his master's tastes. Errin walked down the marble steps and splashed into the bath. After a few minutes Boran entered with his robe and the nobleman stepped into it. 'How do my eyes look?' he asked the servant. Boran peered at him.

'Bloodshot, sir. In fact you do not look well.'

'You should see them from this side. What shall I wear?'

'After the meeting, the Duke has arranged a hunt, so I have laid out your riding outfit.'

'The black leather with silver trim?'

'No, sir, the red.'

'Make it the black. I'll leave the red to the Duke's guest.'

'Yes, sir. Might I suggest some breakfast, sir?'

'No,' said Errin, shuddering as his mobile stomach heaved.

'You may be glad of it while bouncing up and down on a horse.'

'Bouncing? One doesn't bounce, Boran. One rides.'

'Indeed, my Lord. Perhaps a little dry bread?' Errin nodded and walked through to his bedroom, waiting while Boran fetched his clothes. The trews were fashionably cut from soft black leather, ending at the calf. Over these Errin pulled a pair of knee-length black boots. His tunic was of wool, black and unadorned, while his riding coat was of black leather, double-shouldered and trimmed with silver thread.

'You will need a cloak, sir; there is a vicious wind.'

'I'll take the black one, with the sheepskin lining and the hood.'

'It needs to be oiled, sir. I will have it ready after the meeting.'

After breaking his fast with bread and a little cheese, Errin walked across the courtyard to the main hall. Some members of the Council were already inside, waiting to be summoned through to the inner chambers.

'Good morning, Lord Errin,' said a portly man dressed in riding clothes of green velvet. Sweat shone on his brow.

'It is pleasant to see you, Lord Porteron. I missed you at the feast.'

'Yes, yes. I had work to attend to. I am told it was a fine affair.'

'Yes,' agreed Errin, turning to greet a newcomer. 'Lord Delaan, good morning. You look wonderfully refreshed considering your exertions on the dance floor.'

The slim young man in the brown tunic grinned. 'Youth, my dear Errin. My, my, you do look a little frail.'

'I guarantee that I look better than I feel. You know Lord Porteron?'

'Of course. How are you, sir?'

'I am well. Very well. Couldn't be better.'

During the next few minutes the other lords and knights made their entrance. Last to arrive was the Lord Seer, dressed in robes of white. Errin greeted them all and sent a message to the Duke that the

Council was assembled. As always the Duke kept them waiting the obligatory ten minutes, then they filed into the inner chamber where a long table was set with six chairs on either side and two at the head. The Duke was sitting talking to Cairbre.

As the nobles entered the Duke waved them to their seats and Errin strode the length of the table to sit alongside Cairbre. The man seemed greatly refreshed; his eyes were clear and there was colour in his pale cheeks.

'I see that you slept well, Sir Cairbre,' said Errin.

'I am well rested. Thank you for your concern.'

The business of the day proceeded much as always. Tax gathering was discussed, and the greater incidences of robbery close to the forest. There was talk from Porteron of a problem with runaway slaves in the west and a shortage of skilled workers for the fields. It was agreed to ship forty slaves to his estate.

'What is causing the shortage?' asked Errin. Porteron blinked and rubbed at his sweating face with a handkerchief.

'It is not a great problem, Lord Errin.'

'I take your word for that, of course. But is it disease?'

'No, no. Naturally we have followed to the letter the decree of our dear – and revered – monarch, but we have . . . had a large number of resident Nomads. They have been sent to Gar-aden, and . . . temporarily you understand . . . we are short of workers.'

'I see. Thank you.'

'We expected short-term problems of this nature,' said Okessa smoothly. 'But the land, and its nobles, can only benefit from the removal of these tainted souls.'

All around the table heads nodded in agreement. 'You have a further point to make?' Okessa asked.

Errin shook his head. 'No, my Lord Seer. I understand that in Mactha there is now a shortage of bread, since the local baker was dispossessed.'

'The shortage arose, Lord Errin, because the filthy Nomad burned down his own premises. He should have been hung.'

'May I say a word, gentlemen?' said Cairbre, rising. 'I know – as does the King – that the removal of the Nomad vermin is bound to cause immediate hardship in many areas. But the ultimate goal is a worthy one . . . a crusade, if you will. Less than thirty years ago, the Lords of this kingdom ruled the entire continent. For two hundred years we brought laws, education, civilization to nations of barbarians. But we allowed ourselves to become weak, tainted with the blood of lesser peoples, and now we rule only the land of the Nine Duchies. Our strength, both physical and spiritual, has been polluted. A great cleansing is needed. Until this year the economy of the realm has been largely in the hands of the merchant class, who are predominantly Nomad. The King was becoming powerless in his own land. Now the treasury is ruled by the King and his wisdom is beyond question. The future, gentlemen, stands and beckons. When the realm is rid of all impurity, we shall rise again and become pre-eminent among nations!'

Cairbre sat down to stunned silence, which was immediately broken as the Duke applauded, followed by the entire Council. Errin clapped hands with the rest, but less enthusiastically. Words and phrases flashed in his mind: *Lesser peoples. Vermin. Impurity. Taint.*

'Thank you, Sir Cairbre,' said Okessa. 'Your stirring words have brought us to the most delicate of matters. As you will know, the King has decreed that all of Nomad blood are to be sent to Gar-aden. I have, on the Duke's insistence, begun examinations of all families with known Nomad connections. It seems we have two noble families in Mactha with tainted blood.'

Errin's eyes flickered around the table. Lord Porteron's face was chalk-white.

'Sadly, our duty to the King necessitates that these also be sent to Gar-aden,' Okessa continued.

'I have always been loyal,' said Porteron, rising. 'My family has fought in three wars for the King and the crown.'

'Your loyalty is not in question, sir,' said Okessa with a thin smile. 'And I am sure the King will arrange your speedy return to us.'

'This is outrageous! Insane!'

'Be so kind, Porteron,' said the Duke, 'as to wait outside. There are men waiting there who will take you to your quarters.'

'Sir Cairbre!' shouted Porteron. 'Surely the King cannot mean to destroy the noble families? The Nomad line in my House goes back to my great-grandfather.'

The Red Knight rose, his eyes cold. 'Already you have shown the worth of your Nomad blood. A direct order from your Duke to leave has been disobeyed . . . moreover, you have willingly sent to Gar-aden people from your district who have even more tenuous blood links than your own. Had your true blood been in the ascendancy, you would have come to the Duke and confessed. Now get out of my sight.'

Porteron staggered back as if struck and stumbled from the room. Errin had guessed that Porteron was out of favour when he had been instructed not to invite him to the Feast. But this?

'You mentioned two noble families, Lord Okessa?' said the young Lord Delaan.

'It is no one present, sir,' said Okessa. 'I refer to the Lady Dianu, whose mother was of Nomad extraction.'

Errin felt his heart hammer in his chest and his hands began to tremble.

'The Lady Dianu's mother died in childbirth,' said Errin. 'She was from Cithaeron, and there is no record of any Nomad involvement in her blood line.'

'Sadly that is not the case,' said Okessa, unable to keep a triumphant grin from his thin lips. 'She was the daughter of a man named Kial Orday, who was born on the eastern steppes into a Nomad tribe called the Wolves. There is no doubting her tainted line; she has been summoned to Mactha and will be sent to Garaden.'

Errin bit back any further argument. 'My congratulations, Lord Seer. As ever, you have been meticulous in your endeavours.'

'Meticulous enough, Lord Errin, to have discovered that you planned to marry this woman. Thankfully you are now spared the prospect of coupling with a Nomad whore.'

The words were sent like arrows, but Errin had been expecting something of the like. 'Indeed, my Lord. I can hardly think of the words to thank you.' Okessa's disappointment was obvious and it brought a taunting grin from Errin, who leaned forward holding to the Seer's gaze. 'Happily, sir,' said Errin, 'there is no doubt as to your bloodline. Your mother was a fine Gabalan of good stock, who plied a trade among the sailors near the docks at Furbolg. I am confident they were all good Gabalan sailors, and there was not a Nomad among them.'

'How dare you?' stormed Okessa, surging to his feet.

'How dare I? How dare the son of a common prostitute abuse the name of a noble lady of this realm!'

'I take it, Errin, that you will champion her? You will demand trial by combat?' Okessa hissed.

Errin froze as the words hammered home. All he had been taught as a Knight and the son of an earl screamed at him to accept the challenge in the name of chivalry, but all that he had learned as a man warned him to beware. He was no swordsman and he knew what had happened to the champion Elodan. He took a deep breath. 'I will consider that option,' he said. Aware that all eyes were upon him, he transferred his gaze to the table and fought to quell the anger within.

'You will consider the option,' sneered Okessa. 'How gallant of you!'

'That is enough,' snapped the Duke. 'The Lord Errin has every right to take time on this issue. We are . . . were . . . all fond of the Lady Dianu. But if her blood is tainted, then it is right that she travel to Gar-aden. The King's word is law; we all accept that. Now let us move on.'

Errin sat in a daze throughout the rest of the meeting, images racing through his mind. Dianu had told him that evil was rampant in the land, and now she would pay, perhaps with her life. He thought of her being brought to Mactha, derided and alone, to endure the sneers of serpents like Okessa. And what would she find in Gar-aden? Stripped of wealth and privilege, she would be forced to live in a desert hut making a living as best she could among other Nomads. But what skills did she have that could make her life bearable? None – save her beauty. They might just as well kill her, he realized. When she was brought to Mactha he would have to avoid seeing her; he would not be able to meet her eyes. And when they took her away, he would have to live every day of his life in the knowledge that he had done nothing to save the woman he loved.

Love. At the thought of the word and the emotions it conveyed, his throat swelled. He swallowed hard. Yes, he loved Dianu. He always had, ever since they were children together. Could he bear to live, knowing he had done nothing to aid her?

In that moment he knew he did not have the courage to turn away from her.

He blinked and stared around the table. The meeting

was obviously over and all eyes were on him as his voice came surprisingly clear and strong.

'My sword will speak for the Lady Dianu,' he declared.

Okessa smiled as he sank back in his chair and switched his gaze to the stunned Duke.

'My Lord, you must name someone to champion the King's cause.'

'Retract, Errin,' whispered the Duke. 'This is madness.'

'I cannot.'

'I think you should,' said Cairbre softly. 'For I must champion the King's cause, and that will mean us facing one another.'

Errin shrugged. 'What will be will be.'

'I hope,' said Cairbre, 'that you are a fine swordsman. But think on this. I am the man who cut the hand from Elodan, and he was the best I ever fought.'

A storm broke over the forest as Ruad, Gwydion and the three magic hounds reached the shelter of the trees. Ruad led the way east into the thickest of the woods, seeking a haven from the driving rain. Mortally tired, Gwydion slipped on a muddy slope and fell heavily. Ruad walked back to help him to his feet.

Calling one of the golden hounds, Ruad lifted Gwydion to its back.

'Such is the fate of old men,' said Gwydion, with a weak smile, 'to be mounted on a dog.'

Ruad chuckled. 'At least it is a magic dog.'

'Have you been here before, Ruad?'

'Two years ago I came looking for herbs. There is an old cabin about a mile further along the trail. It was uninhabited then. Now?' He shrugged.

'This is a gloomy place,' said Gwydion.

'It will look better by sunlight, I promise you.'

They continued on the trail and Gwydion found his mount not entirely to his liking. The metal back made a poor seat, the plates grinding and pinching the skin of his thighs. But it was a great deal less arduous than walking.

Ruad's recollection of the distance was faulty, and it was two hours and almost midnight before they came to the cabin. It was no longer empty and no longer solitary; four other homes had been built close by.

'I hope we will be welcome,' said Gwydion.

Ruad did not reply. Boldly he stepped to the first door they came across. Warm golden light showed through the gap in the shutters of the window as he rapped his fist against the door.

It was opened by a young man, carrying a broad-bladed knife.

'What do you want?' asked the man. Then he saw the golden hounds; his mouth gaped and he stepped back, the knife forgotten. 'A wizard!' he shouted to someone behind him.

Ruad moved swiftly into the house. 'Indeed I am,' he said, forcing a broad smile to his face. 'But a friendly wizard, seeking shelter for the night. We mean no harm to any here, I promise you. And we will pay for shelter.' Inside the one-roomed cabin was an elderly woman, three young children and a younger woman in a bed by the fire. The man was in his early twenties, stockily built, with thick dark curly hair.

'What else can go wrong?' he shrugged, dropping the knife to a rough-cut table. 'For what it is worth, you are welcome. But the beasts stay outside.'

'Of course.' Ruad helped Gwydion into the house and the hounds sat outside the door, the rain streaming from their metal hides. Inside once more, Ruad removed his soaked leather jerkin and stood before the fire, enjoying the warmth. The children sat quietly staring at him, their eyes wide and fearful, while the old woman returned to the bedside, where she sat dabbing at the brow of the younger woman.

'Is she sick?' Gwydion asked. The young man looked away and sat at the table staring at the wall. Gwydion struggled out of his white woollen robes and laid them over a chair by the fire. Dressed only in a loin-cloth, he dried himself by the blaze and then moved to the bedside. The young woman was skeletally thin, her skin almost translucent. Dark rings had formed beneath her eyes. When Gwydion lifted her wrist, the pulse was weak and fluttering like a trapped butterfly.

'May I take your seat?' he asked the old woman. 'I am weary from my travels.' She looked up at him, her eyes dull, then stood and moved away, shepherding the children to their beds by the other wall. Gwydion placed his hand on the dying woman's brow, closing his eyes and seeking the Colours. The Red was still powerful, yet less so than in Mactha; he rose through it to the outer edges of the Harmony, fastening to the Green. Slowly he linked with the woman, flowing with her blood, pulsing with the rhythms of her life. He found the cancer; it had spread across both lungs and down into her stomach.

'Fetch me a piece of meat,' he said.

The young man ignored him, but Ruad walked to the table and touched him on the shoulder. 'Bring some meat to my friend.'

'Dying people give him an appetite, do they?'

'It is not to eat. Do as I ask. Please?'

The young man rose and fetched a joint of ham from a hook in the pantry, carrying it to Gwydion. 'Put it in a bowl on the bed,' said the elderly Healer. The old woman fetched a bowl and the ham was placed in it. Ruad joined them. Gwydion soared into the Colours. One bony hand rested on the woman's brow, the other on the meat in the wooden bowl. Gwydion's face grew ever more pale and he began to tremble. Ruad moved alongside him, waiting. The young woman groaned.

'What is he doing?' the young man asked.

'Be silent!' hissed Ruad.

The old woman gasped and stepped back, her hand over her mouth. The meat in the bowl began to writhe and darken; white maggots appeared, and the stench of corruption filled the room as the ham grew slimy, edged with blue. Maggots crawled over the old man's fingers.

The young woman's face seemed less translucent now, and her cheeks showed colour. Gwydion's hand slipped from her brow and, as he toppled, Ruad caught him and carried him to the fireside, where he laid him on the goatskin rug before the hearth. 'Get a blanket!' ordered Ruad. The old woman brought two and covered the sleeping Healer with one, making a pillow of the other which she eased under his head.

'Ahmta!' cried the young man, as his wife's eyes opened.

'Brion,' she whispered. 'I have been dreaming.'

The young man's eyes filled with tears and he leaned over the bed, taking Ahmta in his arms. Turning, the old woman began to weep. Ruad patted her shoulder and moved to the bedside.

'How are you feeling?' he asked the woman.

'Tired, sir. Who are you?'

'Travellers, passing through. Sleep now. In the morning you will feel better.'

'I doubt that, sir. I am dying.'

'No,' Ruad told her. 'Tomorrow you will wake and rise, and all will be as it once was. You are cured.'

The woman smiled, disbelieving, but faded into sleep as Brion lifted the blankets around her, then rose.

'Is it true?' he asked, his face still wet with his tears.

'I do not lie. Well . . . not often. Gwydion is a Healer, a great Healer.'

'I have no way to repay you. I . . . do not even own this cabin. Food is short. But what I have is yours.'

Ruad grinned. 'A roof for the night and, perhaps, a little breakfast. I am afraid the ham is ruined, and I should take it from the house before the stench reaches us all.'

The young man took the decomposed meat from the house and hurled it into the undergrowth. When he returned, he offered Ruad a goblet of water. 'We have no wine or ale,' he apologized.

'This will suffice.'

'Are you truly men?' asked Brion.

'Yes. Do we look so strange?'

'No, not at all. It is just . . . you are an answer to prayer, and it comes to me you may be . . . gods?'

'If I was a god,' said Ruad, grinning, 'would I have made myself so ugly?'

Ruad lay beside the sleeping Gwydion on the floor by the fire, his thoughts sorrowful.

Gwydion had cleansed the cancer from the woman, Ahmta, but to Ruad the scene was only a grim reminder of the malignancy eating at the heart of the realm. And Ruad knew that he, as the Armourer Ollathair, had helped that cancer to grow. Despite his wisdom – perhaps even because of it – he had fallen victim to the god of Folly – Pride.

When the new King, Ahak, fresh from his triumph in the Fomorian Wars, sent word to Ollathair of the world beyond the Gate, it had seemed the answer to prayer. All his life Ollathair had sought to excel – first to impress his father, Calibal, and then to be the greatest Armourer in the long history of the Knights.

He could still recall with total clarity the night the King's messenger brought him the letter. A visitor had come to Ahak, claiming to be from a land called the

Vyre; this land was beset, said the messenger, by great evil. They needed the legendary Knights of the Gabala to come to their aid. In return they offered gifts of medicine and knowledge that would eradicate sickness and disease, that would bring a new era of peace and contentment to the Gabalan people.

At first Ollathair had been sceptical, but the King sent a silver mirror imbued with a magic more powerful than anything Ollathair had ever experienced. Using the mirror, he could focus on any part of the realm and see it clearly. More, he could pierce the mystic curtain between the worlds of the Gabala and the Vyre. And he found, as the messenger said, a land of great wonders: a white, many-towered city, peopled by angelic beings, was surrounded by impenetrable forests in which dwelt creatures of nightmare. It was the jewel of Paradise, set amidst the horrors of Hell.

Ollathair made contact with a man named Paulus, a councillor of the Vyre Elders. Paulus begged the Armourer to send his Knights and Ahak also urged the Armourer to respond.

For Ollathair this was an opportunity his pride forbade him to ignore. He had the chance to outdo his father, Calibal, and to earn his place in history as the greatest Armourer. He had called Samildanach to him, and the Lord Knight had questioned him until dawn. If Hell surrounded the Vyre, how could they survive? How could they combat the screaming demons with their long talons? How could they return, once Olla-thair was no longer with them?

He answered all questions with promises: he would make finer armour, he would create swords that would never dull, he would re-open the Gate between Worlds at prearranged times, beginning one month after they had passed through. And he would stay in contact with them, using the magic mirror.

Samildanach was enchanted with the idea, and with

112

the gifts promised by the Vyre. He longed to be the Knight who brought an end to disease and despair.

Ollathair had opened the Gate on Midsummer's Eve six years ago and Samildanach had led the Knights through – never to return.

Ollathair had hurried back to the Citadel and taken up the mirror, but only his reflection stared back at him. He tried the Colours: Black under the moonlight; Blue under the sun; Red with his own blood; but the mirror had lost its power.

Fear began to gnaw at him and he tried in every way to breach the Gate with his spirit, but it seemed that a wall – invisible and yet impenetrable – had been set before him. He contacted the King, to see if the messenger was still at Furbolg, but the man had returned to his own land. Ollathair was beside himself; all his powers were useless.

He had one great hope – Samildanach, greatest of warriors, finest of men. A descendant of kings and the most complete Knight Ollathair had ever known. Whatever perils lay beyond the Gate, the Armourer was sure Samildanach would overcome them.

The days drifted by with agonizing slowness until the month had passed and Ollathair cast the spell that opened the Gate. Screeching creatures of nightmare gathered in the darkness beyond, but the Armourer's powers hurled them back. Of the Knights there was no sign.

Night after night Ollathair conjured the Gate, until his powers were spent, his strength wasted.

Finally he had travelled to Furbolg. The King had greeted him like an old friend and had entertained him royally for several weeks. But then he had been asked to create weapons of power for the monarch and he had refused. As the Armourer of the Gabala Knights, he was not under Ahak's rule.

The King had ordered him arrested, claiming his

refusal bordered on treason. For days he had suffered torture – his eye burned from his skull, hot irons scorching his flesh. Then he had feigned death and been hurled into a shallow pit outside the city walls.

He had escaped, but it was almost a year before his strength and power returned. Then he had taken the name Ruad Ro-fhessa and moved to the north. And for three years had explored every means of breaching the world beyond.

At last he was forced to the inescapable conclusion that the Knights – *his* Knights – had been slain.

Samildanach, Edrin, Pateus, Manannan, Bersis, Cantaray, Joanin, Keristae and Bodarch – all dead. Ruad Ro-fhessa carried the blame like a burning coal in his heart.

Yet now, here on this wooden floor, the pain was worse than ever before. For the King had embarked on a reign of terror and had gathered to him other Knights, dread warriors strengthened by sorcery. And the world needed the true Knights more than ever.

At last Ruad fell asleep, but his dreams were of fire and blood and Knights in crimson armour hunted him with knives of cold steel. He awoke sweating in the pre-light of dawn. Gwydion slept on, as did the household. He sat up and added tinder to the ashes, stirring them and blowing the flickering embers to life. Brion awoke and stared down at his sleeping wife. He kissed her lightly and her eyes opened.

'It was true,' she whispered. 'I am healed.' Ahmta sat up. 'There is no pain.'

'When I woke I thought it was a dream,' Brion said, cupping her face in his hands.

Ruad grinned and rose from the floor. 'Good morning to you both. You slept well, I trust?'

'Yes, sir,' said Brion, sliding from beneath his blanket and standing. 'I promised you breakfast and you shall have it – eggs, bacon, and I shall borrow ale from Dalik.'

A low metallic growling came from outside and Ruad ran to the door and opened it. A small crowd had gathered silently to examine the hounds, and one man had tried to prise a golden scale loose. As Ruad appeared the crowd fell back. Brion ran from the house and swiftly explained the presence of his visitors, and the magic they had wrought.

Within an hour the news had spread to settlements nearby and a larger crowd had gathered – many of them sick, or with boils, or deep cuts, or swollen joints.

Ruad woke Gwydion. 'You had best eat, my friend. I fear you have a busy day ahead.'

For most of the morning Gwydion plied his trade on the porch of the cabin, receiving payment in copper and silver coin, goods – a battered knife and two hatchets, three blankets, a small sack of flour, a side of ham, a barrel of ale, a pair of boots, a cloak, two chickens, seven pigeons and a silver ring set with a black stone – and occasionally just the promise of food and a bed for the night should he desire it.

By noon the old man was exhausted and he sent away the fifteen or so who were still waiting, promising to see them tomorrow. He gave the chickens and the ham to Brion and then Ruad, he and the family enjoyed the small barrel of ale.

'Had I known my powers would be so great here, I would have come five years ago,' said Gwydion. 'The Green is easy to find, and very strong.'

At dusk a rider came to the settlement. People hid behind locked doors, watching the man from behind barred shutters as he reined in his stallion before the house that boasted the three golden hounds.

'Ollathair!' he called. 'Come forth!'

Ruad opened the door and stepped into sight. The man looked familiar, but his face was hard to see, for he wore a helm and though the visor was up the sun was behind him.

'Who calls for Ollathair?' Ruad asked.

The man dismounted. 'One who knows him well,' said the rider, approaching the Armourer. All colour fled from Ruad's face as he recognized the workmanship of the battered helm and the grey eyes of the Once-Knight.

'Manannan?' he whispered. 'It cannot be!'

'It is Manannan,' said the Once-Knight. 'It is the traitor, Manannan. I have no right to ask this of you, but it would be pleasant if you would remove this damned helm. I fear the beard within the neck-plates is strangling me to death. I have worn it for six years.'

'How did you get back?'

'I never went. As Samildanach beckoned us forward, something inside me snapped. Fear swept through me like a storm, and I turned my horse away into the shadows.'

Despair struck Ruad anew. 'Then you do not know what became of them?'

'No. Will you help me?'

'I cannot, Manannan. If I could, I would do it in an instant. But the spell I cast was to protect you in the inferno beyond the Gate and the Gate is the key. All spell-locks were made to be undone the moment you passed back through the Gate.'

'What are you saying? That I am doomed to die in this metal cage?'

'No,' said Ruad softly. 'I am saying you must pass the Gate and return.'

The Once-Knight staggered as if struck. 'Pass the . . . alone? When I could not do it surrounded by the finest warriors in the world? Impossible!'

'You would at least know the fate of your friends. You might even find them and bring them home. The gods know how they are needed now.'

'And that is the only way for me?'

'Yes.'

'Let me inside, Ollathair. Let me sit and think.'

6

The country estates of the Lady Dianu covered six hundred acres, at the centre of which was a wooded valley. On the high ground to the west, some twelve miles from Mactha, was the old castle – derelict now, but still used by the local villagers for the May Dance and for open-air banquets in the summer. Beside it was the New House built by Dianu's grandfather and boasting forty bedchambers, a central hall, two libraries and a lower hall with sleeping quarters for sixty slaves.

The windows were wide and the house had been built without concern for defence. At present only twelve servants were in residence, and the two upper floors were closed.

On the ground floor in the main, circular library, Dianu and her sister Sheera were meeting with the merchant Cartain, who had arrived in the night, travelling alone with false papers.

'You must leave now,' Cartain snapped. 'Why do you not understand the danger? Okessa has been researching your family records. Believe me, there will be troops on the way.'

'Errin would have warned me,' said Dianu. 'Have no fear, Cartain. Take Sheera and the two Nomad servants. I will meet you in Pertia Port.'

The sun was shining through the open window and Dianu moved to the sill, enjoying the scent of the roses below. The gardener waved at her.

'I think we should listen to Cartain,' said Sheera. She was dressed in riding buckskins, wearing tight well-fitting trews under a brushed hide tunic.

'I do not think it becomes you, sister, to dress like a man,' said Dianu. 'Whatever will the servants think?'

Sheera shook her head. 'You still think he is coming, don't you? You believe that Errin will surrender his status and his lands to journey with you to Cithaeron? Well, he will not. Cartain has risked his life to help us escape. I think your attitude is selfish – and very foolish.'

'I have five men waiting in the woods, my ladies,' said Cartain. 'If we leave now, we can be in Pertia Port in four days. Much of your wealth has already been shipped. You achieve nothing by delaying your departure, Lady Dianu, but you risk much.'

'I do not believe the risk is as great as you say,' Dianu maintained, smoothing the front of her white silk dress. 'But very well; you go ahead with Sheera. I shall follow tomorrow, I promise you. I will need to pack, and I have ordered five wagons to be delivered here.'

'Ordered . . . are you mad?' hissed Cartain.

'How dare you use that tone with me, sir! You think I would leave here without my mother's heirlooms?'

'This was to have been a secret departure, Lady Dianu. How secret will it be when it is known – as known it will be – that you have ordered five wagons?'

'The people of Mactha have been loyal to my family for generations, Cartain. They will say nothing.'

The merchant shook his head and turned to the taller sister. 'Will you travel with me now, my lady?'

'I will, Cartain,' she agreed. Sheera rose and walked to her sister. 'I think you are wrong, Dianu, but I hope to see you in Pertia Port.'

'Safe journey,' said Dianu, leaning to kiss her sister's cheek. 'I will be several days behind you. The wagons will be slow-moving.'

'Might I ask,' enquired Cartain, 'how you intend to

protect this valuable cargo when you pass Groundsel's realm?'

'I have hired soldiers to escort me,' Dianu told him.

'I thought you might have done,' said Cartain softly. 'You will not, by any chance, have trumpets sounded as you leave?' Without waiting for an answer, he spun on his heel and strode from the room. Sheera caught up with him by the doorway as he stepped into the sunlight.

'You should not have been rude, Cartain.'

He breathed a deep sigh. 'No, I should not. Her rank demands respect, but her stupidity is hard to bear.'

'It is not stupidity, sir merchant. It is stubbornness. There is a difference,' she said, swinging herself into the saddle of a tall black gelding.

He mounted his own bay mare. 'Yes, there is,' he admitted, 'and I will accept your point if she is proved to be right. But we are dealing here in life or death. And to risk life for a few pretty pieces of silver is not wise.'

He spurred his mount down the gravel path as Sheera swung in the saddle. Dianu had leaned out of the window and plucked a red rose, which she waved at her sister.

Sheera raised her arm in farewell, then thundered her mount after the merchant.

Dianu was arrested by the soldiers she had hired to protect her and brought under guard to Mactha – her servants with her, her wagons piled with her possessions.

The Duke visited Errin with the news. 'You realize, Errin, that you can no longer stand for her? She is now an accepted traitress, never mind her Nomad blood. It frees you from this insane battle.'

Errin sat by the narrow window, staring out over the countryside. He looked at the Duke and smiled.

'How does it free me, my Lord? I love the woman; I cannot stand by and see her shipped to Gar-aden.'

The Duke poured himself a goblet of wine and drank deeply. 'She will not be sent to Gar-aden,' he said, his voice almost a whisper.

'What? Why?'

'That is for Nomads.'

'What are you saying?'

'You know what I am saying, Errin. She is to be tried as a traitress and sentenced to death, probably at the stake.'

'Sweet Heaven, is the world mad?' said Errin, rising and slamming his fist against the stone of the sill.

'There is nothing you can do. Nothing! Cairbre will kill you in seconds – and what will it achieve? One more noble line ended. Is a stupid gesture worth your life? It would be different were you an Elodan, but you are not. Errin, my page could best you with the sword.'

'I fear that is no longer the point, my Lord. What sane man would desire to live in a world such as this? And how could I look at myself in a mirror, knowing I had done nothing to save the woman I love?'

The Duke poured a second goblet of wine and drained it; he was looking tired, and his eyes were bloodshot. 'Cairbre does not want to fight you. He has asked me to see you . . . to implore you to reconsider.'

'I will be at the field tomorrow and it will be decided by the laws of the Gabala,' said Errin. 'I am sorry, my Lord. You must find another Lord of the Feast for the King's visit.'

'You realize this is what Okessa wants? You know that his is the only victory?'

'I care nothing for Okessa. He told me I would die in five days – and that is tomorrow. Long may he laugh.'

'Would you like me to practise with you?'

Errin gazed at the Duke and realized the man was sincere. It touched him. Greedy, cruel, lustful – all these vices the Duke had and yet, still, there was a place for compassion. 'Thank you, but no,' said Errin. Suddenly he chuckled. 'You think I can become a champion in one day?'

The Duke smiled. 'You remember the year I won the Silver Lance? You were my page. You brought me my sword and the scabbard slipped between your legs, sprawling you to the dust. I knew then you'd never be a knight. Come Errin, let us get drunk.' He offered his friend a full goblet of wine, but Errin shook his head.

'Will you allow me to see Dianu?'

'Of course . . . for as long as you want.'

'Privately?'

'I guarantee it, my friend.'

An hour later Errin was led through the dungeon corridor to a long room at the end. Dianu was there. There were no chains, and a comfortable bed and two chairs had been placed at her convenience. She was dressed still in her riding clothes, a grey velvet doublet and black hose. Her dark hair flowed free now, making her seem younger than her nineteen years.

Errin heard the door close behind him and opened his arms, but she just stood by the bed staring at him, her eyes wide, her lips trembling. He moved to her, drawing her to him.

'They are going to burn me alive,' she whispered. 'Burn me!'

He could say nothing, except perhaps to tell her he would not be alive to see it – and that would bring her scant comfort. So he held her in silence.

After a while she pulled back from him. 'I love you,' she said. 'I have done so ever since I was small and you used to come to our palace with your father. You remember the games of hunt-and-find in the gardens?'

'Yes. It was always easy to find you; you always moved.'

'I always wanted to be found,' she said. 'By you.'

'I wish I had come with you. I wish we had gone on the night of the Feast. I wish. . . .'

'Is it true that you are going to champion me, Errin?'

'Yes.'

'Against the Red Knight?'

He nodded. 'You would expect me not to?'

'No, I have always known you were the bravest of men, but can you win? And even if you do, will they allow me to depart?'

'I cannot answer either of these questions. Tomorrow we will know. But today, now, we have each other, and today may . . . be all that we have. I don't mind if we just sit quietly, saying nothing. I just want to be here with you.'

'We will not be disturbed?'

'No, the Duke has promised.'

She unfastened the laces of her doublet and said, 'Then be with me, Errin, be part of me.'

At midnight Errin slid from the bed – leaving Dianu sleeping – and tapped on the door, which was opened by a burly guard. The man closed the door quietly and locked it. He would not meet Errin's gaze and led the way silently to the upper levels.

As the guard turned to go, Errin touched him on the shoulder. 'Treat her gently,' he said. The man said nothing and glanced down at Errin's outstretched hand; two gold Raq nestled in his palm. The guard took the money and walked away; then he stopped and spoke without turning. 'I would have done so anyway,' he said, 'but I need the money.'

Errin smiled. 'Let her sleep for as long as she will. Tomorrow will be a long, fearful day.'

He returned to his own apartments, where Boran had placed his battle armour on a wooden stand. Errin stood and gazed at the weapons laid out on the narrow table before the stand: longsword, battle-axe, mace and chain. He had worn the armour only once, at the coronation of the King seven years ago; he had never fought in it. The helm was cylindrical, with a broad slit across the face. Errin lifted it and placed it on his head; it was lined with cushioned velvet and sat snugly in place. He could hear his own breathing, like the sound of a wolf creeping forward in the darkness. His vision through the eye-slit was limited. Removing the helm, he tossed it to his bed. The sword was double-handed and he hefted it, trying to recall the advice of Swordmaster Pleus more than a decade before. But all he could remember was the man shaking his head and telling him he was too clumsy, and that he had two left feet.

Errin sat at the northern window with the sword in his lap until the dawn streaked the sky, when Boran entered silently.

'My Lord, will you eat breakfast?'

'No. I have no appetite.'

'If I may say so, respectfully, you are not being wise. To fight, a man must have strength – and this comes from the food we eat. I have prepared some honey-cakes. Please eat something.'

'It ill becomes a man to die on a full stomach, Boran. I have seen dead men; their bowels open, you know, and they stink. I have no wish to stink.'

'On the field today, sir, there will be two men with swords. Now swords have no brains, they go where they are directed. Sir Cairbre may be a wondrous warrior, but he might slip in the mud just as you strike. Best to be prepared. I shall fetch the honey-cakes.'

As Boran turned the door opened and Sir Cairbre entered. He was wearing his crimson armour and carrying his round, plumed helm under his arm. He approached Errin and bowed.

'Good morning, my Lord,' he said softly. 'Have you reconsidered this unwise action?'

'I have not, sir. Nor shall I!'

'Leave us!' ordered Cairbre, but Boran stood his ground.

'I take no orders from you, sir,' he said, reddening.

Errin rose. 'Thank you, Boran. Fetch the honey-cakes if you please, and some fresh water for our guest.'

The servant departed and Errin, realizing he still held the longsword, hurled it to the bed where it clanged against his helmet.

'I applaud your courage, Lord Errin,' said Cairbre, 'but it will avail you nothing. The Duke has explained to me that you are no swordsman, and I have no wish to walk on to the field for the purpose of simple butchery.'

'But that is the law, Sir Cairbre – the King's law. I have the right to champion my lady – is that not so?'

'Indeed it is, sir. But even if you win – you lose. As the Lord Seer Okessa has pointed out, even if you defeat me you will only establish the Lady Dianu's innocence of the charge of treason. She will still be a Nomad and thus required to travel to Gar-aden. And at that point you will be arrested for treason.'

'How so? I have never spoken against the King.'

'But, sir,' said Cairbre, smiling softly, 'you are about to fight the King's champion. Therefore you are setting yourself against the King, and that makes you a traitor.'

'That is logic of the most dubious kind, Sir Cairbre. The right of the accused to be championed has been with us for a thousand years. In one stroke you remove that right for men – or women – deemed the King's enemies?'

'Traitors should have no rights,' Cairbre declared.

'And how then are we to decide who is a traitor?'

'The facts should judge, not the skills of swordsmen.'

'And who decides the facts?'

'The King, or the King's judges.'

'I see,' said Errin. 'An interesting hypothesis. Let us say that a farmer has a complaint against his liege lord. Is it fair that the liege lord decides his case?'

'We are not talking of farmers, but of the King. His word is the law – and his wishes are above the laws of men,' said Cairbre. 'Despite knowing the Lady Dianu is of Nomad blood, you have decided to champion her. Thus you are championing the cause of all Nomads – regardless of their rank. Can you not see that you are defying your King?'

Boran returned with the honey-cakes and then left. Errin poured Cairbre a goblet of water. 'Can *you* not see, sir Knight,' he said persuasively, 'that in history there have been bad kings as well as good?'

'What point is there in such a question? Are you saying the King is bad?'

'No, no. Do not put words in my mouth, sir. I am saying that the past shows us that a bad king, or an evil king, or a foolish king can make appalling decisions which are not good for the realm. If we say now that the King is above the law, then in a hundred years a bad king may abuse such a position.'

Cairbre smiled and sipped his water. He sat down on the edge of the bed. 'That will not happen in this case, Lord Errin, for we will have the same King in a hundred years. Indeed, in a thousand years. For he is now immortal . . . even as I am.'

Errin said nothing, scanning the Knight's eyes for any sign of madness. Cairbre chuckled. 'I know how this sounds, Lord Errin. Truly I do. But look at me. How old am I? Twenty-five. Thirty? I am nearly fifty.'

Errin could not believe it. He stared into the warrior's face, seeking the tell-tale lines, but the

Knight's skin was pale and smooth, his dark eyes glowing with health.

Cairbre finished his drink and stood looking down at the silver goblet. His slender fingers contracted suddenly and the goblet crumpled in his hand. 'Youth and strength is mine,' said Cairbre, 'and the King's. Do you see now what I was trying to tell the Council? We are going to build an empire – the greatest empire of all time. Faithful friends of the King will become immortal; they will never taste death. This is what you are throwing away. We need you, Errin. Your blood is pure, your line without blemish. Give up this foolishness – and join us in our crusade.'

Errin's eyes grew cold and he stepped back from the Knight. 'I will meet you, sir, on the field at noon. When I am dead I ask – as one Knight to another – that you allow me to be buried alongside Dianu. I think it is inappropriate for us to talk further.'

Cairbre sighed and stood. He drew his sword and tossed it to Errin; it was wondrously light and razor-sharp.

'The blade has magic properties,' he said. 'It will enhance your skill and cut through anything – ultimately even this armour I wear. Use it today and I will take your blade.'

'It is not necessary,' said Errin.

'No, it is not,' Cairbre agreed. 'But at least your lady will see a battle for her life and not a meaningless slaughter. Until noon, then.'

The jousting field, hemmed by stakes and fenced by purple ribbons tied between them, held two thousand people. It seemed that the entire town of Mactha had emptied for the occasion and Errin was distressed to see fires burning and steaks being fried. Vendors were selling food and drink, and children were playing at

127

knights, fighting each other with wooden swords. Errin stood alone at the centre of the field, his helm tucked under his arm. He could scarcely believe that people could turn an event of life and death into such a festive occasion. The sky was clear and blue and despite the presence of autumn it was like a summer's day, bright and warm. His armour felt heavy and, even though Boran had greased the joints, it was difficult to move.

He remembered a day such as this in Cithaeron, when a champion had stood for the life of a noble. He himself had not bothered to watch. He had caught the eye of an attractive lady and they had repaired to her apartments for a lazy afternoon of exquisite pleasure; he had not even troubled to enquire as to the outcome of the battle.

Now he stood alone at the centre of the grass-covered field. There should have been two friends beside him, but none had come forward. Considering Cairbre's talk of treason, he was not surprised.

Dianu was brought into the field on a wagon, and the crowd began to boo and jeer. A tremendous sense of anger engulfed Errin, but his eyes remained fixed on her. She stood with head held high, ignoring the taunts from the crowd. The wagon was followed by the Duke and the Lord Seer, and behind them came the Lords and Knights of the Council.

A herald blew a single blast on a silver bugle and the crowd fell silent.

The wagon was brought to the centre of the field and Errin approached it. Bowing to Dianu, he took her hand and kissed it. He could think of nothing to say, but answered her nervous smile with one of his own.

Sir Cairbre rode into sight and dismounted at the far end of the field. Then he walked slowly to the centre and bowed to Errin. Once more he was wearing the red helm and his eyes were hidden in shadow. He drew his sword – Errin's sword – and pushed it into the earth.

'Do you still wish this affair to continue?' asked Cairbre, his voice muffled and metallic.

'I do.'

'Then let us begin.' He dragged the sword clear and raised it two-handed, dropping the point until it covered half the distance between them. Errin put on his helm, drew his sword and touched the blade to Cairbre's.

Both men looked towards the Duke, who raised his hand. 'Begin!' he bellowed and immediately their swords clashed together, sweeping and blocking, cutting and parrying. Errin had never handled such a blade as Cairbre had given him; it seemed almost to have a mind of its own, saving him three times from deadly slashes.

The screams of the crowd grew louder as the battle continued, but Errin heard nothing above the harsh sounds of his own breathing inside the cushioned helm. Cairbre stumbled, his sword dropping down to expose his left side, and instantly Errin's borrowed blade hammered home into the red armour, smashing several plates from it. He heard Cairbre grunt in pain, and the Red Knight backed away. Storming after him, Errin lost his footing and at once Cairbre crashed a blow to his helm, tearing it from his head. Errin staggered back, blocking cut after cut. Cairbre's speed was dazzling and he felt panic welling within him. He saw Cairbre's sword flash for his head and his own blade leapt to block, but at the last second Cairbre rolled his wrists and sent the blade crashing into Errin's side. He felt his ribs crack, though his armour held. A second blow to the calf broke the bone and Errin fell to his knees, his neck exposed.

He glanced up at the upraised sword . . .

'No!' screamed Dianu. 'Stop it! I am guilty! Guilty!'

129

The blade swept down, halting just as it touched Errin's neck. He did not feel it; his vision swam and he fainted.

He awoke in the fading light of dusk, in his own room. Boran was beside him, bathing a wound in his temple. Errin struggled to rise, but Boran pushed him back. 'Be still, my Lord. You have broken ribs, and they may pierce your lung if you struggle.'

'Why am I alive?'

'The Lady Dianu shouted her guilt and that ended the battle. She saved you, my Lord. Now there is someone to see you.'

'I wish to see no one.'

'I think you will wish to see this man; he is in great danger.'

'Who?'

Boran moved aside and there, sitting beside the bed, was Ubadai.

'You fought pretty good,' said the Nomad. 'He was pretty much better.'

'You must help me,' Errin whispered. 'We must save Dianu. We must!'

'First we save you. Your new man here – good man – he hear they come for you tomorrow. You, me, we go, yes? We run. Get to Cithaeron.'

'Not without Dianu. Now help me up.'

'Gently,' ordered Boran, lifting Errin to a sitting position. A sharp pain lanced his side.

'We help the lady,' said Ubadai, 'but first we get you out of castle. There are horses – you can ride?'

'I can ride,' said Errin. 'Get me some clothes, Boran.'

'It is already done, my Lord. The dark brown leather with the sheepskin cape. I have also packed food, and some coin. You only had three hundred Raq, but it should pay for the passage to Cithaeron.'

Errin looked down at the tightly-bound splint on his left leg. 'Will it support me?' he asked.

Boran shrugged. 'I hope so, my Lord.'

'Help me into my clothes,' said Errin. As Boran moved to obey him there came the sound of marching feet from the courtyard below and Ubadai ran to the window and looked down.

'A squad of men,' he whispered, 'coming this way.'

Errin groaned as Boran gently lifted his arms into the leather shirt. His ribs were bandaged tightly, but the pain was intense.

'Better be quick,' he urged Ubadai as a hammering came from below.

'Open up, in the name of the Duke!'

'Use the side stair-well, my Lord,' said Boran. 'I will detain them for as long as I can.' Errin called Ubadai to him, then levered himself upright by gripping the Nomad's shoulder. He felt the bones of the broken leg grind together and almost screamed. Ubadai half carried him to the small door leading to the servant's stair-well, where Errin stared down into the dark depths. There was no hand-rail.

'I can't climb down there,' he said.

'Much trouble, you,' said Ubadai. Turning, he threw an arm around the back of Errin's thighs and lifted him over his shoulder. Errin's broken ribs grated and he groaned. 'No noise!' Ubadai hissed, slowly descending the stairs.

At the main door, Boran lifted the bolt and bowed to the officer.

'What can I do for you, sir?'

'Where is Lord Errin?'

'He is upstairs sleeping. He was wounded badly today; he has a broken leg.'

'Our orders are to take him into the custody of the Lord Seer.'

'I take it you have a stretcher,' said Boran.

'No. I . . . no one mentioned a broken leg.'

'It was diagnosed by the Duke's surgeon. The Duke

himself was here earlier to enquire after his friend. Who did you say ordered his arrest?'

'The Lord Seer, Okessa.'

'Ah, well, it must be correct then. I am sure the Duke must have authorized it. You have his seal?'

'Seal? Look, you, the Duke's seal is only used for arrests made away from Mactha, in order to prove the identity of the Duke's officers. Why in the devil's name would I need a seal?'

'I am not arguing, captain. I know little of such matters, having never arrested a cousin of the King. Please go about your business.'

'Cousin of the King? Lord Errin?'

'So I understand. Well, go upstairs and drag him down. I've not been in his employ for long, so I have had no time to grow fond of him.'

'I'm not "dragging" anyone anywhere. I was told to arrest the Lord Errin. Haven't you got something we could use for a stretcher?'

'Well . . . you could take his bed, I suppose. It would take more than six of you, though. Are there any more men back at the barracks?'

The officer spun on his heel. 'Medric, Joal, go back and get a stretcher. And see if the Duke's orderly is about; I wouldn't mind an official seal on this one.'

'Very wise, captain. Perhaps you and I should go upstairs and carry Lord Errin down, ready for the stretcher?' suggested Boran.

'Do I look like a labourer?' snapped the captain. 'I'll wait here.'

'Then allow me to fetch you some wine, sir. The very best western wine, aged in the cask for twenty years.'

'That's very decent of you,' the captain thanked him.

'Not at all, sir.'

At the rear of the apartments Ubadai opened the door to the yard and stepped outside. The alley was deserted save for the two horses tethered at the gate.

He eased Errin down, then lifted him to the saddle and led the horses towards the eastern gate. This was mainly used for traders, and Ubadai guessed that news of Errin's arrest would not yet have been circulated to the gate sentries.

He was right, and the two men rode unhindered from Mactha fortress and down through the town.

'It seems deserted,' said Errin. Ubadai grunted and pointed to the nearby hills.

'What is happening?' asked Errin, his mouth suddenly dry.

'Tonight they burn the Lady.'

'Sweet Heaven! I must get there.' Errin lashed the reins across his stallion's neck and forced him into a mad gallop across the fields. Ubadai raced after him, leaning over to grab the reins.

'Stop!' said the Nomad. 'One stupid deed a day is enough.'

'Leave me alone!' shouted Errin, hitting out weakly, his hand cracking against Ubadai's face.

'Think!' ordered Ubadai. 'One man, all broke up. Useless. He is going to ride through the Duke's soldiers and rescue the Lady. You could not even get off horse.'

'There must be *something* I can do.'

'Yes,' said Ubadai. 'Something. Only thing.' He lifted Errin's bow from his saddle horn.

'I can't!'

'Then let us ride to forest and leave this cursed country.'

Errin swallowed hard and took the bow and quiver. Then he pushed his stallion forward, edging it to the cover of some trees near the brow of the hill. A great mass of firewood had been laid around a central stake and as he approached he saw Dianu being led forward by Okessa. The Duke was nowhere in sight. The Red Knight sat his unearthly mount away from the crowd, his gaze fixed on the doomed girl.

Tears stung Errin's eyes and he blinked them away as Dianu was led up on to the pyre and tied to the stake. Her eyes scanned the crowd, but she could not see him in the shadows of the trees. When she was tied, Okessa and the men with him drew back and climbed down to the ground. Then the Seer took a burning torch and thrust it into the tinder at the base of the pyre. Flames and smoke leapt instantly.

Errin took an arrow from his quiver and notched it to the bow.

Heeling his horse forward into the light, he shouted, 'Dianu!' He saw her head come up, and watched in anguish as hope flared in her eyes. 'I love you!' he screamed . . . and drew back the bowstring. He saw realization replace hope and she closed her eyes. He loosed the shaft. It sped through the air to slice home through the blue doublet that covered her breast. Her mouth opened – and her head fell. An angry roar came from the crowd and hands reached out to seize Errin. He was beyond caring but Ubadai rode forward, lashing a man across the face with a riding whip. The Nomad seized the reins of Errin's mount, wheeled it, and the two men thundered from the hill as the flames of Dianu's funeral pyre lit the sky.

7

Lámfhada watched as Arian measured out her paces.
Satisfied, she took a piece of chalk from her pocket and
drew a rough circle on the thick bole of an oak, some
two feet from the ground. Then she returned to where
the youth waited. He loved to watch her walk – her
movements smooth, almost liquid, her eyes alert. She
grinned at him.

'Are you ready?' she asked.

'Yes.'

'Then string your bow.' Lámfhada removed the
string from his borrowed hip-pouch and looped it to
his longbow. As he had been shown, he attached it first
to the foot of the bow, bending down the top to meet
the second loop.

'That tree,' said Arian, 'is thirty paces away. Now
we have practised at thirty paces, so you know the
pull.'

'Of course,' he agreed, drawing an arrow from the
doeskin quiver and notching it to the string.

'Then imagine that chalk circle is a pheasant – and
kill it,' she told him. Slowly he drew back the string
until it touched his cheek, focused on the chalk circle
– and loosed. The shaft hammered into the tree some
seven feet above the circle. He was instantly angry,
grabbing for a second arrow.

'Wait!' she ordered. 'Look at the line of flight and
tell me what you see?'

'It is a clear line, unblocked by trees.'

'What else?'

He stared down at the target. 'It is downhill.'

'Precisely, Lámfhada. And, like sighting across dead

ground, the eye will betray you. Remember this: You will shoot high, when aiming downhill; low, when sighting uphill or across water. It is also difficult to judge distance in the woods. Now, sight on the target and aim some three paces in front of the tree.'

He did so and the arrow flew to the chalk circle as if drawn there by magic.

'I did it!' he yelled.

'Yes; a fine strike. Now turn to your right and plant an arrow in the trunk of the pine over there.'

Lámfhada notched his shaft to the string and stared at the tree. Judging it to be around forty paces, he pulled for fifty. Smoothly he released the string and the arrow sailed towards the target – then dropped to slice into the earth. 'I don't understand,' he said.

'Pace it out,' she told him. Slowly he walked the distance; the tree was seventy paces away.

'You must learn to judge such things,' she said, walking beside him. 'The reason it fooled you was the number of trees pushing in on the line of flight. They destroyed your perspective and shortened the distance. Come, let us retrieve your arrow from the oak.'

'Am I improving, Arian?' he asked, desperate for a word of praise.

'You have a good arm and your release is without tremor. We will see.'

A good arm! Lámfhada felt like a king.

The rain had passed during the morning and the afternoon was bright and clear as he sat with Arian on the hillside overlooking the settlement. Below them the newcomer Elodan was trying to chop logs using a short hatchet. His movements were clumsy and the blade kept missing the chunks and bouncing from the hardwood ring.

Every day Elodan practised and his improvement – if improvement there was – was slow and frustrating.

Lámfhada was over the worst of his wound, which now itched mercilessly as the scabs peeled on his back.

'So, young magician, tell me of the Colours,' said Arian, leaning back on her elbows and grinning at the embarrassed youth. He had tried to impress her with his knowledge of magic, and had shown her Ruad's boots. But when he put them on and whispered the name Ollathair, nothing happened. The magic had been exhausted during his flight from the Lord Errin and the hunters. She had mocked him then – not spitefully, but he had taken it hard and spent many hours trying to find the Black in order to recharge the power. And he had failed.

'First, there is the White,' he told her. 'That is the Colour of Calm and Serenity. Then the Yellow, which is of Innocence and the laughter of children. This is followed by the Black, which is of the Earth and brings strength and speed. Power, if you will. The Blue is of the Sky, and gives the magic of Flight. The Green is of Growth, and Healing. And the Red is of Fear, and Lust.'

'Does the Red have no good powers?' she asked.

'Oh yes. It is of aggression and, used wisely, can aid all other Colours. But it takes a mighty wizard to use it so.'

'A mighty wizard like you, Lámfhada?'

He blushed and grinned. 'Do not mock me, Arian,' he urged. 'I was only a poor apprentice, and even then I had little time with the Master. But I did make a bird of bronze that flew for a little while; it was a beautiful bird, and it took nearly a year to create.'

'I would like to have seen that bird,' said Arian. 'But now to your education, for I have little time to spend with a wounded boy. Name that tree over to your left.'

'A sycamore,' he answered instantly.

'How do you know?'

'It has leaves with five lobes, and winged seeds.'

'And that?' she asked, pointing to another tree.

'Maple. It is like the sycamore, but the leaves are a lighter green, and the bark is grey and finely furrowed.'

A bird swooped down to perch on a branch of the maple. It was white-breasted, its head grey, and its eyes looked as if they wore a black mask.

'Before you ask,' said Lámfhada proudly, 'that is a grey shrike. It feeds on mice and other birds – Llaw Gyffes told me.'

'And what does it signal?' she asked.

'Signal? I . . . don't understand.'

'It signals the coming of winter. You rarely see it in the summer months. Now I suggest you help Elodan with the wood; you can stack it against the north wall for him.'

'Where will you go?' he asked, painfully aware that his time with her was over as she rose smoothly and gathered her bow.

'I am taking Nuada to Groundsel's camp. The poet's fame is spreading through the forest,' she replied.

'Will it be dangerous?'

'Do not fear for me, Lámfhada. I am no country milk-maid. Anyway, Groundsel has offered safe conduct and he will abide by it. Even in the forest there are rules which will not be broken.'

'But the men Elodan killed, were they not from Groundsel's camp?'

'He did not kill them all, boy,' she snapped. 'I took one of them.'

She wandered away and he cursed himself for annoying her. During the last ten days he had found her constantly on his mind, making him twist and turn in his bed, unable to sleep. He strolled down the hill and began to gather the wood around the ring.

'I will do that,' said the dark-haired Elodan, his face grim and bathed in sweat.

'I have been told to do it,' stated Lámfhada. 'They are finding tasks to make me feel useful.'

Elodan grinned. 'It is the same for me. But I'll be damned if I can make my left hand work. It is a question of balance, you see. A man is not just right-handed, but right-sided: foot, eye and hand working together. Now I am just clumsy.' He sat down. 'It is hard to be useless.'

'You are not useless,' Lámfhada told him. 'You rescued Arian single . . . on your own,' he finished lamely.

Elodan laughed. 'Do not fear to say single-handed. It is not as if your words bring home any truth I do not know. How is your back?'

'Almost mended. Arian is teaching me the use of the bow and when I can hunt and bring meat to the settlement, I shall feel much better.'

Elodan wiped the sweat from his face and smiled at the blond youngster. Any fool could see the lad was in love with Arian. Sadly, Arian could see it too. The boy wanted to impress her, but never would, for despite their similarity of age Arian was a grown woman . . . and already in love.

'What brought you to the forest?' Lámfhada asked.

'A dream. A quest. Both have proved to be without foundation,' replied Elodan. 'I shall stay for the winter and then try to get to Cithaeron.'

'What dream did you have?'

'Gabala is awash with rumours of a revolt led by a great hero,' Elodan said, shaking his head. 'His name is Llaw Gyffes, and he has a mighty army gathering in the Forest of the Ocean. I came to join that army.'

'It is not Llaw's fault that stories about him have grown,' said Lámfhada. 'All he did was rescue some prisoners from Mactha.'

'No, it is not his fault. Now I must continue with

my work, and you should start gathering.' But Lámfhada saw he made no move to pick up the hatchet.

'Why did you go against the King?' the youth asked suddenly.

'You are full of questions, Lámfhada – but then so was I when young, and my questions were always of the empire. One of my ancestors marched with Patronius to conquer Fomoria and Sercia. Another fell when the Eagle was carried to the east and the Nomad tribes destroyed them. Twenty years later, his son led the Five Armies that smashed the Nomads and established cities across the Steppes to the Far Sea. Always the empire.' Elodan picked up the hatchet and stared at the curved blade. 'But – as all empires will – the Gabala failed. There is a truth that cannot be ignored. Empires are like men; they grow to maturity, then they age and wither. When there is nothing left to conquer, decay begins. A sad truth to understand. Ten years ago the Fomorians and the Sercians hammered that truth back at us with an uprising. Ahak led a brilliant counter-attack – and he won. But he knew the victory would be short-lived, so he gave the lands back to the rebels and marched home.

'I worshipped the man then; I saw in him the seeds of greatness. But he is an old-style Gabalan and he could not let the past rest. We talked of it often. Tell me, Lámfhada, what separates the civilized man from the barbarian?'

'Learning, culture . . . architecture?'

'Yes,' Elodan agreed, 'but even more basic than that: an abundance of food and wealth. The barbarian must battle for every crust. He has no time for the weak or the infirm. They die and only the strong survive. But we *civilized* people, we learn to care. We help the weak and we ourselves grow fat and lazy. We promote the seeds of our own destruction. Three hundred years ago we were a lean, barbarian people. We conquered much

140

of the world. But twenty years ago the greater part of our armies were mercenaries from conquered barbarian tribes; only the officers were Gabalan. Do you see what I am saying?'

'Not really,' admitted the youth.

'The King believes he can reverse the process: eradicate the weak, the tainted. Burn away the fat, and the Gabala will rise again.'

'And that is why you went against him?'

'No,' said Elodan. 'At the time I believed in everything the King was planning. But I stood for the nobleman, Kester, when he was accused of being tainted.'

'Why?'

'To repay a debt, Lámfhada. I killed his son.'

'Oh,' said Lámfhada, swallowing hard. He could not think of anything to say and his next question sped from his lips before he could stop it. 'Was it a terrible thing to lose your hand?' He looked up into Elodan's eyes, which grew cold and distant; then his lean face relaxed and he smiled at the youth.

'No. The terrible thing was to find a man who could cut it from me. Now let us work.'

The girl was not frightened when she was brought to Cairbre's room by two of Okessa's most trusted servants. Nor was she concerned when the Knight approached her in the candlelight, his armour still strapped to his lean frame. Her fear began when he smiled, and she saw the whiteness of his teeth and the cold gleam in his eyes.

An hour later Cairbre sat in the middle of the room, the curtains drawn, his eyes swamped in crimson. The girl's body lay on the bed, curiously shrivelled like a tanned leather sack.

Cairbre placed his hands together as if in prayer.

The candles guttered and died; the room began to glow and seven circles of amber light formed before the Knight, swelling and brightening, coalescing into faces.

'Welcome, my brothers,' said Cairbre. All the faces were strangely similar, with short-cropped white hair and blood-filled eyes, yet one stood out from the rest. The eyes were almost slanted, the cheekbones high, the mouth full; it was a strong face, a leader's face.

'The Red is growing,' said the leader. 'Soon, we will have it all.'

'How are your plans faring, my Lord?' Cairbre asked.

'Furbolg is quiet. We have begun to take our nourishment far from the city, where panic is less contagious. Also there are Nomad women, and none care when they disappear. But that is a small matter. When the Red takes control, the King will gather his army. The east will be the first to feel the might of the New Gabala. Now tell me, Cairbre, what of the wizard Ollathair?'

'He escaped, my Lord. Okessa sent men to apprehend him, but they were terrified by his demon hounds. I believe he has sought refuge in the great forest.'

'Have you located him?'

'Not yet. It is a perplexing matter, but the Red does not seem to be growing there at the same rate. The White is strong – and the Black. I do not understand it.'

'Ollathair is there,' said the leader. 'Perhaps that is the answer. It does not matter; he will be found and destroyed. I am loosing the Beasts.'

'Will they not slay indiscriminately?' asked Cairbre.

The leader smiled. 'Of course they will; it is their nature. But do not concern yourself, Cairbre. The forest is a breeding ground for traitors. Loyal men do not go there. Therefore any life that is lost is already forfeit.'

'And if the Beasts leave the forest?'

The leader's eyes hardened. 'Be careful, Cairbre, your weakness has not passed without comment. Why did you loan your sword to the traitor Errin?'

'Because I was bored, my Lord. Without it he would have been dead in an instant.'

'And yet, in giving it to him, you allowed him to wound you. That is why you needed the nourishment. You are a brother to me, Cairbre, you always were. But take no more foolish risks. The fate of the kingdom rests with us – and the future of the world. Our crusade against the evils of corruption and decay must not be allowed to falter. We have made great strides with the gradual elimination of the Nomad curse. Soon will come the real test.'

Cairbre bowed his head. 'I am ready, my Lord.'

'There is great talk in Furbolg of a rebel force in the forest, led by a man named Llaw Gyffes. What do you know of him?'

'He is an outlawed blacksmith who killed his wife and one of the Duke's relatives. He escaped from the dungeons of Mactha.'

'Rather too many of our King's enemies are escaping from Mactha,' snapped the leader. 'Llaw Gyffes, Olla-thair – and now this rebel lord, Errin. Is the Duke a sympathizer?'

'I do not think so. He is an opportunist.'

'Watch him carefully. At the first sign of treachery, depose him and install Okessa in his place. *His* loyalty is without question.'

'Indeed it is, my Lord, but the man is a snake.'

'Snakes have their uses, Cairbre. Now, to return to Llaw Gyffes: is he building an army?'

'I have no reason to believe that he is. But then the forest covers several thousand square miles and in it there are many valleys, and mountains and settlements. It is difficult to know what is being planned there.'

'And the White is too strong for you to observe their plans?'

'Yes, my Lord. I flew as close to it as I could last night, but the light almost burnt my soul and I had to flee to my body. That is also why I needed the nourishment.'

'The Beasts will aid the Red, for they will inspire fear – more than fear. Stark and naked terror will radiate from that damned rats' nest.'

The faces faded, and Cairbre was alone.

Terribly alone . . .

Bighorn sheep and a few wild long-haired cattle were grazing together on the hillsides, while a small herd of deer were drinking at a stream which bubbled over white rocks on its journey to the river far below.

At the brow of a hill, where marble boulders had been formed into a rough ring, the air began to crackle. Several sheep stopped their feeding and looked up, but their watery eyes could see no predator and there was no smell of wolf or lion upon the breeze. Warily they milled about. Lightning flashed from the boulders, and the sheep ran. A huge bull, his curved horns scarred by many battle trials, swung to face the boulders. A curious smell reached his nostrils, acrid as smoke, leaving a strange taste in the bull's mouth. The air rippled before him, and a dark shadow fell across the hillside.

There in the circle of boulders stood a huge creature, its head elongated and vulpine, its grey-furred shoulders ridged with muscle. It ambled forward with jaws gaping – long, wicked fangs dripping saliva to its leathery chest. The bull had seen enough; he backed away.

The creature raised its snout as the wind changed and caught the scent of sheep and cattle. Its eyes widened and long talons slid from their sheaths in the flesh of its fingers.

It stood stock still for a moment, then raced at the flock with surprising speed. The sheep scattered, the cattle stampeding towards the stream. His cows threatened, the bull ducked his head and charged. The creature dropped to all fours as the bull approached and at the last second it leapt, high over the bull's head, to land on its back. Long talons sliced deep into the dark flesh, then ripped clear.

Blood gushing from several gaping wounds, the bull bellowed in pain and rage and, in a wild effort to dislodge its tormentor, rolled to its back. The creature leapt clear. The bull's head came up as it struggled to rise, exposing the huge jugular. Talons flashed out. The jugular parted and blood fountained from the dying bull as it sank to the grass, hooves scrabbling weakly. The creature snarled and launched a final murderous assault, ripping and smashing through skin and bone and muscle to finally tear out the heart of the bull . . .

This it devoured. Then, more calmly, it began to tear and bite at the carcass. Hunger satisfied, its head dropped back with snout pointing to the sky. An eerie, unearthly howl echoed through the hills. The deer raced for the sanctuary of the trees and the sheep ran in terror from the hillside.

The first of the Beasts had arrived in the Forest of the Ocean.

'You are an idiot, poet,' said Llaw Gyffes as the slender Nuada packed his spare clothes into a large travelling pack. 'Groundsel is a notorious liar and a foul-mouthed thief. If he doesn't like your stories, you could end up staked out on a hillside.'

Nuada chuckled. 'Come with us, mighty hero. Protect us!'

'Us?'

'Yes. Arian is accompanying me.'

Llaw's face flushed and his eyes showed a murderous gleam. He stroked his red-gold beard, struggling for calm. 'You think it is wise to take a child into Groundsel's lair?' he asked.

Nuada laughed aloud and hoisted the pack to his shoulders. 'Child, Llaw?' he mocked. 'Are you blind? She is a woman – and a damned fetching one. Surely you have noticed?'

'What I notice, or don't notice, is my own affair,' snapped the outlaw. 'How long will you be gone?'

'Admit it, you'll miss me. Go on, be a man, admit it.'

Uttering a foul curse, Llaw rose and stormed from the cabin, almost colliding with Arian but stopping at the last minute by grabbing her shoulders. Mumbling an apology, he stalked off towards the hills. Nuada was right. Llaw would miss him. He was bright company and his stories wove webs of magic that could make a man forget he lived in a forest, in a dark cabin. They could ease the pain of loss and make the world seem a place of heroes and enchantment. Without him this was merely another mud-swamped settlement with no hope and no future.

Llaw's thoughts flew to Lydia, the wife of his heart – a beautiful woman, strong and yet caring. He found his feelings for Arian a betrayal of Lydia's memory, and hoped her ghost would forgive him. Seeing Lámfhada and the cripple, Elodan, working to build the winter wood supply, he tried to walk past without stopping, but Elodan waved and he knew it would be churlish to ignore them.

'How goes it?' he asked.

146

'There will be fuel for the winter,' replied Elodan. 'Has Nuada gone yet?'

'No.'

'He will be missed here, I think. I hope he is not away too long. I've never heard a finer story-teller,' said Elodan. 'I first knew him in Furbolg. He put on a performance for the King. It was the tale of Asmodin. Superb! The King – may the Gods rot his soul – gave Nuada a ruby the size of a goose-egg.'

'He doesn't have it now,' said Llaw gleefully.

'No, I understand he gave it to a lady for a single night of pleasure.'

'The more fool him,' snapped Llaw, thinking of the two-day journey the poet was about to undertake with Arian. But then all Nuada could now offer her was a second pair of woollen leggings and a threadbare blanket. Even so, the slender poet was a handsome man! Llaw cursed.

'What is wrong?' Elodan asked.

'Nothing!' said Llaw, striding off.

'Is he sick, do you think?' Lámfhada whispered.

'No, he is in love,' answered Elodan, chuckling. 'But then, in my experience, that is very much the same.'

Llaw stopped at his cabin and sat staring at his spartan surroundings. Then with a muttered curse he packed his belongings in a canvas shoulder-sack, tucked a double-headed axe into his belt and walked from the settlement without a backward glance.

Cithaeron was the place to be, he decided. He could get work in a smithy there and build a new life.

As he topped the line of hills he heard a distant howl. It chilled his blood. The wolves were out early this year, he thought – and walked on.

Nuada stepped into the sunshine and watched the outlaw crest the hill; Arian stopped beside him. 'What are you looking at?'

'Llaw. I think he is leaving us.'

'Ridiculous!' she snapped. 'He is making his life here.'

Nuada looked at her and grinned. 'Lead on, lady,' he said. 'I shall follow your beauty to the ends of the earth.'

'Fool!'

'Indeed I am. It is the fate of poets.'

He hoisted his pack to his back and waited. 'What about weapons?' she asked.

'I have little use for them. But I have no fear; you will be there to guard me from the evils of the wild.' His violet eyes sparkled with humour. Arian was unsure of Nuada; in the days she had known him he had made no secret of the fact that he found her attractive, yet not once had he made a move to court her. But then, she reasoned, this was a man who had moved among the ladies of the court, with their soft perfumed skin and their clothes of silk.

'Let us go,' she told him, moving off across the settlement. He strolled some paces behind her, enjoying the swaying of her hips in the tight buckskin leggings.

Once more the strange howling came from the distant north. It was answered by a second howl to the east . . . and another from the south. Nuada shivered.

'Wolves?' he asked.

Arian stopped. 'It must be a trick of the wind,' she said, 'or a twisted echo. Anyway, it will not trouble us. Wolves keep well clear of people – except in the worst of winter, when food is scarce. But even then they can be scared away by a hunter with nerve.'

'That howling went through me like a winter wind,' he said.

She smiled at him. 'That's because you are a city man,' she told him.

'So you are not concerned by it?'

'Not at all,' she lied.

*

148

Manannan, the Once-Knight, sat alone with Ollathair the Armourer. The cabin was empty, for Gwydion and the family had wandered out into the settlement square. Ruad waited for Manannan to speak, but the Once-Knight sat silently staring at the table. Finally Ruad spoke.

'We need them, Manannan. If they are alive, they must be brought back.'

'I cannot do it; I cannot pass the Black Gate.'

The Armourer reached over and gripped Manannan's arm. 'The nation is in great danger. The Colours are in disarray; the Red is swelling. Nomads are being murdered. Lust, greed and evil are swamping the Harmonies. Do you understand? The King has gathered to him eight Knights – Red Knights. I sense their evil. They must be countered, Manannan. Only the Knights of the Gabala could hope to stand against them.'

'Then you should not have sent them,' said Manannan, fixing his gaze to Ollathair's.

The older man looked away. 'You are right. It was folly of the worst kind. But I cannot put it right.'

'Go after them yourself.'

'I cannot. There is no one to open the Gate this side, and the spell may not be reversible in the other world. You must go.'

Manannan laughed and shook his head. 'You don't understand; you never did. I came to you the night before the quest began. I told you then of my fears. It was not death that troubled me. I knew that if I passed the Gate my soul would be in peril. But no, you would not listen. Well, they are gone, Ollathair. You cannot bring them back. They died in whatever Hell they found beyond the Gate.'

'You cannot be sure.'

'No, I can't. But if Samildanach and the others were alive, they would have found a way back. I am sure of

that. Samildanach was almost the wizard you are.'
Manannan poured water into a clay cup and drained
it; then he stood and looked down at Ollathair. 'On
that last night, I saw Samildanach saying farewell to
Morrigan; she cried and he left her. I went to her and
dried her tears and she told me she had dreamt strange
dreams of blood and fire, of angels and demons. In
her heart, she said, she knew she would never see
Samildanach again. What could I say? But when we
stood before the Gate and I felt the cold wind blow
through it, my courage died. It is the same now. But
you do not understand, Ollathair. You never did. You
never felt the fear that gnaws away at the soul. You
could never understand what it is to find yourself a
coward. Oh yes, I can face men in battle. I am confident of my skills. But faced with the Gate, I was lost.
Even now when I think of it my heart races, my breath
seems short. I panicked, Ollathair. I did it then – I
would do it now.'

He walked to the door and turned. 'I am truly sorry.'

'Manannan!' called Ruad and the warrior swung to
face him.

'What is it?'

'I have known that fear . . . when the King had me
in chains and they burned my eye from me. But a man
must overcome his fears, or they will overcome him.
You are not a coward. It is not death you fear; it is the
dark, the unknown, the journey into night. Will you
not try to conquer it?'

'You still do not understand,' said Manannan
wearily. 'If I could do it, I would. Can you not see
that?'

'What I see is a man who was once a Knight of the
Gabala – a man who swore an oath to protect and
defend the Order. Go from here, Manannan. I free you
from your oath. Now you can do as you will.'

'Farewell, Armourer,' said the Once-Knight.

150

Outside in the sunlight, he mounted Kuan and rode from the settlement. Death was now assured, he knew; but then, death came to all men. He would find a place high in the mountains and he would cheat his fate. When the pressure on his throat grew great, he would find a way to die that pleased him.

He rode throughout the afternoon, ever higher into the tree line, passing cabins and skirting other settlements. Towards dusk he heard a high-pitched howling from the forest. Kuan's ears pricked and Manannan felt him shudder.

'You have nothing to fear from wolves, Greatheart,' he said, patting the stallion's neck. 'It is not yet winter.'

He rode on, following a narrow track peppered with the spoor of deer. The trees were thicker here and he ducked low over his saddle to avoid overhanging branches. At the bottom of the track the ground opened out and he saw a cabin and a tilled field. Before the cabin lay a man with blood seeping from a terrible wound in his side. The Once-Knight drew his sword and rode warily towards the body. The man was dead; his right arm and half his chest had been torn from him. Kuan whinnied as the smell of blood came to him. By a roughly-dug well lay a woman, her head smashed; there was no other wound in evidence.

Manannan dismounted and searched the ground. There was no spoor in the immediate vicinity, but he followed a trail of blood from the man's body until he reached softer earth. Here he found paw-marks of great size – like the pad of a lion, but almost a foot across. He knelt by the track and stared off into the undergrowth. The beast had obviously moved off to feed. But why? The bodies could have been devoured where they lay. The beast must have been disturbed.

By his arrival? If so, that meant it was still close by. He stood and backed away from the undergrowth. A beast of this size was not something to anger.

At that moment a child came running from the trees, saw Manannan and screamed. She was around nine years old, with long blonde hair, and wearing a tunic of homespun wool.

A creature from nightmare moved out behind her. It was huge and double-headed, in part like a lion but wider at the shoulder. Its fangs were long and curved, and each head showed two great incisors long as sabres. In that instant Manannan realized the beast had not been disturbed by him but had moved off in pursuit of the child. He ran towards the girl, but knew he would never reach her before the beast bore her down. He cut to the left, shouting at the top of his voice.

The creature's heads swung towards him.

'Here, Ugliness!' Manannan bellowed. 'Come to me!'

The sound of its roaring filled the clearing – and it charged!

The Once-Knight stood his ground, his sword held double-handed over his right shoulder, ready for the slashing sweep. As the beast closed on the slender figure, Manannan saw it crouch for the spring and as it leapt he dropped to one knee, his sword flashing in a disembowelling arc. The blade buried itself in the beast's side as it swept over him, and was almost torn from his hands. In his desperation to keep his grip, Manannan was dragged several yards; he rolled swiftly, but the beast – blood gushing from its side – turned and was upon him. The stallion, Kuan, galloped forward and hearing the sound of the charging warhorse, the monster hesitated. Manannan gained his feet and hammered the blade through the neck of the nearest head. The great jaws snapped shut and the head toppled to hang by a sinew. Blood fountained from the neck. Kuan turned his back on the beast, lashing out with his hind legs, his hooves thundering against the creature's body and hurling it into the air.

Manannan rushed in and clove a mighty blow to its remaining head; his blade smashed the skull asunder. The beast reared and a massive claw raked out at Manannan, catching his helmet. The Once-Knight was torn from his feet as the beast fell and died.

Manannan rose. Never had he seen a beast like this – nor heard of any such in the Worlds of Civilization.

The sound of sobbing broke across his thoughts and he turned to see the child kneeling by her mother, pulling at the woman's arm. He sheathed his sword and walked over to the child, lifting her to his chest.

'She is dead, girl. I am sorry.'

Several men came running from the trees, carrying bows and lances, but they stopped, awe-struck, by the body of the beast. As the Once-Knight carried the child to them, her arm reached up to touch his helm and the metal slipped. Swiftly he passed the child to a waiting man and took hold of the helm. The claw had torn away a hinge at the top of the neck-plates and he raised his hands to the metal, but at that moment a thick-set man spoke.

'What is this creature?' he asked, staring down at the two-headed monster.

'I don't know,' replied Manannan. 'But I hope it lives alone.'

The man held out his hand. 'I am Liam. We saw you tackling the beast, but we did not think we could reach you in time. Are you a King's man?'

'I am no one's man. Excuse me.' He walked slowly away from the group and lifted his hand to the spring bar on his helm. It slipped sideways . . . His mouth was dry, and he was almost too frightened to raise the helm. Taking a deep breath, he gripped the metal and straightened his arms . . . the helm grated against the neck-plates and then slid loose. His matted hair caught in the rotting leather padding within, but he tore it free. Without the helm in place the neck-plates fell away, draping his shoulders. The wind was cool on his face; his beard was matted and filthy, and sores stung his skin.

'How long have you been wearing that?' asked Liam, moving to stand beside Manannan.

'Too long. Do you live far from here?'

'No. You are welcome to eat with us.'

'Hot water and a razor would be a blessing beyond my power to describe,' Manannan told him.

In the distance came a terrible howling.

'Something has tasted blood,' said Liam.

8

Ruad heard the screaming and ran from his cabin. In the square beyond, a scaled creature was dragging a man back towards the trees. The beast was over ten feet long, with six legs, and a long snout which had fastened to his victim's leg.

Several villagers ran at the creature, hammering at it with picks and axes. It released the screaming man only to lunge at a villager, who jumped back. The beast swung, and Ruad watched as its tail cracked out like a whip to circle the legs of one of its attackers and haul him towards its gaping jaws. Ruad knelt beside his golden hounds and whispered the word of power, then he pointed at the beast and spoke again. The hounds leapt across the square. The first sprang to the creature's back, sinking its steel fangs through scale and bone. The second lunged for the beast's throat, ripping apart flesh and artery. The third fastened its terrible teeth to the tail trapping the villager; the jaws snapped shut and the tail parted, green gore pumping from the wound. The ruined tail thrashed wildly, spraying blood across the square, and the hounds backed away. For several seconds the creature snapped its great jaws at the air, then it settled slowly to the ground and died.

The villagers gathered round the wounded man and Gwydion came running from a nearby hut to lay his hands on the man's gashed leg. The blood stopped flowing immediately, and Gwydion ordered the injured villager to be carried to his hut.

The hounds padded back to Ruad. He touched each on the head – and they froze once more into statues. For several hours the villagers, armed with bows and

155

axes, searched the woods for more of the creatures. At dusk they returned, having seen tracks but no monsters.

Brion dropped the club he had been carrying and walked to where Ruad sat beside his hounds. 'What manner of beast are they?' he asked.

Ruad shrugged. 'It is too complex to explain, my friend. But they are not from here.'

'I know that,' the villager snapped. 'Speak plainly.'

'They are from a world beyond our own – summoned here by a sorcerer of great power.'

'For what purpose? Merely to kill? Who does that serve?'

'I do not know,' answered Ruad, turning away, but Brion was not to be ignored.

'It seems strange to me that first you come with your magic beasts, and then these things follow. I am not a fool, wizard. Do not treat me like one.'

Ruad looked into the young man's square, honest face. 'It may be that they were sent to kill me. I do not know – and that is the truth. The world outside this forest is sliding inexorably into evil.'

Brion was about to say more when the sound of horses' hooves came to them and a rider cantered into the village. He appeared tall, and his freshly-shaven face was ghostly pale. He rode to the cabin and hurled a helm at Ruad's feet; it bounced against the door, rolled, and came to rest against the flanks of a golden hound.

'There,' said Manannan, 'is your magic helm – the one that could not be released save by the magic of the Gate. Explain that to me, liar! And be convincing, Armourer. Much depends on it.' He dismounted and stalked to stand before Ruad.

'Be so kind as to leave us, Brion,' requested Ruad, placing his hand on the young man's shoulder. 'I will be leaving tonight, and your home will be your own

156

once more.' The young villager nodded, gave Manannan a long stare and then backed away.

'I am pleased for you,' said Ruad. 'And yes, I lied. I wanted you to pass the Gate. The spell on the helm was loosed the moment we spoke. Are you going to kill me?'

'Can you think of a reason why I should not?' Manannan retorted.

'Only that I desire to live – and I think I am needed,' admitted Ruad.

Manannan shook his head. 'I never was one to kill for the sake of it.' He glanced at the dead beast, still oozing green blood to the dust. 'I killed a creature with two heads today. Now this . . . what does it mean, Ollathair? Where are they from?'

'Beyond the Black Gate. Someone has decided to bring terror to the forest.'

'And that someone is . . . ?'

'I know of no sorcerer powerful enough. But ultimately it must be the King's doing. Perhaps they are looking for me. Perhaps for another. It seems to me that evil never needs a sound reason for such deeds as this. Will you help me, Manannan?'

'To do what?'

'To fight the evil. To be what you were trained to be: a Knight of the Gabala. Once it meant a great deal to you.'

'That was a long time ago.'

'But you have not forgotten?'

'How could I forget? What would you have me do?'

'You know what is needed.'

'No!' hissed Manannan. 'It is folly.'

'The Knights must return; I can see no other hope. It is my belief that this evil emanates from the Red Knights of the King. Only the true Gabala can stand against them – surely you see that?'

'What I see is a man with a lunatic dream. The

past is gone, Ollathair. Dead. Find yourself some new Knights – I'll even help you to train them.'

'We do not have five years, Manannan. We may not have five months. Ride through the Gate,' he pleaded. 'Find Samildanach and bring him home. He was the greatest warrior I have ever known; the finest swordsman and the noblest of men. He could help me with the Colours; he could stand against the Red slayers. Together we could rid the land of this evil.'

'Now there is a story I have heard before. Rid the world of evil! I did not accept it the first time.'

'That was an abstract. And I was wrong! Wrong! Is it so terrible to be wrong?'

'My friends died for the privilege of you being wrong.'

'You do not know that, Sir Coward-Knight!' snapped Ruad.

'No, I do not.' He swung on his heel and walked out into the darkness to stand on the porch, feeling the freshness of the night air on his face. He pictured again the Black Gate and heard the hideous sounds of the hidden beasts beyond. His heart raced, his hands trembled. He could not pass that portal. He had told Ollathair he was afraid for his soul but that had been a lie – a falsehood enabling him to save face.

It was death in the dark . . . just like the tree of his childhood. Trapped in the blackness with ants crawling on his skin. He shivered.

And yet, would any beast be worse than the horror he had faced today?

Even the monsters of the dark?

I can't! I'm afraid!

'Come inside,' said Ruad behind him. 'There is someone I want you to see.' He turned and stepped into the doorway, where the one-eyed sorcerer held out a silvered mirror. Manannan took it and gazed at a face he had not seen for six years. The eyes accused him and he looked away.

'You cannot run away any more, Manannan. You cannot live your life wondering if your friends are trapped in some deep, dark dungeon. I know you; it will haunt you all your days. And you are no coward; I would never have chosen you otherwise.'

'Why did you choose me?'

'Because you were strong in the broken places.'

'Always riddles with you, Ollathair. I am free now, you said that yourself. Free of my oath – free of that cursed helm. I do not have to pass the Gate.'

'You are correct in that. It is your choice. But if it would please you, I will beg – I will beg on bended knees.'

'No,' said Manannan softly. 'I would not like to see that. I will journey with you to the Gate and I will sit Kuan as I did before. But I promise nothing, except to try.'

'I will open the Gate here in the mountains,' said Ruad, 'and once through it you will find a city. They will have news there.'

'And they are friendly?'

'They are gods, Manannan. Wise and immortal. And you will find Samildanach; I know you will.'

Groundsel sat in the long hall staring at his treasury – three oak chests, the first half full of gold coin, the second brimming with silver, the third a gleaming pile of jewels and rings and brooches. The Royal Road was now a rich source of income, as Nomad families streamed along it to distant Cithaeron in the hope of a ship to safety. At first Groundsel had robbed and killed the merchants as they travelled, but the numbers of refugees had halted that simple plan. Had he continued, the Road would have become choked with bodies. Now he levied a toll on the escapers and soon he would be rich enough to leave this accursed forest and sail for warmer climes, where he would buy a palace and fill it with nubile slaves. Groundsel squirmed in his seat at the thought. He knew he was not a handsome man: short, squat, wide-shouldered and bulky, he had none of the clean lines of the athlete. His muscles were ridged and ugly, his body hairy, his arms inordinately long. As a slave he had been called Ape, and the masters and other servants laughed at him. Then he became Groundsel, for his job was to collect seeds for the feeding of the chickens. The name had weighed on him like a rock.

He leaned back in his carved chair, his small button eyes closing so that he could the better re-live the memory of the last day. He had been given a beating by the senior servant, Joaper, and the whip had peeled away the skin of his back. He was taking it as he took all beatings – in a grim and defiant silence – when he saw the master's wife grinning by the door of the barn. That dreadful smile carried all the weight of his anger and his shame, and it smote him with tongues of fire. He crouched and turned, grabbing the whip from Joaper's hand and smashing a fearful blow to the servant's face. The man crumpled without a sound. Then Groundsel had leapt upon the startled woman, dragging her back into a hay-covered stall and ripping her clothes from her. She had been too terrified to scream and his rage turned to lust.

When he had finished with her, he stood and retied his leggings. Then he tapped his chest and looked down at her.

'Groundsel,' he said. 'The Ape. Now you are the Ape's leavings. What does that make *you*?'

He strode from the barn with blood seeping from his whipped back and walked up the marble stairs into the house. A shocked servant tried to stop him, but he rammed the man's head into a wall and climbed the winding stair. The master was sitting in his study with his son, an arrogant young noble fond of riding and whoring. It was the boy who reacted first.

'Get out, you miserable peasant!' he ordered. Groundsel smiled and hammered his fist into the boy's face. The older man ran towards his desk and swept up a dagger, but Groundsel was upon him before he could draw it from its scabbard and dragging the man to the wide balcony he pushed him against the edge.

'I have raped your wife. I will kill your son. Die with that thought!'

The old man screamed once as Groundsel toppled him from the high balcony to crash to the marble flagstones. The rebel slave grinned as he saw his master's head split like a melon. Taking the dagger, he cut the throat of the unconscious youth, then walked back to the stables and saddled a gelding. The wife still lay where he had left her; he thought of killing her, but decided that to leave her was a greater punishment.

And he rode for the forest. He had been foolish then, for he had not robbed the house, and it was two years before he had gained mastery of the first outlaw band he joined. Now, five years later, he was the undisputed master of the Western Wood. Five settlements paid tribute to him, and the Royal Road was making him richer than he had dreamed possible.

He had thought to give himself another name – a proud name. Yet he had not. Groundsel was how he saw himself, and the sound of the name added fuel to his hatred.

He closed the chests and dragged them back to their hiding-place in the false wall. It was not much of a hiding-place, but few would dare to approach Groundsel's quarters in his absence. He rubbed at his close-cropped black hair. Rich, you are, he told himself. Yet something was lacking.

It was curious, but until today he had not known what it was. Then the girl Arian had walked into the settlement, along with the poet Nuada. Groundsel watched her hip-swinging stride, her honey-gold hair blowing in the breeze, her high proud head – and need flared in him like a summer fire. He felt hot as he drank in her beauty; his mouth was dry. He rubbed the back of his hand over his face and then glanced at his fingers – noticing for the first time in days that they were filthy. Ducking back inside the hall, he rummaged through another chest which contained clothing he had stolen from his first forest victims. He found a shirt of yellow silk and took it out, along with a pair of brown leather trews and a belt emblazoned with silver circles. Then he ran from the rear of the Hall to the stream. Some women were washing clothes there, so he moved upstream and bathed, scrubbing himself with mint leaves and lavender blossoms. He wiped the surplus water from his body with his hands and dressed swiftly. The shirt was on the large side, but the sleeves were far too short; he rolled back the cuffs and pulled on the trews. Again they were too long. Removing them, he took his knife and cut several inches from each leg. Once dressed, he returned to the hall to welcome his guests.

Like many others in the forest he had heard of the poet, and his first invitations had been courteously refused. Then Groundsel had sent a messenger with a gold coin – and the promise of more.

The man had better be worth it, he had decided, or he'd cut his ears off. Arian and Nuada were waiting in the cool of the southern entrance when Groundsel appeared. Nuada gave a courtly bow – which pleased the robber – while Arian merely smiled. Groundsel's delight was complete.

'Enter, enter,' he said. 'Welcome. I have heard

wondrous tales of your skill, master poet. I trust you will not disappoint us, poor folk that we are.'

Nuada bowed again. 'My Lord Groundsel, I can only hope that my poor talents prove worthy of the trust implicit in your invitation.'

'I am no Lord,' said Groundsel, sitting back on his chair and ordering wine to be brought for his guests. 'Just a poor man trying to do his best for the people who need him. These are hard times. But I am not a Lord – nor would I want to be.'

'A Lord,' said Nuada, 'is a man who commands respect from those who serve him, or fear from those obliged to serve him. He should also be a man of courage and leadership. Last year, I am told, a great fire sprang up, and men turned to you to save them. You organized bands of workers, dug a fire ditch, cleared the ground before the blaze and yourself worked alongside your men. That is heroic leadership, my Lord, sharing the dangers and inspiring your followers.'

Groundsel was lost for words. The fire would have destroyed his granary and winter would have brought starvation and an end to his leadership. Could the fool not see that? But the words were pleasing, and he was beginning to see the value of his investment in the poet. He turned his attention to the girl, asking her name and straining to be cool and pleasant.

He talked with them for an hour before having them escorted to an empty hut at the western edge of the village. When his men returned to explain that the woman and the man were not together, and desired separate accommodation, he was overjoyed. He ordered a second dwelling cleared, the resident family being moved to an overcrowded hut to the north. Naturally, there was no argument.

Back at the first dwelling, Arian turned to Nuada. 'You flatterer! Oh, my dear Lord Groundsel, what a hero you are!' she mocked.

163

Nuada grinned at her. 'And you, I suppose, offered nothing by way of flattery yourself?'

'What do you mean by that?'

'He all but climbed into your breeches, but you just stood by smiling provocatively. Do not think to lecture me! I was raised at court, where the wrong word or look could see a man ruined – or worse. This is no different. Groundsel is like a king here and to go against him could result in unpleasant consequences.'

'We are here on safe conduct,' she reminded him.

'Oh, grow up, Arian. Safe conduct? The man is a savage. However, he is a rich savage, so that gives me a reason for being here. But if you will take my advice, you will leave as soon as it is dark.'

Arian had already decided on that very course of action, but the poet's words stung her.

'I shall do nothing of the sort. I will leave tomorrow after breakfast. I wouldn't miss your performance before these rabble for . . . for a gold piece!'

He shrugged. 'As you will. I should have known better than to advise a woman so worldly-wise. But when he drags you to his bed, I think you will find there is a pig inside that silk shirt.'

'Jealous, poet? Are you attracted to men?' She hurled the question like a barb, and was furious when he laughed at her.

'You are angry, Arian,' he said. 'Was I not attentive enough on the journey here? Did you expect me to ask you to share my blanket? How remiss of me!'

The truth of his words made her blush furiously. Had he so invited her she would have refused, but she had expected him to make an advance. Her hand snaked out to crack against his cheek. For a moment anger flared, then he smiled, bowed and left the hut.

Arian watched him go, then swore under her breath. The poet was right; it was foolish to trust Groundsel's safe conduct. And yet she had only risked this journey in the hope that it would inspire some concern in the heart of Llaw Gyffes. In that she had failed miserably. She pictured Groundsel and his lust-filled eyes and slowly pulled the hunting-knife from its sheath at her side. The edge was honed to razor-sharpness and curled up into a double-edge crescent. *Drag her to his bed?*

She slid the knife back in its scabbard. And waited.

Arian sat beside Groundsel as Nuada stood on a central table and wove his spell over the seventy or so men who had crowded into the hall. His talent filled the room – his voice mellow and musical, his words rich and rolling, his stories vivid and compelling. Even Arian, who often found the battles of men incomprehensible, was swept along by his tales of heroes and maidens, swordsmen and sorcerers.

His delivery was subtly different here, she noticed – more quickfire and the stories less romantic, as if he had gauged his audience in the moment that he stepped to the table. The heroes he spoke of were common men, who had risen to the ranks of the great or who had fought against the evils of the monarchy in times past.

Groundsel was as spellbound as his men, his dark eyes fixed on the poet. Nuada closed his performance with the tale of the great fire, and Groundsel's part in it, emphasizing the strength of character and the powers of leadership that were gifts from the gods to men of certain futures. The hall exploded with applause and Nuada bowed to the audience, then turned to bow even lower in Groundsel's direction.

The outlaw leader stood and returned the bow. Bathed in sweat Nuada leapt from the table, swept up a flagon of ale and downed it.

'You are a man of great talent,' Groundsel told him as he joined the outlaw and Arian at the far end of the hall.

'My talent would be as nothing without the exploits of heroes, my Lord.'

'How did you come to hear of the fire?'

'Everywhere I have travelled men talk of it,' Nuada answered. Arian leaned back and shook her head. She said nothing. Early in the evening Groundsel had put his arm around her, stroking her neck or patting her thigh. But when Nuada had begun speaking he had forgotten her presence. It was galling. And as for the fire . . . everyone knew how Groundsel had done nothing until his own granary was threatened. Three villages were destroyed and fourteen people died before he even stirred from his own settlement.

In that moment, Arian came close to hating Nuada for glorifying the incident.

Groundsel turned to her and grinned. Sweat had drenched the yellow silk shirt and it was creased over his bulging belly. His hand pawed at her thigh. 'You are a fire in my blood,' he whispered, pushing wet lips against her cheek.

She blushed deeply and pulled away from him, but his brawny arm circled her shoulder to drag her in against him.

The door at the far end of the hall opened and two men entered. The first was drenched in blood; the second was Llaw Gyffes.

Llaw supported the wounded man, helping him to a chair. Men rushed towards them, blocking Arian's view. Groundsel leapt to his feet and ran forward, knocking aside any in his way.

'What in the devil's name is going on?' he roared. Llaw stood and faced the shorter man.

'There are beasts loose in the forest. I have never seen their like. I found this man crawling in the undergrowth about a mile away to the east; he said his family had been slaughtered. I carried him half-way here, then I saw one of them – eight to ten feet tall, with the head of a wolf and a body like a bear. It was feeding on a slaughtered bull and ignored me. In the distance I saw a second creature; I would swear it had two heads.'

Noise erupted all around them, for many of the men at the hall had homes in the woods and valleys beyond and had travelled in to hear Nuada.

'Silence!' bellowed Groundsel, kneeling by the wounded man and ripping the blood-drenched shirt from him. Four jagged tears had gouged his chest and it was obvious from the lines that it had been a single slash. That made the paw a prodigious size. No bear could match it, not even the towering black grizzly of the high mountains. 'Carry him to the witch woman,' ordered Groundsel, 'or he'll bleed to death.'

As the man was carried out, Groundsel turned to Llaw. 'You saw two of them. How do you know there are more?'

The tall warrior scratched at his red-gold beard. 'The howling,' he said simply. 'The beast by the bull let out a howl, and it was answered from many points.'

'Aye, I heard the strange howling,' said a man. 'It was from the north. I thought it a trick of the wind.'

'And I saw a track,' put in another. 'On the way here, Groundsel. Big, twice the size of a lion's.'

Other men began to shout and the clamour grew.

'What a night for heroes!' came a voice and the crowd swung to see the poet standing on his table once more. 'If there are two beasts savaging the countryside, are there not heroes enough here to hunt them down? We have Groundsel, the Lord of the Fire, and Llaw Gyffes, who freed the prisoners. And as I look around me I see other men – strong men, proud men. There is a saga waiting out there – and I shall sing it. We will place the carcasses at the far end of the hall and build a fire, and dance. And your bravery will become immortal.'

167

Those in the crowd screamed their approval and moved to the walls to gather their bows and knives.

'Wait!' yelled Groundsel. 'It will be dawn soon and I'll have no wild men rushing around in the darkness sending shafts after everything that moves. We'll kill more of each other than any beast.'

Llaw nodded. 'We'll need to lure them into a trap. I have no wish to walk into a darkened lair hunting the things.'

'Get some rest,' Groundsel told the men, then stalked back to his seat.

Arian rose as Llaw approached. 'I did not expect to see you this far west,' she said. 'Are you lost?'

'I had intended to leave for Cithaeron, but the howling disturbed me,' he told her. 'I tried to skirt it, but I sensed the beasts had my scent so I cut west. What do you make of it, poet?'

Nuada shrugged. 'There are many songs in legend about werebeasts, but I have never seen one. It is said that, far to the east, there is a rich land where the mines are dug by giant ants with the heads of men.'

Groundsel swore. 'It is always far to the east, or the west, or the north. It seems to me that legends always originate far from where men can study them. However, that hardly matters. I too have heard the howling, but I doubt not that the size of the creatures is exaggerated. We are dealing with a rogue bear – large, but still a bear.'

Llaw reddened. 'It is not wise to call a man a liar – especially a man you do not know.'

'You have it right, Stronghand. I do not know you – therefore I have no reason to trust either you or your judgement. I say it is a bear. The dawn will tell.'

'Indeed it will,' agreed Llaw. 'Until then, I will sleep.'

'I'll show you to my hut,' said Arian swiftly and now it was Groundsel whose colour darkened.

'Is this your man?' he demanded, his eyes bright.

'No,' she replied. 'He is a friend of my family.'

'Good,' said Groundsel. 'I look forward to the hunt with your "friend of the family".'

Llaw tensed, but Arian seized his arm and the two of them left the hall and wandered out into the night. The gates of the stockade were once more shut, and guards patrolled the wall.

'Why did you come here?' Llaw asked. 'You want to be bedded by that son of a sow?'

'How dare you? I go where I will. I am not your daughter; you have no right to question me.'

'True enough,' he admitted. Just then a piercing scream echoed from the woods and Llaw ran to the stockade wall and mounted the rough-cut ladder to the palisade. 'Can you see anything?' he asked the sentry.

'No,' replied the man, 'but Daric slipped out about ten minutes ago. He was trying to get back to his family. What is the beast?'

'I do not know,' replied Llaw, 'but it's no damn bear.' A black shadow moved from the trees, halted in the moonlight and looked up at the stockade. The sentry stared in horror at the grisly remains it was dragging.

'Daric did not make it,' stated Llaw.

'I want no part in hunting that thing,' said the sentry.

Llaw watched until the beast moved back into the trees, then he slapped the sentry on the shoulder. 'Think of the saga,' he said.

The man's reply was short, foul and to the point, and Llaw chuckled.

Arian still stood staring into the blackness of the forest. 'Can such a beast be killed by arrows?' she asked.

'It lives and breathes,' said Llaw. 'Therefore it can die. Now show me this hut.'

*

Llaw Gyffes could not sleep as he lay on the narrow cot bed in the small hut. He could hear Arian breathing beside him and yearned to reach out and touch her, to draw her to him. Guilt washed over him. Lydia had been the love of his life and their few years together had filled him with a happiness he could never have known without her. As a young apprentice he had courted her for four years, and had worked hard to save the money for his own smithy. Lydia's father had always maintained that he was not the man for her, and had dreamed of marrying her to a young nobleman. He had disdained their wedding, and had not spoken to Llaw again; he died three years after the marriage. Lydia's mother had moved north to be with her family, but she at least had always treated Llaw with courtesy, if not with love.

Through it all Llaw had been filled with a burning desire to make Lydia happy. But at the end her father had been right. Lydia died a terrible death – one that would have been avoided had she not married the giant smith. He would never forget the sight of her lying on the bed, her dead eyes staring up at the ceiling.

Yet now he lay with another woman, and his thoughts were not innocent of desire.

He rolled to his side, facing away from Arian. He could smell the perfume of her body and see, without seeing, the oval beauty of her face, the sparkling challenge of her eyes and her mocking smile.

'Are you awake?' she whispered, and he heard her body move on the bed. He did not reply; there was nothing to say. He was being betrayed by his body, which yearned for her, and even his mind was at war. It is natural, he told himself, for a man to desire a mate. Tragedy could not change that. And yet . . . and yet . . . If he found peace and love with another woman, would not that make him forget Lydia? And then she would be truly dead – lost and forgotten, as if she had never been. He could not stomach that thought. She had not deserved her fate and did not deserve this treachery now.

Llaw lay silently until the dawn, then rose and watched the rising sun. Beside him Arian lay sleeping, her arms tight against her body, her long legs curled up like a child. Llaw looked down at her; his fingers brushed the hair back from her cheek and he felt the softness of her skin.

Her eyes opened as he touched her. 'Did you sleep well?' she asked, yawning and stretching. Her shirt slid up to expose an inch of midriff and Llaw moved away to the door. Outside the men were gathering and he saw Groundsel, dressed now in hunting leather and carrying a bow. The squat outlaw leader was also wearing two short swords with curved blades.

Llaw gathered his double-headed hand-axe and joined the men. Nuada waved and approached him.

'It should be quite a day,' said the poet, grinning. 'The sun is high, the sky is clear. Tonight will be a fine time of feasting.'

'You have no idea of what today will be, poet. This is not a stag hunt. Are you coming with us?'

'Of course. How can I tell the saga if I do not witness it?'

'That does not seem to have affected your talents thus far,' observed Llaw.

The group split into three sections and scouts were sent out to search for spoor. Llaw went with Groundsel, Arian, Nuada and three others, and led them back along the trail to where he had seen the beast feeding. They found traces of blood, and a few split bones and several enormous tracks, but of the creature there was no sign. They stopped at midday by a stream and sat in a circle around a small fire.

'It has gone to ground,' said Arian. 'I think it must

be sleeping in a cave somewhere. But the ground to the north is rocky, and we'll not be able to track it.'

'Then we must bring it to us,' stated Groundsel. 'Last night it slew one of my men, so we know it has a taste for human meat.'

'You keep saying *it*,' Llaw remarked. 'But there are more of them.'

'So you say,' snapped the outlaw leader. 'This is my plan: We will journey back to the point of its last feeding and wait. It has probably buried some meat there and will return after dark.'

'You will fight this creature at night?' Arian whispered. 'What if the clouds gather? Without a hunter's moon the archers will be useless.'

Groundsel grinned. 'We will sit by a fire – your friends here, and I. And we will talk, swap stories. You and the other archers will be hidden nearby in the trees, out of harm's way. I think the beast will come to us.'

'That is madness,' said Arian. 'And what will it prove?'

Groundsel's eyes flickered towards Nuada, then he shrugged. 'Can you think of a better plan, Llaw Gyffes?'

'As you wish,' Llaw muttered. 'But I think you should gather in all the hunters. This creature will withstand many arrows.'

After the meal Groundsel ordered one of his men to sound the horn and the hunting parties converged to meet at a pre-selected spot, on a high hillside overlooking the stockade. Here a change was made to the original plan, for the first hunting group had found the remains of Daric's family half-buried in a tree-shrouded hollow.

'It will return,' said Groundsel. 'Did you leave the bodies where they were?'

'We did,' replied a tall lean hunter named Dubarin, his face still grey with the shock of the find. 'Believe me, Groundsel, the beast is large. Its stride length is over seven feet; it is no bear.'

'As the poet said, we will nail its carcass to the hall doors tonight.'

Some of the men were sent back to the stockade but Groundsel, Llaw, Nuada and Arian journeyed into the hills with twenty bowmen, arriving at Daric's cabin an hour before dusk. They were led to the bodies by Dubarin, who stopped short of the grisly grave and waved them on.

'I have no need to see it again,' he said, turning aside.

'I don't want to see it at all,' declared Nuada, backing away, but Llaw Gyffes grabbed his arm and hauled him forward.

'Come now, poet, you can't sing of it if you haven't seen it!'

Nuada struggled, but Llaw's grip was like iron and he was dragged to the shallow grave. An arm jutted from beneath the earth and the half-eaten corpse of a young woman lay exposed, her entrails covered in dirt. Part of a child's body lay close by. Nuada gagged and twisted away to vomit on the ground. Llaw knelt beside him. 'Now you see,' he said. 'This is not some song. There are no Elven princes, no flame-breathing dragons. I shall listen to your tale with interest – if we survive this hunt.'

'Leave him be,' said Arian. 'It is hardly his fault that he has never seen death.'

Llaw stood and wandered to where Groundsel was issuing orders to the men. There were trees all around the hollow and he ordered the archers to climb them and prepare for a long wait. Arian took Nuada by the arm and led him to a thick-boled oak, helping him to climb to the lower branches. Groundsel moved some twenty paces from the bodies and built a fire; Llaw gathered wood and joined him.

'You know, of course,' said Llaw, 'that there is no need for us to sit out here in the open like this? The beast will return anyway.'

'It will smell people. I want it to see there are only two of us.'

'There is no one to hear us, Groundsel. What you want is to impress the girl. I am not a fool; I see the way you look at her.'

'And I you,' snapped the outlaw. 'How is it you haven't bedded her?'

Llaw sat down and removed his tinder-box from the pouch at his belt. Swiftly he lit the fire. 'Maybe I will – when the time is right.'

Groundsel chuckled. 'You think you'll survive the night?'

'If I don't, I will not be alone. You may have ordered one – or more – of your archers to cut me down, but I won't die until my axe is buried in what passes for your brain.'

'I have ordered nothing of the kind,' retorted Groundsel. 'I need no help to kill a man. I was thinking of the beast.' He strung his bow and removed three shafts from his quiver; having checked them for warp, he stuck them in the earth beside him. 'Have you ever heard of a beast of this size?'

Llaw shrugged. 'No. A merchant once told me of great cats in the east that could kill a bull and leap a fence carrying its carcass. But this is no cat.'

The sun sank slowly behind the mountains and the two men sat quietly, Llaw feeding the fire. Neither man stared directly into the flames, for the brightness would cause the pupils to contract and leave them virtually blind if they needed to scan the undergrowth. After a while, Groundsel spoke.

'If you deem it unnecessary to sit here, why do you do it?'

'Perhaps for the same reason as you?'

'To impress the lovely Arian? I don't think so. You worry me, Llaw. Could it be that you want to die?'

'You think, perhaps, that if we sit quietly in a safe place we will live for ever?' responded Llaw, removing his axe from his belt and laying it in his lap.

'Did you really kill your wife?'

Llaw swung on Groundsel, his hand curling around the black haft of the axe. For some seconds he could not speak.

'My wife was . . . strangled by the Duke's nephew. He raped her and killed her. I killed him. Do not – ever – repeat that calumny. You won't understand what I am to say to you, but I'll say it anyway: I loved Lydia. More than life. Much, much more than life.'

'So, you *are* looking to die here? Not a good end. You think to join your Lydia? Believe me, Llaw, there is no one to join. Look in that pit over there. That's death, and that's all there is. Darkness and corruption.'

'When did you become a philosopher?' hissed Llaw.

An owl screeched in the night and the two men froze, listening to the wind sighing in the leaves. Groundsel glanced up; the clouds were gathering.

'It will be a dark night,' he observed.

'The night of the beast,' said Llaw. His words hung in the air.

Groundsel hawked and spat. 'Are you frightened?' he asked.

'Of course. And so are you – I can smell your sweat.'

Groundsel chuckled and drew his swords. 'I stole them from a Nomad merchant. Silver steel, Llaw, the finest I have ever seen. They are from the east.'

'There's good ore there,' said Llaw. 'They make impressive blades - and horseshoes that will last a year. I'd like to have gone there and learned the craft. May I?' he asked, holding out his hand. Groundsel reversed a blade and handed it hilt-first to the former smith. 'Yes,' said Llaw, running his fingers reverently along

the curved blade. 'Beautiful work. Layer upon layer of
fine steel, tempered with the blood of the craftsman.
The hilt is held in place by a tiny sliver of ivory.' He
tapped it out and removed the blade. 'See? Here is the
mark of the craftsman. Ohei-sen. This sword is over
three hundred years old.'

'It's worth a lot then?' Groundsel asked.

Llaw slid the hilt back in place, locking it with the
ivory. 'Worth? Tonight you will see what it is worth.
But in the east you would receive maybe 200 Raq – in
gold – for each sword.'

'That much? Then maybe I'll go there one day.'

A movement in the undergrowth caused Groundsel
to reach for his bow, while Llaw eased himself to his
feet, wiped his sweating palms on his leggings and took
up his axe.

The undergrowth parted and Arian walked to the
fire. 'I was getting cold,' she said, dropping her bow
to squat by the blaze and holding out her hands to its
warmth.

'Perhaps   you   were   missing   me?'   suggested
Groundsel.

'Behind you!' yelled Nuada and Llaw swung as the
beast exploded from the undergrowth, charging across
the small clearing on all fours. For a moment Llaw
froze. The size of the creature was beyond anything he
had imagined. Groundsel swept up his bow and loosed
a shaft which glanced from the monster's skull. As the
beast neared, Llaw – realizing Arian was behind him –
hurled himself forward. Arrows flashed into the racing
form, but did not check its speed. Llaw's axe hammered
down to smash into the creature's shoulder, but its
weight struck him – hurling him back, the axe torn
from his grip. Arian dived to her right as the beast
turned towards her, its great paws scattering the fire.

Groundsel had sprinted some yards to the left and
hastily he notched another arrow, sending it to punch

home into the grey fur of the beast's back. More than twenty shafts bristled from the creature. The hunter Dubarin leapt from a nearby tree and ran at the wolf-beast with a lance. As he approached the creature sprang forward, sweeping aside the weapon with a great paw. Talons raked down, ripping Dubarin's face from his skull. Coolly, Arian loosed two shafts and the beast turned, its red eyes focusing on the slender bow-woman. Groundsel ran forward with his two swords in his hands. The creature rose on its hind legs and Groundsel ducked under a vicious sweep of its talons and buried his right-hand blade in its belly. Its forelegs swept around him, the talons lancing into his back. He bellowed in rage and pain and rammed his left-hand sword into the beast's armpit. Then Llaw Gyffes, axe once more in his hand, leapt to the creature's back, hooking his fingers into the shaggy mane of its neck. The axe rose and fell, again and again. Finally the wolf-beast released Groundsel, who staggered back into the arms of Arian.

Two men now ran to aid Llaw. The first died as talons ripped into his belly, the second plunged a lance into the beast's breast. It tried to retreat back into the undergrowth, but more men ran in to encircle it . . . and all the while Llaw Gyffes clung to its back, hammering his axe against the corded muscles of the creature's throat. At last it grew weaker and fell forward. Tearing a lance from the hands of a man near him, Groundsel moved in to help Llaw. The beast's huge head came up and Groundsel buried the point of the lance in its mouth, using all his weight to drive the weapon through its spine.

Llaw stepped from the monster's back just as the clouds cleared and moonlight bathed the scene. The creature was dead.

Snow began to fall as Groundsel pulled the spear clear of the gaping mouth and used it to measure the

177

beast's length. It was over nine feet long from taloned toes to gaping maw.

'We'll never drag this back to the stockade,' said Groundsel. 'Cut its damned head off.'

'We ought to see to those wounds,' suggested Arian. 'You're leaking blood badly.'

'There's no good way to lose blood,' responded Groundsel and kneeling by the creature, he tore one sword loose from its belly. The other was snapped just below the hilt; he swore, and looked up at Llaw Gyffes.

'You know, before tonight this would just have been a broken sword. Now it's 200 gold Raq lost. There's a moral there.'

'You can always steal another,' suggested Llaw.

Groundsel's eyes narrowed as in the distance an eerie howl echoed in the forest. 'Tomorrow,' he said, 'we go after the others. I'll not have these creatures in my forest. Now where's that cursed poet? I want to hear my song.'

9

Errin opened his eyes and almost wept with joy at the absence of pain. By his bed sat an elderly woman in a high-necked dress of blue wool edged with silver thread. 'You are healed, young man. The bone is knit.'

'Thank you, lady. Your magic must be very strong.'

'And expensive,' she told him. 'But do not thank me – thank the Lord Cartain, who has paid handsomely for my services.' She rose and walked from the room and Errin sat up. He was in a small bedchamber with two oval windows; a fire was blazing in the hearth and he could hear the cries of gulls from the roof above. He lay back on the pillows. The ride along the forest road had been a torture beyond his ability to endure; his broken leg had swollen and a fever had taken him. Vaguely he remembered Ubadai tying him to the saddle. And there were people . . . His hazy recollection was of a column of refugees snaking their way along the Royal Road as the snow began to fall. And weird cries in the night . . . the howls of wolves? It was difficult to remember anything but the grinding pain.

Ubadai entered, bearing a tray on which was a bowl of broth and a plate of fruit. 'Better you eat,' he said. 'You still look bad.'

'Where are we?' Errin asked the stocky tribesman.

Ubadai set the tray on the bed and wandered to the window, pushing it open against the snow on the sill. 'Pertia Port,' he answered. 'Our ship leaves tomorrow for Cithaeron.'

Errin finished the broth, which carried just a hint of the flavour of beef, and ate two of the apples on the side plate. With the window open he could smell the sea. He smiled and felt good to be alive.

Alive?

Suddenly he saw again Dianu tied to the stake . . . the flames curling up beneath her, the look in her eyes as he rode through the mob, the hope dying as he bent his bow, the flight of the arrow as it ended her life.

He groaned and Ubadai strode to him, his dark slanted eyes full of concern. 'Old witch said all pain gone.'

'I am all right,' Errin told him, blinking back the tears from his eyes.

'Then why cry? Not good for a man.'

'Tears for the dead, Ubadai. That's all.'

The Nomad tribesman grunted. 'Leg healed; you should stand. Test it before the witch leaves.'

'It's fine. I'll get up in a while. Who is this Lord Cartain?'

'No Lord,' replied Ubadai. 'Nomad merchant. He is waiting downstairs. Shall I send him away?'

Errin chuckled. 'The man has just seen to my health. Why on earth would I send him away?'

Ubadai sniffed. 'Nothing for nothing,' he said, returning to the window. 'Good ship. Makes Cithaeron trip three . . . four times a year. Good time to sail. No storms.'

'What is bothering you?'

Ubadai swung to face his young lord, but Errin could read nothing in the flat, expressionless face. 'You want me to bring him to you?'

'Yes, I would like to thank him.'

Ubadai shook his head. 'I think, maybe, we miss that ship.'

'Nonsense. Bring him up.' Errin swung from the bed and moved to the chair by the window, where his clothes lay neatly folded; they had been cleaned and perfumed. He dressed swiftly and was pulling on his

180

thigh-length riding boots when Ubadai returned. Behind the tribesman was a tall hawk-faced man, dark-eyed and wearing a gold circlet on his brow. The man bowed.

'It is a privilege to meet you, Lord Errin,' said Cartain.

'I cannot see that it should be a privilege,' answered Errin, offering his hand.

Cartain shook it briefly. 'You risked your life to save the Lady Dianu – and fought one of the dread Knights. You are a man of courage.'

'I failed,' said Errin. 'Let that be an end to it.'

Cartain smiled. 'May I sit?' Errin nodded and the merchant arranged his flowing purple robes and sat in a high-backed chair.

'Why have you helped me? Were you a friend to Dianu?'

'Not a friend exactly. I arranged her . . . escape. I was retained to organize the removal of the family wealth and saw to it that Dianu's sister was safely escorted here. I was waiting for the Lady Dianu herself to follow us, but then word came that she was delayed . . . hoping, I think, that you would join her. And then . . .' He spread his hands.

'Still you have not explained why you helped me?'

'There is nothing sinister in my actions, Lord Errin. I am now the . . . trustee, if you will, of the lady's estate. I take my duties seriously. The Lady Sheera is now the beneficiary and I had hoped to deliver her to Cithaeron.'

'Had hoped?'

'She is not here,' said Cartain, his dark eyes locking to Errin's own. 'She has it in her mind to avenge her sister and unbeknownst to me or my people, she engaged two men to lead her back through the forest. I believe she plans to kill Okessa.'

'She is a child,' said Errin. 'Her scheme is madness.'

181

'I know she has spent a number of years in Furbolg, Lord Errin, but to be seventeen is hardly a child. She is tall, well-formed and remarkably headstrong. I fear she has betrayed herself. Here in Pertia – though we are mercifully free from the terrors of the Realm proper – there are spies and assassins aplenty. And I had word yesterday that the King has ordered the fleet to Pertia; they will arrive in around ten days, and from then on the port will be closed to Nomad refugees.'

'You said you feared Sheera had betrayed herself? Explain.'

'One of the men she hired is known to be a King's man. He is a spy and a killer; his reputation is loathsome.'

'I do not see what I can do for you?'

'Who else is there to bring her back? Your man here is said to be one of the finest trackers in the western lands. And there is something else, my Lord. There are strange tales of monsters loose in the woods. I would not like the Lady Sheera to suffer the fate of her sister.'

Errin sat back on the bed. 'Nor would I, sir. But I am no warrior. Violence sickens me and I have no skill with weapons. Could you not find a more worthy rescuer?'

'It is my experience, Lord Errin, that you can rarely measure a man's worth by his ability to deal injury to his fellows. But in that, at least, I can help you.' With his left hand he lifted an apple from the discarded tray and, with his right, drew a dagger from his belt. With a flick of the wrist he tossed the apple in the air. His dagger flashed in a blur of movement and the fruit dropped neatly into his left hand. When he opened his fingers, the apple fell into four pieces.

'A splendid trick, sir, but how does it help me?' Errin asked.

Cartain stood and unbuckled the silver-edged leather

belt he wore, passing it to Errin. 'Please put it on, my Lord.'

'I have a belt.'

'Not like this. This was made by Ollathair, greatest of Craftsmen. Merely touch the buckle and whisper his name, and you will find your speed of hand and eye increased. It has saved my life on three occasions.'

Errin buckled the belt in place. 'Now go to the far wall and say the name, my Lord.' He did as he was bid. The buckle felt warm as his fingers touched it. 'Ollathair,' he whispered.

He watched as Cartain slowly rose. The merchant's arm drew back and his dagger sailed towards Errin, who reached up and caught it easily. Ubadai, with uncharacteristic lack of speed, drew his own dagger and made his way on leaden feet towards the merchant.

Errin touched the belt once more. 'Stop!' he shouted, as Ubadai leapt for Cartain.

'He tried to kill you!' the tribesman stormed.

'No,' said Errin. 'He was proving a point. I take it you hurled that dagger with all your might?'

'I did indeed.'

'This is a precious gift, Cartain; I have never seen the like. Why would you do this? It is more than merely a duty to a client.'

'Yes. I fled Furbolg when the killings began, but even I did not realize how far the slaughter would go. I am now actively involved in financing an army to destroy Ahak – and hopefully all that he stands for. But it will take time. I need men like you, Errin – good men, loyal men, men of good family. No one will flock to the banner of a Nomad merchant, but they will to men like yourself. Fetch Sheera back within ten days and we will sail for Cithaeron and raise a force to free Gabala. Will you do it?'

Errin grinned as he heard Ubadai curse. 'Of course

I will do it. Tell me all you can about the men with Sheera.'

Cartain did so and they spoke until dusk. Then the merchant rose to leave. 'I will have horses and provisions ready for you at dawn. There are snow-storms over the forest, and I understand the Royal Road is blocked. And there is one other thing you should know, Errin.'

'What is that?'

'Sheera hates you. She sees you as the reason her sister stayed behind, and she knows it was your arrow that killed Dianu. It is not just Okessa that she seeks to kill – you understand?'

Errin nodded. 'I understand very well.'

Manannan waited in a grove outside the village while Ruad Ro-fhessa, the Armourer Ollathair, worked his magic in a granite cave hidden by the trees. Kuan cropped grass nearby. The Once-Knight had shaved and the wind felt good on his skin.

As dusk approached the wizard stepped from the cave and stretched. His face was grey with exhaustion as he walked wearily to Manannan and sat beside him on the grass.

'It is ready,' said Ruad. 'One Word of Power will open the Gate. But I am too tired; give me a few moments to gather my strength.'

'Take all the time you need. I am in no hurry.'

'I am sorry for all that I have caused,' said Ruad. 'I hope you can believe that. I wanted only what was good – for the Knights and the Realm.'

'I know. I should have gone with them at the first. I too carry guilt, Ollathair. And I wonder what became of Morrigan. I should have gone to her; I know she never loved me in the way she cared for Samildanach, but I owed it to her to go.'

'You would not have found her. I went to her home and she was gone. Her parents told me she had run off in the night, taking no clothing nor money. They think she took her own life.'

'Poor Morrigan,' Manannan whispered. 'To fall in love with a Knight pledged to celibacy and then to watch him ride into Hell. Are we fools, Ollathair? We rode to the Nine Duchies. We strove to bring justice. And what did we achieve? Look at the world!'

'The Knights of the Gabala were a force for Harmony for centuries,' said Ruad. 'What did we achieve? I ask your own question of you. Look at the world now the Knights are gone! Now come with me, I have a gift.'

Ruad pushed himself to his feet and led the way inside the cave, where two candles were burning. On a wooden tree, shining like ghostly silver, was Manannan's armour restored to shimmering beauty. A new white plume had been added to the helm.

'Put it on. I will help you.'

'How did you do this?'

'I made another Gate to the Citadel and retrieved it. Come, wear it, in pride and honour.'

Manannan stripped his clothing and donned the leather under-tunic, adding the mail habergeon. Slowly he buckled on the breastplate, fastened the shoulder-plates and stood while Ruad settled the greaves into place. He pulled on the silver gauntlets and lastly lifted the dread helm.

'This held me prisoner for six lonely years. Will it do so again?'

'No. There are no special spells, but the armour is still magic and will protect you against most weapons of evil.'

Manannan lowered the helm into place and twisted the neck-plates into the grooves at the base of the helmet. He lifted the visor. 'It feels larger.'

'You have no beard, Manannan. You are as you were on that night six years ago. Have you prayed?'

The Once-Knight smiled grimly. 'Not for a very long time.'

'Then do it now – Knight of the Gabala.'

'To do so now would be hypocrisy. Come, Ollathair, open the Gate.'

They walked out into the waning light and Manannan called Kuan to him. He stepped into the saddle and waited. Ollathair knelt in prayer for several minutes, then lifted his arm and spoke two Words of Power.

Before the horseman the darkness gathered, forming into a great square. A hiss of escaping air came from the centre of the blackness and a long tunnel appeared, from which blew an icy wind.

Kuan backed away, but Manannan whispered words of comfort.

'Ride now!' shouted Ollathair. 'I can hold it for but a few moments more.'

Fear rose in Manannan's heart, colder than the wind from the tunnel. His body began to tremble and his heart pounded erratically. 'Dear Gods,' he whispered. Kuan reared as unearthly screams came from the tunnel and Manannan dragged his blade from its scabbard.

'In the name of All Holiness – ride!' screamed Ollathair.

Lifting a gauntleted hand to his helm, Manannan pulled shut the visor. Then, with a bellowed battle-cry, he kicked Kuan into a run and rode, sword in hand, beyond the Gate.

Lámfhada groaned in his sleep and began to shiver. Across the hut, Elodan stirred and sat up; he moved across to the youth, who was now rolling his head and moaning.

Elodan touched Lámfhada's shoulder. 'Wake up, you are dreaming.'

Suddenly Lámfhada screamed. His hand rose and a golden flash of light exploded from his fingers to hurl Elodan across the floor. The Knight struggled to his knees, gasping for breath, as Lámfhada awoke and swung his legs from the bed.

'Are you all right?' he asked, seeing the Knight crouched on the floor.

'What the Hell did you do, boy?'

'Nothing. I heard a noise and woke,' answered Lámfhada, mystified.

Elodan rose. He lit a lantern and held it in front of his chest; the skin was red and burned in a wide circle from his neck to his belly.

'What is that? How did you do it?' Lámfhada asked.

'*I* didn't. *You* did. You were dreaming; I tried to wake you, then lightning flashed from your hand.'

'I don't remember anything – except the hooded man. It was a nightmare – I have had it often: A man chanting on a hillside; then he turns into a giant wolf. And there is a mist and a sword. But it is all hazy now.'

'Well, the lightning was real, Lámfhada. You have a magic in you.'

Elodan moved back to his bed and sat down, while Lámfhada added fuel to the dying fire in the brazier and stoked it to life. The Knight sat in silence for some moments, lost in thought, then he glanced up at the blond youth. 'A traveller came to the village today. He talked of a wizard and a Healer in the forest to the east of us; a one-eyed wizard, Lámfhada. I think it must be the man you spoke of.'

'It is,' said Lámfhada softly. 'I sense his presence in

the forest when I fly the Yellow. I wish I could go to him.'

'Why should you not?'

'I would be lost as soon as I passed out of sight of the village.'

'Does he have a great power?' asked the Knight.

'Yes.'

'Could he . . . heal this?' Elodan raised the stump of his right arm.

'I do not know. I think that he could . . . I think he can do anything he wishes.'

'Then I will help you to find him.'

Lámfhada looked away. 'He may not be able – or willing – to help you, Elodan. He can be a hard man.'

The Knight shrugged. 'Then I will be no worse off than I am. We will leave in the morning.'

'I don't know . . .'

Elodan smiled grimly. 'You are thinking of the stories of the beasts in the greenwood. Have you seen any?'

'No, but old Tomar saw one and he said it was ten feet tall. And the howling . . .'

'You think these village huts would stop such a creature? Well, they would not. You are no safer here than out in the forest. Will you travel with me?'

'Yes, I will. I need to see Ruad again.'

'Good.'

They set off into the snow-shrouded forest at first light. Elodan had borrowed a thick sheepskin jerkin and a cloak of white wool. He wore a small canvas pack filled with oats and dried meat, and carried a hatchet with a large curved blade. Lámfhada had cut slits in two blankets and wore them both like capes, belted at the waist. He took Arian's spare bow and a quiver of arrows. By mid-afternoon the walkers had travelled some eight miles to the east.

Twice they had seen large tracks, and once had heard a weird howling to the north.

Just before dusk they arrived at the banks of a wide river. A thin sheet of ice had formed on the surface.

'How do we cross it?' asked Lámfhada.

'We'll search for some narrows,' said Elodan, setting off towards the south. They walked for another hour, but found nowhere to cross. At last they came to an abandoned hut; inside Elodan built a fire and they ate some oats and meat.

In the night Lámfhada awoke to the sounds of bestial screams. He walked to the door and looked out into the darkness, but could see nothing. He built up the fire and settled down once more.

At dawn the travellers emerged into the cold air. Elodan stopped and pointed at the ground before the hut where huge paw-marks could be seen in the snow.

The Knight stood and examined the hut walls. They were made of thin timbers, crudely nailed into place. 'Help me,' he said. Then he walked to the corner of the building and wedged his hatchet-blade between two timbers, levering an edge loose. Lámfhada took hold of the wood and between them they ripped out a plank some ten feet long and two feet wide. 'One more,' said Elodan. They carried the planks to the river's edge and Elodan moved up and down the bank, seeking out a place where the ice seemed thickest. Then he slid one plank out on to the ice and, lifting the other plank to his shoulder, carefully stepped on to the wood. The ice crunched and crackled, but did not give. He walked slowly out on to the river, then laid the other plank in front of the first and stepped on to it. 'Now you,' called Elodan. Black cracks snaked out from the ice and Lámfhada moved swiftly forward.

Together they eased the first plank round and pushed it to the front.

Slowly, and with great care, they inched their way across the frozen water. With the opposite shore close they heard a hideous growl and Elodan turned.

Behind them on the bank stood a towering creature with black scaled skin, grey-furred at the shoulder. It dropped to all fours and charged across the ice towards them.

'Run!' Elodan ordered Lámfhada.

'But the ice!'

'Damn the ice! Run!' Lámfhada leapt from the plank, slithered and almost fell, but then began to run. The ice crunched beneath his feet, but did not give until he was almost at the bank. He dropped into a few inches of water and pulled himself to solid ground. Swinging round, he saw Elodan standing on the plank, axe in hand. Then the Knight leapt from the platform and moved to his right where the ice was weakest. Lámfhada saw him dive forward, his arms and legs spread, and watched his body slide further out on to the ice. The beast changed direction – and charged Elodan. The Knight rolled to his belly and lifted the hatchet smashing it to the ice again and again. Great cracks rippled out. A sheet of ice tipped Elodan into the water. The beast tried to stop, but another sheet gave way and with a great splash it toppled into the river. For a moment only its head came clear, then it was sucked away below the surface. Lámfhada saw Elodan holding on to the ice. The youth stood and ran along the bank, seeking a way through to the knight.

Elodan saw him. 'Stay back,' he shouted and tried to pull himself up on to the ice, but with only one hand he could not gain purchase. The ice gave once more . . . and Elodan slid from sight.

'No!' Lámfhada screamed.

He scrambled along the river bank for almost a mile, for he could see the dark form of his friend floating beneath the ice. But after almost half an hour he knew it was hopeless.

Lamfhada sat down on a fallen tree. Fatigue and shock hit him and he began to weep, but at last his tears ran dry and wearily he stood and looked out over the river. Some thirty paces downstream he could see the black shape he knew to be the body of Elodan under the ice near the bank. He moved closer to it. The current created the sensation of movement in his friend, the arm appearing to thud against the ice. Lámfhada took up a heavy branch and smashed it against the surface. Twice more he struck – and the ice parted. Reaching down, he grabbed Elodan's jerkin and hauled the body clear.

'Get a . . . fire . . . going, for . . . pity's sake,' whispered Elodan. Lámfhada dragged the Knight back from the bank and into a small hollow shielded by trees. He cleared snow from the ground for a fire and gathered wood and tinder, but his fingers were too cold to hold the fire flints. He rubbed them furiously and tried again and at last a small flame began to flicker. Carefully he blew it to life and added small twigs and branches. After what seemed an eternity, a bright blaze burned. He helped Elodan from his frozen clothes and rubbed life into his arms and chest. Then he removed one of his blanket capes and lifted it over Elodan's head. He built up the fire until the flames were over three feet high.

'I would not want to go through that again,' said Elodan at last, some colour back in his features.

'How did you survive so long below the water?' Lámfhada asked. 'Are you also a magician?'

'No – but I know nature. Between the ice and the water there is a gap of around two inches. I swam on my back, cutting across the current, looking for a place near the bank where the ice was thin. But it was the cold that almost beat me; I did not have the strength to break through.'

'It was brave of you to risk your life against the beast.'

Elodan shook his head. 'Do not confuse courage with

necessity. When a man has only one choice, it is not a question of bravery.'

'You could have run.'

'The ice would not have supported me.'

'You do not know that, sir Knight,' said Lámfhada.

'No, I do not. Now let us speak no more of it. Tomorrow we will seek out your wizard. But for now – I must sleep.'

The wounds in Groundsel's back required more than forty stitches, yet still he was sitting in his chair when Nuada stood on the central table to tell the gathering of the fight with the beast. Llaw Gyffes and Arian sat beside Groundsel and the hall was silent as the poet began.

He spoke first of the heroes of the past – his words lyrical, almost hypnotic. Then gradually, imperceptibly, the tone changed. He talked of blood and death, and the horrors of the damned. Men shivered despite the blazing fires. He spoke of evil, and the works of evil.

'Nothing is untouched by it,' he said. 'For it is like a plague, spreading through the hearts of men. Some it touches and corrupts instantly, others carry the seed within themselves. Only the very strong can withstand it.' He paused, his eyes scanning the crowd. There were more than one hundred and fifty men gathered here, many having arrived that morning with their families to escape the beasts roaming the forest. 'Only the very strong,' he repeated. 'Now we have heard how these Demon-beasts came among us. One was seen by a boy; he watched it appear in a flash of lightning on a hillside. Perhaps it was that very creature,' said Nuada, pointing to the giant head impaled on a lance at the back of the hall. 'Now in the Elder times such beasts were well known, and knights and heroes rode out to slay them, armed with magic swords or lances, their bodies encased in armour strengthened by spells. Yet last night a group of men, ordinary men, walked the same perilous path as those legendary heroes. But there were no magic swords, no sorcery – only strength, and courage. Two of those men are not here in the flesh; they gave their lives to end the terror. But they are here in spirit, honoured guests among their comrades. They stand proud. No matter what deeds they may have committed in life, in death they are forgiven and exalted. Their names, which will live for ever in song, are Askard and Dubarin. There they stand, by the fire. Let them know how much you value them.'

All around the hall men raised their weapons – swords, lances, knives and axes – and a great cheer went up.

Nuada waited for several moments, then raised his arms for silence.

'And now my friends, my heroes of the forest, Askard and Dubarin, will hear their tale for the first time. And then they will rejoin the other heroes of history in the fabled Halls of Heaven, to drink of the Wine of Life, to savour the joys of glory.'

Groundsel leaned forward and winced as the stitches pulled at his flesh, but his eyes shone as the events of the night before came to life. The tracking and the grisly find, the bowmen in the trees, the leader and Llaw Gyffes sitting in the open by the fire. The nerves, the fear, the dread anticipation – all were recaptured by the poet, and Groundsel felt himself back by the fire waiting, waiting . . . saw again the massive jaws of the Demon-beast as it bore silently down upon him, felt the stomach-wrenching panic as its forepaws closed around him.

'And seeing the lovely bow-woman in mortal danger, Groundsel flung himself at the towering monster. Look! Look at the fangs, and picture it in life with its dreadful talons. But Groundsel did not flinch from the danger. With two short swords he charged, burying them deep into the belly of the beast. Its talons ripped into him . . . as he knew they would. But other heroes were close by.'

The story moved to its climax and Groundsel tore his eyes from the poet and gazed at the men in the room. Their faces were shining, their eyes fixed as the tale neared its end. Askard and Dubarin had given their lives. Llaw Gyffes had clung to the monster's back. And every man had followed Groundsel, conquering their fears, to slay the Demon-beast.

Each feverish, horrific moment blazed into life. Sweat dripped from Groundsel's face and his heart hammered wildly within him. He felt he could take no more, wanting to run from the hall. But the tale ended, with Nuada swinging to point at Groundsel and his companions. 'And there, my friends, are the leading heroes of the tale. The warrior maiden who stood so recklessly before the beast, the man of the axe who rode the demon, and the Forest Lord who stepped into its deadly embrace and lived. Let them hear your cheers.'

A mighty roar went up and Arian could feel the timbers vibrating beneath her feet as men stamped and cheered. Groundsel stood, but his legs were weak and he staggered. Llaw Gyffes rose beside him, supporting his arm. The crowd surged forward, knocking over tables and chairs; seizing Groundsel, they lifted him high as the applause thundered around the hall. Arian took Llaw's arm and led him out into the open air.

'He told it well,' she said, 'but not like it was.'

'Where was he wrong?'

'Groundsel did none of it for pure motives. He wanted to be in another tale of heroes – and he wanted to show me how brave he was.'

'Is that so terrible? Did he not save you from the creature?'

She hooked her arm in his and led him to the stockade wall. The forest was dark and menacing, but there was no howling to be heard. 'Yes,' she admitted, 'he saved me. So did you. What I did was foolish, and I too enjoyed being part of the new forest legends. Will we have some peace now, do you think?'

'Peace? We will kill all the beasts, but that will not bring us peace. Why are they here? What force sent them? No, we will have no peace, Arian. I think this is the beginning of a war.'

'You believe the King is sending these demons to the forest?'

'No, not the King. One of his sorcerers.'

'Then maybe you are right. Maybe we should leave the forest and head for Cithaeron.'

'We?' he asked, drawing back.

'I want to be where you are, Llaw. You must know that I love you.'

He took her by the shoulders, holding her from him. Her eyes were bright with tears, and her hair shone silver in the moonlight.

'The last woman I loved was brutally murdered. I am not ready, Arian, to suffer such pain again. I think I will never be ready.'

And he left her there, alone on the ramparts.

10

As she sat in the cave, feeding the fire, Sheera knew she had made a terrible mistake. The two men had been courteous and respectful when the innkeeper introduced them, but once into the forest they had changed subtly. Strad, the taller and more gregarious of the two, had become silent and almost sinister, while Givan had taken to openly staring at her, letting his eyes linger on her breasts and hips. Neither of them had touched her, and outwardly they remained eager to please, but the journey through the winter forest had begun to worry Sheera. They had sheltered through two blizzards, yet when the skies cleared she had seen from the sun, and the later stars, that their route was curving like a crescent moon back towards the sea.

Last night she had wrapped herself in her blankets and pretended to sleep, straining to hear their conversation. After a while Strad moved over to her and softly asked if she was comfortable. She did not stir and he returned to Givan.

'Only a couple more days of this foul weather,' said Givan. 'Then it is warm beds and warm women. By the Gods, I'll be glad to see the back of this forest.'

'You and I both,' agreed his friend.

Sheera's mind raced. A couple of days? How could that be? It was at least a ten-day march in good weather! She should have listened to Cartain, who had urged her to come to Cithaeron and aid him in gathering the exiles together to form an army. But her anger was great, and the thought of leaving Okessa and the others unpunished could not be tolerated.

Now, stretching her long legs out before her, she

pushed her back against the wall. She was a tall girl, with close-cropped, tightly curled black hair and dark almond-shaped eyes. Her mouth was too wide to be considered beautiful, but her lips were full and her teeth white and even.

'Thinking of some man, are you, princess?' asked Givan, moving to sit near her. He was short and fat, and a widening bald patch on the crown of his head gave him the look of a lustful monk.

'I was thinking about my sister.'

'Yes? Sad business. Very sad. I saw her once in Mactha, riding to the hunt. A well-made woman. You remind me of her, save I think you are taller and maybe a shade slimmer.'

'How soon will we reach the southern valleys?' she asked.

'Oh, about eight days, more or less. Do not worry, we have plenty of provisions.'

'The provisions do not concern me, Givan; they are your responsibility. I understand there are outlaws in the forest?'

'Don't worry your head about them; they'll not be out in this blizzard. And anyway we've got nothing worth stealing – though I dare say there are those who would consider you a prize worth taking.'

She forced a smile. 'How sweet of you to say so, but then I have you and Strad to protect me. It is a very comforting thought.'

'Oh, we'll protect you, princess, don't have no worries on that score. I wouldn't like to see nothing happen to you; I've grown quite fond of you, I have.'

'I think I will sleep now,' she said, turning her back on him and pulling her blankets over her. For a moment she could feel his presence close to her, but then he moved back to where Strad was sitting in the cave-mouth.

'Best forget that sort of stuff,' whispered Strad.

'There's plenty of women available in Pertia – especially after we get paid.'

'She's in my blood, boy. I've got to have her. Will they care that she's soiled? All they'll see is another filthy Nomad. No, I want her worse than anything I can remember.'

'She doesn't want you,' Strad pointed out.

'That's what makes it sweet, boy.'

Sheera waited until both men were sound asleep and then slipped from her blankets. Swiftly she rolled them into a bundle and moved through the cave to the entrance. Outside the blizzard had died, but the wind was bitterly cold. She wrapped herself in a sheepskin cloak and pulled on a second set of woollen leggings. Glancing back at the sleeping men she hooked her pack to her shoulders, gathered her bow and quiver of arrows and stepped out into the night.

The stars were bright and she headed along the line of the Spear Carrier.

She walked for almost an hour, then searched for a camping place, finding a small hollow out of the wind. There were several fallen trees and one of them had crashed down upon a group of boulders. Sheera clambered under the snow-covered branches and found herself in a snug, shallow shelter – the foliage making a thick roof and the boulders a wall around her, save to the west. She gathered tinder and cleared a space for a small fire, which she lit at the first attempt with the tinder-box her sister had given her at the last Solstice feast. With a tiny blaze giving warmth, she settled back in her blankets to sleep.

Awaking to the sound of curses, she cast an anxious look at her little fire. It seemed completely dead.

'Damn that last snow shower,' snapped Givan. 'But she cannot be far away.'

'I don't know why she ran in the first place,' complained Strad. 'You think she knew . . .'

'Shut up you fool, she might be close.'

'More likely died in a drift. We've lost a fortune – and all because you couldn't keep the lust from your eyes.'

'It was nothing to do with me. I think she knew more about the direction than we gave her credit for. Twice I saw her checking the stars.'

Sheera edged her way to the west of her shelter and bellied down to peer under the branches. The first man she saw was Strad; he was searching the ground.

'Found anything?' asked Givan.

'No. But I can smell smoke. Can you?'

Sheera swivelled. The fire she had thought was dead was beginning to smoulder.

Just as she prepared to turn and deal with it, a terrifying scream came from outside and she pressed her face to the branches in time to see a huge shape bearing down on Strad. It seemed to be covered in white-grey fur, but she could see only the thick legs and a part of its hide. Something splashed on her face and hands and looking down, she saw that it was blood. Strad's body fell close to her, the head torn from the shoulders.

She could hear Givan shouting, 'No! No!' But this was followed by a low snarling growl and the sound of bones being crunched and split.

Sheera eased her way back into her shelter and, as silently as she could, fed twigs to the smouldering fire, blowing it to life. The branches to her left quivered, and she heard the beast snuffling beyond them. Forcing herself to stay calm, she continued to work at the fire. A small finger of flame licked at the wood, then gathered itself; she picked up a dry branch and held it to the flame. Snow tipped into her shelter as the beast beyond pushed its snout forward. With great care Sheera took the smoking branch from the fire and turned, lifting it to where she could almost see the beast's head. Acrid smoke curled into the creature's nostrils and it snorted hard, pulling back abruptly.

Sheera returned the branch to the fire and waited. She could hear it feeding beyond the shelter.

But would it return?

Nuada was awakened close to dawn by a rough hand shaking his shoulder. He sat up, his eyes bleary, his body aching from the intake of ale. A lantern had been placed on the table by the bed and he recognized Groundsel's squat figure sitting beside it.

'What . . . why are you here?' asked Nuada. His mouth was dry and he reached for the tankard beside his bed; it contained flat beer, but even this was welcome. He shivered. Outside the snow was falling fast and a cold wind blew through the gaps in the rough-hewn door-frame. He pulled a blanket around his shoulders. 'Is something wrong, Lord Groundsel?'

'No,' answered the man. 'At least, I do not believe so. You spoke well this evening. I could not sleep, so I thought we could talk.'

Nuada swung from the bed and moved to an iron brazier in which the fire was dying. He stoked it with sticks and twigs until a flicker of flame began at the centre, then he added larger chunks of wood.

Groundsel sat quietly, his eyes unfocused. Nuada returned to his bed and waited. The outlaw leader had discarded his silken shirt and now wore the familiar brown leather jerkin of the forester.

'What troubles you, my Lord?'

'Nothing. I fear nothing. I want for nothing. I am no fool, Nuada. I know that – had you chosen to – you could have made me a villain, a swine or a murdering dog. Those men who cheered me could just as easily have been persuaded to hang me. I know this . . . and I know I am not a hero. I know . . .'

Nuada remained silent while Groundsel scratched his short-cropped hair and rubbed at his round ugly face. 'You know what I am saying?'

Nuada nodded, but still he did not speak. 'I enjoyed your tale,' said Groundsel, his voice dropping to a near whisper. 'I enjoyed being cheered. And now I feel . . . I don't know how I feel. A little sad, maybe. You understand?' His dark button eyes fixed on Nuada.

'Is it still a good feeling?' asked the poet.

'Yes and no. I've killed a lot of people, Nuada; I've robbed and I've cheated; I've lied. I am not a hero; that fire threatened to destroy all I've built. And the monster? I wanted to impress the girl. I am not a hero.'

'A man is whatever he wishes to be,' said Nuada softly. 'There are no rigid patterns, no iron moulds. We are not cast from bronze. The hero Petric once headed an army which looted three cities. I have read the histories — his men raped and slaughtered thousands. But at the end he chose a different road.'

'I cannot change. I am what I am: a runaway slave who murdered his master. I am the Ape. I am Groundsel. And I have never had cause to regret what I have become.'

'Then why are you troubled?'

Groundsel leaned forward, resting his arms on his knees. 'Your tale was a lie. A flattery. And yet it touched me . . . because it ought to have been true. I have never cared about being loved. But tonight they cheered me, they lifted me high. And that, poet, was the finest moment of my life. It does not matter that I didn't deserve it — but I wish I had.'

'Let me ask you something, my Lord. When you stood before the beast and you saw its awesome power, were you not frightened?'

'I was,' Groundsel admitted.

'And when it bore down on Arian, did it not occur

201

to you that you could be killed as you charged to rescue her?'

'I did not think of rescue.'

'But you saw that it was about to slay her?'

'Yes, that is true.'

'And you charged the beast – and almost died. Every man there saw the deed. You are too hard on yourself. It was heroic, and it touched all who saw it.'

'You confuse me,' said Groundsel. 'Tell me, does Arian love Llaw Gyffes?'

'I think that she does,' answered Nuada.

The outlaw leader stood. 'I was going to have him killed. I was going to take her – willing or unwilling. But now I owe him, for if he had not leapt upon the beast, I would now be dead and I would have missed the only moment of magic in my life. Gods, I am tired. And there's too much ale in this fat belly.' He walked to the doorway but Nuada's voice halted him.

'My Lord!'

'Yes,' answered Groundsel, without turning.

'You are a better man than you know. And I am glad I told the tale well.'

Groundsel walked out into the snow and Nuada settled back on his bed.

For five days a blizzard raged over the forest. Teams of hunters roamed the western wood, seeking signs of the were-beasts. One gigantic wolf creature was found dead in a drift and the howling was heard no more. The winter tore at the forest and the mountains, temperatures dropping to forty below zero. In the stockaded village families stayed inside for much of the day, only emerging to gather wood for their fires. Of Groundsel himself little was seen; he took to walking the hills, avoiding his men. Nuada spent time with Arian and Llaw, and soon began to feel that boredom would kill him before the winter ended. There were few unattached women in the village, and those there were plied a trade he felt loath to patronize.

As the days passed, the lure of Cithaeron grew. He had the gold pieces Groundsel had given him – more than enough to pay for his passage. And he imagined the marble palaces, the beautiful nubile women and – most of all – the warm golden sunshine. Soft beds, good food – cooked with spices, or in wine – clean clothes and hot baths. He pictured himself swimming in a blue sea, the sun on his back.

He talked to Groundsel's men. Apparently the Royal Road to Pertia Port was less than half a day's walk away; once on the road it was two days to Pertia.

Even so, Nuada did not relish the journey.

But then Groundsel ceased his lonely walks and took to sitting in the hall, gloomy and sullen, his eyes on Arian. If Llaw noticed he gave no sign of it, but the outlaw leader tried to goad him on several occasions. The former blacksmith would have none of it. But Nuada knew it was only a matter of time before the two men came to blows, and he did not want to be in the village when the violence came.

He liked Llaw, and in a curious way Groundsel also.

On the morning of the sixth day Nuada slipped away from the village, continuing his way west through the frozen forest, seeking the sanctuary of the Royal Road with its inns and taverns. He walked for most of the day and made his camp in a shallow cave out of the wind. There he lit a fire and berated himself for his stupidity. The village had at least been warm and welcoming; out here death stalked him with icy fingers. The following morning, cold and frightened, he continued on his way, but the paths he had been told of were disguised by snowfall and the grey, lowering sky offered no clue to direction. He stumbled on, his feet numb, his body trembling, and by noon he was hopelessly lost.

There was no cave to help him here and he made a camp behind some boulders where he struggled to light a fire, but the wind blew it out. A great weariness settled on him and the cold seemed to lessen. He was filled with the desire to lie down in the snow and sleep.

Don't be a fool! he told himself and rising, he forced himself to move on slowly. His foot sank into a snow-drift and he almost fell. Reaching out, he took hold of a snow-covered branch jutting from the ground. The branch gave, the snow falling from it. Nuada screamed – what he was holding was no branch but an arm, frozen and black. He threw himself to his left and his body struck something solid beneath the snow. He scrambled to his feet as the snow fell away to show a man's upper body – the face grey, the teeth exposed in a sickening parody of a grin.

Nuada looked around him. Everywhere there were signs of death. Panic swept through him as he backed away from the icy graveyard.

I won't die here! I won't!

The smell of woodsmoke came to him. Somewhere, someone had built a fire. The wind was in his face so he headed into it, calling out. He staggered on, falling into a drift and pulling himself clear. The smell was stronger now. He called again . . . and fell. He began to crawl.

'Over here!' he heard someone call and hands pulled at his arms.

Nuada awoke in a deep cave, where a huge fire was blazing. He sat up, pushing back the sheepskin-lined cloak that covered him. Seven men and four women were sitting round the fire, their faces thin and gaunt.

'Thank you,' he said. 'You saved my life.' The men ignored him, but a young woman with raven-dark hair moved to sit beside him.

'It is a temporary rescue, I am afraid,' she said. 'There is no food and the roads are blocked.'

'Where are you from?'

'We are from nowhere,' she told him. 'We are non-people now, trying to reach Cithaeron. We left the realm four days ago and joined with a caravan of refugees. Then the snows came.'

'Where are the others?' he asked.

She waved her arm towards the cave entrance. 'They are out there. Some have built wind walls; others have tried to force a path through to the coast. They are dying.'

'How many are you?'

'Two hundred started out. I don't know how many have died.'

Nuada stood and fastened the cloak around his shoulders. He walked to the cave entrance and looked up at the sky. There were no clouds and the stars were shining like diamonds. 'I will fetch help.'

'You almost died out there. Do not go back. Even if you conquer the winter, there is still the killer Groundsel.'

'Let me borrow the cloak,' he said, 'and I shall return with food. Gather as many of your people here as you can; tell the others not to wander.'

'Why would you do this for Nomads?' she asked him.

'Because I am a fool,' he told her. 'Gather your people.'

He stepped out into the night and began to climb towards the east, following the pointing finger of the Star Warrior and lining his path with the Great Spear.

On the point of exhaustion he found a cave where he rested for two hours, warmed by a small fire. Then he pushed on.

By the middle of the following afternoon he found himself on the hill overlooking the stockade. Weak from hunger and cold, he slipped and slithered down the

205

hill. Llaw Gyffes saw him from the parapet and climbed down to meet him.

'Welcome back,' said Llaw. 'Was it an enjoyable stroll?'

'There are people dying back there, Llaw, starving to death. We must help them.'

'First let us help you, poet. Your face is chalk white.' He led him to Arian's hut, where the girl was sitting by the brazier. She rose as he entered and laughed at him.

'Ah, the mighty hunter is home! Did you catch anything? Apart from frostbite?'

Llaw helped Nuada from his frozen clothes and began to rub at the poet's skin, forcing circulation back to the surface. Arian warmed a towel by the fire, then held it to Nuada's face. He lay back as they tended him and his eyes closed . . . When he awoke, Llaw was sitting by his bed.

'There are two hundred people trapped in the forest,' Nuada told him. 'They are Nomads. They have no food, and there is no way out to Cithaeron.'

'A stupid time to try and escape,' commented Llaw.

'I would imagine it was that or die,' said the poet. 'We must help them.'

'Why? I do not know any of them.'

'*Why?* What do you mean why? They are people, Llaw, like you and me.'

'No, they are not. I am safe and warm in a hut, and I have food. I am not trapped.'

'I shall go to Groundsel,' snapped Nuada, swinging from the bed. He stood and moved naked to the fire where his clothes were drying.

'A pretty sight,' said Arian. 'Such fine, pert buttocks.' He turned slowly to face her.

'Make your jests, Arian. Laugh while babies die of cold. Laugh while women sob at their loss.'

Her smile faded. 'I do not laugh at them,' she said.

'No, you do not even think of them. You disgust me – the pair of you. You are no better than the King; in fact, you are worse. He condemns them to death in order to steal their wealth, but you condemn them for no reason at all.'

He dressed and tramped across the snow to the hall where some forty men were present – drinking, eating, telling stories. His arrival was greeted by a cheer and he waved to the men and moved on to stand before Groundsel.

'I am glad you are alive,' said the outlaw. 'I missed you.'

He told Groundsel of the Nomads dying in the forest and the man shrugged. 'They chose a poor time to run. Still, the snow might clear in a few days. Some of them will get through.'

'Will you not help them, my Lord?'

'Is there a reason why I should? Can they pay me?'

'I do not know. But tell me – that magic moment we spoke of, how much was it worth?'

Groundsel's eyes narrowed. 'What has that to do with this?' he whispered. 'I was drunk . . . soft in the head. I regret what I said.'

'Then put a price on your drunken words. How much gold is such a memory worth? Ten Raq? Twenty? A thousand?'

'You know the answer,' hissed Groundsel. 'It is priceless.'

'And that, my Lord, is how those people can pay you. No monsters to slay. No acts of courage. Just a gift to those who need it.'

'And you, Nuada, what do you give?'

'I have nothing.'

'You have the twenty gold Raq I gave you, for your passage to Cithaeron. Will you pay that for grain?'

'Yes, of course, but . . .' Nuada blinked as Groundsel

held out his hand, then opened his leather hip-pouch and counted out the coin.

Groundsel put the gold to one side and leaned forward. 'And will you stay in the forest until I give you leave to go?'

'Stay? I . . .' He saw the look of dark triumph in Groundsel's eyes and swallowed hard. In Cithaeron he could be rich again and live in a palace, with beautiful women to wait on him. The sun was bright and warm, the climate temperate. But here, amid the towering boredom?

'Well?' insisted Groundsel.

'I will stay. But I too have a condition, my Lord. No more thefts from Nomads. I'll stay for the hero Groundsel, not the robber killer.'

Groundsel chuckled and slapped Nuada's shoulder. 'I agree to your condition. Groundsel, the lying oath-breaker, the thief and the killer, gives you his word. For what it is worth.'

Despite the heavy cloak and the sheepskin gloves, two pairs of woollen leggings and fur-lined boots, Errin was bitterly cold. For two days he had followed Ubadai through the frozen forest, riding at a snail's pace for fear of injuries to their mounts. Some trails, simple in summer, had become death-traps for riders, with ice-covered stones, holes part covered by snow, and trees heavy laden and ready to fall at a breath of wind. Ubadai had said nothing for the whole of the first day and when they had camped he had built a good fire, rolled into his blankets and slept until the dawn. Errin knew the tribesman was angry, and the Gabalan lord felt a large measure of guilt over it. He had freed Ubadai and the Nomad had no reason to follow him back into danger. But then he had had no reason to ride into Mactha fortress in order to rescue his former master either. It was baffling.

On the third morning, as the sky cleared, Errin gazed up at the rising sun.

'Which way are we heading today?' he asked Ubadai, as the tribesman rolled his blankets and strapped them to the saddle of his horse. Ubadai pointed to a trail through the trees.

'But that's east, isn't it?' asked Errin. Ubadai nodded, but said nothing. 'Oh, come on, Ubadai, speak to me. Why are we heading east?'

The tribesman grunted something inaudible, then turned to face Errin. 'No tracks, yes? Everywhere fresh snow. No chance to find woman. We go back.'

'We ought to search a little longer – we've only been here two days.'

'This is search. Two choices. The men either good or bad, yes. If good they walk through near Royal Road, to the south. If bad they swing back. Wait till Cartain is gone, deliver woman to Pertia Port when fleet comes in, yes? If they are good men, we have lost them. If bad, I think they come this way.'

'That's just a guess,' said Errin.

'Yes. But I am tracker, not wizard. They travel eastwards on first day – not very good reason for that.'

'How do you know that?'

'The cave yesterday where we rested? There were remains of two fires, and tracks to show three people – one with small feet but long stride. Only three people? Then why two fires? Woman sits apart.'

Errin shrugged. It was little to go on, but Ubadai was the master in this venture. 'You do not want to be here, do you?' he said as he climbed into the saddle.

Ubadai mounted his horse and gave a sour grin, gesturing to the ice-covered trail. '*You* want to be here?'

'That's not what I meant; it is a duty for me. But

why did you agree to come? Why did you come back for me in Mactha?'

'Plenty stupid, maybe,' muttered Ubadai, edging his mount forward.

For two hours they rode until they slithered down a steep slope towards a small grove of pine trees. Ubadai drew his mount to a halt and slipped his bow from under his saddlebags. He strung it, then blew on his fingers to warm them.

'What is it?' asked Errin, coming alongside.

'Smell the air,' ordered Ubadai and Errin lifted his head but could detect little, save perhaps a hint of woodsmoke and a subtle, faintly unpleasant odour reminiscent of the farmyard.

'What do you make of it?' asked Errin.

'Death,' whispered Ubadai. 'And something else. Animal – wolf, maybe.'

'Why are we whispering?'

'We are downwind. It will not know we are here. Better ride back, maybe.'

'If it is a wolf pack, we will scare them away. It might be Sheera . . . in trouble,' he added swiftly.

'I do not like the feel of this,' said Ubadai. 'My skin crawls. I have good skin and it knows where it wants to be . . . and it doesn't want to go in there.'

Errin grinned. 'You've hunted wolves before. And bears – even a lion, if I recall. We're both fine archers.' An eerie howling came from the grove, the sound magnified beyond any wolf call Errin had ever heard. 'On the other hand,' he said, 'you might be right. I think this is a case for discretion.' But just as he was about to wheel his horse back to the slope, another sound broke the silence – a woman's scream.

Errin cursed and spurred his horse into the trees. 'You have no bow!' shouted Ubadai, galloping after him.

Errin's mount thundered into the clearing, saw the

210

giant wolf creature with its sabre talons and huge snarling jaws and desperately tried to swerve. But the ice under its hooves offered no purchase and it slid to its haunches. Errin hurled himself from the saddle as the stallion cannoned into the beast and both animals went down, the beast slashing its talons through the horse's neck. Blood fountained over the monster's grey-white fur. The dying horse lashed out with its hooves, hurling the beast to the snow. The stallion struggled to rise, but the beast was upon it once more, rending and slashing. Errin climbed to his feet and drew the curved short sword given to him by Cartain; it was razor-sharp and beautifully made, but it seemed like a child's toy now, as he stared at the enraged beast. Errin swung his head – Sheera stood nearby, white-faced, holding a smouldering branch. He ran to her. The beast looked up from the dead stallion and climbed slowly across its carcass, staggering and almost falling. Rising to its hind legs, it moved towards the man and woman. Errin stepped in front of Sheera, placed his hand over his buckle and whispered, 'Ollathair.'

Instantly the advance of the beast seemed to slow. Errin waited until the creature was almost upon him, then ducked under a slowly moving sweep of the taloned arm and rammed his sword into the beast's belly.

Sheera appeared alongside him, thrusting the branch into the creature's mouth. In that instant Errin could see the talons moving towards the girl and he let go of his sword and dived at her, dragging her clear.

Behind them Ubadai leapt from the saddle, notched an arrow to his bow, drew and loosed his shaft which sped through the air to punch into the beast's neck. The creature staggered and fell on all fours; then it rolled to its side and died.

Errin climbed to his feet, his eyes scanning the clearing for any further monsters. To his right there was a human leg and across the clearing lay the grisly remains of another victim. Satisfied there were no other beasts, he once more touched the buckle of his belt and turned to Sheera.

'Are you all right?'

'Yes, I . . .' Recognition showed in her eyes and she stepped back from him.

'Errin? What are you doing here?'

'I was looking for you. Cartain was worried; he said the men you were with were probably in the employ of Okessa.'

'I think they were. But of all the men to rescue me – why did it have to be you?'

He shrugged. 'It is pleasant, lady, to have succeeded in something.'

Her face darkened. 'Do not think it absolves you from blame over my sister's murder. It does not! Nothing ever will.'

'I loved Dianu and I would have done anything to save her. But I did not ask her to stay for me, nor did I know she was in danger. I do not much care whether you believe that; it is immaterial to me.' He moved to the beast and dragged his sword clear, wiping it clean of blood on the creature's fur. Reversing the sword, he pushed it at Sheera. 'You want to kill me, lady? Do it! Go on, take the sword and push it home.'

She turned away. 'I was angry when I told Cartain I wanted you dead. I do not desire that – but neither do I desire your company.'

'You have little choice in that, Sheera. I am here to escort you to Pertia Port and then to Cithaeron. Once there you can do as you please.'

'I am not going to Cithaeron. I will find Okessa and see him dead. And if there was any sense of honour in you, you would do the same. You say you loved Dianu? What a way to prove it – running to Cithaeron.'

Errin took a deep breath, pushing back his anger.

'In Cithaeron we can raise an army. Here we can do little save run around a winter forest hoping we do not get lost, which may be all right for spoilt little girls but it doesn't suit me. Now gather your things.' As he turned away from her she grabbed his arm to swing him round and her fist cracked into his jaw. Ubadai winced as he watched the blow crash home. Most women did not know how to punch, but he had to admire the smooth swing and the explosive contact. Errin was unconscious before he hit the snow.

Ubadai strolled across and knelt by the unconscious nobleman, then he looked up at the astonished Sheera.

'I like you, girl,' said Ubadai. 'You plenty stupid.'

11

Nuada was furious when Groundsel told him bluntly that he would not be allowed to accompany the rescue party. The outlaw leader had gathered thirty men together and each was carrying food – bread, dried meat and fruit.

'You need me to show you the way,' protested Nuada. 'You need me!'

'I can find the Royal Road, Nuada, without any help. But look at you – you are on the verge of collapse. You could not stand the journey.'

'I'll get him there – and back,' said Llaw Gyffes. The snow had begun to fall thickly once more and Llaw, like the rest of the men, was warmly clad in oiled sheepskin and high wool-lined walking boots. A hood covered his blond hair and a long scarf was wound around his neck.

Groundsel walked over to Nuada and placed a hand upon his shoulder. 'Every step that you slow us down could mean a death on the Royal Road. You understand that?'

'I won't slow you down, I promise you.'

Llaw pulled Nuada aside and offered him a drink from his canteen. Nuada accepted it – and choked.

'Gods of chaos!' he spluttered. 'What is it?'

'It is a raw spirit distilled from grain – a little goes a long way. You feel warmer?'

'I feel as if someone just lit a fire in my belly.'

'Good. Now, let's go.'

Groundsel set off at a good pace, feeling his way through the snow with a staff, thrusting it deep into drifts to test the footing. The men behind moved without a sound. There was no conversation and Nuada knew that most of them could not understand the nature of their mission.

'Why did you want to come?' asked Llaw, as they walked some way behind the rescue party.

'I told them I would – but also they fear Groundsel.'

'They are right so to do. You are leading the wolf into the lamb-pen; do not be surprised if he behaves like a wolf.'

'I will not be surprised, Llaw. Now tell me why you came with us?'

Llaw chuckled and helped Nuada to climb a sloping drift. The wind picked up, howling ice and snow into their faces, and further conversation became impossible. A journey which had taken Nuada a day and a half was made in less than four hours by the rescue party.

They came across the first bodies lying huddled by a dead fire. There were two women, an old man and a child. All were frozen stiff.

Groundsel hawked and spat. Ice had formed on his dark brows and short beard. 'Stupid!' he said. 'Had they built the fire twenty paces over there, by those rocks, they would still be alive. How could they think a fire in the open would warm them?'

Leaving the bodies where they lay the men pushed on, coming to the cave at mid-afternoon. Some forty people were crowded there; four were dead. Groundsel led the men inside and they broke out the rations. The two fires were dying down and Llaw Gyffes returned to the forest for fuel. Nuada scanned the gaunt, weary faces, glimpsing the girl at the back of the cave. She was squatting beside an elderly woman and he pushed his way through to her.

'I came back,' he said simply.

'She is dead,' replied the girl. 'She died an hour ago.'

Nuada gazed down on the serene face. The woman

was in her late sixties, he guessed, and she had the look of the patrician. 'Then nothing can harm her now,' he said. 'Come, there is food.'

'I am not hungry.' He put his arm around her slender shoulders and pulled her to him.

'Would she want you to die also?' he asked. 'Follow me.' Taking her by the arm he led her to Groundsel, who gave her some bread and a canteen of water.

'The cave could not take all of us; there are others still outside,' the girl told them. Groundsel turned away and sent three groups to search the forest. Llaw Gyffes went with them. In the cave a woman fell at Groundsel's feet, hugging his legs and crying quietly. Embarrassed, he pulled away. A man came to him, seizing his hand and pumping it; others joined him. Groundsel accepted their gratitude with ill grace and pushed his way out into the blizzard. He walked alone for a while and watched the men searching the snow; there were bodies everywhere.

He was about to return to the cave when he heard a whimper from close by and looked around, but there was no one to be seen and the sound ceased. Taking his staff he probed the bushes, but could find nothing. He stopped and listened, but the howling wind obscured any lesser sounds. He crouched closer to the ground . . . still nothing. To his left there was a small drift of snow. As he looked, the wind caused it to flurry and he caught sight of an edge of cloth. Moving to it, he dug away at the snow. Buried here were a man and a woman, huddled together, frozen in death, but they had curled themselves around a small child wrapped in a woollen blanket. Groundsel could imagine their last thoughts: protect the child until the end, their bodies shielding it from the wind and the snow. The child's head moved and its mouth opened. Groundsel swiftly lifted it clear of the snow and ran for the cave. Inside he forced his way to the fire and pulled away the frozen blanket, rubbing at the little girl's slender limbs. Her hair was short, but tightly curled and golden, and she was thin, terribly thin.

'Akis!' he called. 'Where the Hell are you?'

A stocky man came forward. 'Did you bring the milk?' asked Groundsel.

'It's mostly gone, my Lord,' replied the man. Ever since Nuada's saga of the beast, men had begun to echo the poet's style of address.

'Get some here. Now! And warm it.'

'Yes, my Lord.'

The girl's head sagged against Groundsel's shoulder. 'Don't you die on me!' he shouted. 'Don't you dare die on me!' He shook her and rubbed her back and she began to whimper. 'That's it,' said Groundsel. 'Cry! Cry and live!'

'Shall I take her?' asked a woman.

'Leave me alone,' snapped Groundsel as Akis returned with some milk, warmed in a wooden bowl. The outlaw leader lifted the girl's head and held the bowl to her lips; the milk dribbled to her chin, as she shut her mouth against it. 'Pinch her nostrils,' said Groundsel and a woman crouched down beside them and followed his bidding. The child's mouth opened. At first she choked on the milk, but then she began to swallow. When the milk was finished her head sagged again to his shoulder. He was about to shake her when the woman touched his arm.

'She is asleep,' she said. 'Just asleep. She will be fine. Wrap her in a warm blanket and leave her with me. I'll take care of her.'

Groundsel was reluctant to part with the child, but he did so, brushing the hair back from her brow. 'She is pretty,' he said, 'and tough. I like that in a child. How old is she? I am not good at judging ages in babes.'

'I would say around two years old. She might be a little more, but she is very thin and small.'

'You look after her,' said Groundsel, rising.

'Yes, my Lord.'

'I am not a Lord! See to her.' He saw Llaw Gyffes helping a young couple into the cave, which was now becoming seriously overcrowded.

'It's a nightmare out there,' said Llaw. 'There are bodies everywhere, must be close to a hundred.'

'How many survivors?' Groundsel asked.

'I've seen around thirty. There's no room for them here and if we don't find shelter of some kind, many more will die.'

'There are deeper caves about three miles from here,' said Groundsel, 'but bears inhabit some of them.'

'At least you can kill a bear,' muttered Llaw, 'but we can't beat this cold.' Other survivors began to crowd into the cave entrance, shouting for room to be made. Those at the centre were being pushed too close to the fires and arguments broke out.

Groundsel stepped on to a boulder so that he could see over the heads of the milling refugees.

'Silence!' he bellowed. All movement ceased. 'We will need to march out into the blizzard. I want the strongest among you ready to move in the next hour. The rest can stay here; I will leave men and food and we will come back for you when the blizzard dies down.'

Some of the refugees began to shout, refusing to leave the sanctuary of the cave. 'You will do as you are damn well told!' Groundsel roared. 'Or else I'll leave you all to starve! Now, there are deeper caves around an hour's march from here. There we can build fires to keep you alive. Anyone who believes they can make the journey, move to the left of the cave. Those who wish to remain, move to the right.'

Slowly the refugees began to shuffle into place.

Groundsel stepped down and an elderly man approached him.

'I thank you, sir, for your help. Tell me, are you the hero, Llaw Gyffes?'

'No, I am the devil Groundsel.' The man's eyes widened and he backed away.

'Those on the left, move out of the cave. Now!' shouted Llaw Gyffes. 'Come on, make room.'

Groundsel found the woman nursing the child he had saved and leaning down, he took the sleeping girl. 'You are going to take her out into the cold?' said the woman. 'Is that wise?'

'I'll keep her safe,' promised Groundsel, opening his sheepskin jerkin and closing it around the child.

Outside, the blizzard had eased and the snow was falling less thickly as Groundsel took the lead and the thin column set off. Akis, Nuada and four others remained in the cave, distributing food and building up the fires. There was more room now, and the group was mostly made up of the elderly or the young. Nuada was tired, more weary than at any other time in his young life. But he felt curiously lifted and filled with a sense of quiet joy. He sat back against the cave wall and looked at the people sleeping by the fires. *His people*. His by blood, and by deed. The raven-haired girl sat beside him; her mother's body lay at the back of the cave, a thin linen sheet over her face.

'My name is Kartia,' said the girl. She was still cold and he lifted the blanket from his shoulder and drew her in. He said nothing and leaned his head back against the rock wall; it felt like a feather pillow.

And he slept, without dreams.

The journey to the deep caves took more than four hours, but the snows held off and the temperature rose marginally. Even so many of the weaker refugees needed assistance, and Llaw Gyffes and two others followed some way behind the column, watching out for those who fell by the wayside. Llaw gave some of them a mouthful of the fiery spirit, hauling them to their feet. Only one man died during the trip, his heart giving out as he struggled to climb the last hill.

Once at the caves huge fires were lit and the refugees gathered gratefully around them. The child Groundsel was carrying awoke, and he fed her with the last of the milk. Llaw Gyffes watched him with the girl, his pale eyes betraying no emotion. Feeling himself observed, Groundsel passed the child to a middle-aged woman and walked back to the cave mouth where he sat down opposite the tall warrior.

'I like children,' Groundsel remarked, his dark eyes staring challengingly at Llaw.

'So do I. I think the blizzard has passed – the worst should be over for now.'

Groundsel gazed at the sky. 'No clouds. It will get colder yet.'

'What will you do with them all?' asked Llaw. 'How will you feed them, take care of them? And how did Nuada talk you into it?'

Groundsel shrugged. 'I have a full granary and they can work for their food. They can fell trees, gather wood. The younger women can whore for my men; we've not enough women as it is. Three men were killed recently in a fight over a woman.'

Llaw nodded. 'And the last question? Why?'

'I don't answer to you, Llaw Gyffes; I answer to no one. If I choose to do a thing, I do it. I may choose to kill them all tomorrow. My choice. Why did you come?'

Llaw shrugged. 'I needed the exercise. I felt like a dog in a cage. How's your back?'

'I heal fast.'

'You'd better watch for infection. I've seen animal scratches turn bad, very bad.'

'Not here,' said Groundsel. 'The air is good for wounds. Not one case of gangrene have I seen since I came to the forest.' He was silent for a moment, remembering the pain and the fear when the talons sliced home. 'That was a mighty beast, was it not?'

'Damn near broke my axe,' said Llaw. 'Has it occurred to you what fools we were to sit in the open?'

'Once or twice,' Groundsel admitted. 'So far my hunters have found six more of them, dead in the snow. But there is no clue as to their origins. No one has ever heard of anything like them before. I have even sent men to seek the Dagda and ask for his counsel.'

'You know where he lives?'

'No, but the men will go to all the settlements seeking news of him,' said Groundsel. 'He will hear of it – wherever he is.'

'The important question,' said Llaw, 'has to be: Who sent the creatures? And why?'

'Sent them?' responded Groundsel. 'They were not a hunting pack of hounds. I saw no leashes. And no man alive could train those creatures.'

'Remember the boy? He said he watched it appear from the air, in a flash of lightning. Our own hunters found tracks that just appeared on a hillside. No. Someone wants to bring death into the forest – we need to know who.'

'We do indeed,' Groundsel agreed, 'if you are correct. But I am not convinced. There are parts of the forest that have never been explored – high valleys, lonely canyons. The beasts could have been driven down by lack of game – or even curiosity.'

'Maybe,' said Llaw, 'but you saw the wolf creature. It was not completely covered in hair; its chest and belly were dark-skinned. Such a beast would be unlikely to live high where the air is cold. And the other creature that was found dead in the drift? The cold killed it. What forest beast have you heard of that does not prepare for winter?'

'It's a compelling argument, but where does it take us? Some sorcerous animal trainer releases his pack in the mountains? How would we find him? Or recognize him if we did?'

'Find him? We cannot,' admitted Llaw. 'But another wizard could.'

'I take it this is leading somewhere?' Groundsel snapped. 'You don't exactly find yourself surrounded by wizards about here.'

'There is a lad at my village who claims he was an apprentice to a man of magic named Ruad Ro-fhessa. When the snow clears, I will seek him out.'

Groundsel stood and stretched. 'That means leaving the sanctuary of the forest. A risky venture, Stronghand. With that red-gold beard and that pale hair you are an easy man to recognize. And how would we poor forest folk fare if our great hero was taken from us before he could raise his army?'

'I think you would manage, my Lord Groundsel – Great Slayer of Beasts and rescuer of small babes.'

Llaw stood and gazed down at the smaller man. Groundsel smiled, but it did not reach his eyes. 'I think I like you, Llaw. I really do.'

'That's good – and very reassuring.'

'Don't be too reassured. I've killed men I've liked before.'

'I'll remember that.'

For five days Ruad waited, opening the Black Gate each evening and holding it for an hour. Once a giant lizard with serrated teeth tried to force its way through and he sent it scurrying back with a burst of white fire. On the sixth day he was too weak to attempt the Power spell and walked wearily back to the village.

Gwydion said nothing as he entered the small cabin that had been cleared for them. The old man merely put his hand on his friend's shoulder. Ruad shook it loose.

'I've lost him,' he said, slumping to a chair. Gwydion sat beside the Armourer, staring into the broad ugly face and seeing his own reflection in the bronze eye-patch. Ruad cursed. 'I sent him to his death, just like all the others.'

'He was a man, he made his own decisions,' said Gwydion. 'And Gods, Ruad, it was worth the risk. If the Knights of the Gabala could assemble once more, we could sweep the land clean of this evil – we could raise a rebel army.'

'They are all dead, Gwydion. Let me rest.' Ruad stumbled to a straw-filled mattress set against the wall and stretched himself out.

Gwydion moved to him. 'I will give you sleep,' he said, touching his finger to the wizard's brow. Ruad's eye closed, his breathing deepening. Gwydion reached effortlessly into the Colours, marvelling at the strength of the Green, feeling the power flowing from the millions of trees and the birds and animals drawn to them. He replenished his strength and opened his eyes. The candle was burning low and guttering, so he lit another from the stub of the first.

A light tapping disturbed his thoughts and he moved to the door and opened it. A youth stood there, pale hair glistening in the moonlight. Behind him stood a taller man, dark-haired and dark-eyed.

'Yes?' asked Gwydion. 'Is someone sick?'

'No, sir,' said the youth. 'I am seeking Ruad Rohessa. I was his apprentice; my name is Lámfhada.'

Gwydion reached out and touched the youth on the shoulder. There was no evil in him. 'Enter,' said the old man, 'but talk softly, for Ruad is asleep – and he needs his rest.'

The newcomers entered the cabin and Gwydion stoked the fire, hanging a kettle over the coals. 'Would you like some herb tea? It is sweet and aids gentle dreams.'

'You do not remember me, do you?' said the hard-faced man. He thrust out his right arm, exposing the leather-covered stump.

'Elodan? I heard you were dead. I am glad to see the story was untrue. You must forgive me; I am growing old and forgetful. When last I saw you it was as a Knight arrayed in silver armour, a black-plumed helm on your head.'

'Long ago, Gwydion. Another age. The world has changed since then – and not for the better.'

Gwydion poured boiling water into a copper pot and added dried leaves, stirring the mixture with a wooden spoon. He let it stand for several minutes and then transferred it to three round-bottomed mugs.

'Why are you here?' asked the old man.

'I have hopes that the wizard can mend my arm,' said Elodan. 'Lámfhada tells me he can do anything.'

'How did you find us?'

Lámfhada grinned. 'I have been practising with the Colours. I cannot master the majors, but I can now fly the Yellow. And I sensed Ruad was in the forest, though I could not tell where except that it was to the east of where I was. Then we heard of a healer and a wizard, and men were speaking about the three golden hounds. I was there when Ruad was working on the last of them, so I knew it was him. Do you think he will be angry that I sought him out?'

'I do not believe so,' said Gwydion, 'but he has suffered a terrible loss and you may find him . . . changed. Have patience, Lámfhada. And you, Elodan, do not expect overmuch. Ruad is a wizard of great power, but some things are beyond mere men.'

'My hopes were never high, Gwydion. But we will see.'

Gwydion turned his attention back to the youth. 'The Yellow,' he said, 'is a wondrous colour. I too learned my skills in such a way. It is the Colour of Dreams.'

'And yet it has no power,' said Lámfhada.

'No, no, you are wrong. The Yellow leads us to all the other Colours. It is a guide. Without it there would be no wizards, no healers, no mystics, no seers. Tell me, as you ride the Yellow, what Colour do you find pushing at the edge of your mind?'

'None, sir.'

'In time you will find yourself drawn to another Colour, which will intrude as you fly the Yellow. For me it was Green and I became a healer; for others, like Ruad, it is Black. For some, sadly, it is the Red. But the Yellow will lead you to the Colour of your life, for good or ill.'

'Are all men governed by Colours, then, even when they are not sorcerers?' Lamfhada asked.

'Of course. The Colours are life. Look at Elodan – what Colour does his soul wear?'

The warrior said nothing, but Lámfhada swung to look at him. 'I do not know,' said the youth. 'How does one tell?'

'It takes little magic, my boy,' said Gwydion. 'A farmer is a man who loves the land and the yield of the land. His is the Green of growth. But a warrior? What other Colour is there for a man who lives to strike his fellows with a razored blade, or a deadly mace, or a flashing lance? Elodan's Colour is Red, and he knows it. He has always known it. Am I right, King's champion?'

Elodan shrugged. 'There will always be a need for warriors. I feel no shame at what I . . . was.'

'Ah, but then you were not a warrior because of that

need. You chose the path because you enjoyed the fight.'

'That is true. Does it make me evil?'

'No, but neither does it bring you close to sainthood,' said Gwydion, reddening. He took a deep breath. 'Forgive me, Elodan. I have no right to berate you. But much of my life has been spent healing wounds caused by swords or arrows or axes; dealing with the result of hatred, lust or greed. I know you are not evil – but I loathe the men of swords. Come, it is late. Rest here, and we will speak to Ruad in the morning.'

Errin regained consciousness after a few moments and sat up groggily. Ubadai helped him to his feet. 'Bad chin,' said the tribesman, grinning. Errin staggered.

'I'm sorry,' apologized Sheera. 'I thought you'd move or something. I mean, the speed with which you tackled the beast . . . Are you all right?'

'Only my pride suffered lasting damage,' said Errin. 'Can I sit down somewhere?'

'Not here,' replied Ubadai, gesturing at the bodies. 'Blood will bring many creatures – wolves, lions, who knows? You can sit on my horse.'

'No, he can't,' said Sheera. 'It ran as soon as you dismounted.'

'Better and better,' Ubadai grunted. The tribesman scanned the area, then pointed to a nearby hill. 'There should be caves – with our luck, many beasts there. Hip-deep in beasts. Still . . .' He gathered the saddle-bags and provisions from Errin's dead mount, and waited while Sheera fetched her meagre pack from the shelter beneath the tree. Then he supported Errin as they moved slowly uphill. The fresh mountain air soon revived the nobleman. As Ubadai had predicted, there were many shallow caves. He entered one on the south of the hill, but backed out swiftly. 'Bear,' he said. The second cave was empty and the Nomad gathered wood and built a fire.

Sheera settled down beside the fire, grateful for the warmth, and sat watching Errin. 'I really am sorry,' she said.

He shrugged. 'Don't be. I never was very good at defending myself. My old sword tutor said my wrists were as strong as damp lettuce.'

'You moved well enough against the beast, and that sword-thrust all but disembowelled it.'

'Beast was dying anyway,' Ubadai told Sheera. 'You could have killed it with that branch.'

'What is that supposed to mean?' Errin asked.

Ubadai shrugged. 'Sick, maybe. But when it killed horse it nearly fell. It did not charge – it staggered.'

'That's a nice thought,' snapped Errin. 'The conquering Knight kills a sick beast – hardly the basis for a great saga. It didn't look ill to me.'

'Yes, it did,' said Sheera. 'Its chest was almost blue. And it did fall before attacking.'

'It had thin skin,' said Ubadai. 'Not good for cold.'

'Can we stop feeling sorry for the creature?' asked Errin. 'It wasn't exactly a wounded rabbit.'

'You wait here,' said the Nomad. 'I'll find horse.'

After the tribesman had gone, Sheera built up the fire. 'It doesn't matter that the beast was not at full strength, Errin. You still tackled it – and you pulled me clear of the talons with astonishing speed.'

He grinned at her. 'I was rather pleased with that.' He wanted to tell her about the belt, but thought better of it; it was pleasant to be seen in an heroic role. Looking at Sheera, he was struck by her similarity to her sister: the same wide eyes and full lips, the same piercing gaze. Sheera was taller, her hair shorter and more tightly curled, but there was no doubting the blood line.

'What is wrong?' she asked, as she saw his face change.

'Nothing. Would you like something to eat?'

'Not at the moment. I'm still a little queasy from the battle.'

'It was brave of you to stand before the beast with just a burning branch,' he said. 'You looked very impressive there.'

'I didn't have time or space to use my bow. You showed great skill in charging your horse at it.'

'I can't claim too much credit for that; the poor animal was trying to stop and lost its footing.' He looked away and silence fell between them. 'Look . . .' he said at last. 'About Dianu . . .'

'Let's not talk about it,' she said, her face hardening.

'There are some things that must be said. I was a fool; I know that, and no amount of breast-beating will erase it. But I knew nothing of the danger she was in; I did not know you had Nomad blood.'

'You killed her, Errin. Your arrow pierced her heart.'

He closed his eyes, then opened them to stare into the flames. 'Yes,' he agreed. 'My arrow . . . but you do not know what it was like. I had a broken leg and was making my escape. I wanted to rescue her, but I could not get down from my horse. When I rode to the hilltop, she was being tied to a stake at the top of a pyre –'

'I don't want to hear this!'

But Errin pushed on. 'If I had reached her, I could not have freed her. She would either have burnt slowly to death or choked on the smoke. What would you have done, Sheera?'

'All those people around her,' she whispered. 'She must have known many of them. She used to distribute gifts in Mactha – food and coin for the needy. Yet they cheered as she was led to the stake; we heard that in Pertia. And they screamed in rage when you robbed them of their sport. What makes people act like that? How could they be so cruel? So evil?'

He shook his head. 'How can I answer? Some weeks ago a slave boy ran away after I had bought him as a gift for the Duke. I hunted him down, and when he had almost escaped I loosed an arrow into his back. Why? How can any man answer? He was mine; he disobeyed me; I watched him crawl into the forest to die alone. It's been on my mind ever since. I cannot justify it – no more could any man present when Dianu died justify his passions.'

'Are you sure the boy died?'

'No, but the arrow went deep.'

For a while they sat in silence, then Sheera spoke again. 'It is hard to believe how soon the world can change. I spent four years in Furbolg – attending school, enjoying feasts and dances and banquets. I even met the King. He was tall and not old, but his eyes were strange and cold. I did not like him, nor his new Knights. Many rumours sprang up about them. Some men said they were demons from another world; others claimed they were sorcerers who sacrificed living victims on a secret altar. Then the fear began – the arrests, the executions, the mobs chanting in the streets. I used to walk along the Perfumed Path at night – you recall it?'

'Yes,' he said. 'A haunt for lovers. Roses and many other flowers lined the path all the way to the Royal Park.'

'No one used it during my last year in Furbolg. Four women disappeared while walking it, two others were attacked and raped. It became a place of fear. And the murders and robberies! Not a day passed without word of some new outrage, but even that was not enough to concern the nobility. Then one evening at the palace everything changed. The King had ordered a special feast; we arrived late and saw that the palace hall was packed with beds and couches and everywhere people were rutting. The slave at the door told my uncle that no man was allowed to remain with his wife; all had to find other partners. We slipped away then, and that's when my uncle sent me to Dianu and our plan to escape was formed.'

'The King turned the palace into a brothel?' exclaimed Errin. 'And the nobles stood for it?'

'Four who refused to take part were later accused of treachery. That's when the King's champion, Elodan, left his service and challenged the Red Knight, Cairbre. We were already on the road by then, but we heard of the fight.'

'Yes,' said Errin softly. 'Cairbre told me of it. The world has thrown away its sanity.'

'Not the whole world, Errin. Only the Gabala.'

'Perhaps Cartain will raise an army strong enough?'

'No, he will not,' said Sheera fiercely. 'Cithaeron is far away. And, anyway, there is already an army here. You have heard of Llaw Gyffes? Now is the time, Errin. Not in a year or ten years. Now!'

'But the man is a peasant – you can't be serious.'

'A peasant? I would sooner be ruled by an honest peasant than a mad king. But his army would grow even faster if men like you were allied to him.'

Errin shook his head. 'I have heard many stories of the legendary wife-killer, but I have never seen this army. What would it consist of? Killers, thieves, robbers? Would these put an end to King Ahak's reign of terror – or add to it?'

'When I was a child,' said Sheera, 'there was a fire on the estate. Our foresters set another blaze before it, burning all the ground in its path. The first fire was starved and died, and the land was safe. Within a few years you would never have known there had been two fires.'

Ubadai entered the cave. 'No good,' he said. 'Horse bolted and I saw wolf tracks. We walk now.'

'Back to Pertia?' enquired Sheera softly.

'No,' said Errin. 'We'll find Llaw Gyffes.'

'Better and better,' grunted Ubadai.

12

Lámfhada lay in a warm corner of the cabin covered by a thick woollen blanket, his head resting on an embroidered cushion. He could hear Elodan and Gwydion talking in low voices, but the sound washed over him as he reached for the Yellow. He was anxious to see which Colour approached the edge of his vision. Would he be a Healer, or a Wizard, or a Seer, or a Craftsman? He closed his eyes, drawing the Yellow to him and feeling its warmth. His body lost all sensation of weight and he seemed to be floating effortlessly in a warm sea, slowly rolling over and over, yet rising into the glow above. Often he had reached this stage, but mostly he remained a little below it, bathing in the Yellow. Tonight he rose and rose, seeking the Colour of his life. The Yellow deepened into Gold and his eyes snapped open to see the sky was ablaze with colour: Red, Green, White, Blue, Black, Violet – and Gold. They merged and swelled together and he felt himself on a river of magic, whirling above the forest. At first he was frightened and struggled to return, but the Gold brought him tranquillity and he fastened to it.

And from the darkest, deepest corner of the hall of memory came the realization that he had touched the Gold once before – as a nine-year-old child torn by grief at the death of his mother. He remembered the hooded man chanting on the hill and knew him as Ruad Ro-fhessa, the wizard Ollathair. But there was another man close by, he recalled: a man who had sent the frightened boy home. Yet his name was still lost to Lamfhada.

His headlong flight slowed as he reached the edge of

the forest. Gazing down at himself, he saw he was naked and standing on a golden circle. Far below him lay the trees, and he could see a stag running on a hillside, pursued by wolves. He shivered, afraid that he would fall from the circle, wishing it had walls. The circle curved up into a half-sphere and he sat back on a high seat.

This was wondrous beyond his dreaming.

On the hillside the stag had turned to face the pack. Lámfhada watched as it lowered its head. A wolf leapt – only to be hurled into the air. A second wolf moved in behind the stag . . . then another. Their fangs tore at the animal and the stag fell, its throat ripped, blood spilling to the earth. Lámfhada was struck by a terrible sadness, and the golden sphere dropped to the earth. Frightened by the light, the wolves ran off. Lámfhada stepped from the sphere and approached the dead stag. It was old, its fur grey around the mouth. The boy knelt by it and reached out; but his hand passed through the beast, and he remembered that it was his spirit that flew. Golden light flamed from his hand, filling the body of the stag. The wounds closed and the grey hairs vanished. Old, stretched muscles swelled with youth and vitality. The stag's head came up, it surged to its feet and with one leap it bounded from the hilltop. The wolves closed in, but its speed carried it clear as it ran for the sanctuary of the distant trees.

Lámfhada climbed into the sphere and took to the skies, joy flooding him.

At the edge of the forest once more, he gazed out over the realm beyond and saw the Red gathering like a distant sunset. He sensed another presence and saw a man hovering in the sky. He was dressed in red armour and his hair was glittering white in the moonlight – and yet as Lámfhada looked closer, he saw the knight was almost transparent.

'Who are you?' asked Lámfhada.

Blood-red eyes turned on him and the Knight tried to fly closer. But the Gold turned him back.

'I am Cairbre,' the Knight whispered. 'And you?'

'Lámfhada. Why are you here?'

'To see, to learn. Are you with Llaw Gyffes?'

'Yes. Do you know him?'

The Knight smiled. 'I will know him . . . soon. His pitiful little army will see the power of the New Gabala. Tell him I said this. Tell him the King is coming in the spring, with all his soldiers. Tell him there is nowhere to hide from the Red Knights.'

'He would not hide,' said Lámfhada. 'He will not fear you.'

'All creatures of flesh and blood should fear me,' declared Cairbre, 'and all who ride with me. You, boy, what is the source of your magic?'

'I do not know,' said Lámfhada warily. 'I am new to the Colours.'

'There is only one Colour of importance,' snapped the Knight.

'You speak of the Red. Yet it cannot heal.'

'Heal? It can create a form that needs no healing. Why do I talk to you? Begone, boy! I have no wish to slay you.'

'Are you in pain?' asked Lámfhada suddenly. 'Are you ill?'

Cairbre's eyes flashed and he dragged his sword from its ghostly scabbard, swinging the blade at the golden sphere. But the sword bounced back and Cairbre's face grew ever more pale.

He dropped the sword, which floated by his side. 'Kill me,' he said. 'Come on, boy, kill me!'

'Why? Why should I do such a terrible thing?'

'Terrible? You have no idea of the meaning of the word. But you will, when we come for you in the spring. Tell Llaw Gyffes you saw me. Tell him.'

'I will. Why do you hate him?'

'Hate? I do not hate him, boy. I hate myself; to all else I am indifferent.' The Knight turned away and grew ever more transparent, then suddenly he turned, his body bathed in brilliant red. 'Ollathair!' he cried. 'You come from Ollathair!'

Lámfhada shrank back and a wall of golden light sprang between them.

The Knight began to laugh. 'Oh, this is rich! Go to him. Send him my regards. Cairbre-Pateus sends greetings!'

And then he was gone.

Lámfhada fled for the cabin and the safety of his body. He awoke with a start, wondering if he had dreamt his flight, yet he could still see the burning eyes of the Knight.

He sat up. In the opposite corner lay Elodan, fast asleep; Gwydion still sat at the table, staring into a goblet. Lámfhada rose.

'Can you not sleep?' asked the Healer.

'May I speak with you, sir?'

'Why not? There is little else to occupy us.'

'I have found my Colour.'

Gwydion's eyes sparkled and he clapped Lámfhada's shoulder. 'That is good. I hope it is Green; the world has need of Healers.'

'It is Gold.'

'There is no Gold, boy. You are still in the Yellow.'

'No, sir. I floated in a golden boat and saw an ancient stag die. I gave it life, and it rose.'

'Pah! What you had was a dream – but it sounds a damn fine one!'

Lámfhada shook his head. 'Wait! Let me try again.' He closed his eyes and reached for the Colours. The Yellow welcomed him, but of the Gold there was no sign.

'Do not be disheartened, lad,' said Gwydion. 'These things take time. What else did you see?'

'I saw a Red Knight floating at the edge of the forest. He gave me a message for Ollathair; he said Cairbre-Pateus sends greetings.'

Gwydion recoiled, the colour draining from his face.

'Do not deliver that message! Do not speak of it. Do not even think of it.'

'I don't understand.'

'And that's as it should be. But trust me, Lámfhada. Say nothing. It was just a dream . . . just a very bad dream.'

Ubadai knelt by the body that lay across the trail. It had six legs and was covered in scaled skin. The jaws were longer than a man's arm, and were rimmed with three rows of teeth.

'I've never seen anything like it,' declared Errin. 'And there's not a wound on it.'

Ubadai placed his hand on the creature's chest. 'All muscle,' he stated. 'No fat; this one freeze to death.'

'They had many strange beasts in the zoo at Furbolg,' said Sheera. 'Perhaps someone was transporting more from the coast and they escaped?'

Ubadai shrugged. 'Maybe. But I grew to manhood on the Steppes, and I never heard of a lizard with six legs. We should find a safe place to camp. The sun goes down – maybe more beasts.'

Warily they stepped around the carcass and continued on up a winding trail. At the top of the hill the path widened and split, one trail leading to the east, the other south. Ubadai sniffed the air. 'That way,' he said, pointing east.

Errin was too tired and cold to argue; he hitched his saddlebags to his left shoulder and walked on. After another quarter of a mile they came to a bend in the trail, and there ahead of them was a small stone-built house nestling against the side of a sheer rock wall.

Before it, on the snow, sat an old man in faded blue robes. His head was bald and round, but a white forked beard grew to his chest.

'Is he dead?' Errin asked, as Ubadai approached the man.

The old man's eyes opened.

'No, I am not dead,' he snapped. 'I was thinking, I was enjoying the solitude.'

'My apologies,' offered Errin, bowing low. 'But are you not cold sitting there?'

'What has my condition to do with you? This is my home and this is my body. If it is cold, that is its own affair.'

'Indeed it is, sir,' agreed Errin, forcing a smile. 'Look, my companions and I are in need of shelter. Could we prevail upon you to allow us to spend the night in your home?'

'I do not like company,' the old man replied.

'Then sit out here in the snow,' said Ubadai. He turned to Errin. 'Why waste time on a stupid old fool? Let's get inside.'

'No!' said Errin. 'We will find a cave or something.'

The old man grinned. 'I have changed my mind,' he announced. 'You may stay. I expect you will want to light a fire. There is no wood and you will need to gather some. I believe there is an old axe inside.'

Ubadai muttered something under his breath and strode into the house, emerging moments later with the weapon. Errin bowed once more to the man sitting in the snow.

'Why did you change your mind?' he asked.

'Because I am capricious by nature. Now go away and let me think.'

Errin and Sheera moved into the dwelling. There was only one large room, neatly laid out with a bed in one corner and a table with two bench seats set in the centre. The hearth was cold and empty, and there was sign of neither cooking utensils nor food of any kind.

'I'll gather some tinder,' said Sheera. Nodding, Errin dumped his saddlebags against a wall. The stone house was colder than death; ice had formed on the northern wall, where water had flowed through a crack in the roof. He walked over to the bed, where a single threadbare blanket was casually laid. There was no mattress, merely a line of wooden slats.

Errin looked around; the room was stark and inhospitable. He walked out into the gathering dusk, skirted the seated figure and joined Sheera in her wood gathering. In the distance they could hear the steady thud of the axe. For some while they gathered what deadwood could be found and carried it into the house. Sheera started a fire, but its warmth took an age to penetrate the grim cold of the dwelling.

Ubadai came in after an hour and threw the axe against the far wall. His face was red and shining with sweat. 'Need help,' he muttered. Errin and Sheera followed him to a clearing where he had cut down a dead tree, and reduced it to manageable chunks and sections. It was dark by the time they had ferried the fuel to the house, and the fire was blazing brightly in the hearth.

The trio sat round the blaze long into the night, and every once in a while Errin would rise, walk to the door and stare out into the moonlight where the old man was still sitting. It had begun to snow. At last Errin went out to where he sat and squatted down in front of him.

'Excuse me, sir.'

The man's dark eyes opened. 'You again? What is it now? You have the house – what more do you want?'

'Are you trying to die?'

'What if I am?'

'I . . . I know that is your own business, but the

house is now warm and I would feel more comfortable if you joined us. Perhaps we could talk. Death is very rarely an answer to anything.'

'Don't be foolish, boy. Death is the final answer to everything. It is the end of every journey; it is peace and an end to strife.'

'Yes,' Errin agreed, 'but it is also an end to laughter and joy, to companionship, to love. And most of all it is an end to dreams and hopes.'

'Ah, yes, but then death holds no terrors for a man *without* dreams and hopes. Has it occurred to you that the more we love, the greater is our sadness? For ultimately all things end. No dream is ever completely fulfilled.'

'Could it not be said the other way around?' offered Errin. 'The greater our sadness, the greater our joy. How can we recognize one without the counter-balance of the other?'

'Answer me this, young debater: if a man loves a woman for forty years, adores her, lives for her, how great is the pain when she dies and leaves him alone? Given the choice to go back and start again, would he not be wise to avoid the first meeting and live his life without love?'

Errin smiled. 'Does a man who lives in winter regret the summer? Would he choose to spend his life in a perennial autumn? The argument is not a good one, sir. Come inside and enjoy the fire.'

'The fire is immaterial, but I will join you.' The old man rose smoothly, brushed the snow from his clothes and followed Errin inside. Sheera was asleep by the fire and Ubadai was sharpening the old axe. He looked up at the old man.

'Not dead yet, then?' said the Nomad.

'Not yet,' the man agreed.

Errin pushed shut the door and walked over to the fire, holding out his hands to the welcoming blaze. He removed his cloak and outer tunic, allowing the heat to wash over him. 'How could you sit there so long?' he asked as the old man sat beside him.

'Feel my hand,' said the stranger. Errin took it and found it was warmer than his own.

'Incredible. How do you do it?'

'He is a wizard,' said Ubadai. 'I could have told you this.'

'Are you a sorcerer, sir?' asked Errin.

'Of a sort. I am the Dagda. But I cast no spells — you are safe here.'

'What form does your magic take?'

'Don't ask!' snapped Ubadai.

'I tell the truth,' the Dagda answered, 'and I see all the spinning colours in the circle of life: the past, the present, and all of the futures.'

'You tell fortunes,' said Errin. 'Could you tell mine?'

'I could, Lord Errin. I could tell you everything that lies in store for you.'

'Then do so, please.'

'No. You see, I like you.' He turned to Ubadai. 'But you I will tell, should you desire it?'

'Pah! Not me. You shamen are all alike. Death, despair, and bad luck. You say nothing to me, old man.'

'Very wise, Ubadai,' said the Dagda, smiling.

'Will you answer me one question?' asked Errin.

'Perhaps.'

'Can the King's evil be defeated?'

'You are sure Ahak is evil?'

'Do you see his deeds as good?' countered Errin.

'We are talking of the man who led the last victorious army and successfully negotiated a peaceful end to the days of empire. We are talking about the King who introduced legal reforms to aid the poor, who set up a special tax so that food could be distributed among the poverty-stricken. And have you forgotten the free medicines for the sick and needy?'

'I have not forgotten,' replied Errin. 'But nor can I forget the massacre of the Nomads, nor the disgusting events now taking place in the capital.'

'And what does that tell you?'

'That the King has become evil.'

'Indeed, Lord Errin, it does. But the important word is *become*. There is something that has entered the realm, corrupting all it touches.'

'I have no knowledge of that,' said Errin softly, 'but from wherever it comes, can it be defeated?'

'The answer must be yes. Most evil springs from the hearts of men. And all men must die – therefore their evil dies with them. But your question was perhaps more specific. Can this evil be destroyed swiftly, by Llaw Gyffes? The answer, as we sit here, is no.'

'But it could change?' pressed Errin.

'There are many futures, and every man has an opportunity to fashion his own. The Colours are shifting, the Harmony gone. But, yes, it could change. You see, the success or failure of your venture depends on the whim of a thief and a murderer.'

'Llaw Gyffes?'

'No. Get some sleep, Lord Errin. In the morning I will be gone. Rest here until you are ready to leave, then travel east. You will find the man you seek.'

'And where will you go?'

'Wherever I choose,' answered the Dagda.

Groundsel found himself strangely reluctant to part with the golden-haired child he had carried from the blizzard, but once the refugees had been found quarters in the stockade an elderly woman approached him, naming herself as the girl's grandmother. The child's name was Evai, and Groundsel felt both pain and gratification as she wept when her grandmother took her to the makeshift huts being erected against the north wall.

He watched from the doorway as the old woman and the child made their way across the snow, waving when Evai looked back. Arian saw him there and joined him.

'It's going to be very crowded here for a while,' she said. 'I think I'll make my way back home.'

'There's another blizzard coming,' he told her, pointing to the lowering sky. 'Two or three days and it should be safe for a journey. Come inside and share a goblet of wine. It's good; ten years old.' Without waiting for a response he moved back into the hall and wandered to a blazing fire. For a moment Arian stood in the doorway, unsure. But she was lonely; Llaw avoided her company and now Nuada was living with the dark-eyed refugee, Kartia. Removing her sheepskin cloak, she went over to the fire, accepting a silver goblet filled with blood-red wine. She sipped it and sat facing Groundsel.

'An old woman like that is no guardian for a child. She may not last the winter,' he said, staring into the dancing flames.

'You would be a better mother?'

His dark eyes swung on her. 'Do not mock me, girl,' he hissed.

She swallowed hard. 'I'm sorry. I did not mean it the way it sounded.'

He shrugged and the anger faded from his gaze. 'Truth in it, though. I couldn't raise a child; I wouldn't know how. But you could.'

'I'll have children of my own, when I'm ready.'

'I don't doubt it; you've the hips for it. But that's not what I meant. You could stay here . . . with me. We could raise the child – and some of our own. There is no better catch for you in the forest. I have everything here. And when I am ready I'll sail for Cithaeron. And, by the gods, I'll be one of the richest men there!'

Arian took a sip of wine, her mind racing. How could this ugly ape believe that she would marry him? The thought of him touching her made her feel ill. Yes, he was strong – and yes, he would undoubtedly become rich with his thieving and slaying. But a partner for life?

'I have no love for you,' she said, at last, bracing herself for his anger. But his response surprised her.

'Love? You believe it is an arrow from Heaven? It is not. I have seen men and women without love living contented lives. Anyway, love is something that grows through companionship. I do not love you, Arian; I desire you.. But that is a beginning. And I know what you see when you look at Groundsel; I am not blind. I am not tall and handsome like Llaw Gyffes, nor a talented wordsmith like Nuada. But I am strong, and I'll still be here when they are long dead.'

'No,' she said, 'I could not marry you. You talk of desire as a beginning. I believe that . . . and I do not desire you. Your wealth does not interest me, nor a life of riches in Cithaeron. I wish I could say this in a manner less hurtful, but I am not clever with words.'

He nodded, his face showing no emotion. Then he smiled. 'For most of my life I was denied all that I desired. When I broke away and came here, I decided that never again would I be denied anything. I have asked for your hand – as a man should. But I will have you, Arian, with or without your consent. So take a few days to think over my proposal.'

'I do not like being threatened,' she said, eyes blazing. 'And if you think to take me, think again. I will kill you.'

'You think you could?'

Suddenly she laughed. 'Take me to your bed, Groundsel, but be careful never to sleep.'

'It might still be worth it,' he told her.

'You'll never know,' she retorted, rising. Sweeping

her cloak over her shoulder, she moved back into the daylight. Snow was falling fast as she trudged towards her hut. As she approached it, she saw two sentries pulling open the main gates and watched as they bowed to an old man in faded robes of dyed blue wool. His head was bald, but a long, forked white beard flowed to his chest. The sentries backed away from him and Arian stood transfixed. The stranger seemed to float over the snow, leaving barely a trace of footsteps. He stopped in the centre of the village and sat down in the snow. One of the sentries ran to him, bringing him bread; other villagers came from their homes and clustered round him. Puzzled by the commotion, Arian strolled over and Llaw Gyffes joined her.

'What is he doing?' asked Arian, as the old man spread out some thirty black stones on the packed snow before him.

Llaw grinned. 'You have heard of him, Arian – now is your chance to see. He is the Dagda. Have you the courage to question him?' She glanced up into his mocking gaze.

'I'll follow you,' she said, but he shook his head.

'I have no wish to know the future, and I've not the skill to question the old man. He knows it all, right up to the moment of every death.'

'He'll freeze sitting there,' she said.

Llaw turned, then tapped Arian's shoulder, pointing to the hall. Groundsel was walking forward bearing a heavy sheepskin cloak. 'It's part of the ritual in any village he stops in – he will wait for the head man to invite him to his quarters. Very few will refuse.'

'Why? Does he curse them?' she asked.

'Worse than that . . . he tells them the truth.'

The crowd parted for Groundsel, who bowed to the Dagda. The old man gathered his black stones, tipping them into a leather pouch; then he rose and accepted the cloak. The crowd followed as Groundsel led the way to the warmth of the hall.

'Would you like to see his skills in action?' asked Llaw. Arian nodded.

Inside the hall a space was cleared by one of the fires and once again the old man squatted down and spread the stones. He looked up at Groundsel, who shook his head. The crowd stirred. Groundsel pointed to Arian, waving her forward. Llaw came with her and they sat before the Dagda.

'You first,' said Arian and Llaw cleared his throat. The Dagda gave a thin smile.

'Pick eight of the stones,' he said, his voice hissing like a wind through the branches of a dead tree. Llaw looked down at them; they were flat and mostly round, obviously gathered from a stream-bed. Slowly he picked his eight, then the old man turned them over one by one, examining the different runes on each. His pale eyes came up.

'Ask me of your life, Llaw Gyffes.'

Llaw swallowed. 'I do not know what to ask, Dagda,' he muttered, reddening.

'Then shall I tell you all?'

'No!' snapped Llaw. 'All men die – I have no wish to know the time and the place. Tell me if we will have a good spring, with game aplenty.'

'The spring will be fine,' said the Dagda, with another thin smile. 'It will come early, and the game will be more than plentiful. But you will have little time to hunt, Llaw Gyffes, for your enemies are gathering. And they will be here as the snows melt.'

'I have no enemies,' stated Llaw.

'Your enemies are terrible: men of awesome evil. They fear you, Llaw; they fear your army and they fear your name. They must destroy you, and they will come to you with bright swords and dark magic.'

'Then I shall leave for Cithaeron. Let them come there.'

'You will never see Cithaeron, Llaw Gyffes.'

'Can I defeat these enemies?'

'All men can suffer defeat. I see two armies. Do you wish to know the outcome?'

'No. Thank you for your counsel.'

The Dagda smiled and turned to Arian. He turned the stones and spread them under his long, bony fingers. She chose her eight and waited.

'Ask, Arian, and I shall enlighten you.'

'Will Llaw win?' she asked. Llaw cursed and pushed himself to his feet, but before he could retreat out of hearing the old man's voice sounded.

'I see him lifeless on the ground before the forest, and a demon stalking the hill: a red demon with a dark sword.'

'You foolish child,' snapped Llaw, his angry eyes fixed on Arian. 'A curse on you!'

He strode from the hall and Groundsel knelt by Arian. 'Ask him about us,' he whispered. Her face white, Arian shook her head. 'I don't want to know any more. I am sorry, Dagda.'

As she tried to rise to follow Llaw, Groundsel held her arm. 'Ask him! I will abide by what he says.'

She shook herself loose and took a deep breath. 'Tell me of Groundsel,' she whispered. The outlaw leader blanched.

'He too will die in the spring. I see a horse, a white horse – and a rider in shining silver. And a child on a hillside. The demons are gathering, and a great storm will descend on the forest. But Groundsel will not see it.'

'What should we do?' Arian asked.

'Whatever you will.'

'Does Llaw have to die?'

'All creatures die. Some die well, others badly.' He

looked up at Groundsel. 'Would you like to hear more, my new Lord Groundsel?'

'I never asked you about me, but for years you've been longing to tell me, you bastard! Well, I'll outlive you. And when this shining silver rider comes to me, I'll kill him too. I do not believe you, Dagda. Nothing is writ in those stones that a strong man cannot change. I will make my own decisions.'

'Indeed you will. Think on that point when you meet the silver rider.' The old man turned his attention to Arian. 'You asked what to do. I do not advise, I merely tell what is. But I see a one-handed swordsman and a Child of Power. I see a Craftsman, a wizard with a burden. All must come together. A balance must be restored.'

Arian left him then and made her way to Llaw's hut, desperate to apologize. She had not meant to ask the question; it had sprung from her concern. Surely he would be able to understand?

But Llaw's hut was empty, his belongings gone. She ran to the gate and climbed the ladder to the rampart. Fresh snow was falling, but she could see his footsteps leading away into the darkness of the forest.

Llaw Gyffes pushed on until an hour before dusk, ploughing his slow way through drifts, down icy slopes and across frozen streams, determined to put as much distance between himself and the Dagda as possible. The man was a grim legend in the forest. None knew where he lived, but stories of his travels claimed he had walked the Forest of the Ocean for more than a century. Some said he was a former Knight, others that he was a priest, but all agreed his words were double-edged. Yet still men and women clamoured to hear of their futures – dark or bright, joy-filled or pain-borne.

At dusk Llaw had a fire going against the fallen

trunk of an old birch. He built a snow wall to the north to shelter him from the bitter wind and settled down to sit out the night.

Damn the girl! Death in the spring . . . lifeless before an army of enemies he had never courted. What unlucky star had he been born under? Which god had he offended to have his life so ruined? First Lydia – and that blow had been savage – and now a meaningless death.

The stars were bright, the temperature dropping as Llaw built up the fire and gathered his cloak around him. A whisper of movement came from the undergrowth and he drew his axe from his belt and swung his head. Sitting some fifteen feet from the fire, and gazing at him with baleful eyes, was a huge grey wolf. In the light from the blaze Llaw could see that his muzzle was white; he was old, and cast from the pack. From the size of the scarred shoulders Llaw guessed he had once been the leader of the pack; but like all creatures age had withered his strength and a younger male had forced him aside. Llaw reached into his pack, pulling out a section of dried beef which he tossed to the wolf. The beast ignored it. Llaw looked away and added more wood to the blaze. When he looked back the meat was gone, but the wolf still sat.

'Proud, are you?' said Llaw. 'No bad thing, in man or beast.' He tossed another chunk of meat, this time a little closer. Once more the wolf waited until he looked away before scooping the meat into its jaws. There were few recorded instances of wolves attacking men, and Llaw was not worried about his ability to kill the beast. His axe was sharp, his arm strong. But he was glad of the company. 'Come, Grey One. Enjoy the fire.'

Another piece of beef landed before the wolf, but to his right, bringing him closer to the warmth. As he moved to the morsel Llaw saw the marks of recent combat on the gnarled shoulders, jagged fang marks deep along the flank. An old scar could still be seen on his right hind leg, causing him to limp. 'You won't survive the winter, Grey One. Even a tired rabbit could outrun you, and you'll bring down no stags. Best you stay with me for a while.' The wolf settled down on his haunches, grateful for the heat and his first meal in ten days.

The wound on his hind leg had been caused in the summer when a huge brown bear had attacked his mate. He had charged the beast and leapt for his throat, but the thick fur had prevented his fangs from sinking home and a swipe from the bear's talons had opened a long wound in his side. His mate had died, and his own wound had been long in the healing. When the pack had gathered for the winter the challenges had come, as they always did, but he had neither the strength nor the will to withstand them. They had driven him from them many days ago.

He had lived on carrion and the leavings of other carnivores. Then with his strength almost gone he had smelt the man and had been gathering himself to attack him. Now he was unsure . . . but the meat was good, the fire warm. He settled down warily, his yellow eyes fixed on the man, his hunger now less keen.

Llaw delved into his pack; there were three more pieces of meat. He pulled two of them clear and bit into one. The wolf's head came up and he threw the second piece to it. This time the animal ate it at once.

Adding fresh wood, Llaw settled down beside the fire. He did not fear an attack from the wolf. How could he? Did not the Dagda say he had until the spring?

He slept without dreams and awoke in the chill of the morning. The fire had died down to glowing embers and the wolf had gone. Llaw felt a sense of loss. He sat up, shivered and stoked the fire to life, adding twigs he had gathered the previous afternoon. Then he took a copper pot from his pack and filled it with snow, placing it at the edge of the fire. As the snow melted, he added fresh handfuls until the pot was half full with water. Into this he mixed some dried oats, stirring with a stick until it thickened.

The words of the Dagda haunted him still. His enemies were gathering, and he could not avoid them. That left the former blacksmith only one option. He would attempt what the legends said he had already achieved. He would build an army. He would take the war to them.

But how? How could a blacksmith raise such a force?

He chuckled, 'Start with one, Llaw. Find one man . . . then another. The forest is full of rebels.' His thoughts went to Elodan, the former Knight. He at least was versed in the ways of war. And the wizard who had helped Lamfhada, he too could be a help. Llaw ate the hot oats, doused the fire and set off to the east.

13

The Duke was mildly drunk as he sat on the ramparts gazing out over the snow-covered countryside. An iron brazier had been set up beside him, but the glowing coals barely countered the freezing wind.

Far in the distance he could just make out the black line of the forest, and beyond it he could picture the sea and the trade route to Cithaeron. The dawn sky was clear and the doves were waking around the tower, wheeling and diving. The Duke shivered and held out his hands to the coals.

Three days ago he had still nursed hopes of riding the storm of the new age. But then the King had arrived, with a thousand riders. The audience had been short, and when the Duke was summoned to his own hall there had been Okessa sitting at the King's right. And flanking the throne were the eight demonic Red Knights. The Duke had bowed low.

'This is a troublesome Duchy,' said Ahak, Lord of the Realm, Captain of Ten Thousand Lances. The Duke looked up into his red-rimmed eyes and could find no words; the shock of the King's appearance, white-haired and grey of face, unnerved him. 'Well? Have you nothing to say, kinsman?'

'I am . . . heartbroken that you are distressed, my liege. Perhaps the reports have been unnecessarily alarming. We have identified all of Nomad birth, our taxes are collected and have been despatched to Furbolg. Where is the problem?'

Ahak shook his head and turned to Okessa. 'Where is the problem, he asks. Is he slow-witted?' Okessa shrugged and smiled and the King swung on the Duke.

'Where? Is this not the castle from which the rebel Llaw Gyffes made his escape, to form his rebellious army in that cursed forest? Is this not the Duchy that saw your own Lord of the Feast – a man you recommended should supervise *my* visit, and attend *my* person – turn traitor?' Okessa leaned towards the King and whispered something in his ear. 'Ah, yes,' hissed Ahak. 'And what of this wizard Ollathair, who was allowed to escape? And you do not see where the problem lies?'

'My liege, I cannot dispute we have suffered . . . misfortunes. But the man Llaw Gyffes was just a black-smith who killed his wife. And yes, he escaped. But of the men who escaped with him, all but a mere handful were recaptured. And as for Errin, I blame the Lord Okessa for provoking him at the Council. The man was concerned about a woman he loved.'

'A Nomad bitch! Who knows what foul treason they would have plotted? I am displeased with you, kinsman. But I will consider what action to take when I have studied your Duchy at close quarters. Go now.'

Dismissed from his own hall, he had not been summoned to the King's presence since then. But he had seen others who were. Two nights ago three young women from the village had been led into the courtyard by one of Okessa's servants. An hour later, as the Duke lay in bed unable to sleep, he had heard a terrible scream. The girls had not been seen since that night, but the Duke had watched as three sacks were carried from the royal quarters, their contents buried behind the stables. The Duke had slipped out into the court-yard an hour later and found the fresh-turned earth. Digging his fingers into the ground, he had come up with a small skull which he hastily reburied.

The following morning he had ordered his horse saddled for his usual ride across the hills, but was informed by his captain that the Lord Okessa had requested the Duke's presence *within* the castle, in case the King should have need to call on him.

He was a prisoner in his own fortress, guarded by his own troops.

It was barely credible but then neither was the change in Ahak. The Duke had always known the King was a ruthless man. Six years ago the rumours had been strong that he ordered the poisoning of his uncle, the previous monarch, but in those days Ahak had been a powerhouse of physical strength, young and in his prime – his hair was raven-black, his eyes clear. Once, at a feast, he had lifted a twenty-gallon barrel of wine over his head and held it there for ten heart-beats. Now he was a shadow of the man he had been. And yet, how old could he be? Thirty-three? Thirty-four? Certainly no more.

As the coals in the brazier died down, the Duke returned to his quarters. His servants brought him hot water and, with the aid of a silver mirror, he shaved carefully around his thin beard, noting the grey hairs that were beginning to appear at his temples.

His face was lean and strong, the eyes deep and set close together above a curved nose. Not handsome, he knew, but powerful. He put down the mirror and rubbed at his face with a warmed towel.

Rebels in the forest! He wished to Hell there was a rebel army ready to sweep down. But all his spies informed him that the legend of Llaw Gyffes was exactly that: a fable. He smiled ruefully. Even if the legend were true, and the army swept into Mactha, he would still be a prisoner. He was a hated man; it was a lesson his father had taught him.

'A man can rule using either love or fear,' he had said. 'But fear is stronger.' And his words had been proved true. But now, as the Duke waited for news of his fate, he knew there was not a man in Mactha who would assist him and few tears would be shed when his blood ran.

'Breakfast, my Lord?' asked a slave-girl, whose name the Duke did not know.

'No.' He looked at the girl. She was young, dark and pretty. He knew he had bedded her at some time in the winter, but could not remember much of the event. He wandered to his bedroom. He was glad he had never married; he had planned to, of course, in order to sire an heir, but had decided to wait until he was fifty. At least now he would not have the worry of a family waiting to share his fate.

Hearing the thunder of hooves from the courtyard, he walked to the window. Five hundred of the King's black-cloaked riders were galloping from the castle and he watched them for a while as they headed for the forest.

He summoned his captain. 'Where are they going?' he asked.

'I understand the King has commanded them to enter the forest and ascertain the strength of Llaw Gyffes' army.'

'There is no army,' snapped the Duke. 'They will find a few settlements, and they will rape and kill. Gods! The world has gone mad.' The man said nothing.

The Duke waved him away. 'Go,' he said. 'Go and report what I have said; I don't doubt Okessa will reward you.'

The man bowed, moved back and closed the door.

The Duke heard the key turn in the lock . . .

Manannan pushed back the sheets, lifted the girl's arm from his chest and rolled from the bed. He poured himself a goblet of the golden Ambria and watched the sun rise in glory over the mountains. Strength flowed through him and he swung round to see the girl awake; she smiled at him and sat up.

'How are you feeling, Lord Knight?'

He chuckled and returned to the bed, stroking her shoulder and pushing back the long, flowing hair to kiss her neck. Her skin was ivory pale, her body soft. Arousal swamped him . . .

An hour later he watched her leave and lay back on the bed. Sunlight streamed through the open window, bathing his body, and the music of songbirds came floating from the perfumed gardens below.

Manannan drank more of the elixir, then bathed and dressed in robes of blue silk. Wandering to the terraced garden, he strolled there among the blooms and the flowering trees. He found a small group of poets sitting among the camellias, arguing gently with a number of artists on the question of beauty. For a while he listened, but the sound of distant music lured him to a pavilion where women were dancing.

And the sun shone with incredible brightness.

Ollathair had been right. The tunnel beyond the Black Gate was a nightmare to chill a man's soul: glittering eyes in the darkness, the sweat of terror upon his brow. But beyond it was a land of surpassing beauty and a city the like of which Manannan had never seen. White stone buildings towered over the landscape, wondrous statues lined the streets, and there were gardens everywhere, and woods of flowering trees.

He had been met at the city gates by Paulus, a poet and a Magister. The man, tall and white-haired, had bowed low.

'Welcome at last, Manannan. It is a blessing for us that you have come.'

'You know me?' he had asked, dismounting.

'Know you, my dear man? Samildanach has talked of nothing else. Welcome indeed! He will be delighted to hear of your arrival.'

'He is here? Alive?'

'Not here,' said Paulus, smiling. 'But yes, he is very much alive – as are all your comrades. They chose to remain among the Vyre and help us in our troubles. But you are tired from your travels. Follow me to my home; there you can bathe and take refreshment.'

The Magister's home was a palace of exquisite beauty, marble-fronted and surrounded by terraced gardens. Young women came out to greet them and Manannan allowed Kuan to be led away to the stables beyond the gardens.

'You have many slaves,' he said to Paulus as they walked inside.

'Not slaves, helpers. Servants, if you like.' He led the Once-Knight to a suite of rooms and gave him his first goblet of Ambria. As he drank it, Manannan felt strength surge through his limbs.

'What is it?' he asked, astonished.

'It is the bedrock of our civilization. It is life, Manannan. Drink of this and you will never have need of medicine, neither will you age.'

Samildanach and the other Knights were away in the north, he was told, but they would return in about a month. At first Manannan was concerned, and restless. Could he not ride out to meet them? Paulus agreed that he could, but advised him to rest for a few days, gather his strength, and then he would supply a guide. But the days passed and Manannan grew to love the white-towered city. There was something about it that opened his soul: the problems of the Realm seemed so far away, and the world he had left behind so remote and petty.

He bathed in scented water and found no need of food – one drink and his strength returned in seconds. The people here were gentle, and he spent several days roaming the libraries and museums, studying the customs of the Vyre. They were not a warrior race, though once – according to the histories – they had boasted great armies. Now they employed a mercenary force to patrol their borders, but there was little trouble with neighbouring lands.

'Where is Samildanach?' he asked Paulus on the fourth day of his stay.

'He is helping to rescue some people from your own troubled land. Nomads, I believe they are called. He has opened a Gate for them to allow them to settle in our land.'

'That is kind of you.'

'It is not just kindness, Manannan. We have suffered terrible plagues here during the last thirty years, and there are few people left to till the earth or supply our needs. The land needs new blood. There are some two thousand Nomads settled already in the north. Perhaps when Samildanach returns, you can visit the new towns they are building.'

On the fifth day Manannan had been ill at ease. He felt strong as a lion, but on edge. He spoke of his feeling to Paulus, who smiled and clapped him on the shoulder. 'You must understand,' said the Magister, 'that the Ambria is working inside you, rebuilding your body, making it stronger than it has ever been. It is also making you more aware of your body. What you need is a companion for your bed.'

'I am pledged to celibacy,' Manannan had told him.

'Truly? For what purpose? Man was intended to mate. Trust me, Manannan.'

He had sent Draya to him that night, and she was divine to look at as well as being bright, witty and charming. Together they had finished a pitcher of Ambria and made love throughout the night. And Paulus was right. The tension in Manannan was gone; he felt smooth and relaxed, at one with this new world. After Draya he had enjoyed Senlis, Marin and others whose names he could not now remember.

The joy of it all was almost too hard to bear.

The City of the Vyre was close to Manannan's view of Paradise. It had everything except an all-powerful god and, truth be told, that made it somehow even better than Paradise. There were no judges here; the only law seemed to be Joy.

And the days passed. Manannan read the Books of the Vyre, learned their poetry, viewed their painting and sculpture, made love to their women. The Once-Knight was content for the first time in his life.

Soon Samildanach would return and they would ride to the rescue of Ollathair, put the Realm to rights, and then return here to enjoy the rewards of the blessed.

On the sixteenth evening Manannan fell asleep with these dreams in his mind. He awoke in the middle of the night, shivering and cold, and reached for his Ambria only to find the pitcher empty. He swore and rose – he was sure it had been half full when he fell asleep, but Paulus would have more. As he stood, he saw a figure sitting in the chair by the window – her back to the moonlight, her face in shadow.

'Who are you?' he asked. 'Never mind. Just let me get a drink and I will talk to you.'

'You need a drink to be able to talk?' she responded, her voice low and deep. Something stirred in Manannan's memory, but it danced like morning mist, dispersing as he reached for it.

'No, of course not. But I am cold.' He moved toward the door.

'Then put a blanket around your shoulders. You look foolish standing there naked, holding that pitcher.'

'Who are you?'

'I am a friend, Manannan. The only friend you have here.'

'Nonsense. I have made more friends here than in all my life.'

'Come,' she said. 'Sit and talk.'

'I need a drink.'

'There is fresh water,' she offered.

'I don't need water,' he snapped.

'No,' she admitted, 'you need Ambria. You need the Nectar of the Gods. Is it too late for you, Manannan?'

'Do not speak in riddles, woman. I have no time for this; I did not ask you here.'

'You did not. Nor did I ask to be here in this cursed city. But such is the game of life. You are a Knight of the Gabala and once that meant something to the world. Only the strongest, the noblest could dream of donning the silver armour. Are you strong, Manannan?'

'I have never been stronger.'

'Then let me set you a task – not a difficult task. Sit here with me until the dawn – do not leave this room until the sun rises. Is that too difficult, sir Knight?'

'What a ridiculous question. Of course it would not be difficult, but I have no wish to play this game. Now leave me in peace.'

'The call of the Ambria is strong, is it not? I know. I cannot resist it. For me it has been too long, and no one warned me of its terrible properties.'

Manannan hurled the pitcher aside. 'Damn you, woman, does your prattle never end?' He stormed across to her and dragged her to her feet. It was then that she turned towards him and the moonlight fell upon her face. Manannan recoiled as if struck. 'Morrigan? Dear Gods, Morrigan?'

'I am grateful that you remember me.'

'How did you come here?'

'Samildanach brought me. Ten days after you . . . they . . . passed the Black Gate. He came to me in the night, took me in his arms and told me he loved me. He said he would show me Paradise.' She laughed grimly. 'Instead we came here.'

'But . . . this is not an evil place.'

'Because they are cultured and have treated you well? They have done a terrible thing to you, Manannan.'

'Not so. I am strong, and I am happy. What terrible thing is that?'

'And why did you come?'

'To find Samildanach.'

'In order to return home?'

'Yes.'

'To combat the evil in the realm caused by the King and his Red Knights?'

'Yes.'

Morrigan sat down and stared out over the moonlit garden, silent for a while. Then she looked up at Manannan. 'The Red Knights are led by Samildanach. They are your friends, my dear; they are the Knights of the Gabala.'

'I do not believe it. Paulus says they are in the north, resettling Nomads.'

'Indeed they are . . . or they were. But you have not heard it all yet, Manannan. The Nomads are coming here in their thousands . . . but not to till the land. They are the Ambria . . . they are the food for the Vyre. That is what we are here, Drinkers of Souls. That is immortality, Manannan. We suck the essence of life itself from other human beings. We are not immortal, we are merely Undead. That is the drink you lust after – if you still want it. Go and find it.'

'You are lying. It cannot be as you say. It cannot.'

'I want you to try to remember the man you were when you rode here – the dreams that you had. Think back to all you held dear. Think of me as I once was. You have been corrupted, even as Samildanach and the others were corrupted – great men, noble men, who now spend their days gathering human souls for Paulus and the Vyre. *Look* at me, Manannan!'

260

Suddenly she rose, gripped him by the shoulders and bared her teeth.

As he watched, her incisors lengthened into fangs, pointed and hollow. He thrust her from him.

'Can you not see?' she screamed.

'Get away from me! You are a demon – you are not Morrigan at all. Begone!'

'It is too late for you, Manannan,' she whispered as she moved past him to the door. 'I am so sorry.'

'Wait!' he called, as she moved into the doorway. 'Please, Morrigan.' She turned. He was sweating now and beginning to feel nauseous. Taking a deep breath he walked back to the window, sitting down on the sill and breathing deeply of the scented air. She came back into the room, pushing the door closed behind her.

'I cannot believe you,' he said softly, 'but I will listen. And I will accept your challenge to sit out the night.'

She nodded and sat facing him in the moonlight. Her face was pale, and there were silver streaks in her long golden hair, but her eyes were as he remembered – large, dark and almost slanted.

'Samildanach brought me through the Black Gate. Everywhere there were monsters, demons, but he held them at bay with his silver sword and we rode for the city. I could not believe its beauty, and was astonished at the greeting we received. Paulus and several others opened up their homes to the Knights. They fed us Ambria, and we were happy. Never before, or since, have I tasted such happiness. And we changed, Manannan, even as you are changing. I tried to stop drinking the Ambria, but I could not. It fastens to the soul, corrupting . . . distorting. New realities appeared and we learnt that the Vyre were dying, their food sources disappearing. Soon there would be no Ambria.'

Manannan leaned forward. 'How did this happen? Are there not people in this land?'

She smiled. 'The half pitcher you had when I came here would have cost maybe fifty lives. This is a large city, Manannan. To feed it would take a nation of – shall we say – lesser beings? Hence the Nomads. Samildanach and the others returned to the realm, taking with them Ambria for the King. They had new armour then, the magical garb of the Elder Vyre, the warrior race who first conquered this land. They were greeted well and the King took them to his counsel. But the Ambria ran out and the King learned – as did Samildanach – how to draw life from living victims.'

'That is what is so hard to believe,' said Manannan. 'He was always the most noble of men.' He clutched his stomach and groaned. 'Where did you put the Ambria? I just need a mouthful; I will be fine then.'

'Wait! Be strong. You will see. Breathe deeply, Manannan.'

'I cannot. The smell from the garden is too sickly.'

'That is what I am saying. The Ambria shifts perceptions. Look around at the room.' He did as she bade him. The white walls seemed greyer now, and he noticed mould above the window. The silken sheets on the bed were filthy and soiled and the room smelt of decay. He turned back to Morrigan to see that her pale ivory skin was dry, her eyes dull, her lips tinged with blue.

He swallowed hard. 'But is this real? I don't know any more.'

'It is real,' she whispered. 'You are living in the City of the Undead. You are in Hell, Manannan. Samildanach almost saw it, but the Ambria took him.'

Manannan looked out into the garden, where the rockery steps were choked with weeds. He staggered to his feet. 'Is there any water?'

'Yes,' she said, fetching him a pitcher from the outer room. 'But be careful; it will not taste good to you for the Ambria is jealous.' He drank deeply, and choked. 'Have some more,' she urged him. 'It will do you good.'

His stomach rebelled, but he forced down the water. 'We must get out,' he said, 'back to the Gate.'

'I would not know how to open it,' she told him, 'but Paulus would.'

He groaned again. 'What is happening to me? There is such pain.'

'You were becoming one of us. Now your body – your life – is fighting back.'

His head dropped and he rubbed at his eyes. 'Why are you doing this for me? How is it that you are not affected by the Ambria?'

She laughed and rose. 'Not affected, Manannan? Oh, but I am. I drank your half pitcher. When I look around this room I see only beauty – and a man I desire. But I can remember how I felt when first I came here . . . when Samildanach was a god to me. I cling to that memory and I do not want to see you – my oldest and dearest friend – riding out to gather souls for the Vyre.'

'Help me to dress.' He looked around, searching the room. 'Where is my armour?'

'You will need no armour where you are going,' said Paulus from the doorway. Beyond him were several warriors in black armour, helms down, swords in their hands. 'We offered you immortality, Manannan. Now you will merely aid our own.'

The warriors surged forward to pin the arms of the Once-Knight.

Paulus shook his head. 'Such a pity. I thought you were strong like your brothers. But no – even a fallen woman can turn your head from the glories of what could have been for you. Your stupidity offends me. Take him away!'

14

Nuada was surprised when the Dagda summoned him, following the poet's evening performance in the hall. The old man had been allocated quarters close to the hut Nuada shared with the girl, Kartia, and a sentry had come to them just before midnight.

'I don't think you should go,' Kartia told Nuada, taking him by the arm. 'He is a demonic man, and the Lord Groundsel says he never gives good news.'

Nuada shrugged. 'I have met very few genuine seers; I cannot pass this by. But I will ask him no questions of death. Do not fear for me, Kartia.' He smiled at her and kissed her cheek. 'I will return soon.'

He walked out into the cold night air and glanced up at the shining stars. Shivering in the chill, he drew his cloak about him. The sentry pointed to an open doorway, through which he could see the amber glow of a brazier. He stepped inside to see the Dagda sitting cross-legged on a goatskin rug, his eyes closed and his hands spread. Nuada cleared his throat and tapped on the door frame.

'Enter, poet. Be at ease,' said the Dagda, opening his eyes and Nuada pushed the door closed. There were no chairs, nor furniture of any kind, so he sat on the rug next to the old man. 'Is there anything you would ask me?' queried the Dagda.

Nuada grinned. 'Nothing, sir. I have no wish to learn the day of my death.'

'Then why did you obey my summons?' the Dagda asked, his dark eyes fixing Nuada with a piercing gaze.

'To learn of you, sir. I would guess there is a song in your travels and I would be delighted to sing it.'

'Some matters are not suited to song, my boy, and some lives are better left to mystery and magic. But you intrigue me. Are you aware of the Colours?'

'Of course,' Nuada replied, 'though I have no special skill with them. Why do you ask?'

The old man stroked his forked white beard, then rose and added wood to the fire in the brazier. Nuada watched him closely. He seemed older than time, yet his movements were smooth, almost liquid. His hands were slender, yet strong, and there were no liver spots upon their backs.

'The Colours,' said the Dagda, returning to sit before the poet, 'are created of Harmony. We all add, or subtract, to and from the Colours. Even as we talk, the Red is growing stronger over the realm of the Gabala. Everywhere the more vile of emotions predominate. Lust, greed, selfishness rule in Furbolg. Of care and compassion there is little to be seen. How strange then that, in this forest peopled by evil men, the Red should hold little sway. What answer can you offer for this?'

'I have no answers,' Nuada told him. 'I am a saga poet; I merely re-tell stories.'

'Can you see Colours in men?' asked the Dagda suddenly. 'Can you look into a man's eyes and know his soul?'

'No. I take it you can?'

The Dagda grinned. 'Yes, I can. It is both a curse and a gift. I was here last year, in this pit of a settlement. The Red was everywhere. Now it is vanished and the White holds sway here now. Only just, mind. Do you know why?'

'You keep asking me the same question. I can answer it no other way.'

'You are the answer, poet. I watched you tonight, filling their heads with nobility and strength – none more so than the sewer-rat Groundsel. You are the stone that falls into the centre of the lake, sending ripples out into the farthest corners. Now that is a gift worth having.'

'You are beginning to lose me,' said Nuada. 'Are you saying my stories change men's hearts? I cannot believe that. I accept that I can – for a short time – suspend their disbelief. But in the morning, when they wake, I am just a part of the previous night's entertainment.'

'Not so, Nuada. A man is a complex beast and his soul is like a sponge, drawing in emotions in a random manner. Strike him and he becomes angry, his soul Red as blood. Feed him, stroke him, make love to him – and his soul softens, blurs, changes. You fill them with glory, make them all believe they can be better, stronger. You force them to draw in the power of the White.'

Nuada thought for a moment. 'Is that bad? Is it wrong?'

'Not at all; it is close to holiness. A man is what he knows. But his soul will yearn for all that he does not know, for hidden there is all he may become.'

'I take it, sir,' said Nuada uneasily, 'that there is a point to this conversation, and you have yet to make it?'

'There is, and I have. You have many choices, Nuada. I cannot tell you that which you fear; I do not know. It happens with perhaps one man in a thousand. You could live for fifty more years, or you could die in a few days. All depends on the choices you make. But you are a man of power, and this will mean you will draw evil to you. It cannot be avoided. The King is insane; he has summoned his army and is determined to enter this forest and destroy all who live here.'

'Why? There is nothing here – no wealth, no army, and surely no threat.'

'There is a threat here: it is you. As we speak, the King sits in Mactha with his advisers. They turn their eyes to the Forest of the Ocean and they see the Power of the White and the Green. The Red is beaten back . . . their Colour, their strength. They cannot tolerate it. They wonder, as wonder they must, how long it will be before the White pushes back.'

'Are you saying the King and his Knights are right to fear a poet? That is madness.'

'Did I not say he was insane? All evil men are insane, Nuada. The question is – and here is the point – what will you do?'

'Do? What *is* there for me to do? I will tell my stories and move on. In the spring I shall be in Cithaeron.'

The Dagda nodded. 'That is a good choice. You will live long and happily there and breed fine sons.'

'That is good to know, but I see by your eyes you are disappointed.'

'Not at all,' replied the Dagda sharply. 'There is nothing in the world of men to surprise or disappoint. When you go, the White will wither and the Red will gain sway. Many will die – and die horribly. The Forest will become a charnel-house.'

'And if I stay, all will be peace and harmony? I think not, Dagda.'

'You are correct. But there will at least be balance in the contest. And the White could win – with your help.'

'Do I still live for fifty years and breed fine sons?'

The Dagda was silent and Nuada chuckled without humour. 'I thought not. It is not fair of you to put this pressure upon me; I have done nothing to harm you.'

'On the contrary, young man, you have done much to please me. It was not entirely true to say that there is nothing in the world to surprise me. I wander this forest and I see the brutality, the cruelty of Man. It is more than pleasant to see Groundsel behave like a hero; to see him care for a golden-haired child. You have been good for him; he will die well for you.'

'I do not want anyone to die for me – least of all Groundsel. Gods, I even like the little man!'

'And why not?' offered the Dagda. 'There is now much to like.'

'Are you advising me to stay? Are you telling me it is my duty to stand against the King and his Red Knights?'

'It is not for me to instruct you in the ways of duty, Nuada. You are a man – a good man. I am here to tell you the choices you face . . . no more than that. I will not judge you if you decide to make a life in Cithaeron.'

'No, you have merely made sure that I will judge myself. Do not play with words, old man. Tell me what can be done to aid the White?'

'The Knights of the Gabala must ride again.'

'No one knows where they are.'

'They are with the King,' said the Dagda. 'They are his Red Slayers, his Drinkers of Souls. They are Vampyres, Nuada.'

'Then how can they ride again on the side of the White?'

'They cannot. They are corrupted by the evil they sought to destroy.'

'Spare me the riddles then!' stormed Nuada. 'How can the Knights ride again?'

'There must be new Knights to restore the balance. Even more than this, they must reflect the old Knights. We had eight good men who turned to evil; you must help to find eight men who can become good. Seek out a man called Ruad Ro-fhessa. He is the Armourer; he will advise.'

'Where shall I find him? And how many Knights are there in this forest?'

'There is one Lord here – you gave him the title yourself.'

'Groundsel? You think Groundsel would become a Knight of the Gabala?'

'He can be the first, Nuada. The first of your Knights of Dark Renown.'

Ruad was walking alone in the high meadows when Lámfhada came up to him. The youth stood back for a while, waiting for Ruad to acknowledge him. The Craftsman cleared snow from a boulder and sat, removing his bronze eye-patch and rubbing at the withered skin of the socket beneath. 'It itches badly, boy,' he said, gesturing Lámfhada forward. He forced a smile. 'What troubles you, lad? When I awoke this morning, old Gwydion seemed ill at ease? Was it something you said?'

Lámfhada nodded. 'I have been awake most of the night. Gwydion told me I had a nightmare, but I believe I have found my Colour. It is Gold, Ruad. It is all the Colours woven together.'

'Tell me of it,' said the wizard gravely. Lámfhada explained about his first flight as a child, when he had seen the Knights ride through the Black Gate and had destroyed the wolf creature with a blast of golden lightning. Then he spoke of soaring over the Forest of the Ocean on a disc of gold and scattering the wolf pack, and reviving the stag. But he could not yet bring himself to talk of the Knight, Pateus. Ruad listened in silence until the youth had finished his story.

'I knew you had power, my boy. I could sense it in you. And I still recall how the falling feathers of your bird reversed their flight. The talent was buried deep within you; it still is. But it will surface again, and next time it will be stronger. Bear with it. Such power is not granted without reason. You will have need of it.'

Lámfhada stood and looked away. 'I am not wise, Ruad. I do not *know* whether to speak. When I told Gwydion of my flight, and what happened, he grew upset and urged me not to tell you. But I think he was wrong. I hope you will not be angry – but I left something out of my tale.' And slowly, falteringly, Lámfhada explained about the Red Knight, watching with growing apprehension as the colour faded from Ruad's face.

'Pateus? He said his name was Pateus?'

'Yes, sir. Cairbre-Pateus. Who is he?'

'He is a Knight of the Gabala, the eldest of my Knights. He is the sin of pride returned to haunt me.' Ruad saw the fear in Lámfhada's face. 'No, no, boy, do not be frightened. You were right and Gwydion was wrong – very wrong. Some time ago, before I came to this forest, I saw a vision of eight Red Knights. Deep down I knew who they were, and I knew who led them. But I would not face my fears.'

'What happened to them?' asked Lámfhada, returning to sit beside the Craftsman.

'They lost. Simply that. They found evil and it conquered them.'

'How could that be? They were the greatest of Knights.'

'I have no answers, save that evil rarely stalks the land with horns and fire. If it did so, all men would turn from it. Take me, Lámfhada . . . I sent nine good men into an unknown realm, filled with terrible dangers. Was that a good deed? I did it not for the world, but for my own glory. I tell myself it was not evil, but great evil has come from it. Do you wish to debate that with me?'

'I am no debater, sir. But I see no evil in you.'

'No? But then had you known Samildanach, or Pateus, or Manannan, you would have said the same.'

'What can you do, Ruad? Are they as strong as before?'

'If Pateus can now fly the Colours, he is stronger than ever he was. And only the Source knows how

270

powerful Samildanach has become. I need to think, Lámfhada – best that you leave me for a while.'

The youth stood for a moment, wishing he could say something . . . do something to help the man who had befriended him. But there was nothing and he turned sadly away. At the bottom of the hill he found Elodan hurling stones at a target chalked on a tree. None of the missiles came close to the target and his throwing stance was disjointed and awkward.

'A pox on it!' snapped Elodan. Then he saw Lámfhada and grinned. 'Never give up, boy, that's the answer. It's what separates men from the beasts of the herd. The problem is threefold, you see. A man is right-sided or left-sided – eye, hand and leg. I am trying to change the focus of my being: to become left-sided, if you will.'

'Is that possible?'

'I doubt it, but I will continue my efforts until my dying day. I can do no more. I will not sit in some hut until my hair turns silver, dreaming of what once I was. Come, let us find some food.' He glanced at Lámfhada. 'What is wrong, boy?'

The youth told him of his conversation with Ruad and Elodan sighed. 'That is grim news. I knew Samildanach. What a swordsman! It is hard to believe.'

'Ruad says evil is not always ugly, but I'm not sure I understand what he meant.'

'I'll explain it to you, but first we'll eat,' said Elodan as they returned to the cabin, where the three golden hounds sat like statues. Gwydion was absent when they arrived and they prepared a meal of cold meat and cheese, washed down with cool spring water. Then Elodan stoked up the fire and sat facing the blond youth.

'A long time ago, when I was young, I saw a woman who fired my blood. I met her in the King's Park; she and her servants used to gather flowers there. She was beautiful, but she was married to a nobleman twice her age, and very unhappy. We met by chance, and then by design. I fell in love with her – hopelessly, completely. I dreamed of taking her away to my estates in the north, raising a family. But it could not be – not while her husband lived. I grew to hate him – though there was nothing to hate. By his lights, he was a good man. But I would fall asleep at night dreaming of his death. It could not be right, I decided, that someone so young and beautiful should be saddled with such a husband. Anyway, one day I told a friend of mine to whisper my name to the man, and to tell him I was seeing his wife in secret. The husband had no choice then but to challenge me to single combat. He was old, but still canny. But his years betrayed him – and I slew him. And that was an evil deed.'

Lámfhada swallowed hard. 'But what of the woman?'

'She inherited his wealth – and married her lover. I was merely the instrument of her freedom. But I believed I was doing right; I had convinced myself he was evil and cruel. Self-deception, Lámfhada! That is why I stood for Kester against the King. Her husband was Kester's son. You understand now something of what Ruad meant?'

'I'm not sure. There are stories of terrible deeds in Furbolg, of Nomad families being massacred. How can the men responsible not see that as evil? It is not the same as being in love with a beautiful woman and fighting a duel.'

Elodan shrugged. 'We were talking of self-deception. Samildanach loved the Realm the way most men love a woman. If he came to believe that the Nomads were responsible for the nation's fall from power, I would guess he could come to hate them. But I cannot answer for him.'

'They believe Llaw Gyffes has an army and they are

coming here in the spring. I think it will be terrible when they arrive.'

Elodan nodded and gazed down at the stump at his wrist. 'Even were I not crippled, I could not stand against the Gabala Knights. Cairbre took me as simply as I took the husband. Damn Llaw Gyffes!' Elodan pushed himself to his feet. 'I need to return to my work. I will see you later.'

Lámfhada watched him go, then cleared away the plates and cleaned them behind the cabin. Glancing up, he saw a stag in the distance. Suddenly its head came up and it sprinted for cover. Lámfhada scanned the countryside, looking for sign of wolves . . .

And saw the five hundred black-cloaked riders silhouetted against the skyline.

As the riders thundered across the half-mile of snow-covered meadows, Lámfhada raced back into the village shouting at the top of his voice. People streamed from the huts, saw the raiders and began to run for the shelter of the trees. Elodan gathered up a hatchet and joined Lámfhada.

'Get to Ruad. He must not be taken,' said the crippled warrior.

'What will you do?'

'I'll stay with the stragglers.' Some of the men had armed themselves with bows and knives and Elodan bellowed at them to make for the trees: 'Stay together and form a line at the top of the hill.' There were fourteen bowmen in the party, including Brion, the husband of Ahmta.

'Why are they attacking us?' Brion asked, as they ran. 'There's nothing here for them.'

'Ask them when they get here,' snapped Elodan.

The raiders, swords drawn, galloped into the village. An old man – slower than the other refugees – was the first to be caught as a lance took him high in the back, lifting him from his feet. For a second or so his legs flapped in the air, then the lance snapped and he tumbled to the ground beneath the pounding hooves. A child ran from a cabin, screaming with fear; her mother, on the hillside above, turned and sprinted back for her. The child was trampled to death, the mother speared.

Then the soldiers were clear of the cabins and heading for the hillside. Elodan formed the bowmen into a line. 'Ignore the riders. Aim for the horses and bring them down. It's the only way to stop the charge. And do not loose the shafts until I order it.'

Longbows were hastily strung and arrows notched to the strings. 'Draw!' bellowed Elodan. The riders were slowing now as the hill took its toll on their mounts, but still they were closing fast. At forty paces, Elodan's raised arm swept down. 'Now!' he shouted. The arrows hammered home at the centre of the line and horses reared and fell. But the wings of the charging line continued forward, sweeping round towards the bowmen. 'Left!' ordered Elodan. The bowmen smoothly notched more shafts and loosed them. Horses tumbled to the snow, hurling their riders to the ground. 'Now to the right!' The horsemen were almost upon them and two of the bowmen broke and ran for the trees. Elodan ignored them as the remaining archers bent their bows and loosed their shafts at point-blank range. 'Now *run!*' shouted Elodan, turning and sprinting towards the trees. He heard a horse close behind him and turned to see a lancer bent low over the saddle, his weapon aimed at Elodan's heart. The crippled warrior drew back his arm and flung the hatchet with all his might. It sailed over the horse's head to bury itself in the rider's face and he tumbled back from the saddle.

One of the archers was down, hacked to death. The

others were racing for the trees. Elodan cursed. They would never make it.

Suddenly a score of arrows flashed from the undergrowth, ripping into the riders. Then again . . . and again. The soldiers turned and fled down the hillside.

Llaw Gyffes stepped out to stand beside Elodan. 'You are a man of iron,' said Llaw.

'That must be a compliment – coming from a blacksmith?'

'It is. I sweated blood when I saw you form that fighting line.'

'They'll be back, Llaw – and we do not have the men to hold them. But I'm glad you came when you did!'

'A man needs some luck,' said Llaw. 'I came upon a hunting party from this village and they said you were here, so I came with them. Then we heard the screaming and took up positions in the bushes.'

'So,' whispered Elodan, 'the great hero, Stronghand, was seeking me? Might I enquire why?'

'I need a man who understands the ways of war.'

'Then you *are* to gather an army! It's about time, Llaw. Well, this cripple will help you – if you'll have him.'

Llaw clapped him hard on the shoulder. 'That hatchet throw was a good one. I'd say you were coming on.'

'I was aiming for the horse,' snapped Elodan. 'I missed it – at less than ten feet.'

'I'll not tell a soul,' Llaw promised. 'Now let's get back. Brion is heading the villagers for the long caves. But we'll need food, and firewood.'

'Might I suggest something?'

Llaw grinned. 'You are our general.'

'Leave me twenty men and I will form a rearguard while you move on.'

'Be careful, Elodan. I don't want to lose you this early in the fight.'

'They've made it a war, my friend. Now they must learn what that means.'

Bavis Lan, the leader of the raiders, dismounted before the cabin where sat the three golden hounds. He walked under the rough-hewn porch and knelt by the statues.

'By Chera! They're gold,' he whispered. His aide, Lugas, joined him and stood by silently as Bavis examined the statues. 'Well?' snapped the leader. 'Don't just stand there, Lugas. Make your report!'

Lugas saluted crisply. 'We lost eighteen horses and nine men dead. Eight other men have injuries. Shall we pursue them into the trees?'

Bavis stood, a tall, lean man in his middle forties. He removed his helm and ran a hand through his silver-streaked hair. 'No. Once inside the tree line they would pick us off with ease. We hit two settlements today, and we've given them something to think about. We'll camp here, and strike north along the valley tomorrow.'

'Yes, sir.'

'What do you make of these statues?'

'They're beautiful, sir.'

'Aren't they just? I shall take them back to Mactha as a present for the King.'

The cabin door opened and a thickset man appeared. Bavis turned, his hand reaching for his sword. The man was powerfully built and sported an eye-patch of bronze; behind him stood a blond youth, his eyes fearful.

'Who the devil are you?' Bavis asked.

'The owner of the hounds. I fear they are too precious to put before a dullard like Ahak. He would not appreciate them – they have no blood, you see.'

'Your conversation brands you a traitor,' snarled Lugas, dragging his sword clear.

'And your deeds brand you a butcher,' responded the man, dropping his hand to touch the head of the nearest hound. 'Ollathair,' he said.

The hound's jewelled eyes snapped open and as Lugas' sword came up it leapt, sinking its teeth into the officer's forearm. Before he could even scream, the hound's jaws snapped shut and the arm and hand were torn clear. Lugas sank to his knees, staring in horror at the blood seeping from the stump at the end of his arm.

The general was frozen to the spot. The man with the eye-patch stepped back into the cabin, the three hounds following him. The door closed.

A flash of golden light streamed from the open window. Bavis Lan blinked and then ran forward, kicking the door from its hinges. The cabin was empty.

'Help me!' pleaded Lugas. 'Dear Gods, help me!'

'Surgeon!' bellowed Bavis. 'Someone find the surgeon!'

High on the hillside the air split with a flash of light and Ruad stepped clear, followed by Lámfhada and the hounds. The sorcerer's face was grim, and his hands were shaking. He turned and dragged the blood-drenched arm from the jaws of the hound and hurled it out onto the hill.

'A curse on them all!' he hissed.

'We should find the others,' said Lámfhada softly, unable to tear his eyes from the dismembered limb on the snow.

Ruad did not hear him. He stared down at the village, watching the soldiers running to aid the crippled officer.

'I will make you pay for this, Ahak,' he swore. 'Somehow, Ollathair will make you pay.' He turned away and walked swiftly into the trees, the hounds padding alongside.

They reached the long caves at dusk and found Gwydion tending an injured man. Fires had been lit inside the caves and the refugees were gathered round them. Llaw Gyffes approached the one-eyed sorcerer.

'Are you the Craftsman?'

'I am,' said Ruad. He looked closely at the broad-shouldered blond warrior, noting the pale blue eyes and the red-gold beard. 'And you are Stronghand. I hope the name fits you, boy – you'll have need of your strength when the snow clears.'

'I know. The Dagda spoke of the King's army. Will you aid us?'

'I will do what I can. But you should know the King's forces are led by the Knights of the Gabala, and they will prove deadly enemies.'

Llaw smiled. 'If I put my mind to it, wizard, I think I can be just as deadly. Have a little faith.'

'It's not faith I lack, Stronghand. But the Knights wear armour protected by spells, and carry swords of eldritch power – and even without these . . . gifts . . . their talents are extraordinary.'

Llaw put his huge hands on Ruad's shoulders. 'Do not tell me of their powers, wizard. Devote your mind to the problem of defeating them.'

'It is not going to be quite that simple.'

'I do not doubt it. But they live and breathe, so they must also be able to die. Find me a way to kill them.'

15

Manannan relaxed as the guards took hold of his arms, his head dropping on his chest. Then, in an explosive burst of movement, he tore his right arm free and hammered his elbow back into one guard's throat. The man screamed and staggered. Twisting towards the second guard, Manannan rammed his forehead into the man's face. Free once more, he dragged a dagger from the guard's belt and leapt at Paulus, grabbing him by his long white hair and hauling him forward so that the knife-point rested against the wrinkled flesh of his throat.

The four other guards drew weapons, but stood by, uncertain.

'Dismiss them,' ordered Manannan, 'or your life ends here.'

'Get back,' squealed Paulus. 'Leave us!' The guards helped their injured comrades from the room and pulled the door shut. Manannan dragged back Paulus' head and pricked the skin of his neck, allowing a thin trickle of blood to seep down on to his white tunic.

'You will now take us to my armour and my horse,' hissed Manannan, 'and then I might let you live.' He flicked a glance at Morrigan. 'Are you coming with me?'

'Where else can I go?'

'Then lead the way through the back of the apartments. The guards are probably there by now, but we'll walk through them.'

Dragging the whimpering Paulus, they entered the gardens; the smell from the blooms was almost sickening. The black-cloaked guards had gathered, but they stayed back as Manannan followed Paulus' directions to the stables beyond a high white wall. Kuan was there, standing statue-still. Manannan ran his hand over the stallion's back, but the animal did not move.

'What have you done to him?' stormed the Once-Knight.

'We made him better than ever he was,' said Paulus, 'as we were doing with you. Why can you not understand, Manannan? We have given you freely the gift of immortality!'

The Once-Knight flung the old man against a wall. 'Immortality? You almost made me one of you – a drinker of souls.'

'Do not be so romantic,' snapped Paulus. 'Do you not slaughter animals for meat? Where then is the difference? Or will you tell me that a bull has no soul? It is a living being made up of flesh and blood and bone – and that is all a man is. We perfected the elixir of life. What right have you to judge us?'

'I will not debate with you, Vampyre. There is no point. Now, where is the armour?'

Paulus led him to a wide room at the rear of the stable. Here, on wooden trees, were nine suits of silver armour. Manannan's anger soared and he swallowed hard.

'This is all that remains of the true Knights who came here! The proud men who wore these are dead – just as you are dead, Paulus. You may walk under the sun, but you are dead: a ruined, corrupted thing.' He turned to Morrigan. 'Saddle Kuan.'

'The guards are gathering outside,' she told him.

'Ignore them. Saddle my horse.'

'They will not let us leave.'

'Then I shall cut a path through them. Now, saddle Kuan.'

'It is not too late for you, Manannan,' whispered

Paulus. 'I spoke harshly before, but you could still join us. Wait and speak to Samildanach – he is your friend.'

'He is dead, Paulus. I do not speak with the dead.' Morrigan led the cold stallion into the room and Manannan moved to stand before his horse, pulling Paulus with him. He handed his knife to Morrigan. 'If he struggles or moves an inch, kill him. Can you do that?'

'It would be a pleasure,' she said, holding the blade against Paulus' throat.

He smiled thinly. 'And how long, my dear, can you survive in the world of blood without your Ambria? You will need nourishment – and they will hate you for it. They will destroy you.'

Morrigan said nothing, but the Once-Knight saw the truth bring fear to her eyes. He could find no words of comfort and moved to his armour.

'Look out!' shouted Morrigan and Manannan swivelled just as a lance hurtled towards his back. He threw up an arm to strike the missile aside, but the guard who had thrown it stepped from behind a stall and ran at him with sword raised. The Once-Knight reached out and drew his own shining silver blade from its scabbard on the tree.

'You cannot stand against me,' he told the guard. 'Be sensible – and live.'

The guard shouted an obscenity and rushed in, whereupon Manannan countered the clumsy blow and slashed a reverse sweep across the man's throat. The guard's head toppled from his shoulders, body slumping to the hay-strewn floor. Swiftly Manannan donned his armour, buckling the breastplate and sliding the shoulder-guards into place. His stomach heaved and his body shook; sweat trickled from his face into his eyes.

'Be strong, Manannan,' Morrigan pleaded. He forced a grin and walked to Paulus.

'Now, Vampyre, you have one last opportunity to cling to your half-life. Open the Gate between the Worlds.'

'I cannot, not here. The beasts will enter. There must be space for the tunnel.'

'Then you die here,' said Manannan softly, pressing the sword to Paulus' belly.

'Wait!' begged the old man. 'I could reach Ollathair! He could open the Gate.'

'Then do it!'

Paulus nodded and closed his eyes. A golden circle of light began to grow against the far wall and Manannan saw a cave packed with people and Ollathair talking to a tall man with a red-gold beard. He watched as the sorcerer stiffened and turned. Ollathair's voice whispered inside Manannan's mind.

'Do not taunt me, Manannan. Begone! Join your brothers!'

'I need help, Ollathair,' said the Once-Knight, aloud. 'Morrigan is with me. You must open the Gate.'

'If this is some form of demonic trickery, you will answer for it.'

Manannan shook his head. 'Just open the Gate, Armourer. I'll give you answers.'

'Consider it done,' said Ollathair and the vision faded.

Manannan rested his sword on Paulus' shoulder. 'Morrigan, I think it best that you also don a suit of armour. Use the one furthest left; it once belonged to Pateus, and he was slim enough.'

He watched as she slid from her dress, then turned his attention to Paulus. 'I ought to kill you,' he whispered. 'By the Source, you deserve it! But I will not.'

'Do not take a high moral tone with me, Manannan, merely because my ways are different from yours. In your petty world, thousands die in wars and plagues and bloodshed. Their corpses serve no purpose. Here

282

the deaths are relatively few, for we have no battles and no diseases. My people are a cultured race.'

'You live on death, Paulus – on other people's misery. Do you drag them screaming for mercy to their deaths? And do they feel fear as you did a few moments ago? Do they beg for their lives as you were prepared to do?'

'I would imagine they do,' Paulus admitted, 'though the Ambria vats are in the north of the city and I have not found it necessary to visit them. But in your world, do not the kings and princes have men put to death? Do they not own slaves whose lives depend upon the whim of their owners?'

'There is nothing either of us can say to reach the other,' said Manannan. 'You and your race are evil – but then that is just a word to you. You will be destroyed . . . in time.' Glancing back at Morrigan, who was fastening silver greaves to her calves, he waited until she buckled the sword to her hip and then patted Kuan's neck. 'Come, Greatheart, we are going home.'

'He does not hear you,' said Paulus. 'The stallion is dead. But you will find him faster than ever he was; he will not let you down.'

'He would not have let me down in life – and that would have been his choice,' Manannan told him. 'Go, Paulus. You are free.'

The old man turned to find himself facing Morrigan, a sword in her hands.

'What are you doing?' whispered Paulus. 'He said I was free.'

'Perhaps he did,' hissed Morrigan, 'but I am of the Vyre, Paulus, and I am evil. I am what you made me.'

'Don't! Please. I beg you, Morrigan. I will bring you Ambria . . . I will . . .'

Her sword hammered into his side, ripping his

entrails from his body, and he fell screaming to the floor.

Morrigan ran to Manannan and vaulted into the saddle behind him. 'Ride!' she shouted.

The dead stallion bunched its muscles and galloped from the stable. Guards hurled themselves aside as the horse thundered by. Arrows bounced from Manannan's armour – and then they were clear and out into the countryside.

Ahead of them lay the trees and the dark shadow-haunted entrance to the Tunnel of the Gate.

'Why did you kill him?' shouted Manannan.

'Why did you not?' she countered.

Kuan ran on, his pace constant. Arrows jutted from his dead flesh and Manannan felt a great sense of loss and a heavy sadness. They entered the tunnel at a full gallop and all light vanished, but when Manannan held up his sword and shouted 'Ollathair!', the blade blazed with a white light which reflected from scores of eyes to the left and right.

'The beasts are coming,' screamed Morrigan and Manannan glanced back to see a pack of huge, lumbering wolf creatures running along the trail behind them. He turned his gaze to the front – the tunnel was ending.

And still the Gate was shut.

'Was that the enemy?' asked Llaw, as the glowing golden window faded.

'I hope not,' answered Ruad. 'That was Manannan. I sent him through the Black Gate in search of the Gabala Knights and I must bring him back.'

'But you said that the evil beyond the Gate overcame them. How do you know it has not affected Manannan? This could be a trick.'

'If it proves so, he – they – will rue it. I am not

without power. I will return here by morning.' As Ruad moved towards the doorway, Llaw called out to him.

'Shall I send men with you?'

'No. If it is a trap, they will not be able to aid me, and if it isn't I will not need them.'

The sorcerer walked out into the snow, glad to be free of the cave and the hope in the eyes of Llaw Gyffes. How could the man understand the ways of magic? He was a blacksmith and a man of little learning. As far as he was concerned, the enemy were just men. The fact that they possessed enormous power from the Red did not concern him. After all, the great Ollathair was now with the rebels.

'Find me a way to kill them.'

Did he think it was so easy? Samildanach alone had almost been a match for Ruad Ro-fhessa – and that was before they passed through the Gate. Who knew of what terrible deeds he was now capable? Ruad trudged on, reaching a low hill above the cave. The wind howled around him and he walked on into a circle of trees. Selecting a shaded spot, he gathered wood, building a rough pyramid. He needed no tinder. Reaching into the Red, he ran his hand over a branch; flames sprang from within the wood and he thrust it into the pyramid.

For a little while he sat lost in thoughts of all that could have been. Then he straightened his back and reached for the calm of the White.

Soon he would open the Gate, but first he had to think, to plan. If Manannan had been changed, corrupted, then Ruad would kill him. Morrigan, too. If not, he would seek the Once-Knight's counsel and plan – as Llaw urged him – a defence against Samildanach's evil.

Evil? He rolled the word around in his mind. What did it mean? Samildanach had been a Knight, pledged to fight injustice. He had always hated evil. Yet now he was the man Ruad feared above all others. And how did Samildanach view *him?* As evil? Was it all relative? A mere matter of perception? The Gabala Knights had patrolled the Nine Duchies dispensing justice – but they were backed by their skills with lance and blade, which meant that their power was inspired by fear. And fear was a cousin to evil.

Ruad shook his head. This was not the time for such a debate.

He pictured again Manannan's face and the shadowy background he had glimpsed through the window. There was something there, he recalled, that had caught his eye. He concentrated on the memory, trying to bring the image into sharp focus. Something had gleamed in the background. A mirror behind Manannan? No, not a mirror. A warrior in armour? No, not quite. It was inert . . . lifeless . . . and yet, curiously familiar.

Think, man!

He lifted himself once more into the White, cleansing his mind, freeing himself from fear and doubt. All that mattered was the gleaming object. All else faded.

And then it was there: the ornate shoulder-plate he had made for Edrin. It was resting on a wooden armour-tree, and with it was Edrin's silver armour.

Ruad opened his eye – his mouth dry and his heart beginning to hammer. He tried again to find calm, but it was impossible. The original armour of the Gabala Knights was within his grasp, for if Edrin's armour was there, why not the others?

He thought of Manannan. The Gate would need to be opened soon, but there was still time. He needed power and floated towards the Black, filling his body with strength, feeling his muscles swell. Then he sought the Red. Fear touched him as the Colour washed over him – such a powerful spell would radiate far. He must be swift, or Samildanach would locate him and travel the Mist to kill him. He pictured the arms he had made for the Gabala Knights – the ornate helms, habergeons, greaves and gauntlets, and the swords of silver steel that would never dull. He drew the memories to him and reached out. His mind swam. Waves of pain blanketed him.

He had tried this before – six years ago – and been repulsed by a wall of sorcery. But now the wall had disappeared. Sensing the closeness of his creations, he opened the eyes of his mind and saw Manannan and Morrigan racing towards the Gate. The woman was wearing Pateus' armour.

Swiftly he reached out again. There! In a wide room, seven suits of armour and seven swords. He returned to his body, holding the place in his mind, and said aloud the Words of Calling. The air crackled and his head ached; he groaned and felt the wetness of blood flowing from his nose.

Too late now to halt the process. 'Come to me!' he shouted. 'Come to Ollathair!' A flash of light leapt from the ground before him, scattering his fire. He brushed the cinders from his lap and fought his way through the burning pain in his chest. His left arm was growing numb, and he could feel panic welling in him. If his heart gave out now, it would all be for nothing.

Calm! Be calm, he told himself. 'Come to me!' he whispered.

Glowing lights formed a circle around Ruad, shimmering in the moonlight, translucent and almost transparent. He watched as they formed, growing more solid. Slumping back to the ground, he sucked in a deep breath. Around him, like ghostly Knights, stood the armour of the Gabala – and with this, allied to Ruad's own enormous powers, Llaw Gyffes might have a chance. He eased himself to his feet.

He *must* open the Gate for Manannan. He gathered his fading strength, took one last look at the eight silent statues and then began the Spell of Opening. Pain tore at his chest and the fingers of his left hand grew numb.

The Black Gate appeared. Ruad knew he was close to the limits of his strength, that he would only be able to hold the Spell for a few seconds once the Gate was open. It would be more than tragic if he opened it too soon . . . and yet, too late would be no better. He recalled the speed at which Manannan had been riding into the tunnel and reckoned he should be at the Gate soon – if not now. And that meant the Chaos Beasts would be closing on him. He groaned as his agony grew and clutched his chest. His breathing was ragged and sweat dripped into his eyes as he sank to his knees and fought to calm his erratic heart. The pain eased a little. Ruad slowly began the completion of the Spell.

A creaking sound came from his right. He twisted and scanned the circle, blinking sweat from his eyes. All was now silent, the moonlight gleaming on the eight suits of armour. Eight? There should only be seven! A power like unseen hands dragged him to his feet and drew him towards the nearest armour. Ruad glanced up to see the visor slowly opening and struggled to hold his position, but he was too weak. Closer and closer he came, and now he could do nothing save stare at the moving visor. The pull on him ceased. He wanted to run, but could not take his eyes from the plumed helm and the blackness within.

The moon came out from behind a cloud. Silver light washed over the figure and Ruad watched the armour darken until it was deep crimson.

Two blood-red eyes gazed down on him.

'Time to die, traitor!' said Samildanach. Too late Ruad saw the dagger in the gauntleted hand. I plunged into the sorcerer's belly, ripping up through the lungs.

Ruad crumpled to the ground . . .

Samildanach stepped back – and vanished.

The sorcerer tried to roll to his belly, but the pain was colossal. Blood bubbled into his throat and he tried to swallow it back, but coughed, spraying bloody froth which stained his beard and tunic.

Knowing he had scant seconds to live, Ruad fell back and pointed his arm at the Gate.

'Open!' he hissed, completing the Spell. A great warmth flowed through him as he gazed up at the stars and all pain vanished. He saw again the day when he had become the Armourer, and recalled the joy on the faces of his Knights.

'With you at our head we will change the world, my friend,' Samildanach had told him.

'You will not need me for that, Lord Knight,' Ruad had replied.

The stars grew faint as the snow-clouds gathered and Ruad could hear a sound like a rushing sea. 'I don't want to die,' he whispered. 'I want to . . .' A large snowflake touched his eye and melted to become a single tear that flowed down the dead man's face.

Three of the beasts were down – one of them writhing across the path, clutching the stump of its severed arm. Manannan and Morrigan backed away to the Gate as a score more of the monsters advanced warily. The undead stallion, Kuan, stood by unmoving, ignored by the pack; they were interested only in living meat.

A huge creature, larger than a bear, dropped on all fours and rushed at Morrigan. She drove her silver sword into its mouth, plunging it deep down the beast's throat. The impetus of its charge carried it forward, even in death, and it hammered her into the Gate.

Manannan had no time to help her. Cutting left and right, his silver sword held the other beasts at bay, but they were growing more daring – darting in and back, slashing at him with long, curved talons. A gigantic wolf slunk down on all fours, creeping into the shadows on Manannan's left. The Once-Knight did not see the beast until it was too late, when suddenly it sprang and he was hurled from his feet, his sword spinning from his hand. Twisting under the wolf, he crashed a mailed fist into its face. Instantly the other creatures were on him, ripping at his armour, sinking talons into his helm, pulling and tearing, seeking the warm flesh beneath the silver steel.

'Kuan!' he yelled. 'To me!' The undead horse trembled. The shout came again and Kuan backed away, shaking his great head. Then the light of life stirred in his blank grey eyes.

'Kuan!'

The stallion bunched its muscles and charged the pack – hooves hammering, hind legs kicking out with awesome force. They scattered before the horse and Manannan reached up and grasped the reins, hauling himself to his feet. He gathered his sword.

Morrigan eased herself from behind the enormous carcass of the bear-beast and advanced to stand beside him. At first the pack had been dismayed by the stallion's sudden attack but now they were gathering themselves for another charge.

Manannan patted Kuan's neck. 'Welcome home, Greatheart,' he said.

As the pack swept forward the stallion hurled himself into their midst. Manannan tried to stop him, and watched in horror as the dreadful talons tore into his body. A shaft of moonlight lit the scene. Manannan spun to see the Black Gate slowly opening, and beyond it the stars of his own world. 'Back!' he yelled to Morrigan; she needed no second bidding and leapt through the narrow opening.

'Kuan!' bellowed Manannan, but the stallion was beyond hearing. Still it lashed and kicked at the beasts, but grievous were the wounds . . . terrible tears and deep, deep cuts.

'Manannan!' yelled Morrigan. 'The Gate is closing!' For a moment more Manannan stood, watching the last moments of his stallion. Then he turned and ran for the Gate. It shimmered before his eyes and he hurled himself over the last few yards, hitting the snow-covered ground and rolling on his back. When at last he stood and looked back, the Gate had vanished.

Morrigan touched his arm. He swung to see the ghostly circle and the grimly silent Knights of the Gabala.

'Sweet Heaven,' he whispered. Then he saw the still figure of Ollathair and ran to him. Blood had drenched the man's tunic and stained the snow around him.

'Look,' pointed Morrigan. The snow beside Olla-thair's corpse showed a set of footprints that seemed to appear from nowhere.

'Samildanach,' said Manannan. He pulled the gauntlet from his right hand and gently closed Olla-thair's eye.

'What now?' asked Morrigan. 'Without him, what chance do we have?'

The Once-Knight could find no words. A long time ago, Ollathair had been his mentor and his friend. The Armourer had been almost a father to them all, and the Knights had adored him. He had been gentle and wise, and the Colours had brought him many gifts. Now he lay silent in the snow, killed by a friend.

'Not a fitting end for such a man,' Manannan whispered.

'I have no sympathy for him,' said Morrigan. 'He fashioned his own doom when he sent the Knights through the Gate. Let us go from here. It is cold.'

Movement caught Manannan's eye and he watched as a large group of men marched over the hill-top bearing torches. He waited until they approached the circle. A tall warrior with a red-gold beard stepped inside.

'So, you bastard, it was a trap!' said Llaw Gyffes, drawing his axe from his belt.

'I did not kill him,' answered the Once-Knight. 'Look there at the footprints.'

'Defend yourself!' roared Llaw, rushing forward. Manannan ducked under a clumsy sweep and crashed a right hook to the warrior's jaw. Llaw Gyffes hit the ground hard, but rolled to his feet.

'Enough of this nonsense!' said Manannan. 'The man was my friend.'

Llaw gathered himself to attack again, but Lámfhada pushed through the crowd to kneel by Ruad's corpse. As Llaw Gyffes advanced on Manannan, the boy called out to him.

'Look at the wound,' said Lámfhada. 'It was not a sword, but a narrow blade like a dagger. And he has no knife.'

Llaw knelt and examined the wound, then looked up at Manannan.

'I still don't trust you,' he declared, 'but I suppose it matters little now. The enemy is gathering a great army, led by wizard Knights, and we have no sorcerer to defend us.' He turned away and stared off into the distance.

The Once-Knight moved to stand beside him. 'You will grow to trust me,' he said, 'for I do not lie and I am true to my friends.'

Llaw smiled. 'A lot of good that will do us! I am trying to plan a war against an enemy I cannot defeat. I am no general.' He swung to stare at the circle of faces lit by the flickering torches. 'Look at them,' he said. 'Foresters, runaway farmers and clerics. There is not a mail-shirt among them. What do we do when the enemy arrives?'

'Fight or run,' replied Manannan. 'They are the only two choices.'

'We cannot run. A man came yesterday to tell us that the King's fleet has docked at Cithaeron, bringing a thousand soldiers. There is no retreat now; they will hunt us down like wolves.'

Manannan remained silent for a moment. 'Look around you,' he said at last. 'The forest is an awesome size – not the easiest place for an army to force a pitched battle. Do not let the evil deeds of tonight bring you to despair. Come, let us bury Ollathair and say a few words of farewell to his spirit.'

There was a sudden flurry of movement from the back of the circle, and men stepped back to allow Nuada and Groundsel to move forward. The squat outlaw leader looked down at the corpse.

'So,' he said, 'that's the great wizard. Well, he was a big help.'

'What are you doing here?' asked Llaw. 'Isn't this a little far from your normal hunting-grounds? There's no one to rob.'

'Yes, it's good to see you too, Llaw,' said Groundsel, grinning. 'But I am here, so Nuada tells me, because it is my destiny. He spoke to the Dagda and they decided that the hero Groundsel needed to meet the wizard Ollathair. Well, I've met him. It was a short meeting, but that is life. I'll be going home in the morning.'

'Wait!' said Nuada. 'That wasn't what the Dagda said, and you know it. But this is not the place or the time to discuss it. Let us bury this man, and I will say a few words for him.'

'You've never said a *few* words in your life, poet,' said Groundsel. The outlaw looked closely at Manannan, his eyes narrowing, then he turned away without a sound and walked back through the circle of men.

Llaw ordered Ruad's body to be carried to the caves, and other men struggled to bear the Gabala armour. Manannan rejoined Morrigan, who had been strangely silent throughout the encounter.

The Once-Knight stared into her face. It looked sickly and pale in the silver moonlight. 'Are you all right, Morrigan?'

'Leave me alone,' she whispered. 'I must get away from here.'

'Why?'

'I am tired. I need . . . to rest. Let me go.'

'Let us go to their camp. You can rest there. And eat . . .' His voice faded to a whisper. 'That's it, isn't it? You need Ambria, or . . . Listen to me, Morrigan, you must fight it. You *must*.'

'I will. Just leave me for a while; I need to be alone.'

'That is what you do *not* need.'

She tore her arm free from his grasp, her eyes blazing. 'Get away from me!' she hissed, but he stood his ground.

'I know that you only had eyes for Samildanach,' he said gently, 'and I was merely a friend with whom you shared your confidences. But I loved you, Morrigan, I still love you.'

For a moment more the air was electric between them, then she seemed to sag. 'Dear Gods of Light,' she whispered. 'Help me!' He stepped forward and took her in a clumsy embrace, encumbered by the armour they both wore.

'Come with me,' he said, and led her after the torch-lit column.

Once in the caves, Morrigan stripped herself of the armour and ate a little meat and dried fruit. Then she took some borrowed blankets and moved back into the shadows at the far end of the cave to sleep.

Many of the men accompanied Llaw and Nuada to

watch the burial of the sorcerer Ollathair, and to listen to Nuada's oration.

As they made their slow way back to the caves, one man lingered behind the rest. He was tired and he had an ache in his knee from an old injury when his horse had fallen, pinning him to the ground. He stopped and sat for a while on a storm-toppled tree.

He rubbed at the knee until the pain subsided and made as if to stand. Then he saw the woman standing close by. She was young and pale, and beautiful, her hair silver in the moonlight.

'Best be getting back,' he advised. 'It's cold out here.'

'I too am cold,' she said, sitting beside him and resting her head on his shoulder, her hand on his thigh. 'But the cave is so crowded. Stay with me for a while.' He turned towards her and ran his hand inside the blanket she held around her, sliding his fingers up across her flanks and feeling the softness of her flesh. He could hardly believe that she did not stop him . . . his hand curled over her breast.

Her face lifted and they kissed. The cold was forgotten as the man fumbled at her clothing.

'I can't believe it,' he whispered. 'Nothing like this has ever happened to me before. What a night for my luck to change.'

Morrigan said nothing.

And her lips moved to his neck . . .

16

Lámfhada sat with Gwydion, watching the melting snow and the small white and yellow flowers that pushed themselves clear of the ice on the meadow. The sky was gloriously blue and the sun blazed over the mountains. The old man reached out and patted the youth's shoulder.

'Do not despair, my friend,' said the Healer. 'I know there are many who disagree, but I believe our friend is now at peace in a far better place than this.'

'He was good to me,' said Lámfhada. 'He took me to his home, he taught me many things. And I made a metal bird that flew. He opened the world for me.'

'He was a good man – and he died badly. But that is not the end, believe me. You should trust these white hairs; I have seen much in the world, and I have learned.'

Lámfhada shook his head. 'I too have learned. The evil are always strong, and they always win.'

'You have seen only a part of the circle, Lámfhada – for that is what it is. Good and evil chase each other round and round. If you join the circle in the wrong place, you will find evil triumphant. But continue on the journey and you will see it lose, and win again, and lose . . . for eternity.'

'Then nothing is ever achieved?'

The old man chuckled. 'That would depend on how you view achievement. The winning is not important – it is the struggle that counts.'

'What is the point of struggling against the impossible?'

'Hold on to that thought – and examine it, for there

you will find evil's greatest weapon. *What can I do, when I am so small and weak? Why should I not steal a little, everyone else does? Why should I try to be pure, when it leaves me poor and disregarded? How can I change the world?* Yet all ideas, for good or evil, start in the heart of a single man or woman. From there they spread, one to one, two to two, a hundred to a hundred.'

'You are flying too high for me, Gwydion,' said Lámfhada, stretching his legs and rising. 'I cannot follow all of this.'

Gwydion rose beside him. 'Ruad was good to you and showed you a path to follow. You will show others. The more men who follow this path because of you, the greater Ruad's achievement. His death will not stop that. But if you despair, and take another path, his life will have been diminished. That is your debt, my friend.'

'And how do I walk this path without him to guide me?'

'You begin by pushing all hatred from your heart, for that is another weapon of the Great Enemy. We can never beat him by employing his tactics. We can destroy his emissaries but ultimately, if we do so with hatred, we slowly, inexorably, come to replace those we have slain.'

'I am not a scholar, Gwydion, I am a runaway slave. Most of what you say is lost on me. Were I older and stronger, I would take up the sword and follow Llaw Gyffes. I would kill every man who serves the King.'

Gwydion looked away and spoke softly. 'Perhaps the truth will change you. Perhaps not. Try to find peace, Lámfhada.' The old man wandered back down the hill to where the refugees were gathering their possessions.

Lámfhada watched him making his slow way back to the caves. How could he not hate the men who had killed Ruad? Did they not deserve his hatred? He transferred his gaze to the first spring flowers. How easy for them, he thought, for when they died they merely returned to the earth, to the warmth of their bulbs, ready to grow again. Not so with men. The day of the Gold returned to his memory and he saw the old, dying stag, and felt again the joy that he, Lámfhada, had found the power to give it fresh life. But this time the joy was sullied by pain. He had never since managed to find the Gold – had he done so, he might have saved Ruad's life.

Lámfhada closed his eyes and sought the gentle sanctuary of the Yellow. He floated for some time, oblivious to the world beyond, but Gwydion's words echoed in the corridors of his mind.

'*You begin by pushing all hatred from your heart, for that is another weapon of the Great Enemy. We can never beat him by employing his tactics. We can destroy his emissaries but ultimately, if we do so with hatred, we slowly, inexorably, come to replace those we have slain.*'

At no time during his association with Ruad had the sorcerer ever spoken of hate. Even at the last he had felt pity for his fallen Knights. 'I don't hate them,' said Lámfhada. 'I don't hate anyone.' Lost in the Yellow, he began to weep the first tears he had shed for his friend. His mind swam, rolling and twisting in the Colours. At first he did not care, but then an emotion close to panic struck him for he was losing his way. He stretched out the arms of his spirit form and concentrated on the Yellow, but all the Colours streamed by him at dizzying speed.

'Be calm,' he told himself. 'Fear is useless here.' The streaming kaleidoscope slowed until he floated at the edge of the Red. He pulled back, crossing the Black and the Green, seeking the Yellow and the way home. Then the strangest sensation touched him and he realized he was not alone. Yet there were no words, no touch, only a curious certainty. 'Speak to me,' he said, but there was nothing – only the warmth of companionship, the knowledge of friendship. 'Is it you, Ruad?' he asked. 'Tell me. Show me.' The Colours drew back before a blaze of Gold that loomed and engulfed him. On a conjured disc of gold he soared through the rainbow and floated above the Forest of the Ocean far below.

Then he saw a shimmering figure in the sky above the refugee camp. He sped towards it, recognizing the warrior Knight Cairbre. The Red Knight spun towards him.

'Your sorcerer is gone, and this rag-tag army will concern us not at all,' said the Knight. 'What a waste of time and energy.'

'I think you should leave the Forest,' Lámfhada told him. 'You are not welcome here.'

Cairbre's pale face was touched by the ghost of a smile. 'You cannot hurt me, child. You cannot stop me. I travel where I will.'

'Not any more,' said Lámfhada, raising his hand. A golden globe sprang up around Cairbre. He drew his sword and lashed at it, but he was trapped.

'Without Ollathair you have nothing,' stormed Cairbre. 'None can stand against Samildanach.'

'I can,' said Lámfhada. 'Now begone!' The globe flashed away at dizzying speed and the boy sorcerer followed it to the edge of the Forest. The Colours were out of harmony here, the Red pushing all before it. Lámfhada raised his arms and a wall of gold appeared, moving west and east and soaring north over his head. He opened his hand, willing the fingers to turn Red and when they had done so he touched the wall. Burning pain lanced him. He drew back, healed the hand and returned to his body.

The Red Knights would spy no more on Llaw Gyffes, and that would trouble them. Back on the hillside Lámfhada rose wearily. He knew now what he must do – and worse, what must befall them all. But there was no fear . . . for he was not alone.

Manannan convinced Llaw of the need to move to a safer camp in the high meadows, where they could build new homes and watch all the approaches day and night. For two days the one hundred and twelve refugees marched further into the mountains, passing several small settlements. At each, they obtained food and temporary shelter.

On the third day they were joined by Elodan and his rearguard; they had ambushed the soldiers as they rode north, killing five, and had escaped without loss. At last the refugees came to the high meadows, and began the task of felling trees and clearing the ground for new homes. The weather was calm and temperate, but all knew the winter was not yet passed and the crude dwellings were built with speed against the last savage onslaught of the snow.

Llaw Gyffes and Groundsel were tireless in their labours, stripping trees, dragging timber across the frozen ground, organizing work parties and hunting groups. Elodan took his twenty men back into the forest, scouting for signs of the soldiers and directing other refugees to the main camp. Nuada took part in no physical labour, but earned his salt at night around the camp-fires with stories and jests, tales and songs.

Manannan and Morrigan, bereft of armour, worked among the refugees. The Once-Knight had no talent with carpentry or building, but laboured hard to assist those with more skill.

By the seventh night after Ruad's death, a new village had been built with more than thirty makeshift dwellings. Elodan had returned to report that the soldiers had sacked two more settlements and the death toll was high. More than a hundred bodies had been counted at the first, but wolves had dragged away many at the second, making a count impossible.

Nuada asked for a meeting of the leaders and chose, as its site, a deep cave above the meadow. Here he lit a large fire and waited as the men gathered. The Healer Gwydion sat beside Lámfhada and watched the warriors as they seated themselves. Groundsel was the first to arrive; short, squat and bearded, he sat with his back to a wall, his eyes on the cave mouth. Gwydion noticed that his right hand never strayed far from the hilt of his sword. Llaw Gyffes came next, with the hawk-faced Elodan. Gwydion bowed his head to the Knight, who responded with a tight smile. Then came the former Gabala Knight Manannan, once more in armour; he and Elodan could have been brothers, for both had the same aquiline features and both were of patrician blood. Manannan was built more powerfully, his face more square, but it was in the eyes that a subtle difference could be seen. Elodan had tasted the despair of defeat, the pain of the vanquished, and it showed.

Groundsel was the first to speak. 'Well, poet, you have us here. Entertain us, for the Gods know we need it.'

Nuada rose. 'There is no song for you tonight, my Lord Groundsel,' he said, his violet eyes scanning the small group. 'Tonight we decide on a matter of great importance. We have here among us a Knight of the Gabala. Might I ask him first to speak?'

'What would you have me say?' Manannan asked. 'I am here as a man, not a Knight. The Gabala Knights are no more.'

'Then tell us of the Order, and what it stood for.'

'Surely all of us here know the answer to that,' said Manannan. 'What is your purpose, Sir Poet?'

'Bear with me, sir, and accede to my request.' Nuada sat down.

Manannan cleared his throat. 'The history is long, and I will not bore you with it. Suffice to say that the Knights were champions of justice in the Nine Duchies, free from interference and subject not to the power of the King nor any law made by him. They would ride into any castle and have the power to award decisions, to settle all disputes. Is that what you wished to hear?'

'In part, Manannan,' answered Nuada. 'But was it not the case that often you had to fight, to kill, for your cause?'

'Yes, though not as often as legend has it. In the main we . . . they represented the common people in disputes against landowners. Such landowners could demand trial by combat; that was within the law.'

'And why were you needed?'

Manannan gave a nervous laugh. 'Why? Because the weak must also have champions. There is no riddle there, surely?'

'So, then,' said Nuada, 'without the Knights of the Gabala the weak have no one to stand for them?'

'That is so,' agreed Manannan. 'Perhaps one day the Order will be re-established. I would hope that to be true.'

'Why not now?' asked Nuada softly.

'Now, Sir Poet? But the Armourer is dead, the Knights corrupted – and the King has changed the laws.'

'The Knights were never subject to the laws; you said that yourself.'

Llaw Gyffes pushed himself to his feet. 'What are you leading to, Nuada? I thought we were here to talk of sensible things.'

'Oh, but we are, Llaw Gyffes,' said Nuada. 'We are here to talk of rebirth. The Knights of the Gabala must ride again, and the people must know of it. They must ride against the King and his Red Knights.'

'Why not?' said Groundsel. 'We have the armour,

after all. It will be a great boost to morale to have the Knights riding beside us. I like the idea.'

'Do not even think of it in those terms,' snapped Nuada. 'That is not the purpose. The Knights must ride, yes. But *true* Knights, pledged to all the Gabala held dear.'

'It is not possible!' said Manannan. 'Believe me, poet, you have no idea what you are suggesting. There is not a man here who could stand against Samildanach, Pateus, Edrin, or any of the others. At best you would have an arena-show, a carnival. I *was* a Knight of the Gabala. I trained for years for the honour, and for years after it I honed those skills. There is not a man in this forest I could not defeat, with or without a weapon – and I could never stand against Samildanach. Do you understand that? It is not enough for men to wear the armour and ride tall horses. The Gabala Knights were special.'

'Please let me speak,' interposed Gwydion, 'for the debate is moving out of hand. Manannan is correct, the Knights were special. Few people understood this when they rode. They were a force not just to aid the dispossessed, or the weak, but to affect the Colours themselves. What they did was to bring hope to those without hope, and fear to those who would rule by fear. They were the balance. For each dispute they settled, ten . . . twenty . . . a hundred more would be settled *because* the Knights existed. Yet now – out in the world beyond – there is despair and hatred and terror. We need the Knights. And I support Nuada in this. We must find special men, strong men, good men.' He sat down once more beside Lámfhada.

Groundsel began to chuckle; shaking his head, he rose to his feet. 'Strong men? Good men? Here? I am a killer and a thief. I do not say this as a boast, nor am I ashamed of what I am. The world is a harsh place. Watch the wolf as it hunts the stag, or the hawk as it kills the rabbit. You want holy men in silver armour? You will not find them in the Forest of the Ocean. Now, all I am interested in is survival. An army is gathering to destroy us and the route to the sea has been cut off. So the choices are simple: win or die. And I have no intention of dying. If dressing up in those pretty suits of armour will give us a chance, let us do it.'

'And what do you say, Llaw Gyffes?' asked Gwydion.

The former blacksmith added wood to the fire and sat watching the flames. He did not rise, nor did he look at the men around him.

'I lean towards Groundsel's view,' he said. 'The return of the Knights would be a massive blow to the King and would make us the focus of rebellion. But after that the problems would begin. People would expect the Knights to ride fearlessly against the enemy. Could we do that – and survive? Manannan thinks not. I cannot – will not – make a decision here. I think we should vote on it, and only if all agree should we go ahead.'

Elodan stood and raised his right arm, the leather-covered stump glowing in the firelight. 'All my life I dreamed of being asked to become a Gabala Knight. I never was. My friend Edrin was chosen, and I remained. But look at my arm before you decide. I was a fine Knight and a great swordsman, yet I could not stand against Cairbre – much less Samildanach. You – Groundsel – seem a strong man. But I could defeat you even with a near-useless left hand. How will you fare when against a Red Knight? When your body is encased in unfamiliar armour and your vision is restricted by the strips of steel in your visor? And you, Llaw Gyffes, can you ride? Can you control a warhorse with your knees while holding a shield and bearing a lance? And you, Manannan, how long did it take you to master the mace, and the hand axe and the sword?'

'Twenty years,' answered Manannan softly. 'And even then I am less able with the axe than many.'

'We have perhaps a month before we must face the might of Ahak's army,' said Elodan. 'No peasant could begin to master the basics in that time.'

'I have made swords,' said Llaw, 'and hefted them for weight and balance. My arm is strong. I can fight, but I accept what Elodan says and . . .'

'*You* might accept it,' stormed Groundsel, 'but I do not. I do not need some defeated cripple to tell me what I can – or can not – do. Listen to him. Like all patricians, he wants to make us believe there is something extraordinary about a knight. Pigswill! A sword is a lump of iron with which you hammer at an opponent until he is down. Strength, courage and will are all you need. I vote the Knights should return.'

Llaw nodded. 'I agree. Manannan?'

The Once-Knight looked at each man. 'I will agree – but on one condition. If we become Gabala Knights, there must be iron discipline under the elected Lord Knight and the Armourer. No dissension. Total obedience. If that is understood, I agree.'

'And I take it you will be the Lord Knight?' asked Groundsel, sneering.

'No, I could never assume that role. It should be Elodan.'

'Why?' asked Llaw. 'He was never chosen in the first place – you were.'

'He was chosen,' said Manannan softly, 'on the day he quit the King's service and fought Cairbre. Trust me on this.'

'Do not bring religion into this,' said Groundsel. 'I will not have it. He was chosen to have his hand cut off, that is all.'

'Groundsel is right,' put in Elodan. 'It would be inconceivable to have a crippled Knight.'

Manannan shook his head. 'If you are not elected, I take no part in it.'

Nuada raised his hands. 'There are eight suits of armour, therefore we must find eight men. Groundsel, Llaw, Elodan and Manannan make four. Where do we go for the others?'

'Why always men?' said a voice from the cave mouth and they turned to see Morrigan moving into the firelight. 'I can fight with sword, spear or bow. I can ride like a centaur. Ask Manannan. Any man who wants to take my armour can fight me for it – and die.'

'Wonderful,' said Groundsel. 'A cripple leads us and a woman rides beside us.'

'Beware, little man,' Morrigan hissed. 'It is not wise to offend me.'

'Be still, my quaking heart,' jeered Groundsel, but Nuada moved swiftly between them.

'We will not begin such a venture by warring amongst ourselves. Elodan, do you accept the role of Lord Knight?'

'If it is the will of all,' he answered, looking at Groundsel.

The outlaw leader shrugged. 'Why not?' he said.

'Then I accept. But who will be the Armourer? You, Nuada?' Before the poet could answer, Lámfhada pushed himself to his feet.

'No,' he said. 'I will.' Llaw Gyffes looked hard at the youth and said nothing.

But Groundsel burst into laughter. 'Who else could it be but a runaway slave boy?'

Lámfhada raised his hand and looked Groundsel in the eye. 'Please be silent, sir, until I have finished speaking,' he said quietly. 'I studied with Ruad Ro-fhessa, and I have found my Colour. I am not a sorcerer, but I have talent. And I have the will to walk the paths Ruad walked, and the desire to see an end to this evil. I also know how you may choose your Knights and be sure of them.'

'How?' asked Llaw Gyffes.

'Come with me.' The boy turned and they followed him to the wooden armour-trees. 'There, Groundsel, choose your armour.'

The outlaw leader walked along the line of trees. 'There is nothing here to fit me; it will need to be altered.'

'Take the suit that beckons you,' Lámfhada advised.

'What does that mean?' snapped Groundsel. 'I hear no voices.'

'Choose, Groundsel.'

'Do not order me, boy!' He looked around. 'That one; that will do.'

'Now put it on.'

'It won't fit; it's too high and narrow. Oh, all right . . .' Groundsel reached up and took down the breastplate. Manannan stepped forward and helped him into the habergeon, then buckled the breastplate into place. Piece by silver piece the armour was fitted to the squat outlaw, until he stood arrayed in the full splendour of a Gabala Knight. He looked at the helm and lifted it. 'Well, this will never fit,' he said. 'Look at it!' He lifted it to the top of his head and lowered it gently, waiting for the touch of metal to his skull. The helm settled into place. He lifted it clear again. 'So I was wrong. It only looked too small.'

'No,' said Lámfhada. 'Pick up a gauntlet – just one – do not touch the other.' Groundsel did so. It was black, with silver mail across the knuckles. He slid it on and was amazed to find that it fitted his short, thick fingers exactly. 'Now place it beside its partner and observe them,' instructed the boy. Groundsel obeyed and Elodan and Llaw leaned over to see that the gauntlet he had tried was now shorter than the other, the fingers thicker. 'Now the other,' said Lámfhada, and Groundsel was not surprised when the second glove fitted as well as the first.

'The armour is waiting,' said Lámfhada. 'They will choose the new Knights.'

'And what of me?' Morrigan asked.

'You are already chosen, Lady, as are all here. But others will come. Two will be here tomorrow – and one awaits rescue.'

'What has happened to you, boy?' asked Llaw, placing his hand on the youth's shoulder.

Lámfhada smiled. 'I flew too high and saw too much.' Gently he lifted Llaw's hand from his shoulder. 'Tomorrow, Elodan will begin to teach you all what it means to be Knights of the Gabala. But before he does, one fact must be made plain. When the final battle is over, some of you will be dead. You must understand that and accept it, or there is no point in continuing.'

The warriors stared hard at the youth, but nothing was said until Manannan moved forward.

'You have a task for me, I think?'

'Yes,' Lámfhada told him. 'I am sorry.'

'Do not be sorry, Armourer. It is a long time since I felt the Colours move so strongly. I knew before you spoke that you were chosen, as I knew that Elodan would lead us.' He swung to face the others. 'The Gabala Knights are reborn, and I pledge my life to their cause. Any man who disgraces that cause will answer to me. There is no oath to swear, no holy relic to hold. But you will make a promise to yourselves. From this day on no evil shall touch you, and nothing you do will be for selfish gain. From now, until the end, the Knights will represent justice. Win or lose, there is no compromise. If any here feel they cannot live to these ideals . . .' he stared hard at Groundsel, 'walk away now. Do not look back. Do not even consider moving on.'

'I'll do my share,' promised Groundsel. 'I do not

need to be preached at. And the armour chose me –
isn't that right, boy?'

'You were the first to be chosen,' said Lámfhada. 'Is
that not true, Nuada?'

'Yes,' admitted the poet. 'And now, since I am no
longer needed here . . .'

'But you are,' Lámfhada told him.

Nuada swallowed hard. 'I am not a Knight. I cannot
use a sword. I . . .'

'You can hear the armour calling you. Take it.'

'I can't! I won't. I . . . don't want to die here. Do
you understand?'

'We all understand,' said Llaw Gyffes. 'Don't worry,
poet. Go back to the village.' Nuada nodded and
walked away for several steps . . . then he stopped and
turned. His face was ghostly pale and he stared at the
armour. He closed his eyes as if in pain, then opened
them and took a deep, shuddering breath. As the others
watched, he walked forward and touched a suit of
armour. It shimmered and changed. Slowly he drew
the sword from its scabbard and held it before him.
Jagged black lines snaked along the blade, the steel
splitting into shards that tumbled to the floor.

'What in Hell's name does that mean?' whispered
Groundsel.

'Time will tell,' answered Lámfhada, with a broad
smile.

As dawn touched the sky, Elodan walked beside
Lámfhada to the rear of the cave. Ruad's three golden
hounds sat before the armour.

'How did they come here?' asked Elodan.

'I summoned them,' the boy sorcerer told him. 'They
may prove useful, though I hope not to use them. You
know which armour must be yours?'

'Yes,' answered the Knight, moving to stand before

the white and silver helm of Samildanach. An eagle adorned the visor and filigree work of exquisite beauty covered the helm. The breastplate too was embossed with shimmering leaves, as were the greaves and leggings.

'This armour is worth more than my entire estate,' whispered Elodan, reaching out and resting his hand on the metal. 'It is magnificent.'

'Wear it with pride, Elodan.'

'Wear it? I am not fit to touch it.' He lifted his stump. 'And how do I even put it on?'

'I will help you.'

Elodan laughed. 'This is a sorry jest, Lámfhada. The shades of past Gabala Knights would burn with shame.'

'I do not think so, Lord Knight. It always took more than a steady sword hand to be a Gabala Knight. It was a question, surely, of heart and soul? You told me of the woman you loved and the husband you slew. Nothing can wipe away the deed, Elodan. But that is the past, so let it lie. Let it be buried. Be the Lord Knight to the best of your abilities. Teach the others and those who will follow them.'

'I am not worthy,' repeated the Knight.

'None of us is. And we have little time to become so. Come, let me help you into your armour.'

Within the hour Elodan, Llaw Gyffes, Groundsel, Morrigan and Nuada were all fully dressed in the chain and plate of the Gabala. Lámfhada called the poet to him and left Elodan to instruct the others.

'What good will I be to the cause?' asked Nuada. 'I feel ridiculous; it is a sham.'

'No, it is not,' Lámfhada told him. 'The sword broke because it was not needed. You will not be a warrior Knight, Nuada. It is not – thank the Source – in your nature to kill. You will be our herald. You will journey through the forest, to every settlement, and tell them the Knights have returned. You will gather men to our cause. But more than this, you will help the Harmony of the Colours. You must lift and inspire your hearers as never before. You must fill their hearts with hope. Take Kartia with you, and Brion. Go north for two days. You will find a sheltered valley and a man who breeds horses. Purchase mounts for yourselves, and ask the man to deliver seven grey stallions here during the next week.'

'Seven stallions? Does he have that many to spare?'

'He has – and he will part with them. He is a Nomad called Chrysdyn; he is a fair man, and you will meet the price he asks.'

Nuada's violet eyes pulled away from Lámfhada's gaze. 'You have seen the future, haven't you?'

'Yes,' admitted the young Armourer. 'I have seen all the futures. Do not question me, Nuada.'

'No, I won't.' The poet forced a smile. 'You have come a long way since I found you in the forest with an arrow in your back. I think you have found a truth that has eluded me all my life. I wish you would share it.'

'I cannot do so, Nuada – not because it is secret, but because it is not. And you will discover it; you will know, even as I know. Be careful where you ride, my friend.'

The two shook hands and Lámfhada walked with the poet to the cave mouth.

'Where is Manannan?' asked Nuada suddenly. 'I have not seen him this morning.'

'He left last night. And that reminds me: Chrysdyn has lost one stallion and he will search for him most of today. Tell him you will pay for the lost horse, and that it is safe.'

'Manannan has it?'

'Yes. I brought it to him.'

'I take it Manannan will be in danger?'

'We are all in danger, Nuada. But yes, Manannan is riding into the demon's lair. Think of him as you journey.'

17

After five days of wandering in the forest, Errin was footsore and weary. Twice they had been forced to hide from outriding scouts of the King's Lancers, and three days before they had arrived at a ruined village of rotting corpses. Errin could not forget the scenes of destruction; they had filled him with horror and left him nauseous.

Ubadai had wandered over the scene, examining the tracks. 'They rode in from the north and south. At sunrise. Breakfast fires just lit. Villagers had nowhere to run. Maybe a dozen escaped east, but horses rode after them – they would have been caught.'

'Such slaughter is senseless,' said Errin. 'What does it achieve?'

Ubadai shrugged. 'Terror. Good weapon. Make men fear you.'

'You condone this sort of butchery?' asked Sheera. 'What kind of a man are you?'

'What does that mean?' Ubadai demanded. 'Condone?'

'It means,' explained Errin, 'that you agree with this action.'

'I do not agree. I answer question. What it achieves? In my grandfather's day the Khan would ride to war and sack the cities of his enemies. He would go to the first city and give them warning: surrender and they lose only treasure; fight and all would die. They always fought first time. But then the Khan would take all the prisoners out of city and kill every man, woman, child – bar one. This one was sent to next city. They surrender mighty fast.'

'It is still evil,' said Sheera.

Ubadai spread his hands. 'This is the way the world knows. Many people now run from forest. Save families. This makes for small rebel army, you understand? And small army less a problem than big army. We should be in Cithaeron.'

On the afternoon of the fifth day Errin sat down beside the path and checked the soles of his riding boots. One had worn through, the other had split at the seam.

'Look at them,' he said to Sheera. 'You know how much these cost?'

She chuckled. 'Poor Errin! The forest life does not suit you.'

'Be silent!' hissed Ubadai, drawing his short sword from its scabbard.

'What's happening?' Errin asked.

Three men leapt from the undergrowth and Errin dived aside, rolling to the earth. As he rose and reached for his belt, two more attackers jumped to his back, bearing him to the ground. He twisted his head to see Ubadai at bay, his sword ready.

'Don't fight!' shouted Errin. 'Put up your sword!' Ubadai muttered something inaudible and spat, but he sheathed the blade and allowed the newcomers to pin his arms. Errin was hauled to his feet as a young woman stepped from the bushes. She was tall, with honey-blonde hair, and dressed in tunic and trews of buckskin.

'What are you doing here?' she asked.

'Looking for Llaw Gyffes,' said Errin. She smiled.

'For what reason?'

'That is no concern of yours,' he answered. She drew a wickedly sharp hunting knife and placed it against his throat. 'On the other hand,' he continued, 'why make a mystery of it? We are here to join the rebels.'

'I think you are spies,' she said. 'You are no forester;

314

you are a King's man.' Errin managed a smile. The man on his right had firm hold of his bicep, but his forearm was free and carefully he slid his hand to his belt buckle.

'Ollathair,' he said.

'What was that?' asked the woman, but her voice had slowed and deepened. Errin surged free of the men holding him and brushed aside the knife. The man to his left aimed a clumsy blow at his head, but Errin ducked and crashed a fast right-hand punch to his assailant's jaw. The man dropped slowly to the grass. Errin leapt and cannoned his foot into the face of the second attacker, who spun and toppled to the ground with graceful lack of speed. The woman was moving in, her knife sweeping up towards Errin's belly, but he grabbed her wrist, twisted and caught the blade as she dropped it. Raising it to rest against her long neck, he touched the belt buckle.

'As I said,' he told her, 'I am here to join Llaw Gyffes. Will you take me to him?'

'You are very fast,' she said, lifting her hand and gently pushing the knife from her neck.

'Yes,' he admitted. 'But I am no spy. My name is Errin.'

'May I have my knife back . . . Errin?'

'Of course,' he said, reversing the blade and handing it to her. She moved to the fallen men and knelt by them. One was stirring. Errin wandered to where Ubadai and Sheera were still being held. 'Would you be so kind as to release my comrades?' he requested. Ubadai shook himself free and stalked away, muttering curses beneath his breath. Sheera approached Errin and took his arm.

'You are a constant surprise to me,' she whispered. 'I am so relieved she didn't hit you. That *would* have been embarrassing.'

He grinned. 'I enjoy surprising you.'

'I'll kill the bastard!' Errin spun as one of his earlier attackers stormed to his feet, dragging a knife from his belt.

'No!' shouted the woman. 'We'll take them to Llaw.' The man hesitated, but he was unconvinced. Errin swallowed hard and rested his hand on his belt.

The man walked forward. He was tall and black-bearded and his eyes were angry. 'I won't forget this,' he hissed. 'You and I will settle it – you understand me?'

'I believe that I do,' said Errin. The man nodded, rammed his knife into his belt and pushed past them.

The woman approached. 'My name is Arian; I am a friend of Llaw's. If you follow I will take you to him.'

As she walked away ahead of him, Errin's eyes were drawn to her swaying hips. 'I think I'd follow her anywhere,' he said. But Sheera did not smile. Errin looked closely at his companion, but said nothing.

They crested a hill and found themselves looking down on a bustling community. Homes were still being erected, and elsewhere archers were loosing shafts at crudely made targets. On the hillside some wild cattle had been gathered, alongside some bighorn sheep. Errin halted as light flashed from something bright and metallic on the hillside opposite. Four figures in silver armour seemed to be fighting each other; but watching for a few moments, he realized they were merely prac-tising their skills.

'Who are they?' he asked Arian.

'I have no idea. Let's find Llaw.'

It seemed to Errin that the young woman was more than surprised to be directed to the hillside, and to find the legendary Llaw Gyffes arrayed in silver armour.

'What the Hell . . . ?' she began, but Llaw gestured her to silence and approached Errin.

'I think we've been expecting you,' he said, holding out his hand.

Errin shook it. 'You have?'

'Our Armourer told us two would arrive today. I suggest you go up to the cave and speak to him.'

'Now?' asked Errin.

'Unless you have other, more pressing, plans?'

'No, not at all. We will speak later.' Errin, Ubadai and Sheera began the long walk to the cave, while Arian remained behind with Llaw.

As the trio approached the cave mouth, a youth strolled out to meet them. Errin stopped in his tracks, his heart sinking.

'What's the matter?' Sheera asked.

'This is the boy I shot.'

Lámfhada moved to meet them. 'Welcome, Lord Errin, welcome to the Forest of the Ocean.'

'Nice to see you again. Can you direct us to the Armourer? I'd love to stop and talk about old times, but . . .'

'I am the Armourer. And do not fear "old times". The past is dead. And no one here knows that you hunted me.'

'I see. What do you require of me . . . of us?'

'Stand for a moment . . . and listen,' said Lámfhada. Nonplussed, Errin allowed the silence to grow. The sound of distant music came to him; he strained to hear it, but it drifted like the echo of an echo.

'What is it?' he asked. Lámfhada said nothing. 'Can you hear it?' he asked Sheera; she shook her head.

'I can,' said Ubadai. 'It is something in the cave.'

Errin moved to the cave mouth. The sound – if sound it was – was stronger here. It seemed to whisper in the caverns of his soul . . . calling, drawing him in. He turned to Ubadai, who was now standing beside him.

'You can hear it?'

'Yes,' answered the Nomad. 'Let us get away from here.'

'It does not feel threatening.'

'Trust me,' said Ubadai.

'You should listen to him, Errin,' advised Lámfhada. 'If you enter the cave, your life will be changed for ever. Worse, it may bring you pain and an early death.'

'He's right. Let's go,' said Ubadai, grasping Errin's arm.

'No,' whispered Errin. 'I must go in.'

'Why you such a fool always?' shouted Ubadai, but Errin pulled free of him and walked into the cave. It was torchlit, the shadows dancing like ghosts in the dark. Errin walked on until he stood before the three remaining suits of armour. He heard a sound from beside him.

'It is the armour calling you,' said Lámfhada.

'It is Gabala armour; I cannot wear it.'

Lámfhada nodded. 'It is little known, Lord Errin, but one of the most important virtues of all Knights of the Gabala was that not one of them ever expected the honour. To expect it was to lose it. And what you have just said has been said before, a hundred times, by every man who wore the silver.'

Errin turned. 'I am a Lord of the Feast, not a warrior. Never a warrior!' He laughed and pointed to his belt. 'I wear a sorcerer's charm that gives me speed. But it is not from me – not from within.'

'I know all this, Errin. But you have been chosen.'

'By whom? By you?'

'Not by me. But now it is your choice. You can walk away – and no man will judge you.'

'What of the men whose armour this is? What of the real Knights? Supposing they return? Can I give it back?'

'They have returned, Errin. They are the enemy: the Knights of the Red.'

'And I will have to go against them? Cairbre? I fought him once. He is unbeatable; he even gave me his own sword.'

'Then choose your path.'

Errin swung to stare at the armour. Licking his lips, he tried to draw back, but his mind was full of raw memories: Dianu at the stake, the jeering, chanting crowd, Okessa . . . His hand reached out, his fingers touching the metal. Warmth flowed through him and tears started in his eyes.

'Damn you!' shouted Ubadai. 'Always the fool!' The Nomad strode forward and pushed past Errin. He walked to a suit of armour and slapped his hand against it. 'This is mine!' he hissed.

'Why?' whispered Errin. 'You did not have to join me.'

'You know nothing,' said the Nomad. 'Locked in a pantry, you would starve to death.'

The grey stallion walked into the glade with head held high, ears pricked. It saw the man waiting and approached him boldly, secure in its power. The man rose and held out a hand, rubbing the stallion's nose and stroking its neck. The touch was sure.

Manannan smiled. 'You are not Kuan, my friend,' he said softly, 'but I think you will do.' He swung himself to the stallion's back and the beast reared suddenly, but the Once-Knight was ready, his thighs gripped hard to the horse's flanks. 'Steady, now,' he soothed. 'Steady.'

Riding bareback, he headed the horse down from the hills to the ruined village. Several dead horses lay where they had fallen, but Manannan dismounted downwind of them and selected a saddle and bridle.

Within the hour he was riding from the forest towards the distant fortress of Mactha.

He was worried as he rode – and not just for his life, though his peril did not escape his anxiety. His thoughts were of Lámfhada and the new Knights. Only

Elodan had the skill and the training for the role – and he was crippled. The outlaw Groundsel was a man full of barely concealed bitterness, while Nuada was a poet who could never take up arms. As for Llaw Gyffes? Manannan liked him; there was iron in him. But was that enough for a Gabala Knight? A man could eat sparrows and convince himself they were turkeys – but the question of taste remained. And Morrigan . . . poor Morrigan.

For several days Manannan had endured the pangs of withdrawal from Ambria. For Morrigan, the night-mare must have been infinitely worse. And yet she had not complained once. But then the Once-Knight had heard of the disappearance of a man from Groundsel's group, and his fears had begun.

He reached the edge of the trees and looked back. Somewhere within the vast forest an enemy force was riding. Manannan wished he could have ridden against it with Elodan and the others.

Instead he must ride into the lair of the enemy and fight a duel with a man who had been a brother. It would be Pateus, who had now resumed his former name, Cairbre: Cairbre the thinker, the oldest of the Knights. Cairbre the kind, always the first to entertain the village children with stories. Now he was Cairbre the Drinker of Souls. It was almost inconceivable.

Manannan dug his heels into the stallion's flanks.

And rode for the castle . . .

The Duke of Mactha was brought out into the field and the crowds jeered and hissed. He wore a simple tunic of black wool edged with silver braid, dark grey riding trews and boots, and a short leather cape lined with fur. His head was held high and he looked neither left nor right as he was led to the execution cart set before the King's pavilion. Climbing into the cart, he stood facing his monarch. All around the field were the newly arrived soldiers of the King's army, waiting eagerly to see the execution. The Duke glanced to his left at the scaffold and the huge vat of boiling water beside it. A shiver went through him and he looked away. As soon as this farce of a trial was over, he would be taken to the scaffold and hanged. But before he could die, he would be cut down and plunged into the boiling water. Then his arms and his legs would be hacked away. Hanged, drawn and quartered . . . the traditional end for traitors.

The Duke returned his gaze to the King. On his right sat the eight Red Knights; on his left the Lord Seer, Okessa.

Okessa rose and fixed his pale eyes on the Duke. 'You have been brought here before your peers and your liege lord to answer charges of treason, of aiding and giving counsel to traitors. How do you plead to these accusations?'

The Duke smiled thinly. 'I say that they are nonsense. Now shall we get on with the execution? You are beginning to bore me, Okessa.'

'We will see how bored you will become,' Okessa snapped. 'Let us hear from the witnesses.'

For the next hour the Duke listened to a variety of stories from his servants and his soldiers: that he went to Errin and offered to help him escape, that he had condemned the King publicly, that he had suggested to his first officer that if the King were assassinated while at Mactha there was a good chance the Duke himself would be declared the next monarch.

As each witness finished his testimony, the Duke was asked if he had any questions. He had none. At last the ritual came to its close, and now Okessa rose once more, demanding that the traitor should meet his fate at once. The King had sat silently through the trial.

Now he rose – his white hair shining in the sunlight, his pale face glistening with sweat.

'Has the prisoner no words to say in his own defence?' he asked. 'Does he not wish to beg for clemency?'

The Duke laughed aloud. 'I have stood here and wasted a beautiful morning, my liege, listening to lies and deceits. I will not spoil it further by adding the truth. To be honest, though, for a moment, I think this is rather a good day to die. So let us . . .'

His words faded away as the sound of a trotting horse came to him. He turned and saw a Knight in silver armour riding slowly across the field. The crowd was silent as the Knight approached.

'Who are you, sir?' demanded the King.

'I am Manannan, a Knight of the Gabala.'

'That is a lie. The Gabala Knights have gone. You are an imposter.'

'I see Samildanach sitting beside you, my lord. He will vouch for me.'

The King swung to the Red Knight, who rose and removed his helm. His hair was close-cropped and white, his eyes a brilliant blue.

'What do you do here, Coward Knight?' asked Samildanach. 'Have you come to pay homage to your betters?'

Manannan ignored him and fixed his gaze on the King. 'I am here, my Lord, to champion the cause of the Duke of Mactha, and demand the right to trial by combat.'

'A traitor has no rights,' screamed Okessa, but the King waved him to silence.

'You wish to go against Sir Cairbre, who is the King's champion in this Duchy? Is that wise, Sir Knight?'

'Who knows, sire? It would certainly add some spice to the proceedings,' Manannan replied.

'That is true – and it should not be said that the King decries the customs that made our ancestors masters of the world. Very well. Let the fight commence.'

'It is customary, my lord King, for a horse to be brought to the accused, for should he be proved innocent he may desire to ride from his place of execution and not walk like a prisoner between guards.'

'Let it be so done,' said Ahak. 'Are you ready to champion my cause, Cairbre?' he asked. The Red Knight stood and bowed.

'As always, my liege.'

Manannan dismounted, tethered his stallion to the execution cart and waited until a second horse had been brought for the Duke.

'Why are you doing this for me?' asked the prisoner. 'I do not know you.'

'But you do, my Lord. A long time ago, you and I jousted and you unseated me. But that is the past. I do it because it needs to be done. When the battle is over, mount the horse and ride like the devil towards the forest.'

'What of you?'

'With luck I shall be beside you.'

'Can you defeat Cairbre?'

'There is always a first time,' replied Manannan, pulling shut his visor and striding out to the centre of the field, where he drew his longsword and plunged it into the ground by his feet. Cairbre walked slowly down the pavilion steps and marched to stand before him. His visor was open, and Manannan was shocked to see that his old friend appeared to have become once more a youth.

'Surprised, Manannan? You should not be. Paulus, whom you so cruelly slew, could have given you this for yourself. Immortality, Manannan – that is what you threw away.'

'I did not kill him, Pateus; Morrigan did that. And

such immortality as you have, I would not desire. Come, let us cross blades and be done with it.'

'I do not desire your death, Manannan, but I have no choice. I will make it swift for you, I promise you that.'

'Youth has changed you, Pateus; it has given you arrogance.' Cairbre smiled and raised his sword and Manannan's blade swung up to rest against it. Both men looked to the King.

'Begin!' he shouted. Cairbre's sword slashed down, but Manannan blocked the cut with his cross guard and sent a wicked blow crashing into Cairbre's side. Crimson armour-plates sundered and split – but the sword was halted by the chain-mail beneath.

The crowd began to bay and cheer as the Knights circled one another, swords ringing and clashing in the discordant music of battle. Cairbre was slimmer and faster, but Manannan was powerful and his defence sure. Time and again the swords hammered against the defensive plate worn by both men, but neither combatant could land a deadly blow. The battle wore on. Manannan's blade blocked a thrust aimed at the groin, and lashed out to crash against Cairbre's waist. Again the crimson plates parted, and now blood began to seep through the mail-shirt where the rings had been driven into the flesh beneath. Cairbre circled to his left, trying to guard the wound, but Manannan launched a fresh attack – feinting a blow to the head, only to bring the sword slicing down to rip into Cairbre's injured side. This time blood sprayed from the wound.

Manannan surged forward – only to suffer a riposte that all but tore his helm from his head. Even wounded, Cairbre was not an opponent to take lightly. Manannan moved in more cautiously; Cairbre was growing desperate, and the Once-Knight knew that the battle was reaching its climax. Now Cairbre had only one chance – a swift attack and a killing blow to the neck.

plates. Manannan gave him the opening. Cairbre's sword flashed in the sunlight. The Once-Knight ducked beneath the slashing blade and rammed his own sword, point first, into Cairbre's side, driving the blade up, and up, tearing through Cairbre's lungs. As the Red Knight sagged to his knees, Manannan pushed him to his side and tore loose the sword. Cairbre groaned and tried to speak, but blood fountained from his mouth.

In the stunned silence that followed Manannan rose, walked to his stallion and mounted.

He bowed once to the King and wheeled his horse. The Duke leapt from the cart to the saddle of his own mount and the two riders thundered across the field towards a high picket fence.

'Stop them!' shouted Okessa and the crowd ran at them, but the riders approached the fence well ahead. The Duke leaned forward in the saddle and his horse surged up and over the barrier. Manannan followed him, almost losing his balance.

Then they were away and clear.

Manannan glanced back. The King's riders had reacted swiftly and the chase was on.

Bavis Lan was sick of the forest. For sixteen days he and his men had hunted down traitors, destroyed villages and butchered the inhabitants. And at no time had they come across any sign of a rebel army. It was galling to think of the long ride back to Mactha and the sterile report to be made to the King. Two days ago they had captured the leader of a small settlement and he had been tortured to death. Throughout his ordeal, Bavis had questioned him concerning Llaw Gyffes and his army. The man had known nothing.

Bavis hitched himself round in his saddle, looking back at the four hundred and eighty-three men riding behind him. Only seventeen had died during the brief campaign, and that included young Lugas whose severed arm had turned blue with corruption. He had died screaming three nights ago. The slight losses alone should ensure that the King believed his tale: there was no rebellion.

The column wound its slow way down the forest paths and out on to the open ground before a range of wooded hills. Here Bavis raised his arm and signalled a halt for the midday meal. As he did so, three riders came galloping from the woods to the right. He shaded his eyes against the sunlight and tried to identify the men, thinking them to be his scouts. As they neared, he saw that they were dressed in foresters' buckskins – and each carried a bow.

The riders hauled on the reins of their mountain ponies some thirty paces from the column and loosed their shafts. Bavis ducked low over his stallion's neck and an arrow took the man behind him in the throat. The three attackers turned their mounts and thundered away towards the trees.

'First Turma, after them!' yelled Bavis and sixteen riders promptly peeled away from the column and spurred their horses into a gallop. The tall horses of the soldiers were stronger and faster than the ponies, and Bavis could see that the enemy would be overtaken just before they could reach the safety of the trees. The foresters wheeled their ponies and loosed a second volley of arrows. Two soldiers were shot from their mounts; a third swayed in the saddle – a shaft lodged in his shoulder.

Suddenly six Knights in armour of shining silver rode from the trees and Bavis blinked. The newcomers hammered into the charging lancers, swords bright in the sunlight. Horses reared and men died and the charge broke.

'Advance!' roared Bavis Lan, and the entire column galloped towards the fray. The six Knights cut and hacked their way clear of the First Turma and rode back into the forest, their grey mounts barely cantering. Fury filled Bavis. Dragging his sword clear of its scabbard, he screamed a battle cry and set off in pursuit. The trail within the trees was wide and the Knights were just ahead.

A terrible groaning noise came from Bavis' right and he swung in the saddle in time to see a huge tree crashing down behind him. Men were swept from their saddles, horses crushed beneath the falling giant. A second tree fell – and a third. Panic swept through the column as riders dragged on their reins and tried to steer a path away from the trail. Arrows tore into them from the undergrowth. Bavis was lost. The thunderous noise of crashing trees, the pitiful screams of the trapped and dying, the chaos of the ambush, left him unable to think clearly.

'Back!' he yelled. 'Retreat!' But there was nowhere to go. An arrow glanced from his breastplate and tore up into his cheek.

He had to get away! He dragged at the reins and found himself facing the six Knights, who had turned and were once more moving in for the attack. Bavis kicked his horse into a run and swerved from the trail; an archer loomed up before him, but he lashed his sword across the man's face.

Now he was clear and racing for the safety of the open ground beyond. He glanced back to see a single Knight following him. His horse stumbled, righted itself and ran on; the beast was sweating heavily, and foam showed on its neck; the charge uphill had drained its strength. Bavis looked back once more . . . the Knight was gaining.

'Dear Gods of Heaven, save me!' he pleaded as his stallion cleared a fallen tree and galloped out into the open. Far now from the screams, Bavis steered his mount towards a stream at the foot of the valley. If he could just make the stream, he could lose the Knight in the thick undergrowth beyond.

Another look behind him showed that the Knight had not closed the distance between them – but he was still there, grim and deadly.

Bavis' stallion splashed into the stream and stumbled up the bank beyond. The Knight was closer now. Bavis ducked low over the saddle as branches tore at him. The trail narrowed, cutting left and right. He dragged the stallion to a halt and leapt from the saddle, then slapped his hand against the beast's rump. It took off at a run and the general hurled himself into the undergrowth. He heard the Knight canter past, then rose and began to make his way deeper into the trees. The ambush had been terrible and he began to realize the awesome implications for his own career. His thirty Turmae had been destroyed utterly, of that he was in no doubt. The King would not take it kindly that the pick of his lancers had been wiped out by a band of peasant rebels. Bavis sat down on a large rock. He might have won his way clear of the enemy, but his life would be forfeit upon his return to Mactha.

It was all so galling. The success of his foray into the forest had lulled him into a sense of false security. He was convinced there was no rebel army; why in the devil's name had he charged up that hill?

His thoughts were interrupted as a young woman stepped into the glade. She was extraordinarily beautiful, with long golden hair curiously streaked with silver.

'Are you lost?' she asked, moving towards him. He was struck by the sensual grace of her movements.

'Yes. Where are you from?'

She came close and reached up to touch his bare arm. A shiver of pure pleasure came to him as her fingers stroked his flesh. His mouth was dry – the Knight forgotten.

His hands fumbled at her tunic.

How strange, he thought, that arousal could come at such a time.

Morrigan's arm circled his neck and drew him down towards her.

Elodan turned away as Groundsel cut the throat of a wounded soldier.

'Squeamish, Lord Knight?' asked the outlaw leader.

'Yes,' answered Elodan. 'I was not trained for butchery.'

Groundsel laughed. 'You would never guess it! Your strategy was perfect – only one escaped.'

Everywhere the rebels were stripping the dead, gaining armour and swords. Thirty horses had survived the massacre, and these were loaded with weapons and armour and led away, back towards the camp in the high meadow. Elodan walked from the bodies to where Llaw, Errin and Ubadai were sitting in a sheltered glade by a tiny stream.

Errin looked up. 'Unbelievable,' he said. 'You planned it well, Elodan.'

'I feel no pride in it,' owned the Lord Knight. 'So many dead.'

'All enemies,' declared Ubadai. 'I shed no tears.'

'No,' whispered Elodan, 'nor does Groundsel. He'll be searching the corpses for gold teeth next.'

Errin grinned. 'Not an easy man to like, our Groundsel. But he fights well.'

'There is more to being a Knight than that!' snapped Elodan. 'You should know that, Lord Errin. I am ashamed to wear this armour.'

'Do not say that!' stormed Llaw Gyffes. 'Not ever! I know how you feel – but put yourself in my place. I am a blacksmith and an outlaw. As far as history is concerned, I am also a wife killer. I do not know how to be a Knight – but I will do my best not to dishonour the armour. That is all any man can do. Content yourself with this victory; it will give heart to the men.'

'I hope Morrigan is all right,' remarked Errin, as the silence grew. 'One of us should have gone with her.'

'I think you will find she is capable,' said Elodan. 'I watched her during the first encounter. She uses a sword like a veteran and her size belies her strength.'

'Even so, she is a woman,' said Errin.

Llaw chuckled. 'Do not confuse women like Morrigan with the wasp-waisted courtesans you have known, Errin. No – nor Arian nor Sheera. They are women to walk the mountains with. Strong.'

'I am no expert on mountain women, Llaw. I bow to your knowledge.'

Groundsel joined them, removing his helm and rubbing at his sweat-drenched hair. 'When do we eat?' he asked.

'How can you think of food with the stench of death in the air?' responded Errin.

'I think of food because I am hungry. What has the smell to do with it?'

'There is the woman,' said Ubadai, pointing to the hillside. Morrigan rode into the glade and dismounted and Elodan rose and strode to meet her. She raised her hand and lowered the helm visor masking her face.

'Did you catch him?'

'Yes, he is dead.'

'Are you well, Morrigan?' asked the Lord Knight.

'I am fine. The sun is bright on my eyes, that is all. When do we leave?'

'Most of the men are returning to the camp, but I would like you and Groundsel to head west. I am told there is a large settlement there, on a mountainside. It can only be reached by a bridge of chains. Some of the men have been there and they claim that the leader, Bucklar, has more than two hundred warriors. It would

330

be good for us if he could spare a hundred for our cause.'

'West?' she queried. 'That will bring us close to Pertia Port. I thought the enemy was there in force.'

'So I understand. Take what supplies you will need.'

'Does it have to be Groundsel? Why not Errin or Llaw – or even the Nomad?'

Elodan grinned. 'Being the Lord Knight has certain advantages, Morrigan. I do not want him around me, so you have the pleasure of his company.'

'He may not survive the journey,' she said.

The Duke dismounted by the cave and stared long and hard at the blond youth waiting for them. 'What do you want of me?' he asked.

The youth smiled. 'I want nothing, my Lord. All I ask is that you step into the cave and make a choice.'

'No.' The Duke turned to Manannan. 'What is in there?'

'A suit of armour,' said the Once-Knight.

'And I am to wear it? I am expected to fight alongside peasants and outlaws?'

'More than that,' Lámfhada told him. 'You will be expected to die for them, if necessary.'

'What madness! I am grateful that you saved my life – but I did not ask for your help and therefore feel no obligation to you. Why should I fight for your cause?'

Lámfhada stepped forward. 'There is no reason why you should,' he said. 'If you desire to ride on, then you may. We will even give you supplies for the journey.'

'And if I fight for you, what do you offer me?'

'Nothing at all,' came the answer.

'You amaze me, boy. Tell me, Manannan, this suit of armour, is it silver like your own?'

'Yes.'

'You are asking me to become a Knight of the

331

Gabala? It is beyond belief. Ask any man who ever served me and he will tell you I am a hard man, maybe even a cruel one. I have lied and I have cheated and I have killed. All these things I have done to maintain my position – and had Okessa not turned on me I would still be serving the King. Is that the sort of man you wish to wear the silver helm? I think not.'

'That was yesterday, Lord Duke,' said Lámfhada. 'Now let the armour choose.'

'What do you say, Manannan? Should I enter the cave?'

'Why should my opinion make a difference?'

'Because you are a Gabala Knight. Do you want me for a companion?'

'No, my Lord. But I am only a man. The armour is imbued with magic and it will choose. Enter the cave.'

The Duke stroked his thin beard and looked at the cave mouth. Then he shrugged. 'Very well, I will look. But build no hopes, my friends.'

Swiftly he walked into the darkness and approached the solitary suit of armour. It was cold inside the cave and he shivered. Two flickering torches lit the walls, and reflected flames danced upon the breastplate. As a child he had been enchanted by tales of the Gabala Knights, but his father had always dismissed them.

'Fools,' he would say. 'Life is too short to spend riding the country interfering in other men's disputes. What does it matter if a peasant loses a farm, or wins one? Who will care a hundred years from now?'

The words seemed to echo inside the Duke's mind. He remembered his father's funeral; not one tear had been shed.

'And who will cry for you, Roem?' he asked himself, then shook his head. What did it matter? Tears for the dead were a waste of time. The question now was a simple one – did he stay and fight, or leave for Cithaeron? Across the sea, with no wealth, he would find few friends. He would be forced to seek service with other rebels, perhaps as a captain of the guard, or as a Sabreur for some petty tribal chieftain. And here? Here he would fight alongside peasants and outlaws, men with no breeding: men not fit to kiss his hand.

Yet, at least, here he had a chance to regain his position, to win back his father's Duchy.

He sat on the cold stone floor staring up at the armour. What chance of victory did these rebels have – even with the Knights reborn? Realistically? Against Ahak's legions, his lancers and his scouts? Little or none. So what was the real choice? Alive in Cithaeron or dead in the Gabala!

Alive? Penniless and without honour – that was not life.

So then, what else is there, Roem? You can either live out your span, despised by your fellows, or fight alongside men you despise.

He stood and walked to the armour, seeing his lean angular face reflected in the breastplate. 'Put a cloak over your contempt, Roem,' he whispered. 'Stand alongside these men and win back your birthright. And then, when the battle is won, the peasants can be herded back into their place.'

He reached out and touched the armour.

18

Outside the cave in the village beyond, the victorious rebel army had arrived safely home. Women and children streamed to meet them. Manannan sat down on a boulder and watched as Elodan, Llaw, Errin and Ubadai rode up to the cave.

'It is good to see you safe,' Elodan greeted them, stepping from the saddle. 'Did your mission go well?'

'He is in the cave,' said Manannan.

'What of Cairbre?'

'I killed him. Let us talk no more of it.'

'Who is in the cave?' asked Llaw. 'What was this mission?'

Lámfhada moved in front of Llaw. 'The Duke of Mactha,' he said softly.

All colour fled from Llaw's face. 'What mockery is this? The whoreson sentenced me to death for a crime he knew I did not commit. He is a King's man!'

'No,' said Manannan. 'He was on trial for his life; the King was to have him executed.'

'Which just shows that even a bad King cannot be wrong all the time. This is a mistake, but I will put it to rights. Get out of my way,' said Llaw, drawing his sword.

'Put it down!' Elodan commanded. 'This instant!'

Llaw swung on him. 'So? You patricians want to stick together, do you? Fine. What else should I have expected?'

'You are wrong, Llaw,' said Elodan softly. 'I am the man you asked to lead your army. *Your* army. But I am also the Lord Knight of the New Gabala. If the armour chooses him, then he is with us. If not?' He shrugged. 'Then he is yours. Does that suit you?'

Llaw backed away. 'If the armour chooses? Had I known he would be among us, I would never have agreed to wear it myself.' Slamming his sword in its scabbard, he stalked to his horse, mounted and rode for the village.

'Thank you, Elodan,' said the Duke, stepping out into the open, his armour blazing in the sunlight.

'Lord Duke,' said Elodan, 'welcome to the Order.'

'I am the Duke no longer. My name is Roem,' he said, holding out his hand. Elodan shook it. Errin removed his helm and strolled forward.

'I see we have a fine cook,' commented Roem. 'We must be a force to be reckoned with.'

Arian found Llaw Gyffes high on the south meadow in a grove of beech trees overlooking the forest. He was sitting by a small fire, staring into the flames, and did not hear her approach. She sat beside him and reached out to touch him, but stopped. Encased as he was in his armour, there was no point.

'Llaw?' she whispered but he did not turn his head. 'Come, Llaw, speak to me.'

'There is nothing to say. I am lost, Arian . . . lost.' She moved closer to him.

'No, you are not! You are Llaw Gyffes, the strongest man I have ever known. How can you be so down-hearted? You have triumphed over your enemies and your army grows by the day.'

He shook his head. 'None of it matters. My life was destroyed when Lydia died. And now I too must die – just as the Dagda said. And you know what will happen then? Nothing. If the King should prove victorious, the world will go on as before. If we should defeat him, then the Duke of Mactha – or someone like him – will rule and the world will go on as before. We change nothing by what we do.'

'What were you expecting, Llaw? Back in the village, there are people who would now be dead but for you and Elodan, and the others. At Groundsel's settlement there are Nomads who would have frozen to death but for you and Groundsel and Nuada. Ask *them* if you made a difference. Take your eyes from the stars, Llaw. Look to the earth.'

She rose to kneel by his side, her fingers pulling at the leather straps of his breastplate. 'What are you doing?' he asked.

'Get out of this metal,' she ordered. 'Put it aside. Then we will walk for a while in the mountains and you will feel the air on your skin.' He helped her, laid the armour beside the fire and stood. She moved to him and ran her hands along his arms.

'I am tired of waiting for you,' she said. 'And don't tell me you are not ready; I am sick of it. You are a man – so stop running from the past and fearing the future. All we have is the Now. All we will ever have is the Now.'

'Does it not frighten you that I must die soon?'

'Yes, it terrifies me,' she told him. 'But it will be the worse for me if you should be gone having never loved me.'

His arms circled her. 'I love you,' he said simply. 'You are never far from my thoughts.'

She drew him down beside the fire and kissed him, but he groaned and weakly pulled away.

'Forget the stars, Llaw,' she whispered. 'Forget the stars.'

Later, as they lay closely together, it seemed to Llaw that a burden had been taken from him. He could not recall the moment when it had passed, nor even what it was that had weighed him down. He could smell the newly growing grass and feel the wind of spring upon his face. He could hear the birds in the trees above and sense the joy of growth in the forest. The world of kings and knights and peasants seemed a fragile, insubstantial matter as Arian snuggled against him, her right leg curled over his thigh. Rising on his elbow, he looked down at her. She was sleeping. He touched her skin and kissed her hair and her eyes opened.

'I was dreaming,' she said.

'Are you happy still?'

'You fool,' she answered. She rose swiftly and ran to the stream and he followed her, watching her bathe. 'Come in,' she called.

'It looks cold.'

'The great Llaw Gyffes fears a little cold water? Come in.'

He waded in alongside her and sat down. 'Gods of Heaven!' he exclaimed. She laughed and splashed his chest and face; he grabbed her and they rolled under the water.

'I surrender,' she shouted as they surfaced. 'Truly.'

He said nothing and pulled her in to his embrace. 'You should have come to me long ago,' he whispered.

'I did, Llaw, but you were not ready. Will you regret this day?'

'Never.'

'Good. Now get dressed and go back to your Knights - all of them.'

His face darkened. 'I cannot face the man. I think if I did, I would kill him.'

'You are too strong for that. Trust me, Llaw. In this, I think I know you better.'

He stood and shivered. Arian grasped his arm and hauled herself upright. Sensing his changing mood, she remained silent, following him back to the fire. He dressed swiftly and started to walk back to his horse which was tethered to the root of a nearby beech. But he stopped and looked back; then suddenly he grinned. 'Will you ride with me, my lady?'

She pulled on her tunic and trews, gathered her boots and knife and ran to him.

He left her in the village and rode back for the cave. The other Knights were sitting with Elodan and Lámfhada. Llaw dismounted and tethered his horse. No one spoke as he joined the circle and looked across at the Duke of Mactha.

'I am Llaw Gyffes,' he said, extending his hand.

'I am Roem. I am pleased to meet you,' responded the other, taking his hand and gripping it firmly.

'Now the new Order is complete,' said Lámfhada, 'and it is time to prepare for the Day of Blood. Nuada is carrying our banner to all the settlements of the forest. Morrigan and Groundsel are seeking allies close to Pertia Port. The King's army is almost ready to move. They will be at our southern borders within ten days; we must be ready to oppose them.'

'How many men do we have?' Roem asked.

'Close to two hundred now, but the numbers are swelling daily. Nuada's prowess has rarely been put to better use.'

'The King has ten thousand men,' said Roem. 'Two thousand lancers, six thousand foot-soldiers, fifteen hundred archers, and five hundred scouts, used to the ways of the forest. You cannot hold them with two hundred, nor a thousand.'

Elodan raised his hand. 'It is not important that we have a large army, only that the King thinks we have. Now Lámfhada says he has placed a spell over the forest and the Seers of the King cannot breach it. That being the case, all the King has to go on is that his five hundred lancers have been wiped out. I do not think he will immediately venture into the forest in force. He will send in his scouts and then advance slowly. We must eliminate those scouts.'

'That sounds plausible,' said Errin, 'but do we fight a holding action from now until the King dies of old age? Somewhere there must be a conclusive encounter.'

'Indeed there must, and we must recognize the opportunity when it arises,' answered Elodan. 'But until then, as the weaker side, we must hit and run – strike them where we can – make them think they are facing a force ten . . . twenty times greater than we are. And all the time we will be growing.'

Llaw spoke. 'There is something else to consider: supplies. We have the forest and the deer, and sheep are plentiful. The King has ten thousand men and they will need to be supplied from the south. We must have a raiding force behind their lines. Empty bellies make for discontent.'

'I will lead that force,' said Roem. 'It is my Duchy and I know all the roads. Give me fifty men; we will live off the land and force them to send back troops.'

'You will be alone,' Lámfhada pointed out. 'We cannot support you.'

'Do not fear for me, Armourer. I am not ready to die yet.'

'Very well,' agreed Elodan. 'Select your fifty men and train them; you have ten days.'

'What of the rest of us?' asked Manannan.

'Your day is coming,' said Lámfhada, looking away.

Morrigan sat under the stars, her memories vivid and painful. Her love for Samildanach seemed from another age, when the world was young and innocence a joy. Her six years in the City of the Vyre had drenched that innocence in blood and lust and depravity. She could no longer recall the numbers of men and women who had shared her bed, nor see all the faces. All she could remember clearly was the taste of the Ambria, and the surging strength it brought to her limbs. She had told Manannan that Samildanach had tired of her, but it was not strictly true. Faced with the myriad pleasures of the Vyre they had drifted apart – seeking new sensations, more pleasure and pain.

Now Manannan claimed to love her. But he did not know . . . he loved the woman who once had been. She shivered as the night wind rolled down from the snow-covered peaks.

The general had died swiftly, his body shrivelling as his life filled her. He had not even known he was dying. She had left the empty hide-covered sack of bones where they fell. How soon would she need to feed again? A day? Two days?

She could hear Groundsel snoring by the fire. Detestable little man! You will be next, she promised herself. But then what? Manannan? Llaw Gyffes? Or merely another innocent stranger, like the man with the injured knee?

Was life so enchanting that she could not bear to leave it?

She knew the answer. Of course it was. To see and hear, to breathe and feel – how could anyone bear to die?

'Can't you sleep?' asked Groundsel, sitting up and running his fingers across his scalp. 'Damned lice,' he said. 'Nothing shifts them.'

'Try bathing once in a while.'

'What are you doing?' he asked.

'I am thinking.'

'Do you never sleep? How do you manage to keep your strength?'

'I draw it from the company of men, Groundsel. Strangely, I am feeling rather weak at the moment.'

He grinned at her. 'That's the first time I've seen any sign of humour from you, Morrigan. Perhaps you are beginning to like me. Why don't we start afresh? Come and join me; I'll give you a little strength.'

'Beware, Groundsel. I might just do that.'

He yawned and stood. She turned away as he urinated against a tree. 'Who are we supposed to see?' he asked.

'The leader is a man called Bucklar. You should like him, Groundsel – he has built his kingdom the way you built yours, on blood and murder. I think that's why Elodan thought you were the man to accompany me. You think Bucklar will send men to aid Llaw's army?'

'That depends. If he feels threatened by the King, then he will. If he thinks he's safe, he'll wait – and when the other forest leaders send men, he'll attack their lands and extend his power.'

'It is doubly important, then, that he helps us. For without him the other leaders will also hold back.'

'True, lady.' He began to climb into his leggings.

'I thought you wanted me,' said Morrigan, rising and striding towards him.

'I did,' Groundsel said, grinning. 'But you didn't say please. Dawn's coming up; we should be moving.'

Samildanach walked to the coffin and gazed down on the face of his oldest friend. His anger had gone and he was aware of a terrible emptiness deep within him. He knew that he had loved Cairbre as a brother, but that had been so long ago – before the crusade, before the Vyre, before the dawning of the New Age. Now he searched for that love and could find nothing. All he could see was a pale corpse, hands folded across a crimson breastplate.

The other Knights moved forward, circling the coffin and observing the body, and Samildanach looked from face to face. All wore the same expression. A shiver passed through the Lord Knight.

'We all know,' declared Samildanach, 'why our

brother died. He had ceased to take the Nourishment his body desired; he was physically weak. I do not know why Cairbre acted as he did, but it should be a lesson to us all. Our crusade is a holy one. We must restore the civilization and the power of the Gabala and introduce to it the wonders of the Vyre.' His words seemed hollow and they echoed in the high arched tomb. He saw again Manannan riding on to the field, his silver armour ablaze.

They had been friends . . .

Friends? The concepts of friendship, of love, or brotherhood moved in his mind like wisps of smoke, close but unobtainable.

'Are you well, Samildanach?' Edrin asked.

'Yes. I feel there should be words to say over our . . friend. But I can think of none.'

'Then let us cover him and be gone,' said Bersis. 'This place is cold and inhospitable.'

'Yes,' whispered Samildanach. 'Cover him.' He turned and strode for the stairs. The tallest of the Knights, he was wide-shouldered and narrow-hipped, and his movements, even in armour, were smooth and sure. He led the Knights to the Upper Room, where they seated themselves around the oval oak table.

'It is time,' said Samildanach, 'to gauge the strength of the enemy. The boy sorcerer has placed a barrier around the forest, and now is the moment to breach it. Give of your strength, my friends.'

The Knights bowed their heads and Samildanach felt the power soaking into his frame. Standing, he moved away from the table; lifting his arms, he called for the Red. His right hand sliced through the air which parted like a torn silk screen. A cold breeze whispered into the room. Samildanach opened the curtain further and gazed on the night-shrouded Forest of the Ocean. Then he stepped through and sealed the opening behind him. He was in a glade by a rushing river. Silently he made his way to the nearest hilltop and gazed around him at the moonlit landscape. A mile to the north lay the village of Llaw Gyffes. Samildanach sat cross-legged on the grass and closed his eyes, his spirit soaring into the night sky. Picturing the silver armour of the Gabala Knights, he felt the pull of their magic. He found himself floating by a cave. Inside, a fire was burning low and he could see seven sleeping figures. He recognized the Duke of Mactha, and Manannan; the others he did not know. He left the scene and rose once more. This time the pull took him far to the west and he came to a Long Hall wherein stood a shining figure surrounded by scores of warriors. The Knight was telling the men of past glories and great heroes. His voice was compelling and Samildanach could see the Colours blossoming throughout the hall.

This one was a danger . . .

Rising again, he journeyed east and north. Here, in a hollow, he found Morrigan and a squat, ugly peasant. Samildanach recoiled from the man. This was the enemy, he thought? This was the kind of man who now wore the silver? Anger flared in him. His spirit eyes turned to Morrigan, whose beauty in the moonlight was beyond reason. He smiled as she made some cutting remark to the peasant. How could she be here, among these low-born outlaws?

For some time Samildanach roamed the forest, seeking signs of the rebel army. Nowhere could he find any evidence of large concentrations of troops. But he did not have time to search the entire forest, and returned to the cave. There he hovered at the entrance and fixed his concentration on the blond youth who slept beside three golden statues of hounds.

'Come to me,' he said softly. 'Rise and come to me.'

Lámfhada stirred and rolled over. A shimmering light glowed around him and his spirit rose from his body. He blinked and saw Samildanach. The Knight moved back into the moonlight; Lámfhada followed and they floated high above the trees.

'How did you come here?' asked the youth.

'How did you think to stop me?' replied Samildanach. 'Foolish child. It is time to die.'

Suddenly Samildanach's form swelled to dwarf the terrified Lámfhada. Talons erupted from the Knight's fingers and slashed at the boy's chest. He hurled himself back and reached in terror for the Gold, but his mind was too full of fear and panic and it eluded him. He tried to escape, but Samildanach's giant hand circled him and he was drawn ever closer to the huge face.

'I expected at least a battle, child,' said the Knight.

'And you shall have one,' came a voice from behind. Samildanach swung to see a familiar figure floating beside him.

'Ollathair! What a pleasant surprise.'

'Not for me. Release the boy.'

'Why should I? A dead man cannot harm me.'

'Indeed he cannot. But there is a live man standing beside your body, with a knife to its throat.'

The figure faded from sight and Samildanach smiled. 'Well, boy, it seems you are to live – for now.' He released Lámfhada and sped away.

Samildanach opened his eyes and rolled to his right, his dagger hissing from its scabbard. There was no one close, but beside his body were the marks of recent footprints.

'You should have killed me, Ollathair – as I killed you.' He opened the curtain of night and stepped back into the Upper Room.

Once seated at the table, he roused the Knights.

Swiftly he outlined all he had seen; then he turned to Edrin and Bersis. 'I see no real danger to the King's army,' said Samildanach, 'but there are two men who

344

should be dealt with at haste. Edrin, you and Bersis will go to Pertia Port. There you will show the commander the King's seal. Bersis will take command of five hundred men and lead an attack on the Citadel above the Bridge of Chains. Morrigan will be there; I do not want her harmed. But there is one with her who offends me. Kill him. You, Edrin, will take fifty men and move through to the west of the forest. Find a village nestling below the two highest peaks. There you will hear of one of these new Knights. He is a story-teller of great power and, given time, he could raise a force against us. Destroy him. Use any means. You understand?'

'I will not fail you, Samildanach. Be assured, he will die.'

Lámfhada watched the Red Knight disappear into the distance. 'Ruad,' whispered the youth. 'Are you still here?'

'He never was here,' came a voice in his mind. 'Return to your body. I will come to you within a short time.'

Lámfhada did as he was bid; then he stood, wrapped a blanket around his shoulders and silently moved past the sleeping Knights. Outside the cave, he sat on a rock and scanned the countryside. After a few minutes he saw a tall figure making his way up the rocky path. Dressed in long robes of faded blue and ancient leather sandals, the man was old, and completely bald; a forked white beard flowed to his chest and he was using a quarter-staff to aid him on his climb. The newcomer halted before Lámfhada.

'I am the Dagda,' he said, 'and you were born under lucky omens.'

'Thank you for your help. Why did you impersonate Ruad?'

The Dagda shrugged. 'It was a necessary deceit which sowed the seed of fear in Samildanach's mind. Also,' he continued, sitting beside the youth, 'I knew Ruad Ro-fhessa – and I think my deceit would have pleased him. How are you faring, Lámfhada?'

The Armourer shrugged. 'I do my best. I can do no more. But I wish Ruad was here to guide me.'

'That is understandable, but a man is strongest when he is alone. Remember that. You have the Knights, and I think the Source is with you. Even so, there is much you must suffer.'

'I know all this. When I found the Gold I saw all that could be, all that should be, all that might be. What I could not discern was all that *will* be. Good men will die, I know that.'

'All men die, good or otherwise,' said the Dagda. 'And I know what you saw. I was with you when you flew.'

'You were the one whose presence I felt? I hoped it was Ruad.'

'Do not be disappointed. I have waited for you for a very long time.' The Dagda chuckled. 'Precisely one hundred and forty-two years! Does that seem a long time to you, child? I can see that it does. Well, we are here now and you have much to learn.'

'What do you mean . . . waited for me?'

'You – or one like you. Ruad would have told you, had he lived. You walk the Gold, Lámfhada, and that is rare. It is special. All the Colours are subject to the Gold, and it is part of the Great Harmony that when the Colours are threatened the Gold shines. The Red is swelling over the Realm, but its users do not understand the Harmony. They seek to make the Red preeminent, but no Colour exists of itself. If the Red is allowed to dominate, the other Colours will fade and die. Neither can the Red exist alone. So then, those who seek to promote the Red are actually destroying all magic. And without magic, the world would have only one colour: it would be Grey — the grey of the tombstone, the grey of ashes. You understand?'

'No,' said Lámfhada. 'Magic is used by very few. How would the world be harmed if it failed? Trees would still grow, flowers would bloom. Babies would still be born?'

'No, that is not the case. All life is magic, and all men feel it. They see the spectacle of the dawn and they are filled with a sense of wonder. That is magic. See the look in the mother's eyes as she holds her first-born and cuts its cord. She understands magic. In that moment, for that precious second, she understands. But when the Harmony is disrupted — as now in the Realm — and the magic is under threat, there is only cynicism and despair and Man's more brutal emotions begin to surface. No, my friend, the world needs magic as it needs air and water.'

'Who are you, Dagda? What are you?' Lámfhada asked. 'Are you some sort of god?'

The old man shook his head. 'I am a man. No more, no less. A long time ago I was — in the world's eyes — a great man. But I forsook my life and its riches, for I yearned to know all the world's secrets. I came to this forest and met a man — a man who had waited for me for eighty-seven years. He was the Dagda. And though his story was different from mine — as indeed yours will be — we were the same. We were rings in a chain that began when Man first reared to his hind legs, and will end when the stars fall and the sun dies . . . and perhaps not even then.'

Lámfhada's mouth was dry and he wished to be free of this strange old man. As if sensing his fear, the Dagda placed a bony hand upon his shoulder.

'We — he and I, you and I — are the Enchanters. We watch the Colours, and we nurse them. We walk the land and we maintain the Balance. Where all is war, and plague and death, we seek to aid the White or the Green or the Blue. Where all is peace and tranquillity, we strengthen the Red and the Black. But mostly we guard the Yellow, for as you now know, Lámfhada, the Yellow is merely the Gold disguised. And it is the Gold that maintains the other Colours.'

'Why is this not known?' Lámfhada asked him.

'Once it was, boy. And through such knowledge, men made themselves gods and brought calamity upon themselves. Now it survives in folk tales and legend. The Sun worshippers echo the Mystery; they worship the sphere of Gold that feeds the earth. Think of it. All that grows or lives or breathes depends upon the sun. And that is so with the Colours. The Yellow is born of innocence and the laughter of children, fed by the sense of wonder in the young. In its turn, it nourishes the others. But now the truth has become a Mystery, for it is safer that way. I guard that mystery. Now you will guard it.'

'What do you require of me?'

'I? I require nothing. I have completed my task, as the Guardian before me completed his. He was the Dagda . . . now you are the Dagda.'

'I do not wish to be.'

'No more did I. It is lonely, Lámfhada. And yet it is fulfilling – you will find it so.'

'And what if I die? Do you tell me the world will end? I do not believe it.'

'If you die, another will be chosen. And you are only one of many. But you will not die yet. You did not see your own death in any of the futures, only the deaths of your Knights. I know; for I too have seen the futures. I will leave you now – you will need time to think.'

'When will you come back for my answer?'

The old man smiled. 'I will not come back. I have done all that I was required to do. Now I will find a place. I will watch the stars, and I will die at peace and join the Colours.' The Dagda pushed himself to his feet and looked into Lámfhada's eyes. 'You have changed, young man, since I first saw you on that hillside six years ago, when you watched the Gabala Knights ride to a doom they did not deserve. And you will change even more through the long, lonely years ahead. Count the days, and the months and the years. And one day you will look into the face of a newcomer and you will see what I see. Farewell.'

'I don't want it. You cannot do this to me,' shouted Lámfhada, storming to his feet.

But the old man ignored him. He had heard those same words before. One hundred and forty-two years, three months and eight days before. But then it was he who had spoken them.

19

Groundsel reined in his stallion at the top of the rise and gazed down in silent wonder at the Bridge of Chains, spanning the chasm. The bridge was constructed of huge rings of iron from which hung rods connected to more rings. To these were fastened wooden planks. The swaying structure began on the northern slopes of a wooded hill and stretched for almost a quarter of a mile to where it joined a stone promontory set beneath a portcullis gate. 'How did they make it?' asked Groundsel as Morrigan rode alongside him.

'Some believe it was magic,' she told him, 'but my father explained that they first made a simple rope bridge and gradually strengthened it. He said it took over seven years to construct.'

Groundsel switched his attention to the Citadel itself. It was carved from the side of the mountain and reared above the chasm like a giant tooth. As far as he could see, the Citadel was inaccessible from the south or west; only the slender bridge linked it to the forest. The fortress was walled to the north and boasted two square towers above the portcullis. Groundsel could see no sentries, nor movement of any kind on the walls.

'I do not like the thought of riding a horse across that bridge,' he said. 'I have never liked heights.'

'You will find it will support you well enough,' she told him, edging her mount forward. Together they rode down the hill and halted before the bridge, where Morrigan lifted her helm from her head and placed it over the pommel of her saddle.

'Are you ready, Forest Lord?' she asked, grinning.

Groundsel's face was pale, his mouth set in a hard line. He did not answer, but spurred the stallion forward. As the horse moved out on to the bridge, he pulled down the visor of his helm and shut his eyes. Morrigan followed him, riding close to the right-hand side of the structure and gazing down over the iron rings. The chasm was deep, and she could just make out the bright ribbon of a stream running over the rocks below.

She transferred her gaze to Groundsel, who was sitting like a statue, looking neither left nor right. The horses' hooves sounded like slow drum-beats on the wooden planks.

'Enjoying the view, Groundsel?' she called, but there was no reply. Smiling, she kicked her horse into a run. The bridge swayed alarmingly as Morrigan overtook Groundsel and cantered up to the portcullis gate, where she swung her mount and waited while her companion made his slow way forward. Once on solid ground, Groundsel slid from the saddle and sat down beside the gate. He removed his helmet and wiped the sweat from his face.

'You do not look well, my Lord,' she said.

His muttered reply was short and brutal. Laughter burst from Morrigan.

'My dear Groundsel, how could you use such language in front of a lady? A Knight of the Gabala should always be courteous. Shall we go inside?'

Groundsel stood and led his horse through the gateway. As they passed under the portcullis, he stopped and looked up. 'Rusted solid,' he said. 'What sort of fool allows his defences to fall into such disrepair?'

'I don't know,' she replied sweetly. 'Perhaps the man is a peasant. He probably doesn't understand knightly ways. You could instruct him, Groundsel.'

His eyes were cold as he approached her. 'You seem intent on making me angry, bitch. That is not wise.'

'Have I offended you? Oh, I am sorry, dear Groundsel. Perhaps we should kiss and become friends again?'

'I would sooner kiss the rear end of my horse,' he snapped.

'Well, your experience is obviously greater than mine in such matters – but I pity the horse.' She dragged on her reins and cantered into the Citadel. Nothing moved, the fortress seemed deserted.

She headed her mount towards the High Keep and halted before the steps to the double doors. Groundsel rode alongside her.

'There's nobody here,' he said. 'What in Hell's name happened?'

'They are inside,' she told him.

'How do you know?'

Morrigan shook her head and dismounted, wondering how he would react if she told him she could sense their blood, warm and promising. Mounting the steps, she banged her mailed fist against the door.

'Bucklar!' she called. 'You have visitors.'

The left-hand door slid open, creaking on its hinges. 'Don't go in!' called Groundsel, dragging his longsword clear. 'I don't like this at all.'

'Then stay outside,' she advised. She stepped into the cool interior and smiled at the woman who stood holding the bent bow, the arrow aimed at Morrigan's face. 'Do not fear me,' she said. 'I am here with a message from Llaw Gyffes.' Behind the woman were several children, one of whom held a curved dagger. Movement came from the shadows to left and right and Morrigan swung her head. There were some twenty women in the hall; their eyes were frightened, their manner tense and expectant. Then Groundsel entered, grinned and sheathed his blade.

'Wonderful!' he said. 'We've ridden for days to find a fortress of women and children. How many will want to join Llaw's army, do you think?'

'Who are you?' asked the woman with the bow, easing the string forward and lowering her weapon. Morrigan noted that the arrow was still notched and could be loosed in an instant.

'I am Morrigan. The ape in the armour is Groundsel. We are looking for Bucklar. The King's army is about to attack us in the south and we were hoping Bucklar could send some men to aid us.'

'No,' the woman said, 'he won't do that. He can't. We are already under attack. A force has invaded the forest from Pertia Port and wiped out two settlements. My husband – and almost all of the men – have gone after them.'

'What a genius,' said Groundsel. 'Leaving his home base undefended. Come on, Morrigan, let's go.'

'You leave if you wish,' said Morrigan, 'but I have had enough of sleeping on the ground, with ants crawling inside my armour. I intend to stay here the night – and take a bath.'

Groundsel approached her. 'I may not be a Knight by birth, Morrigan, but neither was I born a fool. This is not a fortress, it's a tomb. There's only one way out – over that bridge. And if the enemy gets here before Bucklar returns, everyone here will be slaughtered. Is a bath worth the risk?'

'You worry too much,' she told him.

'Your insults are easier to bear than your stupidity,' he retorted and, turning on his heel, he strode from the hall and mounted his stallion. His helm was hanging from the pommel and he eased it into place. What a useless mission, he thought, as he rode from the port-cullis gate. Four days in the company of a harridan and nothing to show for it.

He swallowed hard as his horse walked out on to

the gently swaying bridge and steeled himself to stare straight ahead. The boards beneath the horse creaked and groaned, the chains to left and right of him grating. Safely on the other side he angled his white stallion up the hill and into the trees, halting to stare back at the Citadel. Morrigan was right, he knew. He was a peasant – and worse, he was a murderer and a thief. How amusing he must seem to her and the other patricians. A movement came on the hillside opposite, and he saw a young boy walk out of the undergrowth with a small grey dog beside him. Now that was a good age to be, thought Groundsel, remembering the early years of his youth, when he had played with the master's hounds, and all the summers were lifetime long and golden and the winters bright with cold magic. He grinned, thinking of the golden-haired child he had saved from the snow. It would be nice to watch her grow in Cithaeron, to see her dance and sing and play. Why waste time on this doomed war? Morrigan's words lashed at him.

'*The ape in the armour is Groundsel . . .*'

A month ago he would have killed her for those words, and thought nothing of it.

Suddenly the boy darted down the hillside and raced on to the bridge, the dog running beside him. Groundsel swung in the saddle. Back along the road were some thirty soldiers, marching two abreast towards the Citadel.

Groundsel chuckled. 'Have a good bath, Morrigan my sweet,' he whispered. He could see movement on the walls of the Citadel; several women were gathering at the gate towers, armed with bows and quivers of arrows. The soldiers marched to the bridge and halted. Loosening their packs, they dropped them at the road side and untied the small round shields that were buckled to them. Finally the officer gathered his men around him, giving instructions.

'Be interested to see how you are going to handle this, Morrigan,' murmured Groundsel.

The soldiers surged on to the bridge and ran forward, holding their shields before them. Groundsel could see that the few archers on the battlements would not stop them. Sunlight sparkled from Morrigan's silver armour as she stepped into sight, sword in hand.

'You've got pluck, at least,' owned Groundsel.

Seeing her before them, the soldiers slowed their charge. Arrows thudded into their shields, or bounced from breastplates and helms. One man went down with a shaft in his thigh. But the rest ran on.

Morrigan sprang to meet them, her longsword slicing murderously through a wooden shield and half-severing the arm beneath. The warrior screamed and hurled himself away from the silver figure, tripping to fall in front of his comrades. Several men tumbled over him and the charge faltered. Morrigan's sword rose and fell in the mêlée, cutting through armour, skin and bone. Several blades bounced from her own armour, but no blade touched her flesh. Five men were down before the attackers regained their composure and Morrigan was forced back, step by step, towards the wider portcullis gate, where they could get behind her and bear her down.

Groundsel decided to watch until she was overpowered. The sound of advancing hoofbeats came to him. Back along the road was a rider . . . a rider in crimson armour. Groundsel's eyes narrowed.

'Poor Morrigan,' he thought, and was about to swing his horse and ride away when a series of images flashed into his mind: the child on the hillside; Morrigan in her silver armour, her white horse behind her in the gateway; and now the Red Knight. The words of the Dagda cut into him like hot knives.

He too will die in the spring. I see a horse, a white horse. And a rider in shining silver. And a child on a hillside. The demons are gathering, and a great storm will descend on the forest. But Groundsel will not see it.'

This was the day then. And the rider would kill him. Don't be a fool, he told himself; you are clear. The Dagda is wrong. Ride away and cheat your fate.

But then he recalled the look in Manannan's eyes, and the promise he had asked of all the Knights.

'Damn you all!' shouted Groundsel. Slapping the stallion's rump, he galloped down the hill. The stallion thundered on to the bridge and raced at the startled soldiers. Groundsel's sword hacked down at the first to come within range and then he was among them, cutting left and right. Morrigan, blood flowing from a wound in her temple where her helm had been dashed from her head, forced her way into the fray, swinging her sword double-handed. In the confined space the soldiers found it difficult to hit out, for fear of injuring their fellows. But Groundsel and Morrigan were in no way so impaired. Groundsel's blade crashed through the officer's helm, dashing his brains to the wooden boards.

'Back!' yelled one of the soldiers – and they fled. Groundsel stepped from the saddle and looked around him. Twelve soldiers were down. Three were still alive, but bleeding heavily; he killed them.

'We are dead,' said Morrigan, her voice flat and cold. Groundsel glanced back to see the Red Knight riding slowly across the Bridge of Chains, a dark sword in his mailed fist.

'Speak for yourself,' returned the former outlaw. 'I never met the man I couldn't kill.' Morrigan said nothing but she backed away, her sword falling from her hand. The Red Knight advanced with terrifying lack of speed, the undead stallion plodding forward. Groundsel rode to meet him, halting his mount in the Knight's path.

A dry metallic chuckle came from within the red

helm. 'It takes more than armour to make a warrior, Knight,' said a voice. 'I shall kill you slowly for your effrontery . . . I shall dismember you.'

'You all want to talk first, don't you?' hissed Groundsel. 'Well, I've heard your boasts, Scumbucket – now let's see how you fight!' He spurred his stallion and aimed a wicked blow at the crimson helm, but the Red Knight swayed in the saddle and Groundsel's sword swept harmlessly by. A thundering cut hammered into Groundsel's neck-plates. Stars exploded before his eyes and he tried to crash his own blade at the crimson figure, but again and again the dark sword clanged against the Gabala armour. His shoulder-plate was ripped from him, then his helm was struck, the visor spinning away. His stallion reared, saving Groundsel from a thrust that would have speared his eye. The horse backed away and Groundsel dragged in a shuddering breath. The Red Knight advanced, and in that moment Groundsel knew the end had come. He could not lay a sword on the man.

The Red Knight began to laugh. 'What a sorry day for the Gabala! You really are the worst Knight in history. I hope there are others better than you. And now, peasant, it is time to send you to Hell.'

Groundsel said nothing – but as the Red Knight moved in, he kicked his feet from the stirrups and dived at him. It was the one move Bersis had not anticipated. With lightning reflexes the Red Knight swung his sword to slice deep into Groundsel's shoulder, smashing through the collar-bone and down deep into the lungs. Ignoring the pain, Groundsel's powerful arms circled the Knight, driving him from the saddle. They landed across the huge rings that held the bridge and swayed there for a second. Groundsel's face was pressed close to the Red Knight's helm, and the former outlaw could see the fear in his enemy's eyes.

'Not talking now, are you, pig breath?' he spat, blood

bubbling down his beard. 'Send me to Hell, will you? Well, you can join me on the journey.'

'No!' screamed Bersis. But Groundsel, with the last of his strength, dragged his opponent over the edge and the two figures toppled out into space.

Morrigan ran to the precipice and stared down. The Red and Silver figures were still locked in a deadly embrace, but now they looked like children's toys sparkling in the sunlight. Smaller and smaller they became, until at last they were dashed against the jagged rocks below.

At the moment of impact Morrigan averted her eyes. The undead stallion fell to the boards, its flesh stripping away, and a terrible stench was borne to Morrigan on the breeze.

At the far end of the bridge the soldiers were gathering for another rush. But suddenly a horn sounded and the hillside was alive with forest men who charged into the startled troops. Morrigan did not watch the slaughter; she moved to the edge of the chasm and looked down at the tiny figures.

'You were a man, Groundsel,' she said.

Sheera watched as the Duke of Mactha led his fifty riders from the village. For ten days she had observed their training, or joined with other groups practising archery or sword work. Of Errin she had seen little, and her patience was wearing thin. She had spurned the safety of Cithaeron in order to avenge her sister's death, but now she felt useless – and worse, ignored. She had seen Llaw Gyffes walking the hills with Arian, but only twice had Errin sought her out – once to see that she was comfortably ensconced in a primitive cabin, and a second time when she received a nick in her upper arm after an over-enthusiastic practice session with longswords.

'Why must you put yourself in danger?' he had asked her as he examined the shallow cut.

'What sort of question is that?' she responded. 'Am I not also a part of Llaw's army?'

'You are a woman,' he stated, as if that answered the question.

'Is Morrigan not a woman? Or Arian?'

'That is different. Morrigan is . . . strange. Arian has been raised in the forest. Anyway, I have no say over the others.'

'You have no say over me,' she stormed. 'The only connection we have is that you killed my sister.'

Now he avoided her completely – which was galling. Several of the forest men had approached her, but these she sent packing with strong words. She had asked the Duke of Mactha if she could ride with him and raid the supply lines, but he had politely refused her request. He had dismounted from the grey stallion and placed his hand on her shoulders.

'I say this to you in confidence,' he whispered. 'We will not be coming back. There is no hope that we can evade pursuit for long. Most of the men with me understand this. I do not want to see you . . . in peril, Sheera. It was bad enough being part of your sister's . . . trial. You understand?'

'You are going out to die.'

'I think so – though I will strive to delay the dreadful day.'

Now he was gone – as Llaw, Elodan and Manannan were gone. The King's army had reached the southern border and most of the Knights had travelled south to prepare the defences and ready the men. Already word had come back that Elodan had ambushed some of the King's scouts and destroyed them in a short battle. Of Manannan and Llaw there was no word.

Sheera joined a group of women for the midday meal of venison and dried fruit, then took her bow and quiver

359

and wandered to the hills. It was she who first glimpsed Morrigan riding slowly along a game trail, followed by scores of warriors. She ran down to meet them.

'Where is Groundsel?' she called up to the silver rider.

'Dead,' answered Morrigan, touching spurs to her mount and riding on.

Sheera joined the column as it wound its way down to the settlement. There were more than two hundred and fifty men, and she soon gathered that they were from a Citadel to the north, they had already fought one battle, routing troops from Pertia Port, and now were pledged to Llaw Gyffes. It seemed that Groundsel and Morrigan had saved many of their wives and children and the leader, Bucklar, had promised to aid the rebellion.

Sheera sat with the Citadel men as Bucklar, Errin and Lámfhada discussed strategy in the cave. Towards dusk the Citadel leader – a tall, stout warrior with greying hair and a trident beard – led his men south.

Sheera gathered her bow and joined them.

Nuada awoke to the sound of bird-song. Opening his eyes, he saw the dawn breaking over the mountains, the sky ablaze with colour, pink banners streaming into the virgin blue, white clouds running before the sun like sheep before a golden lion.

Kartia's head was resting on his shoulder, her arm draped across his chest. He snuggled down into the blanket, feeling the warmth of her body against him.

This was contentment. This was joy.

Far from the front line of battle, an eternity away from the killing and slaying, Nuada was at peace. Kartia mumbled something in her sleep and Nuada's hand slid over her hips. Her eyes opened.

'Dawn already?' she whispered.

'It is a beautiful day,' he told her. 'A veritable prince of days.' Pulling her to him, he kissed her softly.

For an hour they made love without haste, then lay together in comfortable silence. Finally Nuada stretched and sat up. The fire was dead, and Brion was nowhere to be seen. Usually at this time he would be broiling rabbit meat for their breakfast – or pigeon, or lamb. Nuada rose and strolled to the waterfall, wading in to stand beneath the showering water; it was cool, and wondrously refreshing.

Sunlight bathed the pool at the fall's base and rainbows danced through the curtain of water. Paradise could not contain more beauty, Nuada thought, as he towelled himself down with his shirt. Kartia moved to a tall rock and dived into the pool. Nuada envied her the ability to swim; it was something he would have to learn. As he sat back and watched her glide through the water, his thoughts moved to his mission. So far they had visited a dozen villages, and at each settlement his words had inspired a following. More than three hundred men had pledged themselves to the cause, but it should have been more. Many more.

He must have spoken to more than two thousand warriors, he reflected, glancing back at the armour laid on a blanket beneath an overhanging pine.

The Knight without a sword. He felt a pang of guilt. Not because he did not fight, but because he was so *glad* that he did not. It made him feel like a hypocrite.

Go out and join Llaw, all you young men – but not me. No. I am a poet, you see. I just fill your heads with glory, and skim past the maggots and the worms and the pain.

He had tried to paint a picture of the war as a Holy cause: good versus evil, light against dark. But here in the forest all was shade.

'Nuada! Nuada!' called Brion. Nuada rose and saw the burly blond forester running towards the pool.

'What is the matter?' he asked, climbing down from his rock to meet the running man.

'The King's men have surrounded the village; they have herded all the people into the hall.'

'Slow down. Tell me all.'

'I went back just before dawn. I couldn't catch anything for breakfast, so I thought they would let us have some food. When I got close, I saw the horses, so I hid. They gathered in Ramath and all his people. I don't know what they plan, but we must get away from here. We're too close.'

'Why so frightened? We have horses; we can outrun them, surely.'

'There is a Red Knight with them and they have dark magic. You have said this many times, that they are the Evil Ones. We must get away.'

'A Red Knight? Here? Why?'

'I don't know,' said Brion. 'I'll saddle the horses.'

Kartia swam to the shore and rose from the water. 'What is for breakfast, sir Knight?' she asked.

'Nothing, I am afraid. We have to leave. Ramath's village was attacked this morning; it is not safe here.'

'Poor Ramath,' she said. 'I really liked him.'

'So did I. Now get your things together.'

They gathered their packs and tied them to the saddles. Nuada climbed into his armour, which Brion helped him to buckle.

A man stepped into the clearing and Brion's dagger flashed out.

'Ramath!' greeted Nuada, grinning. 'You escaped! Well done.'

The newcomer was tall and lean, dressed in dark skins of polished leather. He approached Nuada and bowed.

'I did not escape, sir, they let me go.' Ramath swallowed hard and looked away. 'It is you they want. I must return with you within the hour, or all my people

die. The Red Knight, Sir Edrin, has promised that we
will be freed the moment you surrender yourself.'

'You can't!' cried Kartia. 'They will kill you.' She
swung on Ramath. 'How dare you come here and ask
this of him? How dare you?'

Nuada pulled her back. 'How . . . how can you be
sure he will keep his word, Ramath?' he asked.

'I cannot be, sir. But what else can I do?'

Nuada's mouth was dry. He lifted a canteen from
his saddle and drank deeply. 'I have a mission, you
see,' he said at last. 'I must raise an army to fight
these . . . evil men. You understand? I cannot . . .' His
voice faded to silence as he saw the look of despair in
Ramath's eyes.

'I have three sons, sir. None has yet reached five
years. They are sitting with their mother, waiting for
the knives to open their throats.'

Nuada turned away. 'Don't listen to him,' Kartia
pleaded. 'Please Nuada. Think of us. Think . . .'

Nuada stooped and lifted his helm, handing it to
Brion. 'Keep this. I will not need it. Take Kartia back
to Llaw and the others. Tell them I'm sorry; I don't
have the strength to refuse.'

Kartia grabbed at his arm. 'They'll kill you,' she
said, tears spilling to her cheeks. 'Sweet Heaven, they'll
kill you!'

He drew her away from the others, his vision misting
as he kissed her. 'I love you,' he said, 'and I think that
this morning's joy was a gift. A last gift. I never saw
a dawn like it.' He pulled her close. 'I don't know what
to say. There are no words, Kartia.'

'Let me come with you. Please?'

'No. Go with Brion. I will feel . . . stronger if I am
alone.'

He strode to his horse and mounted. Then, taking a
deep shuddering breath, he touched his spurs to the
stallion. Kartia ran forward, but Brion pulled her away

as Nuada rode from the glade, not daring to look back. Ramath walked beside him in silence until they reached the last hill; then he reached up and touched Nuada's hand.

'I will never be able to thank you enough,' said the leader.

Nuada smiled, but his mouth was too dry for words and he was trembling. As he guided the horse down into the village, soldiers ran out, ringing him with their lances.

He was ordered to dismount and did so; his limbs were shaking with fear and he stumbled. The villagers flocked out to see him, lining the way ahead. Looking at their faces, he drew strength from their sympathy. One more performance, Nuada, he told himself. Surely you have the strength for that?

He was led beyond the main hall, where only the night before he had held the villagers spellbound with tales of heroism and courage. What he would not give now to see Llaw Gyffes and the other Knights thundering down the hillside to rescue him. Now, there would be a song!

They took him to a dead tree in a clearing and there was the Red Knight, Edrin.

'So,' he said, 'the story-teller returns. Where is your sword, sir Knight, and your helm?'

'I have no sword,' said Nuada.

'I will loan you one. Then, at least, you can fight for your life.'

Nuada shook his head. 'No. If I were to kill you, these people would suffer for it. You made a bargain: me for them. Honour it.' He could see the anger in the Knight's eyes and knew that he had won. For if the Knight had killed him in combat, the word would have spread through the settlements that the new Knights of the Gabala were weaker than the Red Knights of the King. He smiled. 'What now, sir Knight?'

'If you are too cowardly to fight, then you will die like a villain.'

Soldiers surrounded Nuada and his armour was unbuckled and pulled from him. Then he was taken to the tree, his arms spread against the rough bark. Two soldiers came forward with hammers and long nails and Nuada gritted his teeth as the sharp points were placed against his wrists. The hammers struck. Blood spurted from his arms as the nails drove through flesh, sinew and bone to bite into the trunk beyond. Nuada sagged . . . the nails ripped at him. He groaned and tried to raise his head.

The Red Knight took up a bow and a quiver of arrows, carrying them to Ramath.

'You shoot first,' he said. 'Prove yourself a loyal man of the King.'

The leader blinked. 'I . . . can't . . .'

'Do it!' yelled Nuada. 'Or it is all for nothing. They will kill me anyway; you will not be killing me, *they* will. Do it. I forgive you.'

Ramath took the bow and notched an arrow to the string. Swiftly he drew and loosed and his arrow punched into Nuada's chest. One by one the village men were called forward, and each sent a shaft into the lifeless body nailed to the tree.

At last the arrows were spent and the Red Knight strode to his stallion. The soldiers backed away and marched from the scene. Ramath ran forward and began to pull the arrows from Nuada's body, weeping as he did so.

'I'm sorry, I'm so sorry,' he whispered, over and over.

It was to this scene that Lámfhada's spirit came. He had left the cave to scout the north, and had been drawn to the village by the overpowering outpouring of emotion. He hovered in the air over Nuada's body and saw the terrible wounds it bore.

Remembering the stag, he thrust his golden hands into the corpse and poured his magic into the body. The wounds closed, but there was no life to be found.

Ramath and the other men, unable to see Lámfhada, watched as the wounds closed and stumbled back from the tree.

Knowing it was pointless, still Lámfhada would not stop. More and more power flowed into the corpse - and through it into the dead apple tree beyond. The branches trembled and buds grew in an instant from every twig and bough, opening into pink and white blossom which began to fall like snow around the scene.

At last Lámfhada surrendered to the inevitable: Nuada Silverhand was dead. The Armourer rose from the scene and fled, distraught, to the cave.

Then Ramath stepped forward and stooped to lift apple blossom from the ground. He turned to his people.

'He said it was a Holy War. And you have all seen this sign from the Heavens. We will send a messenger to every settlement. Nuada will have his army. By all the Gods, I swear it!'

20

The King's Scouts charged up the hill into a withering volley of arrows. But still they came on and the hidden archers fell back before them. Elodan waited until the Scouts reached the tree line, then raised a horn to his lips and blew a single note.

Scores of warriors dropped from their hiding place in the trees, knives and swords hacking at the attackers. Elodan drew his sword and spurred his horse into the midst of the fray, cutting and killing. The Scouts fell back, streaming down the hillside.

From the woods opposite Llaw Gyffes, Manannan and a score of mounted warriors galloped into sight. The Scouts scattered before them, but many were ridden down as they ran back along the valley.

Manannan kicked his stallion into a furious gallop and rode through the fleeing men. Ahead of him the Scout's standard-bearer was carrying the King's flag, a raven on a field of blue. Manannon cut him down and seized the standard, raising it high for the defenders to see.

The thunder of hooves filled the air and Manannan swung his mount. Riding into the valley were five hundred of the King's Lancers. The Once-Knight cut left and rode for the trees. Several of the Lancers veered after him and, reaching the tree line, he hurled the standard to a waiting rebel and swung again to meet the charging riders; there were five in the chasing group. Lifting his sword, Manannan spurred the stallion at them. He swayed in the saddle, allowing a lance to slice by him, and hacked the rider from his mount. A second lance glanced from his breastplate and his

367

sword stabbed out to cleave the rider through the ribs. Then he was among them. Unable to use their long lances to good effect, the attackers dropped them and drew their swords. It availed them nothing. Manannan tore into them, his silver blade slicing through armour and mail. The last remaining Lancer tried to escape, but as he turned his steed an arrow flew from the undergrowth and hammered into his horse's side. The beast stumbled, throwing its rider to the earth; the man rose, but another shaft took him in the thigh. Rebels ran from the undergrowth to despatch him.

Manannan leaned on to the pommel of his saddle and watched the Lancers thunder into the valley. Llaw Gyffes and the other riders gave way before them, riding up into the stands of pine that circled the hills.

Elodan rode out to rein in alongside Manannan. 'Do you think they'll come up after us?'

'Not if they have any sense. They can't know how many we are, and Lancers are as useful here as a wooden sword. Did we lose many men?'

'About a dozen. Gwydion is looking to the wounded now. Have you seen Morrigan?'

'No, I thought she was with you.'

'She gave chase to some Scouts over to the west,' said Elodan. 'Perhaps you should find her.'

Manannan nodded. He rode for some minutes, alert for any stragglers who might still be hiding in the undergrowth. Then he heard a terrifying scream and drew his blade. The stallion baulked at entering the glade from which the noise had come, but he patted its neck and spoke soothingly to it. The horse walked on for several steps, then stopped again. Manannan dismounted and tethered the beast. He pushed aside the undergrowth and saw Morrigan crouching over a struggling man; her teeth were fixed into his throat and as Manannan watched the body began to shrivel.

The Once-Knight looked on, horror-struck, while

Morrigan rose and wiped the blood from her mouth. She turned slowly.

'Manannan!'

'Take off that armour,' he hissed. 'Now!'

'Wait!' she pleaded. 'Let me explain.'

'What I saw explained everything. Take off the armour, Morrigan – or I'll kill you where you stand.'

'You think you could?' she spat. 'I have the strength of the Vyre.'

'I *know* I could – and so do you. Take off that armour. *Now*. You disgrace everything it stands for.'

For a moment he thought she would attack him, but then she dropped her sword and began to unbuckle the silver breastplate. He waited in silence until she stood before him in a simple blue tunic and grey leggings. 'What now?' she asked.

'Now you go from here. You leave the forest. If ever I see you again, you will die. Get out of my sight.'

'It is not my fault!' she shouted. 'I did not choose to be the way I am.' He did not reply; she moved closer. 'Manannan, don't send me away.'

'If you are still here in one minute, I shall cut your disgusting head from your shoulders. GET AWAY!' he screamed. She recoiled from his fury and ran from the glade as Manannan slumped to the grass, his hands shaking. He was still there when Elodan found him.

The Once-Knight outlined what he had seen and Elodan sighed. 'In one way she was right, Manannan. She did not choose to be a Vampyre; it was forced on her. But she had to go. Will you remove my helm?' Manannan placed his hands on the helmet and twisted it loose of the neck-ring, lifting it clear. 'Thank you, my friend. I feel more useless than ever in armour. You know, left to myself I would not be able to remove my breastplate.'

'You are beginning to fight well,' Manannan told him. 'That is a boon.'

Elodan lifted his left hand and stared at it. 'It is beginning to obey me, but I would not like to meet anyone skilled.' The Lord Knight glanced at Morrigan's armour. 'I suppose we should select another Knight?' Manannan shook his head. He strode to where the breastplate lay and lifted it, carrying it back to Elodan. On the outside the plate shone like polished silver, but inside it was rusted through. Manannan tensed his muscles and gripped the edges hard; the breastplate snapped and fell apart in his hands.

He hurled it aside. 'The armour reflects the wearer,' he said.

'Then why was she chosen at all?' Elodan asked.

Manannan shrugged. 'I do not know. But we have lost Groundsel, and now Morrigan. Who is next, I wonder?'

'Nuada is also dead,' said Elodan. 'Lámfhada came to me in a dream last night. The poet was nailed to a tree; he gave his life to save a village.'

Manannan said nothing, pushing himself wearily to his feet. 'Come,' he said. 'The day is not yet over.' He lifted Elodan's helm and prepared to place it on the Lord Knight. Elodan's eyes were sorrowful as he spoke.

'It must hurt you, Manannan, to see the men who have become Knights of the Gabala: a cripple who cannot dress himself, a thief, a cook, a blacksmith, and a Nomad tribesman who wouldn't understand the concept of chivalry if it bit him.'

'You have no idea, Elodan, how proud I am. No idea.'

The King hurled the jewel-encrusted goblet at the general, who knew better than to duck. The missile took him high in the forehead, gashing the skin, but he remained at attention as a trickle of blood moved down his cheek.

'You imbecile!' stormed the King. 'You incompetent! My troops will starve if it's left to you to supply them. How many convoys have got through to us in the last six days? How many?'

'One, sire,' answered the man.

'One. You have been given five hundred Lancers; you have scoured the countryside. And what have you achieved? What?'

'Nothing, sire. We captured one of their scouts who told us the Duke of Mactha was leading the force. Under torture he gave us their hiding place. But when we got there, the Duke was gone.'

'Who?' hissed the King. 'Who had gone?'

'The Du . . . the traitor Roem, sire.'

'Get out of my sight – and report to Kar-schen. You are no longer a general; you will take command of the next Turma into the forest.'

'Yes, sire. Thank you, sire,' said the man, bowing and backing away through the tent entrance as the King swung to Samildanach, who was standing beside the throne.

'How do you read our situation, Lord Knight?'

'The former Duke is a worthy adversary. His raids are lightning-swift and well planned. He has burned over a dozen convoys for the loss of maybe six men. He knows the land. Far more worrying is the news of unrest in Furbolg.'

'Unrest? A few riots. My troops have seen to them,' said the King.

'Even so, sire, the main army is with us here. Should there be a revolt . . .'

'A revolt? Why should there be? I am well-loved. Is that not so, Okessa?'

The new Duke of Mactha bowed his bald head. 'Indeed it is, sire. But the Lord Knight is right to be concerned – there will always be elements inspired by envy or greed.'

'What do you suggest, Samildanach?'

'I think you should return to Furbolg, sire – with a thousand Lancers. That should put paid to any problems.'

'But I want to see Llaw Gyffes and his rebels punished.'

'You will, sire. Despite their spirited defence, it is now obvious that they lack the numbers to halt a fierce and sudden invasion. In two days the Lancers will advance on the left and right, two miles apart, and converge on the centre. At the same time I will lead the main body of the army into the forest here. The enemy will be forced to fall back.'

'Then I will stay to see it,' stated the King.

'Sire,' continued Samildanach, 'that is only the first move. They will not stand to be destroyed at a single blow. The rebellion will be crushed, but it will take weeks to hunt them all down – and I fear the continuous pursuit through the forest would bore you to tears.'

'Very well, Samildanach, I will heed your advice. But Llaw Gyffes is not to be killed; he must be brought, with the other traitor Knights, to Furbolg for trial and execution.'

'It will be done, sire.'

'And what plans have you for the traitor, Roem?'

'We are sending one convoy from Mactha – but this time, as well as the escort, there will be Lancers a mile distant to the south, west, east and north. He will not escape. I myself will be riding with the convoy.'

'Send me his head. I shall have it placed on a lance over the main gates of the city.'

'Indeed I shall, sire.'

Soldiers ringed the former Duke as he stood, holding his sword double-handed and keeping them at bay. A warrior ran in, but the Duke swept aside his thrust and slashed his own blade down through the man's neck. A half-mile to the west, the smoke from the burning convoy was rising like a giant cobra. Roem grinned. Around him lay the remains of his force; they had fought well, but had been outnumbered and over-powered. Only Roem, in his silver armour, had been able to withstand the many blows.

'Come then, my heroes,' invited Roem. 'Who is next for the swan's path to glory?'

'I fear you are,' said Samildanach, moving inside the circle. 'Do you wish to surrender?'

'Do *you*?' asked Roem.

'I think not. The King has asked me to send him your head and I promised I would. I am a man who likes to keep his promises.'

'Truly? Did you not once promise to aid the poor and the dispossessed?'

'Enough talk, Roem. Defend yourself!'

The Duke of Mactha was a fine swordsman, but never had he faced a warrior more skilled than Samil-danach. With increasing desperation he fought off the Red Knight's frenzied attacks, but as he grew weaker he could sense his opponent growing ever more strong. The dark blade hissed and cut faster and faster. Roem tried to attack, but his blows seemed clumsy and without style against the master he faced. His shoulder-plate was hacked away by a mighty blow, exposing the collar-bone; then his helm was struck, the sword ricocheting to slice open the skin of his shoulder. A second blow loosened the helm and Roem backed away. Samildanach did not follow.

'Do remove it if it troubles you,' Samildanach invited him.

Roem plunged his sword into the grass and lifted his damaged helm clear.

'You are a remarkable fighter, Samildanach,' he said. 'I only ever saw one man better.'

Samildanach chuckled. 'If you fought a better man than I, Roem, why are you still here?'

'I only practised with him. He will kill you, Samildanach.'

'And the name of this paragon?'

'Manannan.'

The smile left Samildanach's face. 'The day has not dawned when Manannan could best me – and I am stronger and faster now than ever before. I think you seek to unsettle me, Roem. Is that not so?'

'You see through me so easily,' answered Roem with a smile. 'But I wish I could be there when he forces you to kiss the grass at his feet.'

'But you won't!' hissed Samildanach, leaping forward. Roem's sword came up – but too slowly . . . the dark blade swept through his neck and his head toppled to the ground.

Samildanach sheathed his sword and turned his back on the corpse.

'See that the head is sent to the King,' he ordered. 'Today. He should be halfway to Mactha by now.'

For five days a thunderstorm swept across the forest, swelling rivers and streams, making paths and trails treacherous, hills impossible to climb. The fighting became sporadic and the army of the King was forced to halt its advance on both wings. At the centre, under Samildanach and Okessa, the infantry pushed forward slowly.

On the sixth day the sky cleared, the sun blazing down upon the sea of mud that was to be the battleground.

Samildanach decided to wait one more day for the

ground to become more firm, and rode for Mactha to report to the King.

In the hills Elodan and Manannan redirected their forces to the east and west, where the advancing wings were meeting little resistance. Lámfhada arrived at the camp at noon.

'They have two thousand men on each side of us,' he told Manannan. 'If we stay here, we will be trapped; the horns will close in, drawing us on to the foot soldiers. We must retreat.'

'I agree,' said Elodan. 'We cannot allow them to force us into a pitched battle; their numbers would swamp us.'

'I can see that,' said Manannan, 'but I don't like the feel of retreating – and I am not speaking of pride. Most of the men are here as a matter of choice. If they think we are losing, they will run for their homes. Every step we march back will see our army shrink.'

'There's truth in that,' agreed Errin, moving with Ubadai to join them. 'We've already lost some of the warriors from Bucklar's force. Twenty men headed home last night as the rain ceased.'

Elodan shook his head. 'You are saying we cannot retreat, yet Lámfhada tells us we are soon to be surrounded and overwhelmed. That does not leave us many choices. We cannot attack. We have not the discipline, or the lines of command. We can only fight as we are. Any suggestion would be appreciated, Manannan.'

Manannan nodded. 'I think a small victory would serve us well at this stage. May I suggest we shift our position and hit their left wing? While the mud is still deep, their horses will be restricted and it should give our infantry a sound advantage. But there is a danger. It will leave their foot-soldiers with no opposition and they could march into the forest and sack all the settlements between here and the mountains.'

'True,' said Elodan. 'And the men will desert in their hundreds – they will have to, in order to save their families.'

'The enemy is short of food,' Errin put in. 'They cannot march too far, for they will need supplies. They cannot live off the land as we do. We have scattered the herds, driving them north, and there are no crops as yet.'

'Food will no longer be so great a problem for them,' said Lámfhada softly. 'The Duke of Mactha has been slain by Samildanach, and all the men with him are lost to us.'

Errin cursed. The others said nothing. Finally Manannan spoke. 'I do not think they will attack in force today; they will wait for the mud to dry out. It seems to me we have only one choice: we must attack them. Hit their camp. But it is a risky venture, my friends, and our losses will be high.'

'I am not a military man, Manannan,' said Errin, 'but I have an idea – it is probably foolish.'

'Speak, Errin,' Manannan invited.

They listened in silence as Errin outlined his thoughts. Ubadai, who had been quiet throughout, stood and walked away.

Towards dusk Okessa left his tent, lifting his long purple robes to prevent them from scraping the mud, and walked out to the hill at the centre of the camp. From here he could see the neat lines of tents and the regularly spaced cook-fires, the long trestle-tables where the men gathered to collect their meagre rations, the picket lines set at right-angles to the tents and the latrine ditches dug downwind of the camp. Tomorrow would see the end of the rebels and the beginning of Okessa's dream. Already he was the Duke of Mactha, and he had the ear of the King. Soon the army of the

Gabala would march into neighbouring lands, sweeping out to the sea – and the riches of Cithaeron. Okessa longed for the day when the King would make him Satrap of a foreign realm – almost a king in his own right. His two acolytes joined him on the hilltop, leading a white goat. They lifted it to the crude altar and Okessa slit its throat, then he disembowelled it and tore the liver from its innards. Dropping the carcass, he carried the liver to where an acolyte held a burning torch. But the organ was diseased and covered with black spots. Okessa swallowed hard and swung on the acolyte. 'Fetch another goat,' he ordered. 'Do it now.'

The man nodded, handed the torch to his master and ran down the hill, slithering in the mud.

'How are the King's fortunes, my Lord?' asked the second acolyte, approaching his master. Okessa's pale eyes fixed on the man.

'I did not sacrifice the goat for the King,' lied Okessa, 'but for the enemy.' He showed the man the bloody liver and the acolyte grinned.

'Tomorrow should be a fine day, sir.'

'Yes,' Okessa agreed. Dropping the liver to the ground, he wandered to the brow of the hill. Below, the soldiers were gathering in rings around the camp-fires. From the west came a troop of Lancers riding slowly, almost wearily. 'Go down to that officer,' called Okessa. 'Tell him to report directly to me.' The acolyte bowed and made his way down the hill towards the approaching riders.

The troop rode into the camp. Some of the men dismounted and gathered torches; others moved on towards the picket lines where more than five hundred horses were tethered. Okessa watched in astonishment as three riders drew their swords and cut down the picket sentries. Fires leapt from several tents to the west, the wind fanning the flames. Suddenly the camp was in an uproar as men surged from the cook-fires, running to their tents to rescue their possessions. The westerly breeze caught the flames, lifting them from tent to tent. A shout went up from the east and Okessa swung to see the horses thundering towards the forest, being chased by a dozen riders – no, not chased, herded! At the centre of the camp all was chaos. Okessa could see swords flickering in the firelight and men falling.

Then he saw the troop thundering from the camp. His own tent caught fire and he began to run down the hill, but his foot slipped in the mud and he tumbled headlong, spinning and sliding until he came to rest at the foot of the rise. His robes were ruined. Cursing loudly, he got to his feet and strode into the camp to see his tent was blazing, his books and scrolls destroyed.

An officer ran by and Okessa grabbed his arm, but the man tore himself free and continued on his way. Thick smoke curled around him and tears started from his eyes as he coughed and spluttered, backing away from the inferno. To the east men were tearing down their tents in an attempt to halt the advance of the blaze. Just as it seemed they were winning, a tremendous crack of thunder rolled across the heavens and the rain lashed down, dousing cook-fires and torches. The flaming tents hissed and spat, but could not compete with the torrent; within minutes the entire camp was plunged into darkness.

Okessa's fury rose, but there was no one to vent it upon. The storm lasted for more than two hours. When at last the moon broke clear of the retreating clouds Okessa, drenched and filthy, located the general, Karschen. He ordered the night sentries to be put to death and the captain of the watch flogged.

He watched the executions at dawn, but they did not lift his spirits.

How could they?

He had seen the King's future.

*

In Mactha, King Ahak was in a better mood. The upper rooms were warm, the food plentiful and the evening promised heady pleasures. He did not need Nourishment, but what had need to do with joy? To take a woman, use her in the way the Gods intended, fill her with new life and then draw her life from her, filling himself. Never had he believed such joy possible.

He remembered the day Samildanach came to him, with the gift of Ambria. That had been incredible. But the first time he had sucked the life from another living being . . . that was indescribable. Now he had it all. Immortality. Power. The King for Ever. Everlasting. He savoured the feel of the words on his tongue.

Strolling to the window, he stared down into the courtyard. Where in Hell's name was his manservant? He should have found a girl by now.

He poured himself a goblet of strong wine and drained it. There was a time when wine had seemed like the nectar of the Gods. But that had been before Ambria, before the pleasures of the Vyre. Now it served only to whet his appetites.

A light, tapping sound came from the door. 'Enter!' called the King.

The door opened and his manservant, Mahan, stepped inside and bowed. 'My Lord, if it please you, there is a woman from the village who wishes to enjoy the pleasure of your company.'

'Bring her in,' said Ahak, sweeping his purple cloak over his shoulder and drawing himself up to his full height.

Mahan stepped aside and ushered in the woman. She was tall and slender, yet full-breasted, her hips delightfully curved. As Ahak moved forward and took her hand, she averted her eyes from his gaze, looking down towards the floor.

'Do not be shy, my dear,' said Ahak. 'I find it a delight to meet my subjects and listen to their cares and worries. It aids me in this lonely role.' He lifted her chin and was rewarded by a soft smile. Dismissing Mahan, he led the woman to the window. 'Will you join me in a drink?'

'If it please you, my Lord.' Her voice was soft and mellow and fired his passions but he fought them down, savouring the moment. Reaching out, he took her hand, lifting it to his lips. He pulled her close to him, his right arm circling her waist.

'Would you do anything for your King?' he whispered.

'Yes, my Lord.'

He released her hand and ran his fingers down her body, squeezing her breasts, stroking her belly. 'You know what I desire?'

'Yes, Lord,' she said, loosening the ties on her dress. When he pushed it back from her shoulders, it fell to the floor and she stepped from it. He led her to the bed, unfastened his cloak and removed his clothing.

For a moment he stared at her.

'You have no idea of the pleasures in store,' he said, sliding alongside her.

'I think I have, my Lord,' replied Morrigan.

Samildanach dismounted and led his stallion to the stable. Then he mounted the steps and pushed open the main doors to the hall. Mahan moved to greet him.

'Where is the King?' asked the Red Knight.

'He is in the Duke's upper bedchamber, Lord. He has a woman with him.'

'I will wait,' said Samildanach. 'Bring me some wine.'

'Yes, Lord. It may take longer than normal; the woman is exquisitely beautiful.' Mahan grinned.

'Exquisite? Here in Mactha? That is a surprise.'

'Yes, Lord. I think the King's luck has scarcely been

better. I found her waiting outside the castle; she was just sitting by the roadside.'

'Describe her,' said Samildanach.

'Tall, with the most beautiful golden hair. She is young and yet it is already streaked with silver . . .'

'Dear Gods!' shouted Samildanach and drawing his sword he raced for the stairs, taking them two at a time. He reached the upper corridor and ran to the bedchamber, but the door was locked. Leaning back, he crashed his foot against the brass key-plate and the door burst open. Samildanach leapt inside . . .

The King's hideously withered corpse lay on the bed. Morrigan was sitting naked on the floor, blood pooling at her feet from the deep slashes in her wrists.

Samildanach dropped his sword and walked over to her. 'Why?' he whispered.

Her eyes struggled to focus. '*Why*? Can you not see what . . . we have become? Oh, Samildanach! We are corrupting everything we . . . touch.' She sagged sideways and he caught her, drawing her to him. Her head fell to his shoulder. 'I loved you,' she said, 'more than life. And now . . . I don't even know what it means.'

'Don't talk. Let me bind your wrists; we can save your life.'

'There is nothing to save. I died back in the City of the Vyre when I became one of the Undead – just like you, my love.'

'You don't understand. We will build a new Gabala . . . New . . .'

'Do you remember loving me?'

'I remember,' he said.

'Not in the Vyre – but before. In the garden on the night you left. You remember?'

'Yes. It was another age.'

'What happened to that glorious young Knight?'

'He is still here, Morrigan. He . . . Morrigan?

Morrigan!' He laid her gently to the floor and closed her eyes.

21

It was two full days before the King's army was ready to march, the infantry pushing ahead down the long valley in phalanx formation with shields locked in four great squares.

Manannan, Elodan and the other Knights sat their mounts to the north of the advancing army, and the mood was sombre. Llaw had sent scouts east and west to gauge the strength of the enemy cavalry and the first report had been swift. Nearly two thousand riders were pushing in from the west. From the east, there was no word.

'We must pull back,' said Manannan. 'We do not have the numbers to break those squares.'

Reluctantly Llaw agreed.

A forester ran from the trees, his face red, his eyes bright with excitement.

'Llaw! Llaw!' he shouted. 'The Lancers have been crushed!'

'What? What's that you say?'

'There are five thousand rebels, led by a man named Ramath. They smashed the Lancers; they are on their way here now.'

'Ramath? I've never heard of him.'

'The whole forest north of us is ablaze with news of a miracle – something about Nuada and the Tree of Life. I don't understand all of it – but they're here!'

'Where?' asked Manannan and the man turned and gestured to the eastern hills where armed men poured out from the trees, racing down the slopes towards the enemy.

'Damn!' shouted Elodan. 'They'll be cut to pieces!'

'Sound the advance!' ordered Llaw. 'We'll hit them from all sides.'

'If they hold formation, they will turn us back like water from a dam,' said Manannan.

'Then pray they don't,' Llaw told him. 'Forward!' He spurred his stallion into a run, the other Knights following, and behind them some eighty riders in stolen armour.

At the centre of the first square, Okessa saw the attackers and blanched; there were thousands of them. 'Back! Back!' he screamed and the marching square faltered. They could hear the panic in the Duke's voice and this, coupled with the wild screams of the charging horde, caused them to break and stream back down the valley. Two other squares sundered themselves but the third, under the general Kar-schen, held firm.

Okessa spurred his mount towards the safety of the plain, outdistancing the running soldiers. He was almost clear when a slender figure loped down the hill and drew back on a bow. The arrow took his horse in the chest and the beast stumbled, hurling him over its head. He hit the ground hard, rolled and came to his knees to see that his attacker was a woman. He fumbled at his belt. 'I have money here,' he said. 'Take it all.'

'You killed my sister,' said Sheera, notching another arrow. Okessa rose and began to run back the way he had come . . . the arrow took him to the left of his spine, cleaving through to his heart.

Sheera turned and ran back up the hill, but none of the soldiers gave chase – they were too intent on escape. Kar-schen saved the day for the King's army, fighting a steady retreat back down the valley. Hundreds of panicking soldiers, looking back, saw the general's courageous rearguard and, finding their courage once more, joined him. The army suffered fearful losses, but was still intact when dusk gave way to darkness.

Samildanach and the Red Knights arrived near midnight and Kar-schen gave his report.

'There was little I could do,' said the burly, ageing general. 'The Duke panicked and the men fled with him. But we still have an army – and we have been joined by two thousand Lancers. If we go in tomorrow, I believe we will rout them.'

'I do not believe that will be necessary,' Samildanach told him. 'You did well, general; very well. I will see that the King rewards you.'

'His Majesty is well?'

'Yes, he is resting in Mactha.'

At dawn Samildanach rode into the valley, halted his horse and planted a white banner in the earth. Then he waited. It was more than an hour before a Knight in silver armour cantered down to him.

'Welcome, Manannan. How are you faring?'

'I do not wish to engage in idle conversation with you, demon. State your business.'

'Once we were friends,' said Samildanach.

'That was another man. Speak, or I ride back.'

'Very well. I have an offer for you. Tomorrow we can push back into the valley and engage our forces once more. Hundreds of lives will be lost – perhaps thousands. Why do we not settle this like Knights? In single combat?'

'What do we fight for?' asked Manannan. 'What do you offer?'

'If you win, the King's army will return to Furbolg and the Forest of the Ocean will be safe. If I win, you disband your force and surrender Llaw Gyffes.'

'No,' said Manannan. 'If we are to talk of surrender, then you can give us Ahak.'

'Very well. No surrenders – merely disband your force.'

'And how do I know that you will keep your part of the bargain?'

'I give you my word as a Knight,' said Samildanach, fighting to control his anger.

'Once I would have walked into Hell on such a promise. But not now, Samildanach. Your word is worth less than pig-droppings. No. I think we will chance the battle.'

'You then are the Lord Knight, Manannan? Or are you the Armourer? Strange – I heard it was the cripple, Elodan, and the boy, Lámfhada. Run to them and tell them of my offer. See what they have to say.'

Now it was Manannan's turn to feel the cold bite of anger in his soul and he took a deep, slow breath. 'You are right, of course. I shall do this. And if your challenge is accepted I will meet you here at dawn. Believe me, Samildanach, I will defeat you. I promise you that.'

'Enough of your empty threats. Carry my message to your masters. I will wait here for their answer.'

Manannan rode back to where the other Knights waited with Lámfhada, seated around a breakfast fire. Ramath, Bucklar and the other leaders stood close by. Manannan outlined Samildanach's offer and immediately stressed that he was against it.

Lámfhada stood. 'We must not dismiss it lightly. It could save – as Samildanach says – many hundreds of lives. Can you beat him, Manannan?'

'Yes, I believe that I can. But I cannot be sure.'

'There is another point to be considered,' put in Elodan. 'If he loses and breaks his word, it will only strengthen our cause. If he wins, we can disband – and perhaps re-form at a later time.'

'I think you are overlooking something of importance here,' said Errin softly. 'We are the Knights of the Gabala. We cannot refuse such a challenge and maintain any pretence to our title. Samildanach knows this. If we refuse we will be condemned as imposters, and then Nuada's death, and the deaths of the others, will count for nothing. Whatever the risk, we must accept and trust in Manannan's skill.'

Elodan nodded in agreement. 'Thank you, Errin. You are correct, of course. It matters not whether Samildanach is sincere. I doubt that he is, but he must be fought. Lámfhada, you agree?'

'Yes. Ride back to him, Manannan. Tell him that the combat will be fought tomorrow.'

Manannan sighed and shook his head. 'As you say,' he said. He mounted his stallion and returned to the valley and Samildanach.

'Tomorrow, two hours after dawn,' stated the Once-Knight.

'Then the challenge is accepted?'

'Yes. I will be here.'

'You, Manannan?' said Samildanach, smiling broadly. 'But that is not how it will be done. I will follow Gabala rules. I am the Lord Knight of the Crimson therefore naturally I will fight the Lord Knight of the Gabala.'

'What trickery is this?' stormed Manannan. 'Elodan is crippled – as well you know.'

'It is not for me to criticize your choice of leader. But you know the Rule of the Sword: my challenge must be answered by my equal. Naturally, if you now wish to ask me to withdraw my challenge, I will consider your request.'

'And then deny it?'

'Of course. I challenged; it was accepted. It would be base of you to withdraw now.'

'How can one such as you use the word *base*? You are a creature of the dark, a servant of demons. You have turned your back on all that is holy and decent.'

'Do not preach, Manannan. Return to your . . . home in the mud, and tell Elodan I will meet him here two hours after dawn.'

*

Lámfhada sat apart from the Knights, watching the stars and feeling the breath of the night wind. Below him in a sheltered glade Elodan was preparing for the morning's battle; he also sat alone, kneeling in prayer. Lámfhada's heart was heavy and his thoughts filled with foreboding. They had been tricked and now must suffer the consequences. Elodan had taken the news well; he had stood and halted Manannan's angry outburst with a raised hand.

'Enough, Manannan, my friend. It does not become a Knight to give vent to such public rage. Samildanach is entirely correct; and I will be there to meet him.'

Lámfhada heard the rustle of bats' wings and watched them circling in the night sky, seeking insects. He shivered and drew his cloak more closely about him. In the previous autumn he had been a slave, desperate to make a bird of metal fly. Now he was the Armourer and the Dagda, the Guardian of the Colours. It was all too much, and tonight he felt his youth keenly.

A shimmering glow began to appear ahead of him, and a shining figure emerged to stand before him. Lámfhada stood and watched as the vision became solid, not knowing whether to speak or to run. As the face materialized, Lámfhada cowered back; he tried to escape, but a powerful hand grabbed his arm.

'Do not run from me, child,' said Samildanach. 'I wish only to speak with you.'

'What do you want?'

'When I almost trapped you, and my hands closed about you, I saw many things. I saw a dying stag made whole – and young. That is power of the greatest kind. Have you considered all its uses?'

'I will not use that power for you, dark one.'

'Not for me, fool! For him!' said Samildanach, pointing to where Elodan knelt in the glade below. 'Think on it.'

He stepped back – and disappeared.

For a long time Lámfhada sat and puzzled over the Red Knight's words. Why would he seek to aid Elodan? What could he gain? Lámfhada closed his eyes and sought the Colours, rising swiftly to the Gold, floating above the forest and then dropping to hover behind the kneeling Knight. He lifted his hands, willing them to burn with all the power of the Gold, then thrust them into Elodan's back. The Knight stiffened and groaned. Lámfhada could feel the heat in his hands spreading through the other's body. Suddenly Elodan arched back, his right arm rising; he began to tear at the leather pad covering his stump, ripping it from his arm. The skin of the stump was pink and bruised, and it writhed and rippled. Elodan screamed and fainted, toppling sideways to the earth. Still Lámfhada poured his energy into the Knight and the stump swelled like a ball, flattening into a palm from which the beginning of new joints sprouted, stretching into fingers. At last Lámfhada drew back and Elodan stirred and pushed himself to his knees. He stared down at his new right hand, tentatively touching it with the fingers of his left.

'It is a dream,' he whispered. 'Dear Gods of Heaven, it is just a dream!'

Lámfhada returned to his body and rose wearily as the dawn was breaking over the mountains. He walked down to Elodan and found the Knight on his knees, weeping piteously.

Lámfhada sought out Gwydion in the hospital area behind the lines. Finding the old man resting on a hillside beneath the stars, he sat with him and outlined all that had happened since the appearance of the enemy Knight, Samildanach. Gwydion placed his hand on the youth's shoulder. 'And this deed surprised you?' he asked.

'Of course. The man is evil.'

'Yes,' Gwydion agreed, 'he is evil. And what does that tell you?'

'I don't know, Gwydion. That is why I came to you. Is there some deep, cunning plan behind his action? Did I do wrong to follow his bidding and restore Elodan's hand?'

The old man sat in silence for a moment, staring at a distant star. He stroked his white beard and then pointed to a wolf, silhouetted by moonlight on a distant hill. 'Is he evil?' he asked.

'The wolf? No. He is an animal, he kills to live.'

'And what makes a man evil?'

'His deeds judge him,' answered Lámfhada. 'Cruelty, lust, greed – all these things signal what is in a man's heart. Samildanach is a killer and a drinker of souls. His deeds show him to be vile.'

'All this is true,' agreed Gwydion. 'And are you evil?'

'I do not think so. I seek only to defend against them.'

'But are you *capable* of evil deeds? Did you not once say – when Ruad was slain – that you wished you could wield a sword so that you could kill every King's man?'

'All men are capable of evil, Gwydion. We all have desires we must resist.'

'And that is the point, my boy,' explained Gwydion. 'I spoke to Manannan about his journey to the Vyre; he was given a drink they called Ambria. Even in the few days he was among them, the drink had its effect. It erodes and destroys a man's *perception* of right and wrong. As far as I can understand, it promotes the sense of Self. What is enjoyable becomes what is right, what is desired becomes what is needed. Can you understand that? It almost happened to Manannan – and he could not see it until Morrigan saved him. But make no mistake, Lámfhada, had Morrigan not warned him he would now be riding with Samildanach.'

'What are you saying? That Samildanach is not evil?'

'Of course I am not. By our perceptions – and those of all civilized men – he is a demon. But by his own perceptions, he is still Samildanach, Lord Knight of the Gabala, acting in what he sees as the best interests of the Realm. He is still a Knight; he will still retain something of his past.'

'Then there is still some good in him, you think?'

'Think of Groundsel: a killer, a rapist, a thief. Yet there was some good in him and Nuada found it. No man is entirely good – or bad. Ultimately most men act out of self-interest – and that is the breeding ground for all that is iniquitous. But most of us – happily – have an ability to judge ourselves and our deeds. We have a moral sense which stands like a wall between us and what is unjust. To commit an evil deed we have to climb that wall, knowingly. But for Samildanach and the others, the Ambria destroyed the wall, obliterating all knowledge of it. They are as much victims of the evil as we are.'

Lámfhada fell silent. A chill breeze blew across the hillside and he shivered. Finally he spoke. 'But if Samildanach believes that all he desires is good for the Realm, how could he help Elodan, whom he must see as a traitor?'

'I cannot answer that, Lámfhada, save with a hope. Samildanach was the finest of men – just and righteous, noble of spirit and bearing. In any age he would have been numbered among the greatest of knights. I do not believe even the dark power of the Ambria could completely destroy such a man. Aiding Elodan was a fine deed. I hope it means that, deep within himself, Samildanach is searching for the wall – struggling to rebuild it.'

'Then perhaps he will not fight against Elodan?'

'He will fight,' said Gwydion sadly. 'With all the strength and skill he can muster.'

'And Elodan will die,' Lámfhada said.

'Did you not tell me you had seen the future, Lámfhada? Surely you already know the outcome?'

'If only it were as simple as that, Gwydion. When I fly the Gold, I see so many possible futures, like ripples in a rushing river. But which will it be?'

'Have you seen any in which Elodan conquers?'

'No, but then I saw none in which I gave him back his hand.'

'And now you do not wish to fly the Gold?'

'No. I cannot . . . will not. I will watch tomorrow.'

'Today,' said Gwydion, pointing at the red streaks of dawn beyond the mountains.

Samildanach waited as the other Knights of the Crimson entered the tent. Edrin, Cantaray, Joanin, Keristae and Bodarch all seated themselves in a circle around him.

'There is a girl being brought to you, Samildanach,' said Keristae. 'She is young and full of life.'

'And shall remain so,' declared the Lord Knight. 'I have no need of Nourishment.'

'With respect, Lord,' said Edrin, 'I think you are wrong.'

'You think I need aid to kill a cripple?'

'It is not that, Samildanach. It is just . . . you are behaving strangely. Indeed, there are similarities between your actions and those of our brother Cairbre. We fear for you.'

'I will have you all with me,' said Samildanach. 'I will carry the strength of your souls.'

Joanin leaned forward. 'Is all well with you? You have not seemed . . . at ease since you returned from the King?'

'At ease? No. You are correct, Joanin. I think we all need to return to the Vyre. As soon as Elodan is dead

392

and the rebels routed, we will go home. Now, I have need of your strength for the combat ahead.'

The Knights bowed their heads and Samildanach felt their souls flowing into his body. A long time ago the transfusion would have filled him with many emotions – now he felt only the rawness of power. Rising, he moved to the tent entrance. The sun was rising. He looked back at the silent, still figures; their lives depended now on his skill.

Across the valley Elodan sat with Llaw, Errin, Ubadai and Manannan. Lámfhada moved to join them.

'I thank you for this miracle,' said Elodan. 'Even if I die today, it will be as a whole man.'

'I am glad for you,' said Lámfhada uneasily. 'I hope it was the right deed.'

'Why should it not be?' Manannan asked. 'It gives us hope in the battle with the demon.' Lámfhada opened his mouth to speak, but the words would not come.

'Tell us, Manannan,' said Llaw. 'What will Samildanach be doing now?'

'He will be preparing, as we are preparing – and he will enter the field as The One.' Glancing at the faces around him, he saw they did not understand him. 'It is a mystic ritual. All his Knights give him their souls, their strengths, their beliefs: the very essence of themselves. If he dies, they all die.'

'And this makes him stronger?' asked Llaw.

'Of course.'

'Then should we not do the same?' suggested Errin.

'You do not know how, and I do not have the years to teach you,' replied Manannan.

Lámfhada rose to his feet. 'I can help you with that,' he said softly. 'I can join you. But the risks are very great.'

'Do it,' Manannan told him.

'No!' cried Elodan. 'It is a burden I could not bear. To risk death myself is one matter, but to know that all of you could die? No, I will not agree.'

'I am not a brave man,' said Errin, 'but the cause is more important than the lives of five men. And if we can give you strength, then let us do it.'

Elodan looked from one to another. 'Only if all are agreed,' he said, switching his gaze at last to Ubadai. 'You speak, my friend. Always you are silent at our meetings. And yet, when Errin led his troop into the enemy camp, you insisted on going with him. You never shirk danger. I would value your counsel.'

Ubadai grinned. 'I say no, and it is no?'

'Exactly,' said Elodan.

The Nomad turned to Errin. 'You want this?'

'I do.'

'You too?' Ubadai asked Llaw.

The warrior shrugged. 'I don't know what extra strength I can supply – but, yes, I am willing.'

'All is madness,' said the Nomad. 'But I am mad too. Angry mad. Let us kill the whoreson together.'

Lámfhada walked to the centre of the circle and sat down. 'I want you all to join hands,' he said, 'then close your eyes and picture Elodan in your minds.' Lámfhada's spirit rose from his body; he covered the circle in a glowing sphere of Gold and moved to Manannan, then to Llaw and Errin, and finally to Ubadai.

Elodan felt the influx of power from the Once-Knight in a surge of confidence that bordered on arrogance. The strength of a man who had never been bested in battle flowed through him. But he rode above it – for he had lost, and in that knowledge of despair lay strength. Llaw's soul came next and with it the extraordinary endurance of the common man – born without wealth or privilege, yet possessing the ability to withstand the many and varied perils of this bloody time. Like an oak was Llaw, deep-rooted and enduring. Errin followed. Nobility of spirit and the courage to overcome his fears flowed with him. Lastly the Nomad Ubadai, fiercely loyal to the master he loved and ready to die to protect him.

Elodan's eyes opened and he gazed at Lámfhada. 'You did well, Armourer,' he said. 'I thank you.' The other Knights were lying back on the grass, scarcely breathing.

Rising, Elodan said, 'It is time, I think.'

'The Source of All Life be with you, Elodan,' said Lámfhada.

Elodan strode to his stallion and mounted. He saw Samildanach waiting, and behind him the army of the King stretching across the valley.

Touching spurs to his mount, the Lord Knight of the Gabala rode down the long hill.

Samildanach watched as the Lord Knight of the Gabala cantered his mount towards him. He had been prepared for combat, but had not anticipated the tremendous shock of seeing his own armour on another man. Worse, he had the impression that he was watching himself ride out to battle. He remembered the sense of pride he had experienced when first he donned the silver helm.

Images ripped through his mind: Morrigan in the garden, and then dying on the floor of the King's bedchamber; Cairbre lecturing him on points of duty and honour, Cairbre in the pale coffin; Manannan debating the chivalric code, Manannan calling him a demon.

Somewhere deep inside him a chain snapped and he shook his head, fighting to force away the memories.

Ollathair, gentle Ollathair, smiling at the success of

a golden bird as it soared under the sun; Ollathair sagging to the ground, Samildanach's knife in his belly.

Stop it! Leave me alone!

Elodan dismounted and walked some yards to the left, drawing his sword and plunging it into the earth. From the forest all around them came the fighting men of the rebellion. Silently they marched down to sit facing the army of the King. Samildanach lifted his leg over the pommel of his saddle and slid to the ground.

Kill him, he thought. Return to the Vyre. There they will tend your restless spirit.

The voice of the girl child as she was led into his chambers the first time he needed Nourishment came to him: *'Please don't hurt me! Please don't hurt me!'*

'Are you ready?' Elodan asked.

'Yes,' Samildanach answered. 'I am ready.' Now Morrigan's voice was echoing in his mind:

'Can you not see what . . . we have become? Oh, Samildanach! We are corrupting everything we . . . touch . . . I loved you more than life. And now . . . I don't even know what it means.'

'Don't talk. Let me bind your wrists; we can save your life.'

'There is nothing to save. I died back in the City of the Vyre when I became one of the Undead – just like you, my love.'

'What is wrong with you? Draw your sword,' said Elodan.

The dark blade snaked into the air and Elodan blocked, but only just in time, and the combat commenced. He fought for his life against the greatest swordsman he had ever known. Cairbre had been more than talented, but Samildanach's skill was astounding. Speed, balance and lightning reflexes confounded all Elodan's attempts to attack. The dark sword crashed against his breastplate, smashing a hinge and severing the brass-edged leather straps. The armour sagged. Elodan ducked under a sweeping blow and thundered a stroke against Samildanach's shoulder that ripped loose a crimson plate. Samildanach staggered back.

'What happened to that glorious young knight?' whispered Morrigan, from the caverns of his soul.

The dark blade flashed forward, but Elodan blocked it with ease and sent a counter that tore through a curved hip-plate, sending it spinning to the grass. Samildanach returned to the attack with a riposte of blistering speed, his sword ripping into Elodan's helm. Stars exploded before the Lord Knight's eyes and his vision swam. He hurled himself back and – more by luck than skill – blocked a sweep that would have torn his head from his shoulders. Samildanach moved in for the kill – and stopped.

'Please don't hurt me!' came the child's voice from his memory.

'Leave me alone!' screamed Samildanach.

Elodan staggered and drew a deep, shuddering breath. His vision cleared and he saw his opponent staring at the sky: 'Leave me alone!'

'Samildanach!'

The Red Knight swung. 'I'll kill you,' he shouted and once more the battle was joined. Elodan fought off the frenzied attack, landing counter-blow after counter-blow against the crimson armour. A great crack appeared down the centre of Samildanach's breast-plate and his visor was hacked away. Yet still he came on. A second blow loosened Elodan's helm, which twisted, partially blocking his vision. Samildanach ran in, holding his great blade double-handed; Elodan ducked sharply and the hissing sword swept over his head. Off balance for the first time, Samildanach stumbled to the earth. Elodan swiftly dropped his sword and lifted clear his damaged helm. Bareheaded, he gathered his blade as Samildanach regained his feet.

'You are not me!' screamed Samildanach. 'You can never be me!'

'I would not wish to be,' replied Elodan, staring into the haunted eyes of the Red Knight.

'None of us is what we would wish to be,' said Samildanach. 'And now it is time for you to die.' His sword hissed down with tremendous force and Elodan dropped to his knees, sweeping his blade above his head to block the killer blow. The swords clanged together . . . and Elodan's silver blade snapped a foot above the hilt.

Samildanach's sword swept up, his eyes gleaming with the joy of triumph.

'What happened to that glorious young knight?' Samildanach froze . . . and swiftly Elodan rammed the broken sword through the crack in the Red Knight's breastplate, plunging it deep into his chest. Blood welled from the wound, spilling over Elodan's hand. Samildanach staggered, but the dark blade rose again above Elodan's unprotected head.

Down it flashed – to stop an inch short of Elodan's neck. The blade tapped gently on Elodan's right shoulder, then crossed to touch lightly on the left. Samildanach dropped to his knees. Inside him all was turmoil, and he could feel the souls of his Knights struggling to be free of his dying body. But he held them trapped.

Elodan moved to him. 'Why did you let me live?' he asked. 'Why?'

'What happened to that glorious young knight?'

'I died . . . a long . . . time ago,' whispered Samildanach, falling forward into Elodan's arms. The Lord Knight laid the corpse on the grass and rose to a roaring cheer from the rebels.

A stout middle-aged man walked out from the King's army. He halted before Elodan and bowed.

'My name is Kar-schen. The war is over, sir Knight. I offer myself – and my regiments – to your cause.'

'I have no cause,' said Elodan. 'I am the Lord Knight of the Gabala.'

'Welcome back,' greeted Kar-schen.

Epilogue

Llaw Gyffes refused the opportunity to march on Furbolg and seize the crown, and Kar-schen returned to the city and the Ebony Throne. Errin and Ubadai surrendered their armour and rode back to Errin's estates. Kar-schen gave Errin the Duchy of Mactha and the new Duke asked Sheera to be his Duchess. She pondered the proposal for four months, and they were married in the temple of Furbolg on the last day of autumn.

Arian and Llaw were wed in a simple ceremony attended by Bucklar, Ramath and the other rebel leaders, after which they journeyed deep into the mountains to build a home where the air was clean, the rivers pure and the stars close.

Lámfhada renounced his role as Armourer and became the Dagda, the Guardian of the Colours. He roamed the Forest of the Ocean as a Healer and a Seer, and waited ninety-four years, eleven months and three days to pass on the mantle to a surprised youth who did not want it.

Elodan and Manannan rode through the Black Gate to aid the Nomads brought as victims for the Vyre.

They did not return.